Prizm Books

Aisling: Book I Guardian by Carole Cummings
Aisling: Book II Dream by Carole Cummings
Aisling: Book III Beloved Son by Carole Cummings
Changing Jamie by Dakota Chase
City/Country by Nicky Gray
Climbing the Date Palm by Shira Glassman
Comfort Me by Louis Flint Ceci
Desmond and Garrick Book I by Hayden Thorne
Desmond and Garrick Book II by Hayden Thorne
Devilwood Lane by Lucia Moreno Velo
Don't Ask by Laura Hughes
The Dybbuk's Mirror by Alisse Lee Goldenberg
The End by Nora Olsen
Foxhart by A.R. Jarvis
Heart Sense by KL Richardsson
Heart Song by KL Richardsson
I Kiss Girls by Gina Harris
Ink ~ Blood ~ Fire by K. Baldwin & Lyra Ricci
Josef Jaeger by Jere' M. Fishback
Just for Kicks by Racheal Renwick
Murder in Torbaydos by Ian James Krender
The Next Competitor by K. P. Kincaid
Repeating History: The Eye of Ra by Dakota Chase
The Second Mango by Shira Glassman
A Strange Place in Time by Alyx J. Shaw
The Strings of the Violin by Alisse Lee Goldenberg
The Suicide Year by Lena Prodan
Tartaros by Voss Foster
The Tenth Man by Tamara Sheehan
Tyler Buckspan by Jere' M. Fishback
Under the Willow by Kari Jo Spear
Vampirism and You! by Missouri Dalton
The Water Seekers by Michelle Rode
The World's a Stage by Gail Sterling

Murder in Torbaydos

Ian James Krender

Murder in Torbaydos

This is a work of fiction. Names, characters, places, and incidents either are the product of the author's imagination or are used fictitiously. While this novel is inspired by historical events, it is a fictionalized portrayal, and the author created all characters, events and storylines in the pursuit of literary fiction, not historical accuracy.

Murder in Torbaydos
PRIZM
An imprint of Torquere Press, Inc.
1380 Rio Rancho Blvd #1319, Rio Rancho, NM 87124.
Copyright 2014 © by Ian James Krender
Cover illustration by Ali Futcher
Published with permission
ISBN: 978-1-61040-835-6
www.prizmbooks.com
www.torquerepress.com

First Prizm Printing: November 2014
Printed in the USA

prizm
there's room under the rainbow
www.prizmbooks.com

Acknowledgment

Thank you to Derek Mason, Craig McGill,
Alison Futcher, and The McTrish

Dedication

For my Grandmother.

Murder in Torbaydos

Ian James Krender

Murder in Torbaydos

Ian James Krender

Prologue: Jez Matthews

I write this book in my twilight years. Though considerable time has passed since these tragic events occurred, there is no doubt in my mind that it will be controversial. Some people will suspect me of profiteering. However, if I am privileged enough to see this work published, then I will donate any proceeds to the affected surviving family members. The money would be of little use to me now, as I am elderly, and I have no heirs.

Perhaps writing this is a form of therapy, a way to assuage my own guilt. Goodness knows, I have spent much time reflecting on the 'what ifs.' Over the years, I have learned to forgive myself the errors of my past. However, I will never forget the pain that I have caused others through my poor decisions.

The accounts of my own actions are as accurate as I can recall them, given the passage of time. Clearly, I was not present or indeed alive in the earlier years this book is set. My historical interpretation of those events has been derived from piecing together old letters and photographs. I have also been able to make extensive use of the Wilsons' diaries, posted to me some years ago. I have spoken and corresponded with numerous people, and I extend my thanks to them for having to relive some unpleasant memories. This includes some of the police officers assigned to the investigation, who have been very understanding. The Internet has proven to be a powerful research tool. I extend my gratitude to the Torquay Library for their patience in dealing with my correspondence. However, I hope you will indulge me with a little poetic license, particularly concerning events in the 1970s and 1919. It has been difficult for me to relive the subject matter described in the following pages, as I am sure it will be difficult for those directly and indirectly involved. Furthermore, it is understandable that communicating with me, given my reputation, has been unpalatable. My earnest hope is that this book will put the record straight. I warn you: What follows may be uncomfortable to read, but I swear by almighty God that it is the truth.

Chapter 1

February 1919: The Kingsleys

February was unseasonably cold in Torquay despite the appearance of snowdrops. A bitter North Easterly wind had edged in from Siberia, bringing daytime temperatures down to freezing and dashing all hopes of an early spring. Pembroke House, Sir Wilfred and Lady Elizabeth Kingsley's holiday home, was situated in the heart of Torquay—a seaside resort often described as the 'Jewel of the English Riviera' and a playground of the wealthy.

The villa, which overlooked the delightful and secluded Meadfoot Beach, was a brisk ten-minute walk to Torquay Harbor. A recently completed railroad had made Torquay, with its relatively mild climate, something of a boomtown. Sir Wilfred's late father had built a considerable fortune from his successful manufacturing business, founded during the industrial revolution. He commissioned the building of the imposing Pembroke House in 1852, at the height of his career.

Accessed through an impressive wrought-iron gate, a sweeping drive led to the pristine cream and white walled building, which glistened in the weak winter sunshine. At the front of the house, large floor-to-ceiling bay windows and a magnificent stained glass entrance porch made a welcoming sight to visitors. Pembroke House had provided a satisfying retreat from the hustle and bustle of London society for two generations of the Kingsleys.

Sir Wilfred's condition had deteriorated to the extent that his physician suggested he be moved from their London home to their secondary residence in Torquay, where the benign climate and fresh sea air might aid his recovery. Since Wilfred was too infirmed to travel by car, several servants assisted Lady Elizabeth in bringing Sir Wilfred to Torquay by first-class rail. They were of the opinion that this journey had not improved his overall health, but it was preferable to continuing to subject him to the thick smog that had plagued London throughout the cold, dry winter.

Sir Wilfred's loyal friend and physician, Doctor Charles Ashcroft, had accompanied Lady Elizabeth and her small entourage to Torquay. This included the dashingly handsome family lawyer and friend, James Partridge, who had taken leave from his duties as a junior partner in the Wigmore Street branch of his firm. The family butler, Albert Henderson, was also present.

Now ensconced at Pembroke House in Torquay, Sir Wilfred Kingsley was sweating profusely as he lay in his four-poster bed in the master bedroom. The beads of sweat on his pasty white forehead were being gently patted dry by his full-time nurse. His breathing was heavy and strained, and he was delirious, drifting in and out of consciousness. This was in part from his malaise, but also because of the potent sedatives administered to him. His flesh was pallid and tight like parchment against his skull, his yellowed eyes sunken into their sockets, and his breathing was labored and wheezy. Doctor Ashcroft listened to his heartbeat using a stethoscope, placed on his chest through his unbuttoned pajama top. He looked concerned as he spoke to Lady Elizabeth.

"It's not good news," he said gravely. "His heartbeat is

erratic, and his blood pressure is dangerously low. I think you need to be prepared for the worst possible news."

Lady Elizabeth was somberly dressed in black, looking very much like the widow in waiting. She had a slim figure and a doll-like complexion with a button nose on a beautifully seductive face, crowned with long, wavy locks of brown hair. This contrasted with her steely eyes, which she used effectively to assert her authority. She was about twenty years younger than Sir Wilfred and not a character to be crossed. However, now she was vulnerable. Her eyes were tinged with sadness, and she looked gaunt from worry.

She nodded silently at Doctor Ashcroft, walked over to the fireplace, and gave the logs a firm prod. The fire spat and crackled in response, bathing the luxurious yet gloomy room in an orange glow. The master bedroom of the villa had high ceilings with ornate Italianate cornicing. The large north-facing sash windows rattled in the icy wind. This penetrated the room, making it drafty and difficult to heat effectively.

Henderson, the butler, entered the room and announced James Partridge, who followed him closely behind. Lady Elizabeth tried hard to retain her stiff upper lip, but she betrayed her emotional state by letting out a tearful sob. James put his arms around her and held her tightly. Despite their attempts at discretion, Henderson and the family servants had observed how close the pair had become during Sir Wilfred's illness.

"There, there, my dear. You have done everything you possibly can."

Henderson stood a respectful distance from them, bowing his head. Lady Elizabeth had requested he stay close to hand.

Lady Elizabeth pulled the cord that operated the bell in the servant's quarters, summoning the maid, whom she beckoned to draw the heavy red velvet curtains to keep out the wind. The sun was edging below the horizon with no cloud cover; temperatures would soon drop rapidly.

"The truth is that Sir Wilfred is now beyond help, Elizabeth," said Doctor Ashcroft.

"Is there nothing you can do?"

"Sadly, any treatment we can provide now is palliative. We can endeavor to keep him comfortable, little more," he said, leaning Sir Wilfred forward and putting an extra pillow behind his back. "I've seen nothing like this in my forty years as a physician. With your permission Elizabeth, I'll administer a sedative to make his passing easier."

Lady Elizabeth nodded her approval. Doctor Ashcroft opened his medical bag and took out a small tablet.

"This will help with the pain, Wilfred," he said softly. He picked up a nearby glass of water and put the tablet on Sir Wilfred's tongue, but Sir Wilfred spat it out.

"No, Ashcroft," he said weakly. "I want to be awake. There are things I need to say."

Mustering what little strength he had left, Sir Wilfred raised his right hand and beckoned James to come closer. James obeyed and leaned over. Sir Wilfred weakly grabbed the back of James' head and guided his ear towards his mouth.

"There is little time left for me," he whispered, barely audible. "You must listen carefully... Your Father was a great man... an associate and a close friend. That is why it is painful that my last words shall be so full of hate."

He paused to suck in a desperately needed breath. His grip around James' head tightened, pulling him closer. James could feel the heat from Wilfred's rancid breath against his ear.

"From the depths of hell, I curse you. I shall have my vengeance on you, Partridge."

His grip weakened, and then his arm fell limply to the bed. His erratic breathing stopped, and his face became blank and expressionless. Sir Wilfred was dead.

"Elizabeth, Doctor, I think he's gone," James said shakily, unsettled by Sir Wilfred's final words.

Henderson was visibly distraught but stood steadfastly in the corner.

Lady Elizabeth wiped away a tear with her handkerchief before she regained her composure. She kissed her deceased husband on the forehead and moved toward the doctor, who was standing by the fire. He bowed his head respectfully, as though aware that his presence may be an intrusion.

Lady Elizabeth started to speak, but a loud smash interrupted her as the crystal decanter on the mantelpiece shattered, soaking her dress in brandy. Looking perturbed and slightly cross, she turned toward Henderson. The fire crackled angrily, followed by a loud bang resembling a gunshot. A red-hot ember spat out of the hearth, landing on her dress. From then, events happened extraordinarily and frighteningly rapidly. Her skirt caught fire, and flames engulfed her within seconds. She flailed around, screaming like a rag doll shaken by an invisible dog. Sir Wilfred's nurse acted quickly and instinctively. She threw a blanket over her in an attempt to smother the flames. However, this itself seemed to be flammable and further fueled the fire. Lady Elizabeth was now a black silhouette inside an inferno of orange. The blanket stuck to her, its melted remains clinging to her skin like wax, creating a dark ghoulish apparition. She lurched toward a terrified James, who backed away too slowly. She gripped him tightly, as if possessed, setting them both ablaze. As they collapsed onto the floor, their bloodcurdling screams were stifled as Doctor Ashcroft and Henderson threw the Axminster rug over them, rolling their smoldering bodies across the room. At last, they managed to extinguish the flames.

Almost not daring to look at their scorched bodies, Doctor Ashcroft unraveled the rug.

"Look away, girl," he snapped at Nurse Summers. "Henderson, call for an ambulance!"

Lady Elizabeth's corpse was charred beyond recognition; her once beautiful locks of brown curly hair were singed away. Her skin was blackened and still smoking, which filled the air with an acrid smell of burnt flesh. Her face was twisted in agony. James Partridge was less lucky. He was still alive, twitching in pain, and moaning. His handsome Latin looks were ruined. His breathing was erratic, and he repeatedly croaked, "I'm so sorry."

Doctor Ashcroft opened his capacious medicine bag and injected him with a large dose of morphine to relieve the pain. Fortunately, he only survived for a few minutes.

"Don't bother with the ambulance, Henderson. We need the coroner and the vicar," said Doctor Ashcroft grimly.

The doctor opened the sash window to let out the smoke. The icy wind had gained strength, blowing through the room, causing the curtains to flap about violently. He left the room, glancing back to survey the carnage behind him. The fire was dying down, the wood turning to ash with the flames gently licking embers from underneath. Sir Wilfred sat upright in bed, his eyes open, as though he was still alive, scrutinizing the scene in front of him, with a look of disapproval. Lady Elizabeth was sprawled lifelessly across the singed floor. James Partridge lay on his back on top of the scorched rug, his face betraying the agonizing death he had endured.

The freezing gale quickly penetrated the room, whistling around unnervingly, but at least it had partially removed the nauseous smell.

This picture will stay with me forever, he thought. *God have mercy on their poor souls.*

He closed the door behind him.

Chapter 2

May 1973: Marjorie Wilson

Stanley, my husband, drove my son Christopher and I past Meadfoot Beach in Torquay and parked our Ford Cortina just outside Pembroke House. We wound up the car windows before getting out, stretching our legs and waiting for the estate agent to arrive. The neighborhood had a pleasing feel to it with a mixture of Victorian and modern houses. The area had well-tended gardens. I always thought that neat hedging, freshly cut lawns, and thoroughly weeded flower beds were signs of being in a desirable part of town. New, polished cars sat on the driveways of the various houses in the street. The house that we were viewing was the exception of the road, as it was without doubt an eyesore. The hedges were very overgrown, so there was little we could see from the road outside. We could only peer through the old wrought-iron gates up the driveway and glimpse the side of the building.

"Let's hope the rest of it is a little better, Marje," said Stanley.

I could not help but agree. The estate agent's particulars had described the property as 'in need of modernization,' but on first glance, this seemed optimistic to say the least.

The journey down from London was arduous with delays along the A380, especially around Stonehenge, so we stopped off for a delicious ploughman's lunch at a little country pub not far from Winchester. The weather was a balmy twenty-three degrees and sunny, with a few wispy cirrus clouds and gentle sea breeze. I was glad that I had chosen to wear my favorite pink floral summer dress. Conversely, Stanley looked uncomfortably hot driving down dressed in his brown suit. The interior of the car was sweltering, even with all the car windows open, and his large girth did not help. My friend's Jaguar had the extravagance of air-conditioning, a tonic on days like today, but we were not affluent enough to afford such luxury.

Our son was in many ways unconventional. He insisted on wearing the latest fashions, ridiculous though they may be. Thus, he dressed in a winged yellow shirt with flared jeans tightly hugging his slender hips and some rather silly white winklepicker shoes. His blond hair was shoulder length and uncombed, despite me constantly nagging him to have it cut.

Let me tell you a bit about my family of whom I am sure you will come to realize I am very proud. I am Marjorie Wilson; my husband and I have been happily married for twenty-four years. We met at the local Conservative Club in Barnet, North London a couple of years after the war ended. Stanley was charming, funny, and had strong opinions on everything. We had a lovely summer wedding a year later at St. Johns Church on the High Street. Things were still tough in those days. We spent the first year of married life using the spare bedroom at my parents' home, whilst we saved for a deposit to put down on a house of our own. I worked as a secretary for a small Jewish firm of Chartered Accountants. Stanley owned a newsagent's shop that he inherited from his father, who had sadly died young from a heart attack. We were both pillars of the Barnet community—churchgoing, small-business owners, Rotarians, and Conservative Party activists. I had what Stanley described as a healthy interest in other people's affairs. It was not without considerable effort on my behalf that Barnet became one of the most desirable London postcodes.

A year into our marriage, I became pregnant with our beautiful son whom we named Christopher. He was to be our only child. As he grew up, he proved to be bent, artistically. He played the violin and piano and was simply wonderful on the stage, always taking an important part in school plays. His teachers agreed that he outshone the other boys. Much as Stanley tried to nurture any latent sporting instinct, Christopher was not interested in football. He is now a tall, handsome man of twenty-two years, who is yet to meet the right girl. None of the young ladies introduced to him have been suitable. As he is fond of telling me, he has high standards. I should also mention that he was the first Wilson to attend university, although strictly speaking it was a polytechnic. He studied drama at Birmingham, but, unfortunately, he had to drop out halfway through his course, as the city air aggravated his asthma. These days, he helps Stanley in the shop, and we are hopeful that his acting break will happen soon.

He did obtain a part as an extra in the BBC1 sitcom *On the Buses* a couple of years ago, but it was a nonspeaking role. Despite this, I thought he stole the show playing an inebriated passenger who staggered into a bus stop.

Stanley lit up a cigarette. "I wish you'd give that up," I said.

"Please don't nag me. I have few pleasures in life."

"You're getting fat!" I said, prodding his stomach that hung over his belt.

"I blame your cooking. What is a man supposed to do when presented with a fried breakfast each morning?"

I used a handkerchief to pat dry the top of his balding head, which was sweating from the heat of the sun, and gently scolded him for picking such a mishmash of clothing. It was always better if I chose what he should wear.

A red Mini screeched to an abrupt halt in front of our car, and the estate agent jumped out, making his apologies for being late. He was an impeccably dressed man in his mid-twenties with a neatly trimmed beard. He introduced himself with a firm handshake as Alan Saxon. He was a junior partner in John Saxon & Son's estate agents. Apparently, his last appointment overran.

He opened the padlocked gates and walked us up the drive, holding a clipboard. He started talking in typical estate agent's patter, telling us what a lovely place the English Riviera was.

"We have more sun hours and the highest annual average temperature in the whole of the UK," he said informatively.

He also told us about some other Victorian villas he had on his books in much better condition than Pembroke House. We discovered that the property had been on the market with him and five other local agencies for several years. This was unsurprising given the rundown state of the building.

"It's a big project with loads of potential," he enthused. "The trust is quite keen on disposing of the property, so I'm sure that they will be flexible on the asking price."

"They want £35,000 for it?" said Stanley. "Damned cheek given the condition of the place, I'd say."

"Dad," sighed Christopher, looking embarrassed.

"Everything is going up, son. Milk, bread, cigarettes. It was thirty-eight pence a gallon for petrol on the A380. It cost over three pounds to fill up the car. I blame decimalization, the biggest con in history. As for going into Europe, don't even get me started. We sold our cousins in the Commonwealth down the river, the bloody fr—"

I interrupted him before he embarked on another of his political lectures. "Alan, if we bought it, we would be looking for it to pay for itself. The idea would be to have it as a boarding house or an upmarket bed and breakfast. Would we get permission for change of use, in your opinion?"

"Almost definitely, Mrs. Wilson. The local authority is actively encouraging the conversion of this kind of building. It brings the life back into them and tourist money into the town. It's hard graft, of course, but a lot of people have been very successful at it."

"Well, we're not afraid of hard work are we, Stanley?"

The steep driveway up to the house was overgrown with weeds coming up through the paving stones. To the left was a gate leading to the main garden, which was an acre of wilderness that had not seen a gardener for decades. The exterior of the house was painted cream with the ornate cornices and windows painted a contrasting white. At least they were at some point; unfortunately, closer inspection revealed the paint badly peeled and cracked. Years of unchecked algae and mildew growth in the damp seaside air stained the walls a dirty, greenish gray color. The original sash windows were unsalvageable, rotten to the point that the wood was like cardboard. The gutters overflowed with leaves. Tree saplings grew from the chimney stacks, and the various outbuildings were on the verge of collapse.

The interior told the same story. The entrance porch had a cracked Minton tile floor, with rendered walls that were crumbling due to rising damp. Upon entering the main hallway, the smell of mold filled my nostrils. There were various cracks in the ceiling and telltale brown patches indicating water ingress. As we explored further, the proliferation of spider webs, threadbare carpets, and holes in the floor became apparent. The agent assured us that it was structurally safe and continued the tour. There was a magnificent staircase and two impressive lounges with high ceilings that Stanley pointed out would make the room difficult to heat. A small but nonetheless impressive dining room led to the kitchen in the east part of the building. It was large, though rotten and filthy with evidence of vermin. The range lay cold and unlit under a chimney breast. Christopher wandered a few paces behind us, looking more interested than expected, but unaware of my increasing excitement.

"There's no electricity," said Alan. "But the house was connected at one point, so it should be easy to fix. You have main sewerage here, so there is no septic tank to worry about. There is a solid-fuel range in the kitchen and numerous fireplaces around the building, but no central heating."

At the rear of the house, there were some servants' quarters and an expansive basement, ideal for additional accommodation or storage. Upstairs, the dank, cold conditions prevailed. There were six bedrooms and two bathrooms. Lime plaster hung in patches from the ceilings, revealing the lathes beneath.

The master bedroom was very impressive, at least forty square feet with a large fireplace. The previous occupants had inexplicably left the walnut four-poster bed in the room, complete with a stained and smelly mattress. It was ghastly, and it would have to go. They had also left an old

Victorian dressing table. An overbearing marble fireplace would need removing at some point. There was evidence of minor fire damage to the room, near to the hearth, as though a log had fallen from the grate and singed the floorboards. As my mind went into homemaking overdrive, I realized that I had already mentally moved in before I had even discussed anything with my family.

The tour ended with a flashlight-lit viewing of the basement. Alan left us to chat and wander around. Before locking up and shaking hands, he said that he would call us on Monday for our comments and wished us a safe journey back to London.

Once he had raced off, I turned to my husband.

"Darling, I love it!"

"It needs a lot of work. It's more than a lick of paint and a few trips to the ironmongers."

"Dad, think of the potential, and it's a snip at that price," said Christopher. "I think it could be amazing."

"There won't be much acting work down here," said Stanley.

"There are two theatres in Torquay, one in Paignton, and one in Babbacombe, not to mention Exeter and Plymouth. Think of the lifestyle, Dad. This would be so much easier than the shop. You need to relax in your old age."

"I'll give you a clip around the ear if you're not careful, son."

"But he has a point. You've had major heart surgery. Your father died young. You get up at five o'clock nearly every morning to put the papers out. Think what we could do with this place—restore the old lady back to her former glory."

"Father built up that newsagent," said Stanley, huffing. "It's been in our family for two generations. He'd turn in his grave if he knew I'd sold it."

"Stanley, Maurice is dead. He worked himself to death. He would not want the same to happen to you. Think about what an opportunity this is. We could sell our house in Barnet, sell the newsagent business and the flat above. We'd have enough money to buy this place outright and a bit over to do it up."

"This is a major renovation, not just a bit of light redecoration. It's going to be a money pit."

"Alan said they would be flexible on the price."

"They'd bleeding well have to be, love."

"Our little palace by the sea," I said longingly. "Working together in the family business. What a perfect life it would be."

"Why has it been for sale for so long? What's wrong with it? I mean, apart from the obvious."

"It was waiting for us."

"We all have a lot to talk about on the drive home," said Stanley. "I want a survey done, so we know what we're letting ourselves in for. As for Christopher, he can't even hang a picture, let alone dirty his hands doing building work. I've got a heart condition, so we'll need professional builders in."

"Dad, I may be no good with a screwdriver, but I have a natural flair for interior design. I'm also great with tradesmen. I bent over backward to accommodate that plumber we employed last winter."

"Yes, he did seem to take a shine to you," said Stanley. "Odd fellow, I thought, but the toilet has never leaked since he fitted that new cock and ball, and he did marvels with the old pipework."

Christopher smirked.

I remember the feelings I had after the viewing as if it were yesterday. It was a mixture of excitement, fear, and a sense of fate. I knew we had to have that house, no matter what. I somehow knew it was going to happen because I would make it a reality. Christopher wanted it too, and we both knew how to press Stanley's buttons. By the time we arrived back in London, we had successfully talked Stanley around. None of us slept on Saturday. We attended evensong on Sunday, and I prayed that we would gain possession of Pembroke House. On Monday morning, Alan from John Saxon & Sons called for our feedback, and Stanley expressed our interest. Typical of Stanley, he made out the price to be extortionate and that we were buying a money pit that nobody else wanted. In fairness, that was not far from the truth. He put in a silly offer, £10,000 below the asking price. Alan said he would consult his client, and half an hour later, he called back. Unbelievably, they accepted our opening bid, which was a complete surprise. In retrospect, perhaps that should have rung alarm bells.

The next few weeks were hectic. We had to put our business and house on the market, and I had to give notice to my employers. Christopher tearfully resigned from BADS, the Barnet Amateur Dramatic Society. Sadly, this meant that no Christmas pantomime would ever be the same without his brilliant renditions of Widow Twankey or one of the ugly sisters. The commercial estate agency sold our newsagent shop to a lovely Pakistani family who were delighted to be moving from down-market Hackney to the much wealthier borough of Barnet. They had a strong work ethic and we felt sure they would make a success of it. We priced our house competitively, and it sold in less than a month. We exchanged contracts on the house, newsagent, and Pembroke House by September, completing in early October. Our second viewing and the survey results had confirmed our suspicions that the renovation work was going to be disruptive and expensive. With this in mind, we temporarily put our furniture into storage and rented a small holiday apartment at a heavily discounted winter rate that Stanley negotiated. It happened to be next door at a sprawling Victorian property called Delamare Court, the owner of which would in due course become a friend of sorts.

Alan, the estate agent, met us at Pembroke House to hand over the keys.

"Good luck," he said cheerily and thrust a box of cheap chocolates into my hands. "Please accept this little gift from the staff at the office."

"Black Magic, my favorite," I lied.

As he drove off, I was sure I could see a wide grin on his face.

We all looked around at what was now our property and my heart sank as the scale of what was ahead finally dawned on me.

Chapter 3

May 2005: Jez Matthews

"You have arrived at your destination," announced the soothing female voice of the car's navigation system. Graham stopped and sandwiched the Audi into a tight parking spot, causing its sensors to beep loudly as he got a little too close to the vehicle behind.

We got out and breathed in deeply, enjoying the fresh sea air after the four-hour drive from Chiswick, West London. I had offered to take turns with the driving, but Graham was very precious about his car and was a nervous passenger. It did not help that I had managed to scrape the front wing against a wall last year in our local Waitrose car park. It was a lovely early summer's day, deceptively hot for the time of year but with a refreshing sea breeze blowing in off Meadfoot beach.

The Marstan Hotel was barely visible through the overgrown hedges and trees. The gates were padlocked, but I could see up the drive through the bars. The garden was unkempt, and the windows boarded up with plywood to keep out unwanted visitors. Nevertheless, I was immediately excited. The property had huge potential, despite its sorry state.

Firstly, a little bit about Graham and myself. The dynamics of our relationship were that he was the sensible business-like person, and I was the creative type. He made decisions in a considered and logical way, whereas I was impulsive and my heart often ruled my head. It was a symbiotic meeting of minds where our personality differences complemented one another. Usually our compromises on major decisions meant that we had made the right choices throughout our time together. We were both passionate about old buildings. Our small terraced house in Chiswick was in an appalling state when we took possession. We gradually restored it over a five-year period, putting back the original features, but reconfiguring it for modern living. In addition to fixing the dry rot, leaking roof, and rising damp, we built a spacious open-plan kitchen diner, a two-story extension, and installed an upstairs bathroom. We derived a great deal of satisfaction from renovating this rundown property. Whilst we realized that it might not necessarily be a lucrative investment, the sense of achievement at leaving a building in a condition fit for another generation to appreciate, more than compensated. The Marstan Hotel would obviously be a larger project, involving relocation and a major lifestyle change. This was no problem for me as I was naturally spontaneous, but Graham struggled with uncertainty.

Graham and I met in a fashionable drinking club called The Shadow Lounge in the Soho area of London. It was midweek, and we were socializing separately with our respective work colleagues. I was instantly attracted to Graham, who was nearly ten years my senior. Intelligent and witty, with a tall, athletic build, he had a good career and was well spoken, the product of a private school education. He was typically handsome with a square jaw, high cheekbones, and glowing skin. His hair was on the long side, parted in the center with foppish curtains at the front. He had a kind face with come-to-bed eyes and exuded confidence. He had a natural presence and stature, yet it was effortless in its delivery. Graham was not a show off; he was not boorish or a boaster, like so many of his type. He was just Graham, a successful commodity trader. He was a stable, astute man with no issues like so many of us gay men. Underneath the manicured exterior, he was a warm, genuine person. It made a difference from so many of the 'queens' that I had met whilst out on the London gay scene. Many were vacuous, compulsive liars and only interested in getting you into bed.

I was a mere twenty-two-year-old, at the time we met. I admit to being a little frivolous and perhaps slightly shallow, but I was not arrogant or nasty. I had my own career in a London-based interior design company. It might be immodest to say this, but I was talented and enjoyed my work immensely. Unfortunately, it paid a mediocre salary, and I financed my rather extravagant lifestyle by means of a permanently overdrawn bank account and creative use of multiple credit cards. To look at, I was the archetypal boy next door. I regularly trained in the gym and played squash, and I freely admit to being a touch vain. I spent longer in the bathroom than the two girls with whom I shared a flat at that time. It took me an hour to do my hair in the morning, and I spent a disproportionately large amount of my salary on clothes and various skin-care products. In fact, I had a Clarins loyalty card. This was all probably down to my own insecurities as the spotty fat boy at school. However, when I think about myself back then, my perception is that of a fundamentally decent man. People said that I had piercing blue eyes and handsome boyish looks. If there were one thing I could change about myself, it would have been my height. I measured a lowly five feet seven. Graham towered above me at six feet, but that aside, I think I had inherited the best of my parents' gene pool. At least there was no sign of baldness in my family.

We spoke briefly whilst each ordering a round of drinks at the bar. Despite the short conversation, we clicked instantly. After our colleagues had left, we sat and drank champagne into the early hours, ignoring the fact that we both had to work the following morning. We exchanged telephone numbers and went home separately. Then it was a waiting game. We had met on Wednesday. The rules of dating etiquette stated that it was too early to call before Saturday. It made you look overly keen, plus somebody as fabulous as me would undoubtedly have a busy social diary at the weekend. In fact, I was doing nothing, and the weekend dragged. I made a mental note to call him on Monday evening. It transpired that it was Graham who text messaged me on Sunday. He said that he had really enjoyed meeting me, and could we do it again sometime. I messaged back and said, "Likewise, but I have a hectic schedule." Direct as always, he replied, "Don't be a prat," which he followed up by inviting me for dinner at his home on Saturday. I accepted by telephoning him, and we had a brief but pleasant chat.

I went to his beautiful apartment in Chelsea, situated in an imposing Georgian white stucco building, the type that you often see as a backdrop on period dramas. I buzzed the intercom beside the tall black door, which served as a communal entrance. His second-floor apartment was spotlessly clean. His furniture consisted mostly of antiques, including canvas portraits of family ancestors in gilded frames. I wondered what he would make of my rented flat share with cheap Athena prints hanging on the walls, or my ancestors, who were rather less distinguished. Should I mention that I lived in Acton, which was a run-down suburb of London that estate agents had been inaccurately describing for two decades as an up-and-coming property hotspot? I had three choices. Talk myself up, and pretend I was something more than I was; embrace my working class roots and hope that Graham liked a bit of rough; or just be myself. I chose the latter.

We ate in the kitchen, which was anachronistic, being minimalist in style consisting of modern units and granite worktops. It contrasted with the rest of the flat. Dinner progressed extremely well. He had clearly put a lot of thought into the menu, having prepared us a romantic three-course supper from one of Jamie Oliver's cookbooks. I had found him handsome when we met, but since I had had quite a lot to drink, part of me wondered if it was beer goggles or my short-term memory cheating me. On more than one occasion, I had exchanged telephone numbers with a Matt Damon lookalike, only to meet up a week later, without the benefit of a bottle of wine, with somebody bearing a closer resemblance to Jabba the Hutt. The low lighting in nightclubs had a lot to answer for.

I was pleased to discover that it was not the case with Graham. If anything, in sober daylight he was more attractive than I remembered. Once again, something clicked between us, and conversation flowed easily. Differences of opinion turned into informed debates, and we discussed many mutual areas of interest with excitement. In fact, given our different backgrounds, it was surprising how much we had in common. There were rarely any uncomfortable silences.

After we had finished eating, we kissed for a while then kicked off our shoes and cuddled up on the floor in front of the television, using the base of the sofa as a backrest. It felt natural to lean against his firm shoulders with his strong arms wrapped around me. I detected a faint smell of Issey Miyake aftershave. We ended the evening by watching a rented DVD of *Love Actually*. It was a cheesy film to say the least but nonetheless enjoyable. At midnight, I was going to ask him to call me a cab, but instead I accepted his invitation to stay over in the spare bedroom.

We spent all day Sunday together enjoying each other's company before I caught a tube train home in the evening.

Subsequently, we saw each other every weekend and at least one day in the week, and gradually we became inseparable. I developed a deep bond with him that to date I had never experienced with anyone else. In my university years, I had both suffered and enjoyed the wild emotions of teenage lust and infatuation several times, but I knew that this was different. I believed that we were building a solid foundation for a lasting relationship. When the lease on my rented flat came up for renewal, Graham invited me to move in with him. I had always considered myself a fiercely independent man, so this was a significant step for me, particularly as we had only been dating for nine months. However, I threw my caution to one side. I knew I had made the right choice when I drove a hired Transit van, containing my few possessions, across London to Chelsea. The overriding emotion that I felt was not of fear, but of contentment.

Another two years passed, and we bought a place together in Chiswick. Although his salary was considerably greater than mine, I insisted on paying my way and sacrificed my expenditure on clothes and partying to save for a deposit. This improved my own self-esteem and earned further respect from Graham. Numerous good-time boys, who littered the London gay scene gay, had taken him for a ride on many occasions, and not that kind of ride—I refer to the financial kind. I was not going to be one of the users. It certainly gave some of his more judgmental friends less ammunition against me. Several of our acquaintances delighted in predicting that our relationship would not endure, as we were too different. His snobbier friends dismissed me as silly. Apparently, I was decent eye candy but not to be taken seriously. Some of my bitchier friends concluded that Graham was into younger men, and that I would be exchanged for a new model once I got older. I think that much of it was jealousy. True, I had landed on my feet and I knew that, but I am pleased to say that their prophecies did not materialize. Ten years later, we are still together. What seemed like a large age difference then is now an irrelevancy.

These days, Graham is a very well kept forty-something, and I am in my thirties. Due to my rigid skin-care program, I do not look much older than when we first met.

We discovered Torquay by accident last summer. It was not a destination that we would have ever considered visiting. We had been traveling to a friend's holiday cottage in Cornwall. The traffic on the journey from London was atrocious, partly caused by a serious car crash on the M4 motorway. At eight o'clock, the car's navigation system was telling us that we still had another three hours to reach our destination.

When we saw signs for Torquay on the M5, we decided to stop overnight. This would punctuate the journey nicely. Our only knowledge of the town was from the BBC sitcom *Fawlty Towers*, which was hardly a positive endorsement. Once we passed the trading estates on the outskirts of Torquay, we had been pleasantly surprised at how beautiful it was. I loved the drama of the hills with the grandiose villas dotted among them. We both appreciated the quaint harbor with the fishing boats in the inner section, and the millionaire's gin palaces moored in the outer part. I thought that this combined with the tropical flora gave it a truly continental feel. The warm climate was partly due to the gulf stream, and that the town was nestled in a large bay, known as Torbay. This protected it from the prevailing easterly winds. It was very different to what I had imagined, and I understood why the locals affectionately referred to the town as 'Torbaydos,' a mildly self-deprecating comparison to Barbados.

Naturally, there were still numerous fish and chip shops, amusement arcades, and the usual vulgar places you find at all English seaside towns, but Torquay, having once been a resort for wealthy Victorians, had a magnificence to it. Aesthetically, it was a little like Brighton, only much smaller, cleaner, and far more relaxed with a small-town rather than a city feel. We drove across the town into what we now knew to be a conservation area, with sprawling Victorian villas set behind cob-stone walls. Some were hotels and others were private houses. We were impressed. We decided to stay somewhere gay, and we made a quick call to a friend in London. He had an old copy of *Gay Times* and randomly picked one of four hotels in the advert section. He inadvertently discovered for us a very nice little guesthouse nestled in lovely subtropical gardens, situated on a leafy road, just a few minutes' walk from the town. We had a delicious meal in a restaurant that used local Devon produce. Lastly, it was a hot, balmy evening, and our visit had just happened to coincide with a massive firework display at the harbor. As we walked back to the hotel, Graham's thoughts echoed mine.

"I'd really like to live here someday," he said.

"Seriously?"

"Yes, I've been thinking about leaving London for some time now."

"Strangely enough, I have too, but I never thought you

would be interested. I always thought your heart was in the city. You love the buzz of it all."

"Well, that's a turn up. I never said anything before because of *your* love affair with London."

"I love it, but sometimes I think a simpler life might be nicer at our age."

"You know I have a stressful job with long hours, office politics, and an obnoxious commute on the Underground. It gets harder each year. I wonder what it is all for. I used to get a kick out of it, and now I just do it for the paycheck."

"Would you not miss our friends, though? We have a great social life."

"We're not talking about the depths of Africa. It's three hours by train to Paddington. People would come and visit I am sure, and we'd make new friends. Besides, can you remember the last time we had a weekend together without having to attend some function?"

"I'm struggling to think of one."

"We both need to think carefully about this, but actually what is there stopping us? I can't think of anything that I couldn't live without in London. We could buy a business together doing something we enjoy. It's seasonal down here. We could get half the year off to travel, maybe even buy a second home in the sun. We've made enough between us to be financially secure."

"You're doing an excellent sales job."

"Why not though?" asked Graham. "Other people do it who are less qualified than us. I reckon there's a market for a posh bed and breakfast. You know, a boutique-style place. With your design skills and my business acumen, we can't lose!"

We procrastinated for six months after that conversation, before the prevarication turned into action. We discussed finance, made extensive lists of pros and cons, read books about running hotels, and registered with estate agents in Torquay. It was clear from looking at the accounts of different companies that the move would involve a reduction in our income, but we hoped the improvements to our quality of life would offset this. Some of Graham's banking friends gave us an idea of how much we could borrow, given our deposit. We considered various leisure-related businesses, including hotels, pubs, restaurants, and shops, but we settled on searching for a small hotel that would give us the lifestyle that we both craved. We put our house up for sale a month later. The real estate market in London was booming at this time, and our property was in tiptop condition and in a desirable area. On the second day of going to market, we received three offers that were all over the asking price. Graham accepted the middle offer, as the purchasers were not in a chain. Whilst the legal processes were taking place, we urgently needed to find a property ourselves and formulate a business plan.

A silver BMW slowed and parked in front of the hotel gates, driven by a tall young man who opened the car door and stepped onto the pavement. Although we had never met him, he was instantly identifiable as an estate agent. He had spiky blond hair and wore a white double-cuffed shirt and a fashionable tie; clothing intended to give him an authoritative air greater than his stature or age. We walked over to him, and he introduced himself with a vigorous handshake as Mike Saxon, the grandson and junior partner of John Saxon & Sons. This was a family-run local estate agent with three offices in the Torquay area. He informed us that they had a historical association with this property.

As we walked up the drive, Mike gave us a brief and edited history of the property, omitting certain less appealing details, which we were to learn about later. The building was constructed in 1852 as a private home called Pembroke House, and it remained in the same family for two generations. Another family purchased it in the 1970s. They sold the land at the rear of the property to a developer, who built apartments. This had paid for a major refurbishment and financed the extensions, enabling them to trade as a hotel. Both Graham and I thought the flats were hideous and the extensions ugly and shoddily constructed. When the father had died, the mother and son had soldiered on without him. Unfortunately, at some point in the 1980s, they had a major feud, and the estranged son moved to Brazil. She then closed the hotel to the public and lived as a recluse until about five years ago when her home help found her dead. She had apparently died of a stroke in her sleep. Immediately after the son inherited the hotel, he put it on the market. Sadly, during her reclusive period, the old lady allowed the house to fall into a state of grave disrepair. This worsened after her death, since the hotel remained unsold for many years. The combination of a grade-two listing and its situation in a conservation area prevented any realistic possibility of development, and thus it was an unappealing prospect for most potential buyers.

The estate agent opened the tatty front door, which was stiff due to its rusty hinges. The entrance vestibule had cheap linoleum on the floor with a fake terracotta tile pattern. The plaster on the walls was crumbling, and the ceiling had collapsed. The hallways were not in too bad a condition, in need of decorating but little else. There were a few telltale signs of leaks given the brown patches on the ceilings, but generally, the building looked sound if not a little damp. That was probably more down to years of being unoccupied and unheated. Sadly, the place had fallen victim to the butchery and dubious fashion statements of the 1970s. All the original fireplaces were bricked up, and low-floating polystyrene monstrosities disguised the high ceilings. It was criminal, sheer vandalism. The family had the foresight to install en suite bathrooms in all the bedrooms, which could have been a good thing, except that they were fitted with avocado suites. There was an abundance of floral patterned wallpaper, woodchip, and artex. This clashed with the worn carpets, dralon curtains, sofas, and pleated bed heads. For some reason, they had covered every flat surface in lace. Outside, the grounds were a neglected wilderness. The swimming pool was full of stagnant green water and the patio seemed to be sinking in the middle, but everything was fixable with enough money. We only wished that we could have seen the inside of the building in the daylight, as unfortunately it was dingy with all the windows boarded up. With hindsight, this may have been a deliberate ploy by the estate agent.

As he walked us around, Mike Saxon talked incessantly. His voice had a mild and charming West Country accent. His enthusiasm was endearing, but his sales pitch was unnecessary. Graham and I had an almost telepathic ability when it came to guessing each other's thoughts. I knew that we were both in love with the place and that we were going to buy it no matter what. It was like fulfilling our destiny. This beautiful, faded piece of English history was going to be ours.

Our tour finished with Mike promising he would call us on Monday. He instructed us to e-mail him if we had any questions. He raced off in his BMW to his next appointment, the throaty exhaust booming loudly as he drove up the hill in first gear.

"Graham," I said. "Can we walk down to the beach and talk?"

"Yes, of course we can."

We walked to Meadfoot Beach and trundled along the coastal path in silence. Then I just burst out with it.

"I love it!"

Graham looked at me with excitement in his eyes. "So do I."

"I mean, it's crazy. It probably needs millions spent on it, but I want it. The house needs us. It needs us to sort it out, to love it. It needs filling with people. It needs to have life breathed back into it."

"Jez?"

"Yes?"

"I love you. You do know I love you?"

"I love you, too. Do you fancy an ice cream?" I pointed to a little cafe overlooking the beach.

"That would be nice. Listen, I won't wait for Mike to call us, I'll phone the agency first thing tomorrow," he said. He lowered his voice conspiratorially. "Now we need to discuss offers."

I feigned being ill to get a sick day off work on Monday morning. I used the old trick of stuffing my nose with toilet paper and calling up in a weak voice, as though I might die any moment. It never failed. Once I was even sent a bunch of flowers from my boss, with a get-well card. Graham was working from home. He called Mike at John Saxon with the telephone on loudspeaker. It was a vendor's market, and we knew that from our own experience of selling the house in Chiswick. This meant that we did not have the option of putting in a ridiculously low offer. However, we knew The Marstan Hotel had been for sale for years, and it was in an appalling condition. The owner was asking £1.2 million for it, so we put in an opening bid of £1.1 million. A few hours later, we received a call informing us the vendors had refused our offer. After some negotiation, we agreed to a final price of £1.15 million.

Lawyers work in old-school time frames. Timesaving innovations such as e-mail seem to have passed them by, so we reluctantly accepted the laborious process of dealing with everything by post. The building survey was the horror story that we had assumed it would be, but essentially the building was structurally sound. There was no subsidence, and everything highlighted in the report was repairable. It gave us some peace of mind to know where we stood. We had a meeting with a mortgage broker who negotiated a competitive deal with Lloyds Bank. Five months from making our offer, we exchanged contracts, and we completed the following week.

On the 12th of October, 2005, we became the proud owners of The Marstan Hotel in Torquay. Mike Saxon met us at the hotel to hand over the keys. He wished us luck and handed us a tin of Family Circle biscuits. They had a whip around at the office apparently. It would take more than a box of Bourbon Creams and Jammie Dodgers to get us over the mountain that lie ahead of us.

Graham and I walked into the dank and dingy building. We had just sold our warm and beautiful house in Arlington Gardens, Chiswick, which was pristine. Entering this hovel almost brought tears to my eyes. What had we done? The Marstan Hotel, formerly Pembroke House, was now ours—lock, stock, and leaking roof. We felt like two passengers strapped into a roller coaster just before it goes over the precipice. There was no going back now.

Chapter 4

September 1973: Marjorie Wilson

Despite living out of a suitcase and enduring the stress of the building work, Stanley and I wasted no time in networking around Torquay's business and political communities. We knew the importance of having contacts from first-hand experience of running a small business in London. We became members of the Conservative Club, a short walk from us at the end of Meadfoot Lane, and as a result of this, we discovered that there was a councilor's position due to become vacant because of an impending retirement. Whilst we were new to politics in the locality, I felt that Stanley would undeniably be perfectly suited for this. Stanley also joined the Torquay Freemasons and the local golf club in St. Marychurch. We were warmly welcomed into the congregation at St. Mathias Anglican Church, and Reverend Andrew Esdale soon became a good friend.

Christopher auditioned and subsequently joined TOADS, an acronym for Torquay Operatic Amateur Dramatic Society. Their production base was a little theatre created from a converted church around the corner from the house. His talent was quickly recognized, and the first play that he performed in was Oscar Wilde's *The Importance of Being Earnest*, in which he was cast as the lead, John Worthing. He was delighted to have received rave reviews from the *Torquay Herald* newspaper for his acting ability. When the pantomime season started, he reprised a favorite role he had played in Barnet, an ugly sister in *Cinderella*. He had auditioned for the part of Cinderella itself, but the casting directors felt that Torquay was not quite ready for it. All three of us became involved in the Torquay Hoteliers Association. Torquay had an abundance of hotels, and we competed for customers, thus it was useful to form alliances and buying groups with proprietors that had complementary businesses.

I resist the temptation to write extensively about local politics, but one significant event was a visit from the Education Secretary, to express her support for Torquay Grammar School, which certain councilors in other parties were attempting to turn into one of those dreadful comprehensives. Her name was Margaret Thatcher, and I thought she was inspirational. In contrast, Stanley was dubious, not least because of her frumpy appearance and shrill voice. He felt that her promotion was due to the fact she was a woman, rather than possession of any political talent, and that her career would be brief. I disagreed with Stanley on this; I found her charming and fiercely intelligent, and I admired her for being a working class woman in the Commons with all those boorish Eton or Harrow educated types with the right connections.

Sadly, she was part of the Heath government that was desperately unpopular. Tough decisions forced upon her had besmirched her reputation. She was known as 'Thatcher the milk snatcher' after scrapping free school milk at secondary schools. I remember her describing the modern Conservative Party as the party for the aspirational and that we were the types they wanted to attract. Stanley was becoming increasingly involved in local politics, and he aspired to serve as an MP in the future. The first-hand political experience that he was gaining could help him to achieve this ambition.

With reference to our fledgling business, we had a mountain to climb before we could open our doors to the public. We needed to make the property habitable. The various quotations from builders were more expensive than we had anticipated. Clearly, it was going to be a challenge to be ready in time for the holiday season. I obtained a part-time secretarial job in a local lawyer's firm to avoid using our savings to cover the shortfall. Stanley had an idea to sell the sizeable area of land at the rear of the hotel to a developer to build apartments. Currently, it languished unloved and overgrown with weeds, the site of a dilapidated greenhouse and an unused well. One of Stanley's golfing partners, a director who had a seat on the Torquay Council planning committee, indicated that he would 'sort it' so we would get permission. To this effect, we engaged the services of an architect who designed a block of four purpose-built apartments. He suggested that a precedent had been set with other properties along the road, should we wish to extend Pembroke House. This was an excellent suggestion that we had not considered. We decided to create a separate annex for Christopher, in order that he would have some privacy. We also asked him to draw up an additional single-story appendage for use as a function room. Stanley wanted to exploit the lucrative wedding market, and this would give us the extra space to host them. We requested that he reconfigure the interior for modern tourism. I was aware that overseas holidays were more popular now, and luxuries like en suite bathrooms were becoming an expectation rather than a bonus. Therefore, I felt that it was justifiable even though it meant reducing the number of the bedrooms. We decided to install a swimming pool to give us an added selling point. After brief negotiations with the planning officers, our architect's designs received approval along with our application to convert from a private dwelling to a commercial premise. It made a lovely Christmas present for us.

We spent Christmas Day at Delamare Court. Mavis kindly invited us to join her, as she was alone over the festive period. She had the whole of the ground floor arranged as her private accommodation, which was palatial in comparison to our cramped holiday-let. It felt very Christmassy with a roaring log fire and a tall fir tree brashly decorated in clashing colors. I helped with the cooking and steamed the Christmas pudding, whilst Stanley carved the turkey. Over Christmas lunch, Mavis talked nonstop for more than an hour, giving us the lowdown on the neighbors. She seemed to know everyone's business, whether it be tittle-tattle or more newsworthy information, and what she did not know she would fabricate. Delamare Court stood on a high vantage point, and she had a powerful pair of binoculars that she used to spy on everyone within range. If any neighbors made a significant purchase, she would know about it. The couple at Twin Pines had bought a new sofa, and the Woodland family from number eight took delivery of an Austin Maxi last week. There were strange goings-on at Meadfoot Lodge; apparently, a white van driver had been making regular visits and entering via the rear gate. I suspected they were having a new kitchen fitted, but Mavis was convinced that something unsavory was going on. Mrs. Howden had undergone a hysterectomy, and the Lytton family from Stanemore House had their Yorkshire terrier put down. Mavis said the vet had diagnosed suspected kidney failure. This information did not come from the Lytton's but the veterinary practice, which Mavis had called as she had noticed the poor thing had not been walked for a week. She prodded and inquired about our business, but we knew her too well to reveal anything of importance.

We all consumed copious amounts of wine. Following the queen's speech, Stanley slumped in an armchair and started to snore loudly, whilst Christopher tackled the washing-up. I was embarrassed about my husband, but Mavis seemed unfazed; she was more concerned that we felt at home. As a divorcee with her two children living in Birmingham, she often complained of being lonely. It seemed that they rarely called or visited. She alleviated her loneliness with the company of seven cats who roamed the house and gardens as if they owned it. I was not fond of cats, particularly the vicious white Persian called Tiddles. It had a nasty habit of rubbing against your leg whilst purring, before biting you as you went to stroke it. Many of Mavis' holiday guests fell victim. Some of the cats did not seem to be house-trained either, and there was always a whiff of cat pee. I did not think that this or the litter trays in the conservatory made an appropriate welcome for tourists. The cats saw our garden as an extension of their territory, and I would be finding ways to discourage this.

We sold the surplus land in January with planning permission in place. The developer started work at the same time as our builders. The profit from the land sale would cover the cost of the renovations and extensions, with some left over. Stanley decided to spend some of this on a new car and bought a Volvo Estate, which was an unnecessary extravagance in my opinion. However, Stanley felt that we needed a more prestigious vehicle to reflect our growing status in the town. The schedule was tight and despite Easter being late that year, I knew we would not be ready by then. With the building covered in scaffolding, most of the roof removed, and a large pit in the garden where the pool would be situated, we prayed for a dry winter. Although the building was still uninhabitable, I used the study as an office. I kept this room free of tradesmen, with the door closed to prevent the worst of the dust penetrating the room. The GPO installed a telephone, and I perched my typewriter on top of a cardboard box. A few weeks into the build, the workmen had put in a rudimentary electrical supply so at least I benefited from heat and light, and they could operate their power tools.

The building project dominated our lives, but we needed to think about creating a business. To successfully market the hotel would require brochures to be printed and advertising in the relevant publications. It was also necessary to appoint suppliers such as butchers, greengrocers, and a laundry company. I oversaw responsibility for the bookkeeping and deposited some working capital into our business current account. Stanley took ownership of marketing and sales. Once we were open, I would cook and clean with a helper, whilst Stanley would oversee the maintenance and operate the bar at weekends. Christopher would wait tables, act as a kitchen porter, and staff the bar during the week. We would employ the services of a gardener, and we would all share front of house duties.

There was much to organize, but I felt that there was light at the end of the tunnel and that we would be ready for our scheduled opening date in May.

Chapter 5

October 2005: Jez Matthews

It was an understatement to say that our first night at The Marstan Hotel was not restful. Firstly, there were strange wailing noises that seemed to emanate from the walls. We chose to sleep in the back bedroom, and overnight there was heavy rain. Graham was woken by water dripping into his ear. Having discovered that this room had a leaking roof, we moved into a different bedroom that at least was watertight. There was a pervading smell of damp, and although we had managed to get the old furnace lit, the radiators were only lukewarm. This was another problem to join the long list. Thankfully, the second bedroom was dry, but unfortunately, the bed that the previous owners had left in situ was rock hard and squeaked. I lay awake listening to the rain patter against the thin glass sash windows, staring up at the stained artex ceiling, wondering what we had done. We had given up our respective careers, a comfortable, warm and waterproof house, and mortgaged ourselves to the hilt to buy a leaky, damp-ridden money pit in the butt-end of Devon. Graham started snoring gently, and eventually I fell asleep but I was restless and disturbed by nightmares. The unpleasant dreams filled me with anxiety, and I kept hearing voices. At one point,

I distinctly heard my name whispered. It was so vivid that I woke up startled, and then failed to get back to sleep.

The following morning, Graham and I tucked into a simple breakfast of cornflakes washed down with a double espresso each. The first thing we had unpacked on arrival was the coffee machine. We sat at the table in our dressing gowns and slippers in the cold, filthy kitchen with the smell of rancid cooking oil that clung to the walls partially disguised by the aroma of freshly ground coffee beans.

"How did you sleep?" I asked.

"Apart from the fact I was woken up by floods of water, and had you fidgeting all night—oh, and the strange noises—fine."

"Did you have nightmares?"

"No, why?"

"I did, horrible ones."

"What were they about?"

"I can't honestly remember, but I was glad I woke up. I kept hearing noises and voices."

"It's an old house, Jez. It'll be the plumbing, and your wild imagination. The only thing I heard was the next-door neighbor's cat meowing."

"Do you think we've bitten off more than we can chew with this place?" I said, looking around.

"It'll be fine. We've got seven months until we open, but we need to get a builder in and soon. We'll need to get a website up and running and think about pricing and where to advertise, then talk about staff. However, the builders take priority. I can't live with this fucking artex everywhere. It's doing my head in."

"It's the carpets in the bathroom that I can't cope with.

They all stink of piss. Minging."

"They can go today. I'll organize a skip to be delivered. Why don't you start phoning builders? In fact, a good place to start would be an architect. I've got an idea."

"And?"

"Let's pull down that hideous extension bedsit thing. It looks foul. I wish we could demolish those awful 70s flats behind, too, but we don't own them. The dining room is shoddily built as well. God knows what they thought they were doing. I was thinking about pulling it down and building a lovely Victorian-style orangery."

"It's a great idea, but that's going to take us well over budget."

"I thought of that, too."

"So long as it doesn't involve borrowing more money. We've got a half million-pound mortgage and no income."

"Well, I was going to tell you this earlier, but..."

"I've a bad feeling about this," I said, glaring at him.

"Okay, you know when I resigned the door was left very open..."

"Go on."

"My old boss Theresa phoned from Anderson Levy Brokers yesterday, to wish us good luck... Well, that was the main reason."

"What did that cow want?" I said. "You know I can't stand her."

"She's always been good to me."

"Only because you're useful to her. She's everything I hate about the human race. The most two-faced person I know. A corporate android in her bloody Versace suits and Clarins lipstick waiting for the next person to stab in the back, so she can climb the greasy pole. I say greasy pole—she's certainly had a few of those in her quest for promotion."

"Now you're being a bitch. She's not that bad, and

you're hardly a saint."

"Excuse me, I've never shagged anyone to get a pay rise, or made-up lies about people I don't like to get them sacked, or taken credit for things that I..."

"All right, if you could stop the attitude for a second, let's get to the point, shall we? My old job has been refilled, but they're looking for somebody to train and mentor a new team in a different department. It's a six-month contract."

"Graham, no. Can't you see what's happening here? Why did we move away from London? Because you were stressed, the commute was killing you, the office politics, hideous hours—Can't you see? We've not even started our new lives, yet you're being sucked back in!"

"They'll pay one thousand pounds a day, four days a week, plus expenses, and the use of the company flat."

"What?"

"They'll pay me a thousand pounds a day. I only have to work Monday to Thursday, so I'd be back at weekends, and it's for six months. This is not permanent. The money I earn will finance making this place perfect."

A silence fell across the room as the reality of the situation sunk in. This was an opportunity that we could not afford to turn down.

"I have to telephone her this morning," said Graham. "If I accept, I start in two weeks."

I stared into space.

"Jez, if you don't want me to, I will phone her now and say no. It's your call," he said.

"What I said still stands. I feel we're selling out, but let's face it. It's six months, and it means financial stability and getting this place done properly instead of compromising."

"Stand up," Graham ordered.

"Why?"

"I want to give you a big hug."

I duly obliged, wrapping my arms around him and holding him tightly.

"And now," he said. "Let's go upstairs and christen that foul bedroom!"

"Now you're talking!" I mumbled, as he pressed his lips against mine.

After our morning's escapades, it was down to business. I found a firm of local architects from the yellow pages. They visited a couple of days later, armed with an array of strange equipment. I gave them an outline of what we wanted, which they indicated would be straightforward. I then received a letter from them requesting a check for £5,000 for the initial draft work. The final fee was much higher. They would act as project managers on the build. This meant that Graham and I could concentrate on the marketing aspects of the business.

Waiting for planning permission was a frustrating period. Despite our eagerness, we could not do much, and it felt as though we were in limbo. Graham worked up in London for most of the week, which made my existence a lonely one, rattling around in that big house on my own. I killed time by taking great pleasure in ripping out and destroying the vile carpets, 1970s furniture, and chintz.

I designed a website, put into place a bookkeeping system, and met suppliers. I visited numerous antique auctions and began to acquire lovely furniture and paintings that the house deserved. It had to be temporarily stored, but I planned in my mind exactly where each piece belonged.

Graham and I hated the name 'Marstan,' and since the hotel had not been trading for over a decade, there was little incentive to keep it. We discussed different ideas—the most ridiculous being Grayjez, a fusion of our two names—but ultimately the choice was obvious. We would revert to the building's original name, Pembroke House, substituting the word 'house' for 'hotel.'

Meanwhile, the mysterious incidents continued unabated. One morning I came down to the kitchen to find half a dozen smashed glasses. The odd noises persisted, but I learned to accept these paranormal events as part of the charm of owning an old property with much history, although I hoped that the spirits would not be too intrusive once we opened. Graham was dismissive and seemed to be oblivious. When I telephoned my notoriously superstitious mother and told her about it, she said my late grandma had possessed *the gift.* I remember when she used to read my tealeaves as a boy, but I just thought that she was inventing stories to frighten me into obedience. Apparently, she used to read tarot and have a Ouija board, but my parents banned her from performing any occultist activities around her grandchildren. I could not help but wonder what she would make of the old place.

Chapter 6

February 1974: Marjorie Wilson

We finally moved out of Delamare Court and into Pembroke House in February. We used an unfinished but habitable bedroom in the east wing. Water and electricity were intermittent, but when we needed a hot bath and could not get one here, we went next door to Mavis. A paraffin heater kept us reasonably warm, and Stanley had managed to get our black-and-white portable television working by jamming a bent coat hanger in the rear socket to function as a makeshift aerial. ITV was a bit fuzzy, but we got a reasonable picture on BBC1.

As the dust affected his asthma, Christopher was staying with a friend he had met at his *Doctor Who* club. Stanley was juggling his campaigning work for the Conservatives in the upcoming election, along with dealing with his duties here. Our MP Martin Breville was expected to win, but there was an element of uncertainty. Martin and Stanley had rapidly become firm friends, and Martin encouraged my husband to stand for a councilor position.

The light outside was fading as the sun descended below the horizon. It was five o'clock in mid-February with little sign of spring. Stan and I were sitting in our overcoats huddled around an electric bar heater in the drafty study. The light came from a single bare bulb hanging from the ceiling that the builders had connected via an extension cable to the newly installed fuse box.

When we had purchased Pembroke House, I had always assumed that we would evolve the name into something obvious, such as The Pembroke Hotel. However, Stanley suggested an idea that at first I found too quirky, but eventually he persuaded me. Since there was no goodwill or trading history under the Pembroke name, he suggested that we call it The Marstan Hotel, using the first letters from our Christian names. When we agreed on this, the house seemed to react angrily by making the light bulb fizz and flicker out. I made a mental note to ask the builders to check the fuse box tomorrow.

Chapter 7

January 2006: Jez Matthews

Early in January, we received a letter from the planning officers approving our application. Finally, it was full steam ahead with the refurbishment project. Although I could escape from the building site to the comfort and warmth of Graham's apartment in the Barbican, I preferred to spend most of my time in Torquay. I slept on a blow-up bed in the study, as the builders had gutted the bedrooms. I removed the old smelly carpet and put a rug down over the floorboards. I hung some cheap curtains to give me some privacy, and I purchased a small television to alleviate my boredom. A microwave served as the only cooking appliance, which I placed on top of a small fridge. The refrigerator had a noisy compressor, which regularly interrupted my sleep. It was not a great living space, but it was bearable. Initially, Graham commuted to Torquay at weekends, but it made more sense for me to travel there, to have a decent shower and a comfortable bed. Although the flat in the Barbican was luxurious, it was not home, and Graham never bothered to unpack. I would catch an early train back to Torquay on Monday mornings, and I enjoyed the view from the carriage as the sooty urban sprawl of London gave way to green fields and eventually to the coastline. It was a three-hour trip on the fast train from London, but I found that the time passed quickly. I enjoyed brunch in the catering car, and then spent the rest of the journey reading *The Guardian* and listening to music on my iPod.

The project manager eliminated the worst of the stress of the construction work. The builders knocked down the ugly 1970s appendages with a wrecking ball in a matter of days, and the work on the orangery began soon after. Living on a building site was hellish, but on the plus side, I had a house full of well-built tradesmen showing off their latest tattoos and talking about football during their numerous tea breaks. There is something wonderfully attractive about grimy, unpretentious builders. One of the apprentices was proud to show me the tattoo on his bottom. I spent a good few minutes admiring the Arsenal Football Club logo that he had indelibly inked on his firm buttock. There were compensations to the inconvenience of all this construction work. They were all straight, of course, but that still did not stop me fantasizing. We encountered a few unexpected problems, such as asbestos discovered in some of the doors, which needed dealing with appropriately. However, even after a month, the difference in the house was stark.

My weekday evenings at home alone were dull. It seemed my life was a daily routine of ready meals, television, and early nights. The highlights were the occasional glass of wine and talking to Graham. The time that we spent apart gave our relationship breathing space, and we always had plenty to catch up on, but in truth, I missed him. I had a broadband connection fitted so I could see and talk to him on Skype, which was better than the telephone. This also meant that I could maintain email contact with friends and work more productively.

It was a Wednesday night in mid-January, and ITV had canceled *Coronation Street* because of a soccer match. I possessed about as much interest in football as George

W. Bush had in promoting gay rights. With nothing to entertain me, I decided impulsively that I would go out to a local pub, which was a short walk from the hotel.

I took a shower in one of the unfinished bathrooms, gelled my hair, and doused myself with aftershave. I changed into a designer outfit, albeit last season's, and headed out to see what the Torquay gay scene had to offer. I walked into The Horn of Plenty, a pub that accurately advertised itself as having a diverse and alternative clientele. I was not expecting it to be busy, but it turned out to be to a charity fundraiser night for Torquay Pride. This meant that it was packed, very noisy, and smoky. As I walked in through the front door, people looked over curiously, and it felt as though there was a spotlight focused on me; I naturally took advantage of the situation, as anybody with my cheekbones would. I was new meat. New chromosomes in a limited gene pool. They were like pigs around shit.

The Horn of Plenty was a stereotypically old-school gay pub, found outside of the big cities. The building itself was charming, being a listed Victorian double-fronted terraced building with large sash windows at the front. These were fitted with Venetian blinds to keep out prying eyes. A small rainbow flag sticker on the door discreetly confirmed that it was a gay venue, without attracting unwanted attention. Inside, it was cramped and chintzy with old-fashioned patterned carpets in need of a deep clean. The ventilation was poor, and thus the air was thick with cigarette smoke. The bar was located in the middle of the pub. The counter was made of imitation wood, and they had an old-fashioned cash register from the 1980s. Mismatched tables and stools were scattered randomly around the place. A raised area served as a mini dance floor or a stage, and the owners had painted the walls in clashing colors, mainly pinks and yellows, upon which they hung signed photographs of gay icons such as Dolly Parton and Cher. It was very different from the trendy London bars to which Graham and I had become accustomed.

I walked over to the bar and waited to be served, holding out a twenty-pound note. Eventually, my turn came, and the barman took my order.

"A large glass of Sauvignon Blanc, please," I said standoffishly.

An older man, who was propping up the bar and holding a half-empty pint of Guinness, eyed me lecherously.

"Things are looking up," he said.

"Not for me," I replied acidly.

The barman that served me was called Dave. He was short, camp, chain-smoked, and had teeth from the Plantagenet era. He weighed about twenty stone and had a personality as large as his girth. He missed nothing that happened in the pub. It was safe to say that he knew everything about everyone, and what he did not know, he would invent.

"Darling," he said loudly in a gravelly smoker's voice, gesticulating with his arms. "Are you visiting the area?"

"No," I said. "My partner and I have bought The Marstan Hotel, or The Pembroke Hotel, as we have now renamed it. We're refurbishing it and turning it into a luxury boutique guesthouse."

"Pem-broke, you *will* be broke darling buying that shit hole," he said, looking very pleased with his humor.

"Well, we have big plans for it."

"We have an extensive choice of wine here, love, white or red. They're blends. If you want rosé, we just mix the two!"

"The white will be fine thanks."

"Daaaaarling," he said walking out from behind the bar, unexpectedly flinging his arms around me. "Welcome to Torbaydos. I hope we will be seeing more of you."

The bear hug lasted a little longer than I felt comfortable with, and I flinched a little against his unwelcome attention, particularly as I detected a whiff of body odor.

His voice hardened, and he said, "And you can leave that fucking London attitude back up there. Your shit stinks just as much as ours."

His words were said half in jest, but he was making a point and it dawned on me how conceited I must have seemed to people. He went back behind the bar and handed me a glass of wine and some change. One of the pub owners came over clutching a book of raffle tickets. His name was Steph, and he was a chain-smoking six-foot transvestite. He was about as convincing at being a female as Dustin Hoffman was playing Tootsie. He had a deep voice and wore a curly blond wig that had a touch of mange. His makeup was appalling, and he had chest hair poking through the top of his dress. He shimmied around the pub making the patrons howl with laughter with his caustic put-downs and bitchy demeanor, all the while dressed in a long navy ball gown that billowed around him, knocking over glasses. I was unsure whether this was a deliberate ploy to increase drink sales, but at no point was an apology or a free replacement offered.

"Would you like a raffle ticket, darlin'? It's to support gay pride next August."

"Erm yes, how much are they?" I said, fumbling in my pocket for change.

"It's a pound a ticket, five pounds a strip, love. Prizes are over there."

The prize collection consisted of a bottle of Blue Nun, a Judy Garland CD, a pair of 'jeweled' marigold gloves, and a £5 bar voucher along with lots of other rubbish that you could not even give away at a car boot sale. I later discovered that the prizes were always the same every year, as when people won they usually just gave them back.

"I'll take two strips," I said eagerly.

He snatched the ten-pound note off me before I changed my mind and tore off the tickets. "Draws at midnight. Good luck, sexy," he said in a deep voice and gave my bottom a squeeze before gliding toward the next customer.

The other owner was called Michelle. I learned later that night that his real name was Michael. He did not like being called Michelle, but people called him that anyway. He was the butch one of the two, but when I say butch, I mean relatively speaking—a bit like saying Graham Norton is butch compared to Lesley Jordan from *Will & Grace*. He was in his forties and quite tall, with a shaven balding head, a goatee beard, and a beer belly. He wore an unflattering Star Trek T-shirt and jeans, and he perpetually scowled.

I sipped my wine, which tasted like turpentine, whilst standing at the bar. I was going to leave once I had finished my drink, but a charming young man walked over to me with his hand extended.

"Hi, I'm Jason. Nice to see a new face."

I studied Jason, who was a lovely looking lad in his early twenties with blond floppy hair, perfect skin and teeth. He was very much the boy-next-door type that I used to be, slim with sparkling blue eyes and a certain naughtiness about him.

"Jason," I said taking his hand firmly. "I'm Jez, short for Jeremy."

"Do you like it in here?" he asked.

"Well," I said. "It's very friendly. It has a sort of rustic charm."

"Friendly? Yes, it always starts out like that, and then they realize you won't sleep with them and it all changes.

Rustic, well I think most of the people in here use straw for bedding," he said, laughing. "You're going to tell me you're in an LTR, aren't you?"

"Yes, I have a long-term partner called Graham. He's working up in London at the moment."

"Always the bloody way. The good-looking ones are married, and I get stuck with this ugly lot. I have to ask this, do you play?" he asked presumptuously.

"No," I said firmly.

"You can't blame a girl for trying. Anyway, that's done with. So you're new to the bay, then? You've bought a hotel from what I've heard."

"Heard?"

"It's been going around the pub."

"You know, Jason," I said, "gays never cease to amaze me. I've been here less than half an hour, and already people know about my business."

"Way it works. You can't sit on the outside. You're either part of it, or you're not. Anyway, you've almost finished your wine. Another?"

"Yes, please."

"Great, I'll have one, too. Cider for me, but not a Stella Cidre—never trust a misspelt cider. I'll have Strongbow."

I could not help laughing at his barefaced cheek. I bought him a drink, and in fairness, he reciprocated later. It was clear that he was shallow and a gossip, possibly even a troublemaker, yet within a few minutes of speaking to him, I knew that we were going to become great friends. I ended up having too much to drink, but nonetheless, I had a cracking evening. They put on karaoke later, and it was hilarious to watch Steph ruin Abba's "Gimme Gimme Gimme", complete with various animated sections involving a dildo and an action man. He lubricated his voice by taking large gulps of wine between verses. The quantity of alcohol I consumed gave me Dutch courage, so Jason and I performed a duet of "Hopelessly Devoted to You" to wolf whistles and applause. The only hopeless thing was our performance. He flirted with me all night and his attentions flattered me, but he respected my boundaries.

It seemed to me that Jason knew everyone in the pub and his or her life stories. He knew, in detail, the incestuous relationships among the indigenous gay population. He knew who had slept with who, and apparently their intimate bedroom secrets. His humor was salacious, but he was hugely entertaining.

The raffle was drawn and the prizes presented to the unlucky recipients. I faired a little better than most as I won a DVD of *Priscilla Queen of the Desert*, a film that I had not seen for a long time, but remember enjoying. At half-past midnight, we were the last two customers in the bar, and the owners chucked us out. Jason and I exchanged numbers before he jumped into a taxi, and I walked home.

My trips to The Horn of Plenty became weekly, then almost nightly, and before I knew it, I was a regular with my drink poured before I reached the bar. They even started stocking a reasonable Sauvignon for my benefit. Jason and I were inseparable partners in crime and people assumed we were having a physical relationship, but we were not.

Jason worked as a window dresser at Hooper's department store in the town, so when I was bored, we would meet up for a coffee or a light lunch. Torquay was beginning to warm up, and the little cafes around the harbor were opening. It was mild enough to sit outside under a patio heater and watch the fishing boats dock and unload their catch. Jason would always have plenty of interesting stories to tell. Whilst I usually spent my weekends in London, Graham would sometimes travel to Torquay. On one occasion, I managed to persuade him to accompany me to the pub. He was not a fan of the experience. He found Jason vacuous and loathed the Saturday night disco and karaoke, but he reluctantly came along and pretended to enjoy himself. After the pub closed, he was happy for me to stay out late with Jason.

After leaving the pub, we would visit Torquay's only gay nightclub for a dance. It was called Bangs, and it was stuck in the dark ages, hidden away up a side street. You had to know about it, as it would be impossible to find otherwise. It was in the basement of a tatty hotel. There was a discreet sign on the outside to avoid drawing too much attention from the general public. You accessed it by descending the highly unsafe steps behind the railings to the lower ground floor. You rang a doorbell, and after a few seconds, the door would open, revealing the scruffy interior. An aggressive lesbian in a fluorescent high-visibility security jacket confronted you to relieve you of £5 for the privilege of attending. The air smelt strongly of poppers, cigarette smoke, stale beer, and vomit. This was all accompanied by the sound of Kylie Minogue blaring out of a sound system designed for a space four times larger. Although it was tacky, it was also great fun. Jason and I would dance until the early hours, taking the piss out of anyone we decided we did not like. The barmen, most of whom Jason had slept with, were arrogant and rude, unless they fancied you. They would practically throw drinks at the clientele, but thankfully, their sarcastic comments were not audible over the din of the music. Jason would often disappear into the toilets with some twink for twenty minutes and come out licking his lips, looking satisfied with himself. The lavatories themselves were filthy. All the urinals leaked, and by the end of the night, the cubicle toilets were blocked and overflowing with tissue paper. The stench was unbearable, but people forgave this and the other numerous faults, as there was a genuinely fabulous atmosphere. Either it was that, or because it was the only gay nightclub within a thirty-mile radius.

Chapter 8

April 1974: Marjorie Wilson

In recent weeks, the building work had slowed down. May was approaching, and there was much to do. Ted Heath lost the general election to Harold Wilson, but thankfully, Martin Breville kept his seat in Torquay. The end of campaigning meant that Stanley had more spare time and he could focus on the business.

The builders joked that the house seemed to be rebelling against the changes we were making. Tools mysteriously went missing overnight, turning up days later in odd places. A black, sooty stain on the wall in the master bedroom inexplicably bled through the new wood chip wallpaper. On a more serious note, part of the scaffolding collapsed for no reason and nearly killed one of the roofers. However, on the plus side, the pool was finished. Christopher had employed the services of a young mustached gardener called Jack, whom he had met whilst on one of his evening walks. Jack, supervised closely by Christopher, was getting the garden into shape, his muscles rippling through a dirty white vest. They had laid new turf and filled the borders with shrubs and bedding plants. Stanley and I never realized that Christopher was a fan of gardening, but horticulture seemed to be his new passion and he was very enthusiastic. The benign climate in Torquay allowed tropical plants to grow that would be more suited to the Mediterranean, and we planted palms, banana, and lemon trees around the pool area. Using a certain amount of imagination, you could believe that you were abroad. The foreman's solution to our timetable slippage was more manpower. After a temporary surge in numbers, at the end of April most of the builders had left, and it was just finishing details that needed to be actioned. The dining room extension was almost completed, needing only the pebbledash and steel casement windows to be painted.

Inside, we rewired the entire house to modern standards. The builders had bricked up the drafty fireplaces. We sold the mantelpieces and surrounds to a scrap yard in Exeter who collected them free of charge, as apparently some people still wanted the ghastly things. Stanley was keen on keeping the heating bills down, so we installed a suspended ceiling in the lounge. This was made of polystyrene tiles fixed to an aluminum frame with modern fluorescent strip lighting, which gave the room a contemporary feel. The walls were so uneven that the plasterer used an artex coating throughout most of the public rooms, skillfully creating a combed pattern. In the bedrooms, we hung wood chip wallpaper that we painted magnolia. This looked lovely, especially with a floral border where the picture rails used to be. All the bedrooms had the latest transistor radios mounted on the wall near the beds. We rectified the leaking roof on the entrance porch and painted the inside, laying down some modern linoleum over the dated tiles. It made a good first impression to our guests.

The en suite bathrooms were a triumph. We fitted avocado-colored suites with dusty pink tiles and luxurious carpeted floors. We had wall-to-wall carpeting with a brown and orange swirled pattern laid throughout the hotel. The new beds arrived with pleated dralon headboards. Stanley and Christopher assembled the furniture that we had purchased at MFI. This was no mean feat as there were eight sets of mahogany effect furniture for the bedrooms, eight teak dining tables, and sideboards for the lounge and bar. I had unpacked my sewing machine and made up some lace tablecloths and nets. Christopher accessorized the rooms and made numerous shopping trips to Woolworth's to buy cushions, lamps, pictures, and candles. He also bought other things that we had overlooked, such as pepper pots and ashtrays. Mavis kindly knitted us eight toilet roll covers as a moving-in present.

In the middle of May, the builders finished the side extension where Christopher would have a private rear entrance to his bedsit with a kitchenette. This gave him the freedom to come and go as he pleased without disturbing us. Stanley and I would live in the main house in a small room at the back, behind the kitchen.

We installed fire extinguishers and an alarm system, at the behest of the fire brigade, to obtain our fire certificate. The magistrates accepted our application for a liquor license. After giving the whole house a deep clean, at last we were ready to open our doors to the public. Our first guests were due to arrive on Friday, the 6th of June, which was three days away.

Finally, our opening day came. Christopher and I spent the morning fretting in anticipation of our first guests arriving. Stanley was wearing a suit and was mentally preparing himself to greet the guests. Whilst we were socially confident, it was still nerve racking, but this was partially countered by our sense of pride in the hotel. The paint was fresh and the beds were all new, having never been slept in. Everything gleamed and sparkled. Christopher bought a bouquet of flowers from the local florist and arranged them in a vase on the coffee table in the lounge. They gave off a pleasing scent, which mingled with the smell of new paint. I only allowed Stanley to smoke in the bar, and already the cigarette smoke was starting to cling to the curtains and carpets in this room. Mavis had dropped in a good-luck card and a box of Terry's All Gold chocolates.

I felt that the house needed life breathing back into it. Converting the building into a hotel would revitalize it and give it a purpose for the modern age. I looked forward to the bustle of guests conversing in the bar and mingling in the public rooms.

We offered the option of evening meals to guests, and I had created a simple menu that changed daily. Tonight, guests had the option of lasagna or fish pie that I had divided into individual portions in small baking dishes. This meant that I would be able to reheat them easily in the oven. Pudding would be a choice of either Arctic roll or sherry trifle. I hoped that the cuisine would leave an indelible impression on our guests.

Finally, at three, the doorbell rang. It was a delightful couple called Mr. and Mrs. Thompson from Staffordshire who were visiting the area for a weekend leisure break.

It was a gentle introduction to hotel ownership, as they were easygoing and appreciative, enjoying the tea and angel layer cake on arrival. Stanley retained his managerial composure, which counterbalanced my informality and Christopher's youthful exuberance. It did unfortunately mean for Stan, that if ever there were complaints from guests, he in his perceived role as the boss would be the person who received them.

At steady intervals throughout the afternoon, the other guests arrived, and I quickly realized what a mixed bag of people stayed in hotels. We had an unmarried younger couple from Birmingham, both factory workers. He had an unsightly tattoo on his forearm and wore scruffy flared jeans and an old T-shirt. She was overweight and as common as muck, but surprisingly they had booked our most expensive room, the master bedroom overlooking the swimming pool. They apparently spent their money on holidays instead of clothes or deodorant. There was an older American couple from Oregon touring England, who found everything in our country quaint, from our tiny cars to our obsession with tea. They loved our hotel, were very sociable, big drinkers, and tipped generously. The rest of the guests who visited were generally pleasant. Our car park was full of new Rovers and Wosleys, which confirmed my belief that we were attracting the right sort.

We served evening meals at six o'clock, after *Jim'll Fix It*. Stanley had assembled a decent wine list with the help of a local merchant whom Christopher had befriended from the amateur dramatic society. Hock and Blue Nun sold particularly well. The diners generally finished by seven and often enjoyed a post-dinner drink and a cigarette in the bar, or watched the color television set in the lounge. Bruce Forsythe's Saturday television show *The Generation Game* always seemed to get a large audience.

The bar proved to be great fun, even if it was sometimes a little tiring. Occasionally, it was raucous, depending on the crowd that was staying with us. Stanley would talk about politics, football, or golf to anybody that would listen, with a cigarette in one hand and a gin and tonic in the other. I tended to be more empathic, listening to people's life stories and their problems. Christopher would usually work the late shift, regaling fascinated guests with stories about his theatrical work and his encounters with some of the showbiz greats, whilst sipping a Babycham.

Christopher usually closed the bar around eleven

and habitually took in the night air with a walk along Daddyhole Plain. He claimed that this helped alleviate his asthma. He seemed to meet a few friends this way too, and they would often drop by for coffee in his bedsit. I was glad that he had made acquaintances so quickly down here, and I hoped that he would meet a nice girl soon as I had planned his future wedding reception in meticulous detail, in my mind at least.

Summer was soon upon us, and the hotel was fully occupied. We enjoyed the lifestyle, and the bank balance was healthy. Even though it was hard work, Stanley and I still made time to pursue our outside interests and maintain a social life. Although Stan constantly complained of disturbing dreams, I had felt more settled living at the hotel than I had anywhere before. It may sound strange, but I felt a symbiotic connection with the bricks and mortar. The house somehow enveloped and loved me. I felt cushioned and protected from the world outside, and I could not imagine living anywhere else. I became more a part of the building and its history as each week passed. Over time, I gained a sense of invincibility as though the house was encouraging and nurturing my ambitions.

Our first member of staff was a teenager called Anna. She lasted a day. She ran downstairs wailing and claimed that an 'unseen assailant' had thrown a bedside lamp at her. Stanley reacted predictably. He was furious, claiming that she had invented the story because she had broken it, and refused to pay her for the morning's work. I will never forget how petrified she looked, though. We now had Elsie, who was a more mature lady and very diligent, always neatly turned out, reliable and trustworthy. I imagined she was in her late 50s, but she was very able with a slim figure and a perfect posture gained from her training as a ballerina in her youth. Whilst at work, she kept her graying hair tied back in a bun, which gave her a slightly severe appearance.

We had a hot busy summer and seemed to lose track of the days. Before we knew it, the nights were drawing in rapidly and we reached September. The school holiday families left, and the hotel filled with an older, more genteel crowd.

Mavis and I met for a weekly lunch at Cafe Blanco, when she would furnish me with the neighborhood gossip. When I wanted intelligent company, I would arrange to meet Tannis Breville, a good friend and the wife of our MP. I also had a circle of friends from the church and the Conservative Club. We had settled into our new life well.

Chapter 9

April 2006: Jez Matthews

The work at the hotel was progressing in leaps and bounds. The orangery was spectacular and overlooked the newly tiled swimming pool and gardens. It was east facing so it caught the morning sun, and I was sure that it would make a stunning breakfast room when we opened. The wood chip, which proliferated around the house like acne, had all been removed, and the artex was now just an unpleasant memory.

We reopened the bricked up fireplaces, and I discovered a reclamation yard near Exeter that stocked original fire surrounds. I spent a king's ransom on two Victorian fireplaces, both made from solid marble. We placed one of them in the drawing room and the other in the bar. They were so heavy that it took four workmen to lift them into place, but it was worth the effort as once cemented into the walls, they looked as though they were part of the original house.

We had demolished the old bathrooms and installed sparkling modern ones with white suites and natural sandstone tiles. The house was totally rewired and plumbed, the woodwork sanded and painted throughout the building, and the walls newly plastered. We fitted luxurious carpets throughout. I now had a blank canvas to fill the building with period furniture and artwork.

When we refitted the kitchen, I managed to get a hold of a gas-fired Aga that one of the neighbors was getting rid of. He accepted £200 for it. Once installed, it put the heart back into the kitchen, transforming it into a warm, welcoming living space. I moved into one of the newly decorated bedrooms above the staff room and made it homely by unpacking our furniture and hanging some of our framed holiday photographs on the walls. It was a relief to have a proper bed with a comfortable mattress.

We turned the old master bedroom into a luxurious suite, and the carpenter installed a reproduction fireplace. One noteworthy event was when the electrician found a sealed letter under the floorboards whilst he was rewiring that room. The writer had scribbled on the envelope, 'A message for the future owners.' I put it in my desk to read later. That is what I loved about old houses; they always had stories to tell. A strange sooty stain seemed to have inexplicably bled through the new plaster, so I decided to have this room wallpapered with a delicately striped Osborne and Little covering that I knew a top London hotel used. It looked fabulous. When we pulled up the linoleum in the entrance porch, underneath we discovered a lovely Minton tiled floor. It took the builders a day to scrape off the glue and clean it up, which was outside of our budget, but I was delighted with the results.

A gruff photographer called Lewis staged and photographed the hotel for the website. He was a man of few words and only two facial expressions, 'I'm not interested' and 'fuck off,' so I left him to it. I did manage to get a brief smile, when I brought him a cup of tea and a slice of homemade shortbread. I use the word 'smile' loosely. It may have been a grimace or perhaps trapped wind.

I talked to Graham on Skype every night. Sometimes I was calm, and other times I was at the point of a nervous breakdown. It was difficult living in the constant mess with builders who could often be unreliable, but Graham was always there to offer solace. He was enjoying his job, and the corporate android Theresa had asked him to extend his contract for a further three months. Although this was not ideal, the money would be handy as we were hopelessly over budget. When spring began to give way to early summer, the hotel was not only in a habitable state but was also a pleasant environment. Our commutes switched around, and he started to travel more often to Torquay at weekends. He was always exhausted but pleased for us to be together. I invariably met him at the station, where he would give me a welcoming hug in the car.

Over the last few months, I had purchased old portraits and furniture from regional auctions and constantly trawled the local antique shops for bargains. I gained the dubious accolade of becoming a 'power buyer' on eBay. One of my more extravagant purchases was a Steinway grand piano, which was a beautiful handmade piece of furniture crafted from walnut. It had a lovely tone, and it was a shame that neither Graham nor I played. It formed the centerpiece of the drawing room, and I imagined us enjoying candlelit evenings with a pianist tinkling away at the ivories in the background. The house certainly seemed to approve of all the attention it was getting. We no longer woke up to mysteriously smashed glasses in the morning, and I felt we had achieved a truce with the house's former inhabitants, who did not perhaps see us as the butchers they initially thought we were. At least, that is what I told myself. In reality, I did not know what they thought; I just hoped that they were not malevolent. Whilst it was full-time work furnishing the hotel, I had never had so much fun. My only regret was that Graham was in London instead of being here to share the experience with me. What he did share was his Platinum American Express Card, and upon reading a statement one weekend, he was furious when he saw how much I had been spending. He issued strict instructions to cut back before we went bankrupt. That included my long, boozy lunches with Jason, of whom he did not approve.

Our website was now online. It had an excellent user interface and did a slick job of promoting the hotel with stunning visual content courtesy of Lewis, the photographer. He may have had the charm and social skills of a chimpanzee, but he knew how to take good pictures. The site was generating strong levels of business, which gave me confidence that we would be able to service our debts. In two weeks, we would finally open our doors to the public, and I could not wait.

Chapter 10

September 1974: Marjorie Wilson

In September, we had one of our most memorable guests, but unfortunately, it was for the wrong reasons. Lesley-Ann arrived by train and walked a mile from the station carrying a large suitcase. It concerned me when guests did this. If they were too mean to pay for a taxi, it often followed that they would be asking for discounts. She wore hippie clothing consisting of a flowing multicolored ethnic dress with a red sari draped around her. Christopher was worried about the ornaments being knocked over, and I was glad that we had bricked up the fireplaces, in case she went up in flames, as there was nothing natural about the material her clothes were made from. She had a mass of curly red hair, a plump, freckled face, and she wore thick NHS tortoiseshell glasses that gave her eyes an unnaturally large and slightly mad appearance. She had those awful huge hooped earrings that seem to be all the rage nowadays, a beaded necklace, and bracelets on both wrists. She did not so much as walk through the hotel as flow and rattle in a kaleidoscope of color.

We gave her our usual welcome with a cup of tea and a slice of Battenberg and showed her to the room that she had booked in the east wing. She had specifically requested a sea view in her confirmation letter, and this room overlooked Meadfoot Beach. Five minutes later, she came downstairs and rang the bell for attention. She was as white as a sheet and spoke hysterically with Stanley.

"I can't stay in that room," she said.

"Is there a problem, Miss... Green isn't it?" said Stanley.

"Yes there is. You see, I am very sensitive to unseen things. Things not of this world. How can I put it...? You might describe me as psychic. I can feel a presence, and believe me, it isn't benevolent."

By now, Stanley and I had heard some strange excuses to get a free room upgrade, but this was a first.

"Miss Green, if there is something wrong with the room, something we can put right, I will, but you must see that—"

"You don't understand," she said, flailing her arms, her wallowing sleeves narrowly missing Christopher's ruby brandy glass full of boiled sweets. "There is evil in this house."

"What on earth are you on about?" Stanley was losing his patience. "Have you been drinking?"

Some of the other residents had entered the lounge, wondering what the commotion was about. In an attempt to take command of the situation, Stanley and I ushered her into the dining room, where we would be out of earshot.

"Please," I said. "Keep your voice down. There are other guests present. Besides, you could trigger an asthma attack—Christopher is very sensitive to tension."

"You don't understand. How could you? I have the gift as did my mother before me and her mother before her. You have to listen to me, I implore you. You are all in terrible danger."

"Look," said Stanley. "This is not some bleeding Alfred Hitchcock film. This is our livelihood. You can't go around making baseless insinuations like this."

"Please do not mock me," she said. "You must have noticed something. Their presence is overwhelmingly strong."

"It's an old house," said Stanley. "There are strange noises. The plumbing is ancient. We get seagulls walking over the roof. It doesn't mean Satan is going to pop up from the basement for a slice of cake and a ritual sacrifice."

"No, I know the difference between a blocked pipe and spirits trapped in eternal torment, trust me. Surely, you must have noticed something more—nightmares, noises, unexplained happenings?"

"Stanley," I said, "there are guests in the lounge. Please, can you see what they want? I will deal with this."

Stanley marched off furiously, and I turned toward Miss Green.

"Leslie-Ann," I began, "my husband and I have never discussed this. However, I know you are telling the truth. I have felt them as well."

"Then what are you doing about them? There's more than one, you know... Tortured, bitter, malevolent. They argue. They hate each other, and they hate us, the living. Their own lives were taken from them before their time!"

"Why do you think they are malignant? We have had nothing other than success and prosperity since we moved in. They are part of the fabric of the house. I have learned to live with them. They don't bother us, except for the occasional broken ornament."

"No, no. Mrs. Wilson, you are so wrong. Nothing good can come from the spirits in this house. I have spent many years talking to my spiritual guides in the afterlife. It takes time and patience to build trust and to understand the emotions of those no longer with us. I sense anger here, anguish. Lives cut short, revenge. I tell you, this house is damned. Leave now, while you still can."

"That's simply not going to happen. This is our home! We have spent a fortune on refurbishment, but your story is fascinating to me. Tell me what else you think you know."

"Please listen to me, Mrs. Wilson"

"Marjorie, please," I interrupted.

"Marjorie, do you know the history of this house? Have you done any research, been to the local library? Looked at any press cuttings?"

"We received basic information from the estate agent. It stood unoccupied and decayed since the twenties... The only inhabitants, apart from the rats and birds, were a group of officers during the war when the army requisitioned it."

"I'm telling you, something happened here, something bad," she said, lowering her voice. "You can call me insane, a silly old fool, but evil lies within these walls. I sense the loathing, the spite, and the hatred. These spirits will trick and betray you. Even now, it may be too late. They will be gaining influence over you, seducing you, feeding off your emotions, corrupting your very souls. You are their gateway to the living. The longer you stay here helps them to become corporeal. Their power over you is growing. I've seen it before. You must believe me!"

She unzipped her bead-covered handbag, and after rummaging around for a few seconds, took out a rosary.

"Carry this with you, and when you go to bed put it under your pillow. It may offer you some protection."

I took the rosary from her and examined it. It was a pewter crucifix attached to a long chain with interspersed oval and spherical turquoise beads between the links.

"How is this going to help me?"

"You must have faith."

"I do have a faith. I'm a Christian."

"Then pray, as I shall be praying for all of you. I cannot

stay here. I will have to find another hotel."

"You are aware that we don't offer refunds..."

"This isn't about money. I don't care about shillings and pence. It's your souls. You must understand you are all in grave danger. You cannot afford to be complacent. I beg of you, leave this place before it's too late!"

Stanley walked back into the dining room, his face beetroot with rage. "Is this nutcase still here?" he said rudely.

"I apologize on behalf of my husband," I said, glaring at Stanley. "Stanley, Leslie-Ann won't be staying with us. Can you collect her bag?"

"With pleasure," said Stanley.

"Remember what I said," she said, crying now. "Nothing good can come from this place."

Stanley handed over her luggage, and she left hurriedly, wheeling her enormous suitcase down the drive.

"One-hundred percent prize nutcase," said Stanley.

"Oh, do be quiet."

"There's nowt as queer as folk," said Stanley. "I mean, have you ever heard such rubbish? You didn't give her a refund, I hope."

"She didn't want one. She believes what she's saying, you know."

"Well, don't let her be filling your head with all her daft nonsense. I know you can be superstitious. There's no such thing as ghosts or poltergeists or vampires or anything else. I will not hear of such talk. I mean, what next? Elves in the garden, trolls on the Teignmouth bridge? She probably overdosed on LSD in the sixties. She looks the sort. Still, it'll be an interesting entry in my diary tonight."

Stanley was dismissive, and his mind closed to such ideas. That was his way, and to be fair on him Leslie-Ann's claims were outrageous... But I knew that there was some truth in what she was saying. I just did not accept that the spirits were evil; I saw them as guardian angels, overseeing and supporting my family.

Chapter 11

May 2006: Jez Matthews

Graham and I sat at the kitchen table, attempting to be business-like in the relaxed environment. The Aga made the room warm and cozy, and there was a pleasing smell of granola baking in the slow oven. A welcome sea breeze blew gently through the open sash window carrying the familiar sound of seagulls with it.

Reservations were materializing even faster than we had hoped. Each morning, the fax machine and our email inbox were full of booking confirmations or inquiries. This would continue throughout the day, and the telephone constantly rang. Already our occupancy rate from July onward was almost one hundred percent. The first guests arrived in May, and the weekends were full with the weekdays filling up fast. We had taken a gamble that there was a market for a boutique guesthouse by the sea, and it seemed to have paid off. There was nothing else like us in Torquay, so with little or no direct competition, we had carved out a niche in the marketplace. We charged rates similar to large hotels but without the overheads, so our projected profits were almost too good to be true. The tourist board had given us five stars and a gold award during their recent inspection. This got a mixed reaction from other hoteliers in the area, ranging from jealousy to kindness and curiosity. The disadvantage of the positive publicity was that competitors started to imitate us. We took a decision that we would not serve evening meals, given the number of good restaurants in the town.

Graham had yet again succumbed to the temptation of an extension of his contract, and it was clear that we needed to recruit some staff. To this effect, I had put an advert in the job vacancy section of the *Torquay Herald*, and we were sifting through resumes. We had decided that we needed a cook, a full-time housekeeper plus assistant, and a gardener. I would do the front of house, accounts, and marketing and manage the staff. Graham would help at weekends in whatever capacity he could. We recruited our neighbor's gardener, who worked freelance on an ad-hoc basis and was grateful for the extra hours. Zachary was a placid hippie sort of fellow who spoke with a slur, as if he smoked cannabis, but he was proficient. The other positions were more crucial, since they were public facing and thus required consideration.

"This one looks well qualified," said Graham passing the CV over. "Two years' experience as the head housekeeper at The Grosvenor in Portsmouth."

"Don't like her perm," I said, pointing at the passport photo attached by a paper clip to the top right of the CV.

"Jez," said Graham. "You have to take this seriously."

"I am! I couldn't employ anybody with a perm like that. She looks like Kevin Keegan attached to a car battery."

"How about this one, then?" he asked, passing over another CV. "He's applying for the chef's job."

"Erm, 'June 2001 through September 2005: Not working due to personal problems.' Don't think so somehow."

"This one then, four years' experience as a sous chef at The Imperial in Paignton?"

"She's ugly," I said dismissively.

"They don't have to be attractive. We're not going to sleep with them, or introduce them as suitors for our friends!"

We spent several hours working through curriculum vitaes, but I was not impressed. Perhaps I had unrealistic expectations or made our advert excessively optimistic. "'Be part of a winning team at Torquay's new boutique five-star hotel. Great working conditions and benefits,'" I said, reading it aloud. "This is depressing. Did I miss something out?"

"At the end of the day, we're paying the minimum wage. We're not going to get Oxbridge graduates wanting to work for us," said Graham. "You've got to be realistic. This is a little seaside town, and we're a small hotel, not Microsoft."

However, I instinctively knew that the house would look after us in the end. The solution came later that afternoon when the doorbell rang. A Czech couple called Lukas and Kristyna had seen our advert and had decided to drop their CVs off in person, which I thought showed initiative. They had both dressed smartly and generally created a good impression, especially as in Torquay it was a bonus if they did not have a facial tattoo.

Kristyna was mousy and subservient. She was also honest and intelligent—not in an academic way, but she was bright and had common sense. Her English, whilst heavily accented, was reasonably good, and she could hold a conversation. She had a smart, petite appearance: about five feet six inches tall, with brown hair tied back in a bun, a slender figure, a thin porcelain face, and little button nose with kind hazel eyes. She looked efficient. Lukas was also eager to please. He was taller and had a rugby player build with a thick muscular torso gained from experience in the construction industry. He was

Slavic-looking with dark cropped hair, brown eyes, square jaw, and a prominent nose. He wore a hand-me-down navy suit that was too small for him, but he looked cute in it. He was not as proficient at English as Kristyna, but this would not be an issue, since he would not be directly involved with guests.

They were an engaged couple in their early twenties and wanted to know whether we could offer accommodation as part of the package. This needed consideration as it changed the dynamics of the house, particularly when we closed in the winter. They had researched us and showed a genuine desire to work hard and learn about the hospitality industry. Lukas mentioned in broken English that he had enjoyed reading the publicity article about us, printed in the local newspaper.

We invited them in for a discussion, with Graham interviewing them in the study, as though he was recruiting the next chief executive of HSBC bank. He asked them questions like, 'What do you think you could bring to this job that others couldn't?' All I wanted to know was could they cook or clean and when could they start. Kristyna had experience as both a cleaner and waitress, so she was ideal. Lukas had a less relevant background but seemed eager to learn. They answered Graham's questions nervously, but I admired them as they took the process seriously. Ultimately, I would be managing them, as Graham would be working away, so whilst the final decision was mine, I valued his opinion.

Graham spent an hour grilling them, and in the end, I left him to it. I was happy to give them a trial, so I put the kettle on and brought them in a gratefully received tray of tea and biscuits. Graham rounded off the interrogation.

"Do you have any questions for us?" asked Graham.

"How much you pay, sir?" asked Lukas.

"Minimum wage plus accommodation, meals, and twenty-day's holiday."

"Is good," he said.

"When you need someone start?" asked Kristyna.

"Our first guests arrive in May," I said. "So ideally in a couple of weeks, to get you familiar with the place and how I like things done."

"Is good, we have reference here, sir," said Kristyna, nervously proffering a sheet of paper from a previous employer.

I scanned it quickly, and it was all in order. Graham nodded at me, indicating his approval.

"The jobs are yours if you want them," I said.

"Yes, we do!"

"In that case, Kristyna and Lukas, welcome to The Pembroke Hotel," I said, extending my hand. Kristyna's handshake was delicate and light; Lukas' nearly broke my hand.

The following week, they moved into the staff room directly underneath our bedroom. It was designed for single occupancy, being about ten feet squared, but they had shoehorned a double bed into it that had previously been stored in the basement. They brought an enormous amount of furniture with them that they had crammed into a rusty old Skoda, which they unloaded and squeezed into their cramped room. I insisted that they parked the car out of sight of the hotel on St. Marks Road behind us, though they ended up selling it a few days after moving in. As a gesture of goodwill, I bought them a little flat-screen television. During the initial weekend that they were here, they insisted on cooking for us, which was the first time either of us had tasted authentic Czech food. It consisted of boiled cabbage, dumplings, and a stew resembling goulash. It was ostensibly peasant food but tasty and filling. Pudding was crepes with peaches. We offered them wine, but they refused, sticking to orange juice. It was a slightly formal but still enjoyable weekend. We learned a lot about Lukas and Kristyna's families and their village in the Czech Republic. They had come to England to save money for a wedding and to buy a house back home, so they were keen to work as many hours as they could, which was fine with us. We also learned that Kristyna had a disabled younger sister, and she asked me if I could transfer some of her salary directly into her mother's bank account. Her parents had divorced some time ago, and she felt a certain amount of guilt leaving her mother to care for her sister on her own. I admired how loyal and close she was to her family. Lukas kept getting his words mixed up, which was quite cute, and it was difficult to work out if he was not being a touch flirtatious. If he was, it certainly went straight over Kristyna's head.

They quickly settled in and proved to be hard and conscientious workers, eager to please and honest. Lukas joined a local gym to keep fit. Kristyna did very little outside of the hotel except attend evensong at the Catholic Church in Warren Road.

Sometimes the pair of them would go out to the cinema or theatre, but they spent most of their evenings in their room watching television. They seemed to love American sitcoms like *Frasier* and *The Simpsons*. Occasionally, I would get a little annoyed with them when they sat at the kitchen table with their mouths open like baby starlings waiting to be fed, but generally, we respected our mutual space and enjoyed good relations.

Lukas proved to be somewhat of a handyman. Before we opened, he mended a leaking toilet and a sticking door. I suspected that these skills would be useful to fix inevitable problems that were likely to occur at the hotel. Lukas had also promised me that he would sort out our garden patio, which despite having new flagstones laid over the old crazy paving, seemed to be sinking in the middle. My preference would have been for the builders to put it right, but once our final check had cleared, they ignored my numerous calls. However, Lukas indicated that it would be easy and inexpensive to mend, and I ordered the materials needed from a local builder's merchant.

Graham came back late every Thursday evening and caught the six fifteen train to London every Monday morning. He was always optimistic, but I could tell the journey was beginning to tire him, and I had made it plain that I did not want him to extend his contract again for the sake of his health and our relationship.

It was the 21st of May, and our first guests were due in the afternoon. There was a nervous anticipation as we waited for the arrival of our first vacationers. Lukas and Kristyna had given the hotel a thorough clean. All the chandeliers sparkled, and each room smelt of polish and fresh flowers. We cleared the swimming pool of leaves and heated it to a comfortable temperature. The garden looked well tended with an abundance of summer flowers. Jason had dropped by to wish us good luck and had thoughtfully bought me a little present, a white mug with my name written on it accompanied by an abysmal photo of me singing karaoke that he had taken with his mobile phone. This had somehow been poorly transferred onto the ceramic. We sat in the kitchen drinking tea, with the delicious smell of a homemade sponge cake cooking in the Aga.

"Now it's just a quick visit, as I had a window in my diary," he said. "I wanted to drop this off. It was in the sale at Robert Dyas. They printed it especially for you, I was going to get you a key fob, too, but I thought I'd save that for a birthday present!"

"Thank you," I said. "It's..."

"Different," Graham interjected.

Graham still did not like Jason. He remained convinced that Jason's motives were disingenuous. Graham compared Jason to a fungal infection. When you thought it had cleared up and it was safe to stop the medication, it would flare up a week later.

"I didn't get you anything, Graham," said Jason snidely. "I couldn't find anything expensive enough for your tastes."

"No problem, Jason. I was going to bring you back something from London, but the charity shop was closed by the time I finished work."

Jason scowled at him.

"Now, calm down, my little rattlesnakes," I said. "This is our big day, let's all play nicely."

"Boring," remarked Jason. "Anyway, I'm off, there's a sale on at Next. I've got a date tonight, and I need a new outfit!"

"You didn't say!" I said.

"It started yesterday. There's up to fifty percent off!"

"No, I mean about the date."

"Oh, that," he replied. "I met him on Gaydar two weeks ago. I think this is the real thing. He loves me. He's a doctor with loads of money, and he has a butt like Matt Damon's."

"Well, good for you, Jason," I said. "We'll have to do a double date sometime when you're a bit more established."

"Deffo," he said casually, shimmying toward the front door. "Laters, girls, my credit card is burning a hole in my pocket. I'll see myself out."

Graham looked at me and rolled his eyes.

"You know that won't last," he said. "He doesn't know the meaning of love."

"I know, you know, and the doctor boyfriend probably knows. Jason is... Well, he's Jason. I wouldn't want him any different, and let's face it: His life is a hell of a lot more interesting than ours."

"What are you saying?"

"Nothing. I love our stable monogamous life together, but the highlight of our weekend is a trip to the garden center. Would you rather have a friend to talk about hardy perennials with, or share a bottle of wine with somebody that has shagged half of Torquay and knows just about everything about everyone's business?"

"He brings out the worst in you, and he brings chaos into the lives of anyone who ever gets involved with him."

"I wouldn't trust him as far as I could throw him, but he's funny! And hey, it's a release sometimes not having to use my brain and just go out, get drunk, and talk shit all night. Besides, the house likes him."

"What the fuck does that mean?"

"The house likes him, I can tell."

"You've been spending too much time in this place. It's a house, Jez, not a sentient being."

The doorbell rang, interrupting our conversation.

"Oh my God, Graham, it's our *first guests*, what am I going to do?"

"A good start would be to open the door."

"Yes, of course. See you in a minute."

I answered the door and started babbling uncontrollably to the guests on the doorstep. I had planned my mini welcome speech to arrivals in meticulous detail, but unfortunately, it all came out of my mouth in one sentence. The poor couple looked at me as if they had arrived at a lunatic asylum.

"Sorry about that," I said apologetically. "I'm just a bit excited, as you're our first guests!" I led them to the drawing room. "Can I offer you a cup of tea and a slice of homemade cake?"

"That would be lovely," the man said, extending his hand. "This is Ruth, and I'm Mike. What a beautiful place this looks, even better than the pictures on the website."

Beaming, I went back into the kitchen and announced to Graham, "They love it! Oh, can you make them a pot of tea? The cake should be cool enough now to cut."

Graham duly obliged whilst Lukas took the luggage to their bedroom. I brought out a well-received tray of tea and cake and gave them a local map of the area.

There is little to say about Ruth and Mike, except that they were a pleasant and appreciative couple in their mid-forties. We had six arrivals that day, and it was clear that the hotel was attracting a broad mix of people. During our first week, the clientele ranged from doctors and lawyers, a famous actor, and a chief executive from a major oil company, accompanied by his secretary. It was obvious that they were having an affair, as the bed in her room remained unused. We had another couple in their sixties who were very prim and proper, but when they departed and Kristyna cleaned their room, there was a bag of sex toys in the wardrobe, including handcuffs and a dildo. I was too embarrassed to call them, so I just put it in our lost property cupboard. Unsurprisingly, they never claimed it back.

We also seemed to attract a lot of Germans, the occasional Americans, and Russians. Whilst the Russian guests were the most difficult to please, they threw £20 notes around like confetti. I enjoyed playing my role as the charming host, and although my social life ceased, I substituted it with being the queen of my own bar. I would stand behind the counter with a glass of Bollinger playing the residents like a comedian works his audience. The champagne flowed, along with the laughter. When we had a receptive crowd, I would keep the bar open late, diligently ensuring everyone's glasses remained topped up, including my own. Every so often, there would be a person whom the house or myself did not like. They usually fell ill on the first night, suffered unbearable nightmares, or were spooked by something and checked out early.

Lukas and Kristyna were gems, and I could not have asked for better staff. Breakfast ran like a well-oiled machine. Kristyna managed the dining room, whilst Lukas cooked and I provided convivial conversation with a dash of naughty humor to the guests. Lukas had become quite adept at cooking. He never failed to make me laugh with his incorrect use of English and accidental innuendoes.

He looked at me one morning with his baleful brown eyes and said innocently in his thick Czech accent, "I have cooked too much sausage this morning, Mr. Jez. Would you like gobble my sausage?"

On another occasion, he asked a woman in the drawing room to 'spread her legs,' so he could vacuum the carpet where she was sitting.

He could not understand why I burst into laughter. Sometimes I thought he was a little too familiar. He liked to give me a big bear hug every morning, but I put it down to his Czech ways.

"Mr. Jez," he would say, as he suffocated me, "I love working here. You nice boss to me and Kristyna. It's good threesome."

Sometimes I corrected him to help him learn, and his English dramatically improved over the next few months. However, I did find his poor grammar endearing. We had most of our conversations whilst preparing breakfast. I could see that Lukas and Kristyna were obviously in love, but he liked to whine about his fiancée, and his comments were often outrageous.

"She no wants cock last night, she on blob."

"You can't say things like that, Lukas," I said. "It's inappropriate and disrespectful."

"It's the true, Mr. Jez, she no wants it. I desperate," he said, looking at my crotch and giving me a wink.

"You are a tease," I said wagging my finger at him and trying to be professional by drawing some boundaries. "And I am your boss, so I will not rise to it."

Lukas burst into laughter, as did I when I realized what I had said.

"You understood that, then!"

Kristyna came in from the dining room, wondering what all the fuss was. Mousy and subservient as she was, paradoxically she had the capability of instantly silencing Lukas with one of her special stares. Lukas continued slicing mushrooms without further conversation. After breakfast, I would clear up and the staff would service the rooms. In the afternoon, Lukas would clean the pool of the leaves that had collected in it overnight. They would dutifully do this without complaint six days a week, but I would always give them Mondays off to recover.

Chapter 12

December 1974: Marjorie Wilson
We were approaching Christmas, which was a busy period for us in the hotel. Stanley and I had closed down for a week at the beginning of December and enjoyed a family holiday in a static caravan on Hayling Island, which had given us some time to recuperate from the hectic summer. As expected, the weather at this time of the year was inclement, but the change of scenery was a tonic. We kept the caravan reasonably warm with the help of a paraffin heater, and we enjoyed some bracing country walks along the various coastal paths.

Upon returning to Torquay, we decorated the hotel for the festive period, and it looked stunning. We bought an artificial Christmas tree from Woolworth's, and Christopher hung tinsel and plastic mistletoe throughout the public rooms. On Christmas Day, we provided the full package of a four-course Christmas lunch, a light Christmas buffet in the evening, and entertainment. We had bought Christopher an electric piano, and he would often sing sea shanties to delighted guests in the evening. I was determined to make Christmas day memorable for our residents. I purchased two enormous frozen turkeys from Bejam, along with a variety of vegetables and all the trimmings.

We had all settled into a routine and the hotel ran

smoothly, although there were occasional unexplained incidents. Unfortunately, affairs in the country at large were not so good. Inflation was rampant, which made trading conditions difficult. We constantly had to increase our room rates in order to pay our bills, which seemed to rise monthly. The gas board sent us a letter stating that they were hiking their prices by twenty percent. There were perpetual strikes, and we were plagued by power cuts. Stanley blamed it all on decimalization and Harold Wilson, the Labour Prime Minister. Politically, there was an absence of discipline in the local and national Conservative Party. We lacked direction and leadership under Heath. There was strong support for a leadership challenge. Stanley accepted a vacant councilor position and was becoming more involved in local politics. We made a substantial donation to the Conservatives this year, which had bought us access to the higher echelons of the party, including the chairman Willie Whitelaw. Stanley's long-term aspiration was to become a Member of Parliament, and I encouraged his ambition, thinking of the prestige it would bring to our family.

Christmas was hard work but also enjoyable with an eclectic mix of guests who entered into the seasonal spirit. Once we had cleared away lunch, we put on the queen's speech in the drawing room, on the color set. Afterward, we provided entertainment by organizing games of charades. Later, Christopher played Gilbert and Sullivan songs on the electric piano. Lubricated with copious volumes of alcohol, the guests danced, sang and made merry, and there was a convivial atmosphere in the hotel.

There was one minor incident on New Year's Eve, when a drunken guest locked himself out in the early hours, but otherwise, it all went smoothly. We put the wireless on at midnight to listen to the chimes of Big Ben, and we celebrated the arrival of 1975 by singing "Auld Lang

Syne". Christopher led this, and made a few mistakes on the piano as a result of too many Babychams. Afterward, we played LPs on the radiogram until about one, when we finally went to bed.

Chapter 13

June 2006: Jez Matthews

It was during a relatively quiet weekday morning in the middle of June that I received a telephone call from a distraught woman speaking in an undecipherable foreign language. Through the wailing, I heard the word 'Kristyna,' so I deduced that it was a relative of hers. It was clear that something serious was amiss.

I took the phone to Kristyna's bedroom and handed it to her. Unfortunately, Lukas had gone shopping, so I waited in case she needed me for emotional support. Kristyna spoke in her native tongue, then burst into tears and put the phone down on her bed.

"Kristyna, what's wrong?" I asked.

She sobbed uncontrollably. "It's my sister."

She did not have to say anything more. Instinctively, I put my arm around her, and she wept, her floods of tears wetting my shirt. I held this poor little creature for nearly half an hour, stroking her soft brown hair as if I were comforting a child. Eventually, she stopped crying, and she spoke weakly.

"She was nineteen. Nineteen years of suffering. Now she's gone."

"I feel awful for you. You said she was disabled. I assumed she was in a wheelchair. I didn't realize her condition was terminal."

"Mr. Jez," she said tearfully, "she had cystic fibrosis. This country is okay—maybe live to forty. My country, when you have that, you no live long."

"I'm so sorry. I cannot begin to imagine your pain."

Lukas came back from town and found us embraced in their bedroom. Kristyna detached herself from me and burst into tears again flinging her arms around Lukas.

I took a step back as they held each other tightly. They spoke in their native tongue, and even though I did not understand a word of the Czech language, I intuitively knew what they were saying. Kristyna's emotions were unbridled, she displayed uncontrolled grief, and for the first time since I had known her, her vulnerability was exposed.

"Please take as much time off as you need," I said. "I will manage."

My presence in their bedroom suddenly seemed to be an intrusion, so I patted Kristyna gently on the back, picked up the phone, and left them to mourn.

A somber mood descended over the house during the next few days. My selfish side wondered how I would cope without a full complement of staff, given the time of year, but I felt compassion for Kristyna. I did not expect her to work whilst she was grieving, so I waited tables and Lukas cleaned the rooms on his own. Kristyna stayed in her bedroom for a few days, emerging for meals and to attend church. Her eyes were laden with the burden of her loss. I booked them onto a coach to London, where they would take a flight to Prague. Their neighbor would collect them from the airport and transport them back home to Pribyslav. Kristyna's trip was one way, as I told her to take all the time she needed to support her mother. Lukas would return a few days after the funeral, so I would only be without him for a week. I hurriedly organized temporary staff cover from an agency. They sent us Patrick from Paignton, who turned out to be useless, and that was on the days he bothered to turn up. The only positive aspect to this horrible situation was that Graham booked the week off work, and it was great to have him around. Over the past six months, we had been living different existences. Although we emailed each other throughout the day and I spoke to him on Skype, I missed him enormously. I felt that the house had a mistress, but it needed its master.

Though we were both working hard, we were together and laughed as we shared anecdotes about the strange guests whom we regularly encountered. However, the nicest thing was cuddling up to each other in bed at night and sleeping soundly after a physically exhausting day. The week passed too quickly. I always hated it when I dropped Graham off at the train station, as I knew I would not be seeing him for a week. It had felt special, having him to myself in our home. This was what it was always supposed to be about, the two of us living the dream away from the big smoke. I really hoped that Graham's work at Anderson Levy would conclude soon. Unfortunately, they kept offering him contract extensions with generous retention bonuses attached. The city was enjoying one of the longest bull markets in history, and Graham's area of expertise was in commodities. These were outperforming almost every other financial sector. The financial institutions in London's square mile paid obscene annual bonuses to city workers. House prices continued their decade-long boom unabated. Banks made record profits each year, and it seemed the party would never end.

"Here we go again," I said, parking the Audi on a five-minute waiting spot at the train station. "Your weekly commute to the capital of the British Empire."

The summer sun was already warm as it rose above

the horizon. The weather forecast had predicted another blistering hot day. Graham took his briefcase and gave me a peck on the cheek.

"This will all be a distant memory before long," he said. "Oh, by the way..."

"What?"

"I love you."

"I love you, too."

I watched him sadly, as he walked off toward the platform.

Chapter 14

January 1975: Marjorie Wilson

Following a busy New Year, the occupancy levels in the hotel fell dramatically as was expected. We used the winter months in 1975 to undertake necessary maintenance and enjoy a rest before Easter. It was strange living at the hotel when it was devoid of guests. One of the novelties was being able to eat breakfast in our dressing gowns, which we could not do when we were open. Christopher largely led an independent life. He usually joined us for dinner but would spend most evenings socializing with his network of friends.

During the period of time that we had lived here, I had become used to the paranormal events that regularly occurred. I had accepted that the house was haunted, and I could do little about it. A date I will never forget was Monday, the 6th of January.

I often felt the invisible presence of spirits in the house. I was sure that they were benevolent, unlike the psychic who had visited us in the autumn, who had claimed otherwise. I frequently heard their soothing voices in my mind. They offered guidance and helped with decision-making. I knew that they were keen to see us succeed in our affairs. Lesley-Anne had given me a rosary to protect me. Despite my skepticism, I had slept with this under my pillow, and for a while, the dreams and my contact with the spirits had stopped. However, the truth is that I missed them, so I threw the crucifix away. I felt this innate sense of destiny living at the house, as if events would always transpire favorably for us. Occasionally, guests would say they had heard strange noises. The master bedroom, in particular, seemed to be a concentrated area of unusual activity, with several guests reporting screams or moaning in the middle of the night. It was in this room that many reported having nightmares, often to do with fires, and they would wake to the smell of smoke but with no obvious explanation.

It was in the early hours of the morning, and I could not sleep. I left Stan snoring in bed, and I crept downstairs to make myself a mug of Ovaltine. As I walked down the staircase, I glimpsed the most extraordinary sight.

I stopped in my tracks about halfway down, rubbing my eyes in disbelief. I saw an apparition floating around the hallway. I could not quite believe what I saw, and if I had been drinking the previous night, I would have dismissed it as an optical illusion or an overactive imagination. One reads descriptions of ghosts in stories, or sees them in films; therefore, it seems peculiar to affirm that my encounter bore a close resemblance to the traditional fictional depiction of ghosts. I saw a tall man dressed in smart Victorian clothes and a top hat. He was colorless and translucent and glided silently from the front door into the drawing room. I could not believe my eyes, and since I was too excited to be frightened, I rushed towards it. I saw the figure disappear into the dining room, then heard a clanking noise. When I opened the door to this room, there was nothing there.

The logical part of my mind forced me to consider if I had been hallucinating. I speculated that the laundry men, who often delivered in the middle of the night, had been walking up the driveway with the van lights behind them and somehow this had created a shadow through the window. I wondered if this potential optical effect, combined with my tiredness and active imagination led to my mind misinterpreting reality. It was not a convincing explanation, and I knew within my heart that it was not possible. The truth was that I had seen something unnatural and inexplicable.

Nevertheless, the experience disconcerted me, much more than hearing voices, and I immediately went upstairs and woke Stanley. As I expected, his reaction was predictable.

"What is wrong with you, woman? It's three in the morning!"

"Stanley, I know what I saw."

"You've woken me up in the middle of the night to tell me this?"

"I knew you wouldn't believe me."

"Now look here, love, I know this house is old and things have happened that neither of us understands, but you're tired. There's bound to be an innocent explanation for it all."

"I swear on Christopher's life," I said. "I saw a ghost."

I never discussed this with Stanley again. I told Christopher in the morning following the experience, and he was a little more open-minded than Stanley. It transpired that he had his own tale of a woman standing beside his piano.

"She was there in the corner of my eye," said Christopher. "She was just as you said your one looked, monochrome, semitransparent, wearing a smart dress. I was playing Cliff Richard's "Congratulations" arranged for the piano, and she appeared. I looked at her, wondering if I'd drunk too much Asti, and she vanished."

"Really?" I asked. "Why haven't you said anything before?"

"I didn't think you would believe me, and I'm not sure I even believe myself. It was late at night, and I was tired. It could have been a trick of my imagination."

"But you don't really think that, do you?"

"No, Mum, I know what I saw. Even so, you know what Dad is like. He loses his rag about things like this, and it's not good for business."

"What did she look like, your ghost? Did you see her face?"

"I only saw her for a few seconds, but she was tall, young, pretty, but very stern-looking, like a schoolmistress. She had an air of disapproval about her. She wore dark clothes, and she had black eyes. Oh, and the room went very cold, my breath condensed in front of me. I've never seen her or anything else since."

"Were you frightened?"

"I was shaken. What about you?"

"I was at the time, but now I just want to see one of them again."

"Somehow I don't think we've seen or heard of the last of this, Mum."

"I think you're right, son."

Speaking to Christopher made me realize I was not insane. Whoever these souls were, I accepted that they lived alongside us in this big drafty old house. I wondered what their connection was with this place and why they stayed here, occasionally revealing themselves to us. Did they have an agenda? Why did they feel the need to break some of my more tasteful ornaments, and why did they frighten some of the guests? These were all questions to which I longed to have answers.

Despite being a little afraid, I was also intrigued,

and I would sometimes sit patiently on the stairs in the middle of the night hoping to see the phenomenon again. However, my patience was not rewarded. It was almost as if the ghosts were teasing me. However, I did go down to the library later in the week and discovered some archived newspaper articles on the old house. It seemed that two members of the Kingsley family had died on the same winter morning—one through natural causes and the other as a result of a fire. The fire had also claimed the life of a young man, who was a friend of the family. I began to piece together the jigsaw puzzle to whom the different voices and images belonged.

I also found a book about the paranormal. This was most interesting. It documented sightings of ghosts in houses around the country, examining common themes and behaviors. The hypotheses were fascinating. I learned the difference between a poltergeist and a ghost. I also agreed with the opinion that the author suggested about ghost's ability to move around a house. He theorized that spirits would remember a building as it was at the time they were alive. They would not be aware of any material changes that could have been made to it. This explained why the ghost that I saw was not visible in the dining room, which was a recent extension, or why I did not feel their presence in the newer additions to the hotel.

I borrowed this book from the library to read thoroughly, as there was much I wished to know.

Chapter 15

July 2006: Jez Matthews

After I dropped Graham at the train station, I endured a frantic morning cooking and serving breakfast on my own. This was stressful but fortunately, we were only half-full, so whilst I coped, I was relieved when Lukas returned in the evening.

He found me in the kitchen reading a copy of *Hello* magazine that one of the guests had left in their room. He looked disheveled after a long unbroken journey from the Czech Republic and in need of a shave and a shower. He let out a weary sigh as he dumped his battered canvas rucksack down on the table.

"I'm back, Mr. Jez."

"It's good to see you," I said, genuinely.

I stood up, and he put his arms around me. I could feel the stubble on his chin brushing against my cheek, and I smelt the airport grime on his skin and clothes. "It was awful, Mr. Jez."

I extricated myself from his muscular arms. "Let me put the kettle on," I said. "You can tell me all about it."

"Kristyna's mother, she no stop crying, no stop whole week."

"She's lost her daughter," I said, filling the kettle with water. "It's the most painful thing that can ever happen to a parent. How is Kristyna?"

"She no good, but she bears up."

"Well, she can have as long as she wants to support her mother. I'll keep her job open here."

"You are kind, Mr. Jez. You are nice boss. You are good to us. I thank you so much."

"Not at all. You are both like family to me."

"These such unhappy circumcisions."

"Cir-cum-stances," I corrected.

"Cir-cum-stances," he said, slowly trying to memorize a new word. "I have little present for you from my family."

He handed me a small package wrapped in purple tissue paper, which I unraveled.

"How lovely," I said. "A set of Russian Dolls!"

"They are Czech dolls," he corrected. "They have Czech flag colors paint on them."

"They will have pride of place in our lounge," I said, looking at them, wondering where I could hide them without causing offence.

"I need to have showered, Mr. Jez. I will work tomorrow as normal and do extra shifts now while Kristyna away."

"That would be appreciated."

"Thank you for tea. I will see you tomorrow."

I finished reading the magazine and retired to our private lounge. I sprawled casually across the sofa with my head rested against a cushion and my feet propped up on the opposite arm and switched on the television. The guests had all gone out for dinner, and I was enjoying a respite from the bar. *Coronation Street* was showing, but there were too many close-ups of Deidre Barlow for my liking, so I turned it off and video-called Graham on the laptop. When he eventually answered, I could see that he was sitting in his apartment with a bottle of Corona and a pile of documents. He looked tired and he had some project deadlines to meet, so I kept the conversation brief.

Shortly after finishing the call, there was a knock on the lounge door. It was Lukas, who looked rejuvenated, having showered and changed his clothes. His short hair was still damp, and he smelt of fresh apples.

"Lukas," I said. "What can I do for you?"

"Mr. Jez, I very lonely in my room. Can I sit with you?"

"Yes, of course," I said. "This can't be an easy time for you, and I'm in the mood for company."

Since I was occupying the entire sofa, I had expected him to sit on the armchair, but he sat beside me, placing my legs over his lap.

"I massage your feet for you, Mr. Jez. You have the long day."

"Erm, no problem," I said awkwardly.

He removed my socks and started to knead the sole of my left foot with his thumbs and forefingers.

"This help your circulation," he said.

My initial reservation of having my personal space invaded rapidly dissipated as my tension ebbed away, whilst he worked his way up from the ball of my foot toward my toes.

"You've done this before," I said, thoroughly enjoying the experience.

"I learn sports massage at evening class," he said. "I want do slide line someday. You have lots of hard skin, Mr. Jez."

He was very tactile, though I winced as he pushed a little too firmly against the bones at the base of my toes. Whilst he busied himself relieving my aching feet, we talked like old friends. Kristyna and the situation back in Pribyslav were understandably playing on his mind. I learned a lot more about him that night, and in the following nights to come. He hated his old life back in the little farming community in the Czech Republic. He loved England, and he enjoyed working at the hotel. In contrast, Kristyna saw England as a means to an end. She wanted to save up for a better life back in Pribyslav, where she and Lukas would have a large brood of children, supported by their respective extensive families that had lived in the village for generations. Lukas had other aspirations, and this divergence of opinions was beginning to cause a schism in their relationship.

"She think small," he said. "There is more to life than farming potatoes in the Czech Republic. I want to see the world, do things, have my own hotel like you and Graham."

"Kristyna is kind, loyal, beautiful, and hardworking. There's a great deal to be said for having a supportive family and a life without complications. You could do worse."

"I know, Mr. Jez. My family loves her, too. Even so, you know where we live. Prague is less two hours travel. It's wonderful city, much culture. How many times have we been? Five times, and four were just to airport to travel here."

"Have you spoken to Kristyna about this?"

"She no wants to know. She is happy with me, television, church. All she wants is the plot of land, small house, babies, and goat."

It suddenly dawned on me how young Lukas was, and how his youth and spontaneity were fighting to burst out of his unsophisticated exterior and escape the straitjacket of his family's expectations. It was the first time I realized that his relationship with Kristyna was not as rock solid as I had assumed. Lukas looked at me with his handsome

Slavic features. He had innocent brown eyes, crowned by his slightly bushy brows, and cropped hair. He stroked my feet and said, "I wish I could meet person like you, somebody who understand me."

A guest rang the bell on the bar. I jumped up and hurriedly put my shoes on without socks. The expression 'saved by the bell' was literal in this instance, and it was a thankful release from an awkward situation. A couple had returned from dinner and wanted a nightcap. I joined them with an extra-large brandy, and then I locked up and went to bed, trying not to dwell on what I think nearly happened.

I wish I could say that I reestablished the boundaries again with Lukas, but I did not. I was his employer and I should have maintained a professional detachment, but I enjoyed his company. I was lonely when Graham was away, and I had to admit that it was pleasing to be in the company of an attractive man. His unintentional flirting was flattering and a boost to my ego. I have to be honest with myself; I was intrigued to see where it was leading. Kristyna had asked for another month of leave to spend with her grieving mother, so Lukas joined me in the private lounge on most nights, when I was not serving drinks in the bar. Lukas unsuccessfully attempted to convert me into liking some of the American sitcoms. However, he did introduce me to *Will & Grace*. The episodes were being repeated on a satellite channel and though I was aware of the series and the characters, I had never watched a full episode. I found it hilarious.

When Graham returned at weekends, Lukas would give us our space and retreat to his bedroom. I had begun to have my suspicions about his sexuality, especially when

I caught him mimicking the dance moves to "Tragedy" by Steps. However, there had been no repeat of the incident in the lounge, so I dismissed it as wishful thinking. He remained a hard worker, and his English was improving rapidly. The pool was proving to be a popular attraction in the hot summer that England was enjoying, and we operated a lucrative bar service for the sunbathers. I taught him how to make cocktails, and we became a formidable team, enjoying each other's company.

Kristyna's extended leave of absence and Paignton Patrick's mediocre attendance record obliged me to contact an employment agency and recruit a replacement member of staff for kitchen and cleaning duties. They sent us Morbid Maureen, the manic-depressive from Marldon. She was a Scottish woman who had moved to Torquay during a messy divorce. If there was anyone who was capable of sucking the life force and happiness out of a room, it was her. She shuffled into the kitchen each morning, with a facial expression as inviting as Morecambe seafront during a rainstorm. However, unlike Paignton Patrick, she was reliable, and in spite of her apparent disdain for human life, she performed her duties well. She was a picture of absolute misery, with bloodshot eyes as if she had been drowning her sorrows in a bottle of vodka the night before, which I suspect she had. I would always politely ask how she was, to which I got the same surly reply of "Don't ask." She would clang and bang her way through the washing-up before changing into her maid's uniform and helping Lukas with the rooms.

Eventually, as the day progressed, she would divulge whatever particular problems she was having. Her predicaments were extensive. Money and health were recurrent topics, her dislike of her noisy neighbors, and generally, the inconvenience of being alive. She did provide us with great conversational fodder, and Graham enjoyed hearing about her when we spoke. Jason visited one morning and managed to persuade her to accompany him to The Horn of Plenty. I am not sure why, as they hardly seemed a compatible pair, but it only happened once and Jason text messaged me the following morning saying, "Never again." Before the evening even started, she was a picture of misery, but apparently, she became progressively depressed the more she drank, which was a lot by all accounts. At the point, she broke down into tears, wailing about how Prince Charles should have married her, if only etiquette had allowed, Jason bundled her into a taxi and headed off on foot to Bangs for a recovery drink.

The hotel was busy, but Lukas was now competent enough to be left in charge for short periods, so I organized a midweek drink with Jason at The Horn of Plenty. I walked in, and the familiar voice of Dave the barman boomed across the room.

"Daaaaaaaaaaaarling," he said leaning over the bar. "Where have you been? You look stunning as always. It will happen one day, gorgeous."

"Preferably when I'm six feet under," I said. Observing the daggered look on his face, that inferred that my joke been received like a lead balloon, I added quickly. "Sorry, I meant underneath a six-foot hunk like you. You look stunning tonight, Dave, if only I was single."

"Good recovery," said Jason under his breath. He had walked over to the bar from the toilets. "That's evil. You don't want to get on the wrong side of it."

Fortunately, the temporary offense was wiped from Dave's face, and I ordered a glass of wine and a lager top.

"So you're a top, eh?" said Dave, cackling. "I could accommodate you!"

"The lager top is for Jason."

"Well, he's definitely not a top darling, at least that's not what it says on the toilet walls down the seafront. He's had more cock inside him than a KFC bargain bucket."

"Bloody cheek," said Jason.

"It's only the truth," said Dave. "At least I insist they have a pulse. You don't mind if they're putrefied."

"Vile," said Jason.

"You leave my Jason alone," I said. "He's my friend, and he's sweet."

"Sweet like saccharin," cackled Dave cattily, handing me my change. "He'll turn on you like he turns on everyone, doll, once he's bored or once he realizes he can't have you."

I ignored the vicious old queen. Over the past few weeks, I had been suffering from cabin fever, the condition that is familiar to many hotel proprietors confined to their businesses, so it was great to escape for a few hours. In summer, the tourists had descended en masse to Torquay and the resort was popular with the gay community, so the pub was full of both local and unfamiliar faces of all ages, sizes, and deviancy. The locals hovered around the tourists like flies around shit. The single, good-looking ones were like sitting ducks, waiting to be ensnared. Many of the pub's regular punters had worked their way through the local men who frequented Torquay's gay venues or those who advertised themselves on the popular Gaydar online dating site, so they were on the lookout for fresh meat. Steph shimmered around in a cerise ball gown, puffing on a cigarette and dishing out acerbic comments to anyone in his path. Michelle leaned against the end of the bar, pint in hand, attempting to look butch. The whole place stank of tobacco smoke and stale beer, and the carpet stuck to your feet. The drinks were overpriced and probably watered down, and people were shagging in the toilets. A feeling of contentment came across me. I was home.

Jason and I sat at the only remaining table, and the gossip flowed like dysentery around a refugee camp. Unsurprisingly, Jason's true love, the doctor, did not last. They never did. Apparently, he had a golden shower fetish, which was incompatible with Jason's Egyptian cotton sheets. He always provided too much information, but that was Jason. He was now bored with Gaydar; apparently it was the same old group of people on it every day, and he had slept with all the attractive ones. Instead, he had joined a dating site called younggayprofessionals. com, which had given him access to people he felt were more of his social standing. He hated his job as a window dresser at Hoopers department store in town and bitched about his tyrant boss for an hour. Halfway into our fourth drink, he asked me what my news was, expecting the usual anecdote about a guest with odd bathroom habits, or the latest saga with the hotel roof, so he was surprised when I told him about Lukas.

"Kristyna is away, so he's spending his evenings with me."

"He's a hottie," said Jason. "I would."

"Jason, you'd shag my pet Labrador given half a chance. Not that I have a pet Labrador."

"Are you accusing me of being promiscuous?"

"They've started awarding you nectar points at the clap clinic, as you're such a loyal customer. You've slept with half the people in Torquay."

"You can piss off. I've only had crabs once. Oh, and Chlamydia, but that was from a toilet seat so it doesn't count. Anyway, stop changing the subject. We were talking about Lukas. He's bloody gorgeous."

"Yes, I had noticed. However, I genuinely enjoy his company. He's good to be around, innocent, eager to learn."

"What's he eager to learn, sucking cock?"

"Don't be revolting!"

"Well, be honest about it. I can't see that you enjoy his company because you like having a good political debate with him. I mean no disrespect, he's as thick as pigshit. The eyes say it all—there's not a lot going on in there!"

"Jason, you are horrid sometimes."

"Let's face it, doll. He's gorgeous, muscular, sporty, with a massive package looking at the bulge his jeans."

"And very straight," I said. "Well, I think so, anyway."

"Dollface, you can't leave me in suspense. Tell me, what has happened?"

"Well, let me start by saying that absolutely nothing has happened."

"Boring."

"Okay, tell me what you think. He came into our private lounge one evening saying he was lonely whilst Kristyna's away."

"Yeah, I'm not really getting the gay vibe yet."

"He then sits beside me, takes my socks off, and starts to massage my feet."

"Now it's getting interesting."

I paused as Steph was gliding past—he had hearing like a fox. After he was out of earshot, I continued.

"Well, I thought it was a little overfamiliar, but it was, you know, not unpleasant. But then he said that he wished that he could meet somebody like me, somebody who understands him."

"He sounds about as heterosexual as Liberace," said Jason. "I mean, are you stupid, Jez? It's staring you in the face. He's either gay or bi-curious, and he wants you."

"We don't know that for sure."

"Of course he is. Straight men don't behave like that. So why didn't you shag? I mean, you're only human."

"Honestly, Jason. Trust you to bring it down to that level. Nothing happened because it's a no-go area. I'm with Graham. He's with Kristyna, *and* he's an employee. It has disaster written all over it in so many ways. Anyway, a guest rang the bar bell."

"So you would have done something if you weren't interrupted? Graham's a hundred miles away, and Kristyna is halfway across Europe."

"No, I wouldn't have done anything. At least I don't think so. I hope not."

"But it's playing on your mind," said Jason. "This is why you're telling me? I don't blame you, he's gorgeous."

"Well, he's come and sat with me every night for the past two weeks, aside from when Graham's been home, and nothing like that has happened since."

"Dollface, he's made the first move. Suck him off, the poor thing. I bet you'd be better than his girlfriend. I doubt she'd swallow. He's waiting for you to make the next move now."

"Well, he'll be waiting a long time," I said.

As soon as I told Jason, I regretted it. I asked him to be discreet, however asking Jason to keep something secret was a bit like asking Jeremy Clarkson to become a vegetarian and be a spokesperson for the Green lobby. It was not going to happen, and it would only be a matter of time before he had one of his slip-ups and told somebody. I knew Jason was shallow, but I stupidly expected him to tell me to be careful. I had hoped he would tell me to remember the solid relationship that I had built with Graham and think about the Pandora's Box I could be opening. I *wanted* a moral lecture; I wanted him to tell me what was right and what was wrong. I wanted disapproval. Perhaps I should have known better. After all, this was Jason, and he was not keen on Graham. Maybe I should have gone to see a priest or called a friend in London. However, I knew the house approved of Jason, and the house would always put my interests first.

We had another drink and moved onto different topics, mostly about how much weight various people had put on since we last saw them. Jason received his usual slips of paper with telephone numbers scribbled on them. At eleven, I staggered home on my own, leaving him in the company of a Welsh rugby player. When I arrived back at the hotel, the bar and public areas were locked, so I went into my private lounge with the intention of sending Graham a goodnight email. I found Lukas sprawled across the sofa in a pair of cargo shorts, revealing his thick hairy legs. His pecs were bursting out of a tight fitting white T-shirt, and he was watching a boxing match on television.

"Lukas," I said. "I didn't expect you to still be up. We have an early start tomorrow."

"I wait up for you."

"You didn't need to do that," I slurred.

"I much care for you," he said, lying across the sofa. His legs were parted, and his muscles rippled through his cotton T-shirt. He had one arm behind his head, which emphasized the size of his biceps.

The words seemed to fall clumsily out of my mouth, as though somebody else was talking. "I care about you, too."

"You go out with Jason. He no good for you. He make you drink too much and gossip."

"Jason is Jason, flawed but funny."

"He is big queen. I not like him."

"Isn't it time you went to bed? We have a busy breakfast tomorrow."

"Please come and sit with me, Mr. Jez."

Lukas pointed the remote control at the television and turned it off. I clumsily fell onto the sofa and looked at him. My vision was blurred, and my judgment impaired. He put his big builder's hand on the side of my face and ran it down my cheek, holding my chin and rubbing it with his thumb. He gazed longingly into my eyes, like a child looking in a shop window at a favorite toy that they wanted for Christmas.

"Lukas, you mustn't," I said weakly. We both knew that I did not mean it.

"If you no want me to, I stop and leave you alone."

"Oh God, I can't believe this is happening. Lukas, I fancy you like mad, but you know we should not be doing this."

"I know, but I can't help way I feel, Mr. Jez."

I put my hand to the back of Lukas' head and pulled him toward me. "I want you, Lukas... so much."

I kissed him, and he responded. It was a sexual fantasy coming true. Despite the erosion of my morality through the deleterious effects of alcohol, the last vestiges of my conscience briefly kicked in. I was very aware I was committing a forbidden act, sleeping with an engaged straight man, who happened to be an employee. My drunken brain was trying to decipher the situation. The logical side of my mind knew that this could spell disaster. In a brief moment of compunction, I pulled myself away. He stroked my forearms gently with his hands. It felt intimate as though we were in a bubble, insulated from the outside world.

"So what we do next?" he asked. "I don't want make you do something you no like to do."

Despite my intoxication, I knew how I had been feeling about Lukas over the last few weeks. There was no longer any mystery as to whether my attraction was reciprocated. The alcohol may have been the catalyst, but

I somehow knew that something was going to happen eventually, so it might as well have been now.

He put his hand behind me and gripped my shoulder, pulling me toward him. My carnal desires overwhelmed me. All memories of Graham and our life together seemed to vanish in a drunken, lustful haze.

"Lukas," I said. "Take me upstairs."

"I do, Mr. Jez, but I have to say I inexperienced, I never do man before, but I want *you*, Mr. Jez. I have ever since I arrived."

He held my hand and led me up to my bedroom. As an employee, Lukas was dutiful, diligent, and bordered on being subservient, but in bed, he was dominant and assertive. He flung me onto the mattress and proceeded to undress me, roughly pulling my jeans down. Then he took off his clothes and revealed a smooth, muscular torso. He had a tribal tattoo across his left shoulder going down the side of his arm. He had a ripped stomach with barely an ounce of fat to cover his six-pack, which had a few wisps of soft hairs traveling up from his waist to his navel.

He told me that it was the first time that he had slept with a man. He had lived a lie for a long time in a backwater farming village in Eastern Europe. He was unleashing years of his pent-up sexual frustration upon me, and I loved every second of it. As I lay there, face down, I saw the picture of Graham that I kept on my bedside table, and an avalanche of guilt swept over me. It was not enough to prevent me from continuing what I had started. I stretched out my arm and tipped over the picture, as if to prevent Graham from seeing what was going on in our bed. Temporarily, he was a distant memory. Then I enjoyed the sensation of Lukas on top of me, moaning with pleasure as he thrust himself inside me. When he finished, he turned me over and kissed me, rubbing his sweaty body against mine until I climaxed.

"You were perfect, Mr. Jez. I love doing you."

"And you were amazing, too," I slurred.

"I love you, Jez."

"Don't be silly," I said.

I took a lingering look at this incredibly handsome man beside me with whom I had just enjoyed the most amazing sex. Then I fell into a comatose alcoholic sleep with my head resting against his chest, as he gently stroked my hair.

Chapter 16

February 1975: Marjorie Wilson

As the protracted winter gradually passed and the days lengthened, the tourists started trickling back to Torquay. The telephone started ringing for brochure requests, and the booking confirmation letters began to arrive, with their much-needed deposit checks. We found the midweek trade to be quiet in winter. It was mainly businessmen; often they were traveling salesmen. They usually stayed for just one night and requested an early breakfast, but otherwise they were low maintenance and Stanley described them as our 'bread and butter.' The weekends were also quiet. It was on the last Saturday in February that we had another memorable guest.

The doorbell rang at three o'clock. It was an elderly, frail gentleman in his eighties. He had a younger female companion. I assumed she was his granddaughter, but it transpired that she was his nurse. She was booked into the room next to his. I answered the door with my welcoming smile and practiced charm and led them to the lounge. He took short, slow steps with the aid of a walking stick.

"May I welcome you to Torquay, and to our small hotel?"

"Yes, yes," he said grumpily. "I'm Albert Henderson. The young lady accompanying me is my help, Miss Jean Smith."

He spoke with an acquired aristocratic accent. He was wearing an ancient brass-buttoned navy blazer that exuded quality, but on closer inspection, it was frayed and no longer fitted his shrunken frame. An impeccably ironed white double-cuffed shirt with gold cufflinks, yellow silk tie, beige trousers, and highly polished brogues created an impression of someone who took pride in their appearance. He suffered from a bad stoop, and paused every few steps to lean on his walking stick and catch his breath. Thinning white hair crowned a wrinkly, liver spotted face, dark sunglasses covered his eyes, and he wore a cumbersome hearing aid. Jean helped Albert lower himself into an armchair.

"Can I offer you a pot of tea and a slice of cake?" I asked.

"Mr. Henderson will have an Earl Gray, please. He will not have any cake. I don't want anything, thank you," said his assistant in a gentle Irish accent. His carer was short, with permed red hair, and wore a neatly pressed nurse's outfit. She carried a small briefcase.

"I believe I booked the old master bedroom at the front of the house," said Albert. "I was most insistent in my booking letter that it be this particular room."

"Yes, Mr. Henderson," I said. "Your booking request made that very clear. It is all as per your instructions, including the fresh flowers you asked for."

"Good, then everything is in order."

I walked into the kitchen and returned with a teapot full of Earl Grey tea on a silver tray. I poured him a cup, which he took gratefully. His hand was shaking, which caused most of it to end up in the saucer.

"What time is dinner served?" he asked.

"We serve evening meals at half past six in the dining room," I said. "Tonight it's a choice of steak and kidney pie or meatballs with rice."

"I'm sure either will be fine," he said. "How long have you owned this place?"

"Over a year now. We have done some extensive renovation work."

"Yes, I can see that. You've ripped the soul out of the place, in my opinion."

"Well, I don't think that's very—"

"Have to interfere with things, you modern types, can't leave things alone the way they should be."

"When we bought the building, it was on the verge of collapse," I said defensively. "Do you have a connection with the place, then?"

Albert smiled. "I think you could say that."

* * *

When he had finished his tea, I led them up to their bedrooms. Jean helped him climb the stairs with a guiding arm. He was very immobile, and I wondered why he had not requested a room on the ground floor.

"We do have ground floor rooms if you prefer."

"I may be old, young lady, but I'm not a cripple," he said tetchily. "Besides, I specifically wanted this room. I have my reasons."

It took a while to help him climb the stairs. Once we were on the landing, I opened the bedroom door for him. He walked in, observing his surroundings with a critical eye and air of disapproval.

"Miss Smith, that is your room there across the corridor," I said, handing her the keys. I looked back at Mr. Henderson. "If there's anything you need, please don't hesitate to—"

"Yes, yes, we will be fine," he snapped.

Jean shut the door.

"Cantankerous old sod," I said under my breath. As

I walked away, I paused and turned back toward the bedroom. I could hear him sobbing loudly. I pressed my ear against the door to listen, but the thickness of the wood prevented me from hearing much, except, "Forgive me, sir!" between cries of anguish.

Chapter 17

July 2006: Jez Matthews

It was seven o'clock, when the shrill electronic alarm from my bedside clock woke me. I leaned over to press the snooze button. Not quite fully awake, I realized that there was an arm around my waist. My initial thoughts were that Graham had returned from London a day early, and then the events of the previous night flooded back. I had hoped it had all been a dream, but Lukas' physical presence in my bed confirmed my worst fears. I had an appalling hangover, with a thumping headache. I was sweating, and my mouth was dry. I turned over and saw Lukas was waking up, too. This was all very wrong, and I cursed my stupidity for allowing it to happen.

"Morning, Mr. Jez, my sweet," he said, staring lovingly into my eyes.

"Morning, Lukas," I said awkwardly. I felt incredibly uncomfortable.

"I wanted you since I saw photograph in newspaper."

He referred to the publicity article that the *Torquay Herald* had written about our refurbishment and subsequent reopening. I had a moment of clarity when he uttered those words. I despaired, as I realized the trap that I had fallen into. He had planned this from the day that I had met him. It dawned on me that his straight country boy act and his accidental innuendos were perhaps not as innocent as I had thought. It had taken me a long time to figure it out, but I realized that he was far from the naive young man that I thought I knew. In fact, he was manipulative and dangerous. This frightened me, as I had much to lose. I accepted that my inferences could be wrong and deep down, I wanted to believe that I was mistaken, but all the evidence pointed toward this conclusion. I was a wealthy, good-looking man, living in a liberal country. I suspected that he saw me as his ticket away from his staid and closeted life back in the Czech Republic.

I felt anxious when I considered the possible implications of my indiscretion. I had enjoyed a monogamous, loving relationship with Graham for over ten years. I had indelibly tainted this, because of a drunken moment of passion with a hormonal, sexually frustrated young man that was barely out of his teens.

However, this was not some random one-night stand. That would have been bad enough. Lukas lived with us, and he was an employee. There was no option of giving him a false telephone number and making an empty promise that we would meet up again soon, hoping I had not caught crabs. A man who created a fake persona, in the way that Lukas had, could not be emotionally stable, and it was worrying that he was infatuated with me. As I lay there, I started to piece together our history over the last few months. He arrived on our doorstep after seeing our job advert and our publicity article, complete with photographs. I thought of all the innuendos, the subtle flirting and lingering hugs, his desire to spend as much time with me as possible, when Graham was not here. It all made sense now. I must have been blind not to notice it.

I climbed out of bed and walked into the bathroom. My reflection in the mirror stared back at me with bloodshot eyes. I stepped into the shower and turned it on. I shut my eyes and tilted my head back, enjoying the water flowing over my hair and face, washing away the stale alcoholic sweat and the lingering smell of secondhand tobacco smoke. Lukas opened the shower door and entered the cubicle, looking like a Greek god. He put his arms around me, nuzzling against my neck. Much as I enjoyed it, I knew that it was wrong.

"No," I said firmly, pushing him away. "You have your own bathroom."

I felt like I had kicked a puppy. He looked crestfallen as he walked away, grabbing a spare towel. My mind was racing, my thoughts a jumbled confusion. I had a choice to make. I could come clean with Graham. I would confess that it was all a terrible drunken mistake, which was the truth and hope he would forgive me. The alternative was to try to forget that it happened and carry on as normal.

I found serving breakfast uncomfortable, because Lukas kept wanting to grope me. I did not think that I would ever be pleased to see Morbid Maureen. However, this particular morning, I could think of nothing better than listening to her droning on about the appeal of euthanasia.

After helping to clear breakfast, I left Lukas and Maureen to clean the rooms. I was in the laundry room, stacking towels and sheets, when Lukas walked in.

"I want speak with you, Mr. Jez."

"Now is not the time, Lukas."

He ignored me and pressed his lips against mine. He pulled me close to him and put his tongue in my ear, then proceeded to nibble the lobe.

"You and me, we are good together. You see, I make you happy."

He started to kiss me, and I could feel that he was aroused.

"Lukas, stop," I said pushing him away gently. "We've got work to do."

"Later, then," he said.

I finished organizing the laundry. I was feeling hungover and depressed. It was obvious that last night was not a one off and was not going to go away. I imagined the hurt that I would cause Graham if I confessed. I knew that he would never be able to trust me again, wondering what I was up to every time he went off to London. I made a conscious decision that I would not tell the truth. Perhaps that was weak, but I also felt it was my cross to bear. I knew that I could not live without Graham. I also knew that it was not an option to sack Lukas, as I ran the risk of enduring an expensive employment tribunal, where the truth would inevitably come out anyway. Besides, I did not have the heart to do it, especially with Kristyna grieving the loss of her sister. There was nobody to blame but myself for the situation.

I had a self-destructive side to my nature, which made my life unnecessarily complicated. I thought that I had grown out of it, but evidently, I had not. Even though Lukas had led me astray, as the older one, I should have known better and should have been able to resist temptation. It was natural for me to blame everybody else, but it was not Kristyna's fault that her sister died, or Graham's because he was working hard in London to finance the refurbishment. It was not even Lukas' fault; he was just a youngster and emotionally immature. No, the blame fell squarely on me. I would cynically take a gamble that Lukas' infatuation was a crush that would soon fade in a short space of time. Then we could put this business behind us and carry on as normal. In Lukas' mind, we had started an affair, but I did not love Lukas, and I knew I never would, as I was in love with Graham.

The hotel was busy, and I thankfully spent the next couple of nights playing my role as the charming, convivial hotel proprietor, so I did not have much time alone with Lukas. However, I knew I could not avoid him forever, and it was important that we set certain rules for when Graham returned. I had washed our bed linen and thoroughly cleaned our bedroom, in a vain effort to cleanse the memory of what had happened. Unfortunately, no amount of fabric conditioner could turn back time. The horrible truth was that I had enjoyed my liaison with Lukas, and despite the risks and the emotional turmoil, I wanted it to happen again. Pushing Lukas away only seemed to make him keener. I wanted the best of both worlds, the security and love that Graham afforded me and the excitement and great sex that was on offer from Lukas. What I did not want was the guilt and self-loathing.

Graham was due back on the eleven fifteen train from London on Thursday night, so I asked Lukas to come into the lounge in the afternoon. He immediately embraced me and tried to kiss me. I turned my head to one side to avoid contact.

"Lukas, we need to talk," I said, struggling against his strong grip.

"We do no need words, Mr. Jez."

"Please, no, stop now. We need to stop."

"But I love you."

"Please, pay attention," I said sternly. "You must try to behave like an adult and understand my situation. Neither of us is single. You are engaged to Kristyna, and I am in a relationship with Graham. They must not find out about this. Do you understand?"

"I want to tell world."

"Just listen to me, please. I will continue to see you

in the week whilst Graham is away. If Graham finds out, you will lose your home and your job and you'll be sent packing to your little village in the Czech Republic before you can say 'Joseph Stalin.' We have to be discreet about this. You understand that word, discreet?"

"I understand, Mr. Jez. We tell Graham dis week."

"No, I said discreet, not this week. Discreet means that we have to keep this a secret between you and me."

"I no want to, I want tell everyone."

"Please, I know this weekend is going to be difficult for you with Graham here, but you must understand we have been a couple for over ten years. This is his home. He owns half. I need you to respect that."

"So I am your bit to slide."

"The expression is your bit on the side, not *to slide*."

Lukas looked hurt.

"Hey, they were your words, I didn't mean that you actually were," I lied.

Although I had not thought about it before, that is exactly what he was, and selfishly that was what I wanted him to remain.

"Look, I enjoy your company. You're sexy and lovely in every way, but think about the lives we will wreck if anybody finds out."

"Okay, I understand."

"You must promise me, Lukas."

"I promise."

"Good, now remember we have to go back to how things were whilst Graham is here. That means you staying in your room and not waving your cock around at every available opportunity."

As if not hearing a word I had said, he placed my hand on his bulging crotch.

"While we alone, you sort this out for me," he said, smiling provocatively.

"No, Lukas, behave yourself or I will end this here and now and tell Graham everything."

Lukas looked dejected and walked back to his room with his head down and his shoulders hunched. I had bought some time, so I could stop worrying, at least temporarily. This was going to be a delicate balancing act, but in spite of my guilt, I felt that if I played my cards right, I could have my cake and eat it. At least in the short term, I hoped that my conversation with Lukas would prevent any problems from occurring this weekend.

I collected Graham from the station and flung my arms around him in the car, holding him tightly.

"I'm so glad you're back, love."

"Is everything all right?"

"It is now, just hold me."

"Something's wrong, isn't it? You're never this sweet."

"I've just had a tough week, that's all."

"Have the guests been difficult?"

"Yes, something like that."

I started the car and drove us home. Seeing Graham had brought me back to reality with an uncomfortable thud. It was difficult to look him in the eye and the remorse that I felt doubled in his presence, but I knew I had to keep it secret. Graham was my first and only true love. I hated myself for behaving this way toward this gentle, kind, and generous man, who loved me unconditionally. Nevertheless, I knew that I had unfinished business with Lukas.

"Have you heard from Kristyna?" he asked.

"No, Lukas speaks to her every day. He says she should be back in a week or so."

"That's a shame."

"Why?"

"I was quite enjoying our chats about Morbid Maureen. It kept me entertained of an evening!"

"Yes, she certainly has given me a lot of material. Even so, it will be good to have Kristyna back. If anything, it will keep Lukas in check, and there're only so many conversations I can take about Maureen's hysterectomy."

I parked the car and carried Graham's luggage inside for him. As usual, he had brought home a suitcase full of dirty clothes for me to wash, even though he had a perfectly useable washing machine in his apartment. The bar was empty, so we enjoyed a brief catch-up over a gin and tonic before locking up and retiring for the night. I did not sleep much, as I had bad dreams. My head was a mess, and I was concerned as to how Lukas would behave at breakfast. In the early hours of the morning, the summer sun streamed through our bedroom windows, shining through the cracks in the curtains. The birds started singing their dawn chorus. The alarm sounded at seven, and I realized that I had slept for a couple of hours at best. I switched off the alarm immediately, to avoid waking Graham, and crept into the bathroom to shower and dress. Graham slept soundly, recovering from the commute and his working week in London.

I went downstairs to find Lukas in the kitchen, preparing breakfast. He planted a quick kiss on my cheek.

"No worry, Mr. Jez, I not do it when Graham around."

Morbid Maureen arrived, complete with her ailment of the day. Today it was a sore throat that she was convinced was a tropical illness that she had contracted from one of our overseas guests.

"You can pick up all number of germs from washing up," she informed.

"Maybe it's Ebola?" I said hopefully.

Graham came down halfway through service and as usual helped himself to coffee and toast. I was relieved that there was no vibe or obvious clue as to what was going on between Lukas and me. For the moment, our secret was safe. I left Maureen and Lukas to clean the rooms and as there were no arrivals, Graham and I took the opportunity to enjoy a walk along the beach, then on into town for an early lunch. I looked at him as we walked. He was really starting to show his age. His hair was graying and his laughter lines were becoming more prominent. Although he was still physically fit, his fatty diet and sedentary lifestyle up in London were beginning to take their toll on his waistline. This did not make me love him any less. He was the man I wanted to grow old with. We had a light lunch in town, sitting outside by the harbor. We shared a pizza and a salad. It was whilst eating that Graham made an announcement.

"The work in London is drying up. They've said that my finish date will be some time in November, so I have another four months at most."

"Well, that's good, isn't it?"

"Yes and no," he said. "Yes, in that I'm sick of the commute every week and I'm missing you, but on the other hand, I know we will both miss the money."

"We'll cope. Graham, the hotel is profitable. We can pay the mortgage, the staff, all the bills, and there's enough to have a comfortable lifestyle. Maybe not as extravagant as we've been used to, but we didn't do it for the money. Anyhow, four months is still a long time."

"I know. I just need some time to adjust to the idea, and you, young man, need to stop buying furniture."

I felt mixed emotions about Graham moving permanently down to Torquay. I knew that it was going to happen eventually, but I had become used to Graham being away. Admittedly, at first I found it difficult, but I had grown to enjoy my freedom. The Pembroke Hotel had become my personal fiefdom. I looked forward to him returning for weekends, but I felt liberated by those four days on my own, and now there was the additional factor of Lukas. Although the situation was complicated, I did not want to give up my liaisons with him. Some careful planning was required.

We strolled around town and did some shopping in Fleet Walk, which was Torquay's answer to the Kings Road, London, with some great boutique clothes shops. Jason had also alerted us to the fact that there was a sale at Hoopers. Graham bought a couple of half-price Ralph Lauren polo shirts there. The town was bustling with tourists and the overseas students who stayed at the language school at this time of the year. This seemed to emphasize the harbor's continental feel. A couple of magnificent yachts had moored in the outer harbor, with their lucky owners sunbathing on the decks. There was also a cruise ship anchored in the bay. It was on days such as this that I appreciated how Torquay had acquired the label of 'The English Riviera.' It made me realize how lucky we were to live in such a vibrant town. I was glad that we had exchanged the traffic, pollution, and noise of London for this.

After a wonderful weekend, once again Graham returned to London. Later in the week, Jason sent me a text message to say that he had booked a couple of days off. At short notice, we hastily arranged a night out. When Jason arrived at the hotel in the evening, he had changed his hairstyle and image yet again. He was wearing a bead necklace and a figure hugging T-shirt, with sunflowers printed on the front. His jeans were baggy and only reached four inches below his waist, leaving a large gap. This revealed a sizeable section of his buttocks that were thankfully covered by a white pair of Calvin Klein boxer shorts. Apparently, the jeans were the latest fashion, but that did not make it right. We sat having a drink in the kitchen.

"I've turned spiritual," he announced.

"Jason, growing your hair a bit longer, listening to Enya, and drinking organic cider does not make you spiritual."

"Ooh, watch the bad Karma, doll."

"So, I presume that we're going to The Horn of Plenty, then?"

"Where else?" asked Jason. "It's *Stars in their Eyes* night tonight."

"That's a new one, isn't it?"

"It's just another name for karaoke."

"Oh for goodness sake, it's always karaoke at that place."

"That's not strictly true. Monday is Bingay Bingo. Tuesday is quiz night. Thursday is lesbian pool night..."

"And it's karaoke on all the other nights. They are so imaginative."

"Don't forget that on Friday, it's karaoke with a twist."

"And what's the twist?"

"It's drag queen karaoke, with a raffle."

"Has my life honestly come to this?"

"Oh, don't be such a killjoy. We can laugh at all the daft queens who think they're the next Justin Timberlake waiting to be discovered."

Lukas walked into the kitchen to make himself a cup of tea. I had left him in charge again.

"Hello, sexy," said Jason, winking at me. He pointed his finger at Lukas and mouthed silently, *He's fucking gorgeous.*

"Hello, Mr. Jason, how are you? I look after reception and bar tonight."

"I am extremely well, Mr. Lukas, and very single, I might add."

I glared at Jason. Lukas looked slightly embarrassed but ignored Jason's clumsy flirting, quickly making his tea, and going back out to the reception area.

"The body on that," said Jason. "He even manages to look good in a Fruit of the Loom T-shirt, bless him."

"Shhhh," I said. "He's only on the other side of that door. He'll overhear you."

"You need to sort out his clothes though. He's a walking advert for Wal-Mart."

"That's Kristyna's business, not mine."

"So, have there been any more developments with Mr. 'I like to massage your feet whilst my fiancée's away?'"

My face betrayed me, as it flushed and turned a bright-red color.

"Oh my God," said Jason. "You haven't. You bloody well have, you lucky bastard."

"It's not like that, it's a nightmare. I was drunk. Look, I need to talk to you *confidentially*, you must not tell anybody. Do you understand?"

"Darling, you know that I am discretion personified. When Steph from the pub got arrested for sucking off that premier league footballer on the A38 lay-by, I didn't say anything for a whole week."

"Come on," I said. "Let's go out. I will confess all, over a drink."

The pub was busy, but we found a quiet corner, away from the noise and the nosy patrons. Dave, the barman, knew that we were talking about something important, as he kept finding excuses to come over. I was convinced that he had hidden microphones underneath the tables. A tubby lesbian was belting out her loose interpretation of Gloria Gaynor's "I Will Survive", with her voice singing in a different key to the music. Steph was hosting the karaoke, wearing an enormous Louis XV wig that measured a foot across, which complemented an outrageous sequin dress. He sprayed his stinging nettle comments at anyone who dared to come close enough. As always, he was drinking heavily, and his native Yorkshire accent became more pronounced with his increasing inebriation. He provided commentary between each song, and his language descended into mixture of insults and profanities. He was like a drunken, camp version of Simon Cowell that had gone through a botched sex change operation.

"And a round of applause for Jenny, who made that song her own. Don't give up your day job, love," he said in his high voice. Then he switched to his low voice, "What a load of fucking shite," before belching into the microphone.

"And next we have two love birds, Mike and Darren, singing a duet of 'Summer Nights'."

The torturous sound of another great song being ruined blared through the speakers, in discordant glory.

Jason came back with our drinks. "Right, enough of this suspense. I want to know everything from the beginning," he ordered.

Confiding in Jason was a little like eating a doner kebab after a night on the town. You knew you should not do it, and you knew that you would regret it, but you could not help yourself. You munched on the greasy, tasteless slivers of meat, wondering which animal it came from. You marveled at how they reformed the connective tissue and gristle into a brown cylindrical shape rotating on the grill. You would be thankful that you ordered extra chili sauce to disguise the flavor, and you realized that it would only be a matter of time until you saw it all again, usually the next morning in the toilet, by which time you would vow to become vegetarian.

So it was against my better judgment that I told Jason the whole story. I related how I came back from the pub last week to find him on the sofa. I told him what happened afterward, then about the snatched moments of affection in the laundry room and the kitchen. He wanted every bit of gory detail, especially about the sex. What I really wanted to talk about was my emotional state and the guilt that I felt.

"What was it like?" said Jason. "You are so lucky. It's every gay girl's dream to bag a hetero, especially one like that."

"It was rough," I said honestly. "But it was also amazing and strangely romantic."

"I bet you couldn't walk for days. He's a big lad. I've noticed that package in those tight jeans."

"Too much information," I said.

"So are you going to carry on with it?"

"I'm not sure... I know I shouldn't. I risk losing everything, but—"

"But he's got supermodel looks, a nine-inch cock, and he's over ten years your junior."

"When you put it like that. So what do you think of me now? Jez, the love rat."

"Dollface, I never judge, except when I watch *Jerry Springer*, or eat in McDonalds, you know that. So long as nobody finds out, then no one will get hurt. Shag him senseless, I'd say, until one or both of you gets bored with it."

"You don't think I should fess up to Graham and get Lukas out of the house?"

"You're applying hetero rules to gay relationships, Jez. How do you know Graham's not shagging up in London? We're sexual creatures. We need to go out and have a bit of fun. It's in our nature, and besides, you're a lot younger than Graham. You've got hormones, and it's not as if you're betraying him *emotionally*."

"Perhaps... I'd just hoped that Graham and I were better than that. Oh, and by the way, I know Graham would never cheat on me, that's what makes it all so unforgivable, and lastly, Jason, please, you must not tell a soul."

"Of course I won't, doll. Mum's the word."

"No, I mean it, if anybody finds out about this, there will be consequences. I want you to give me your word."

"Jez, I'm being serious here. I know when to keep my mouth shut. I won't tell anybody. I promise on my replica Versace sunglasses."

"Good, now pass me the song list. I feel a Boyzone melody coming on. Let's show these queens how to sing."

I left the pub at around eleven. As usual, Jason had pulled. This time it was a camp, bitchy young thing called Simon from Birmingham, who thought he was special because he worked in Debenhams department store and had a lisp. The conversation was not usually that intellectual with Jason's one-night stands, but when they started talking about Kylie Minogue's alleged nose job, I decided that I had had enough. I made my excuses and left them to it. It was a pleasant walk home with a mild sea breeze taking the edge off the nighttime humidity. If I had told almost any other of my friends what I had told Jason tonight, I knew that they would have advised me to stop what I was doing now, or risk losing everything, which would have been good advice. However, in my heart, I did not want to hear that. Somehow, having Jason's approval and even his admiration made it easier to bear.

I arrived back at the hotel to find Lukas had locked up and left me a note saying it had been busy. He had taken about £100 in the bar, which was still in the cash register. There were seven large X's at the end of the note. I later discovered that these represented each day that we had been a couple, in his mind. I put the money in the safe and then went to bed. Lukas was waiting for me, spread-eagled naked on his front wearing nothing but a tight pair of Y-fronts. What was the point of even pretending I did not want him, despite his poor taste in underwear? We went on to have another night of hot sticky sex, with all memories of Graham temporarily forgotten in an orgy of drunken lust.

Chapter 18

February 1975: Marjorie Wilson

Albert and Jean both took dinner at the hotel. Christopher served them steak and kidney pie, and they ordered semolina pudding for dessert. Neither of them had anything to drink, apart from tap water. I warned Christopher that Albert could be a little tetchy, but Christopher had found him congenial.

Albert divulged to Christopher that he was in the employ of the family who owned the building about fifty years ago, when it was named Pembroke House. He also disclosed that he had recently been diagnosed with an untreatable form of cancer. The purpose of his visit was to see his old home and place of work before he died. Christopher was curious to find out more about the building's history, but when pressed, Albert became increasingly nebulous in his responses. After dinner, they enjoyed coffee in the drawing room, whilst watching *Call My Bluff* on the color television set, before they retired for the night.

Morning came, and Christopher and I prepared breakfast whilst Stanley had a lie-in after overindulging with guests in the bar the previous night. Elsie was smartly dressed in her waitress outfit with her hair tied back in a bun. She was pottering around the dining room with a duster whilst we waited for the guests to descend upon us for their bacon and eggs. She always liked to keep herself busy. I put the sausages in the oven, and Elsie came into the kitchen, her face as white as a sheet.

"You had better both come with me. We have a problem," she said.

Christopher and I followed Elsie into the dining room. Jean, Albert's nurse, was waiting for us, her face ashen.

"I'm sorry to be the bearer of bad news, but Mr. Henderson passed away last night."

After a short pause to absorb her announcement, I said, "I'm so sorry, Jean." I put a comforting arm on her shoulder.

"It wasn't totally unexpected," she said. "He was a very ill man, but we thought he had a bit longer."

"Of course," I said.

"I had nursed him for four years. He became like a favorite uncle to me. He could be a bit grumpy sometimes, but he had a good heart."

"I understand."

Whilst I sympathized with Jean, my selfish side worried about the logistical nightmare of dealing with a dead body. It had the potential to damage our reputation, especially if there were police and undertakers wandering around.

"Christopher, go and fetch your father. He'll know what to do."

Stanley came downstairs, looking as if he had dressed in a hurry. As it was a sudden death, we sought advice from the police, who recommended that we leave the body in situ. As a matter of procedure, they dispatched two officers to file a report. We carried on as normal and served breakfast to the remaining guests, the ones that had managed to stay alive. As Stanley rightly said, life goes on. The police officers arrived at eleven o'clock and spent ten minutes here, satisfied that there was no evidence of foul play. The only unusual thing that they had noticed was that the fitted carpet in Albert's bedroom looked like somebody had lifted it up. Neither Jean, Stanley, nor I had any idea as to why this was. After asking Jean and myself a few routine questions, they made a pocket notebook entry and organized an approved firm of funeral directors to collect the body. Since we had uniformed police officers walking about, it was impossible to keep the incident secret from the guests. It was not a pleasant topic, but people were understanding and showed genuine concern for us and for Jean Smith, who was understandably upset.

The police had parked a bright blue liveried Morris Minor on the road, directly outside the hotel, in view of all the neighbors. Therefore, it was inevitable that Mavis would have seen it, so we were expecting her call at any moment. She did not disappoint. The doorbell rang shortly after the police left, and Stanley rolled his eyes at me. Mavis was standing at the door, typically overdressed, having squeezed herself into a poorly fitting cerise outfit made from taffeta. As usual, she reeked of cheap perfume.

"Are you going to a garden party at Buckingham palace?" I asked.

"You are funny, darling," she said. "I'm not one to gossip, as you know, but I saw the police car outside and I've been out of my mind with worry. Are you all okay?"

"Come in," I sighed, leading her to the kitchen. Stanley left us to it.

"Would you like a cup of tea and a French Fancy?"

"Yes, please."

"It's not been the best day," I said, filling the kettle. "One of the guests died during the night."

"Oh my God," said Mavis. "That's every hotel owner's nightmare. How are you bearing up?"

"I'm a bit shaken. These things happen though. I'm sure it's not the first time a guest has died in a hotel room. I just hope it wasn't my steak and kidney pie."

"So who was it, then, and how did they die?"

"It was an older man. The undertakers are due shortly, to take the poor sod away. He was terminally ill, apparently. Sugar?"

"Yes, two lumps, please. Have you taken a look?"

"No, I haven't been in the room. I don't want to either. His nurse found him. She was staying in the room across the corridor. She went in this morning to administer his medication."

"Well, these things are never pleasant," she said with her mouth full of pink icing. "So nothing else to add, then?"

"No, much as I would love to give you a great story about a murder or something else more interesting, I can't. Another thing, I would be grateful if you could keep this to yourself, Mavis. This kind of thing is not exactly good for business."

"Darling, I won't tell a soul. We must do lunch soon, soooo much to tell you. There's been swinger's parties going on at The Hereford Hotel—I mean, you expect it in Paignton, but here in Torquay!"

"Good-bye, Mavis," I said wearily. It had been a long morning, and I was not in the mood.

"I'll see myself out. Ciao, darling."

Stanley came into the kitchen, puffing on a cigarette.

"Not in the kitchen, Stanley!"

He stubbed his cigarette out in the sink. "She's gone, then," he said.

"Yes."

"The whole town will know by lunchtime."

"I know, Stanley."

"She'll be on the phone now."

"I know."

"She can't help herself."

"I know."

"I don't know why you're friends with her."

"Because she's entertaining, and she has a good heart buried somewhere."

"Buried very deep, if you ask me. Well, the undertakers are here, so he will be taken away shortly, poor soul. Listen, I don't want to be the bearer of more bad news."

"What's happened now?"

"I've just been up to the master bedroom. That blooming black stain by the fireplace has come back."

"Oh for God's sake, not again. Christopher says he knows a decorator he met on one of his late-night walks. I'll let him know."

"And another thing," said Stanley lowering his voice. "When I took the undertakers in, I looked at the corpse."

"Oh, please, Stanley, why did you do that?"

"I don't know, couldn't help myself, probably morbid curiosity. He didn't die in his sleep, that's certain."

"Why do you say that?"

"For a start, his eyes were wide open and he was sitting upright in bed, but worse than that Marje, his face—horrible it was, twisted in terror. I've never seen anything like it. He was afraid of something, something terrible. It's as if he saw a..."

"...ghost," I completed, my eyes wide with shock.

Chapter 19

August 2006: Jez Matthews

It was August, and Torquay was basking in hot sunshine. We were extremely busy, and I was grateful that Kristyna was due back on the coach from London this evening. I had decided to keep Morbid Maureen on until September, since she had proven to be reliable and was simply too entertaining to get rid of. I also hoped it would take some pressure off Kristyna, whom I wanted to ease back into work.

I loaned Lukas the car so he could collect Kristyna from the coach station. I had mixed feelings about her coming back. In some respects, I was glad; there was no doubt that she would keep a watchful eye on Lukas. However, it emphasized my feelings of guilt. She had been abroad, burying her dead sister, whilst I had been here, having sex with her fiancée. I did not relish the thought of looking her in the eye. Part of me hoped that when she returned, things would go back to normal. I hoped Lukas' feelings for me and his sexual appetite would somehow dissipate, and he would realize that it had all been a phase. I wanted the old status quo back, where Lukas was the clumsy but lovable husband in waiting, with his devoted fiancée. This way, nobody would get hurt. I knew that it was a vain hope, though, as I was already planning in my own mind how Lukas and I would be able to sneak in some late-night dalliances. It was a big house, and there were plenty of bedrooms. With my warped logic, I justified my actions by convincing myself that I was somehow saving their relationship by giving Lukas a sexual escape, with no emotional strings attached. I did not want flowers, chocolates, or romantic meals; that was what Kristyna was for. I just wanted a good fuck every now and then. My infidelity toward Graham was also justifiable, as in all other respects, I was a great boyfriend, caring and trustworthy. In a few hours, I had almost persuaded myself that I had scruples.

I heard a car pull up the driveway, and I went to the front door to greet them. Kristyna was wearing a suit and white blouse that had become crumpled during her long journey, and she looked weary from her travels. Her eyes betrayed her sadness, and I realized how difficult the last month must have been for her.

"Good afternoon, Jez. It's good to be back," she said, giving me a quick peck on my cheek.

"It's good to have you back, too."

Lukas carried in her suitcase, looking sheepish.

"I can start work tomorrow as usual," she said, efficiently. "Thank you so much for your kindness and understanding. You are good man."

"It's the least I could do," I said, whilst thinking to myself... *And it was great having sex with your future husband whilst you were away.*

"Listen," I said out loud. "Why don't you get freshened up? I've got a roast chicken in the oven for supper."

Our dinner suffered a few interruptions from guests using the bar, but apart from that, it was pleasant. Lukas gave my leg a squeeze under the table, which I ignored. Kristyna remained guarded as always and did not reveal too much or show a great deal of emotion, but her eyes were tinged with sadness. Lukas was giving her a lot of attention, for which I was glad. She spoke briefly about the funeral, before moving on to talk about her nephews and extended family. One positive aspect to the funeral was that she had been able to catch up with friends and relatives. I told her about Morbid Maureen, although Lukas had already given her the lowdown, and I briefed her on a few other operational developments since she had been away. They had an early night, watching television in their bedroom.

After a late evening of amiable conversation with the guests, I quickly sent Graham a goodnight text, then locked up and went to bed. I felt a surge of jealousy as the sounds of Lukas and Kristyna having sex in their bedroom underneath mine permeated the floorboards.

I wondered whether I was emotionally equipped to deal with this situation. I resolved that I would conclude this intrigue at the earliest available opportunity.

Chapter 20

February 1975: Marjorie Wilson

I was in the Wellswood village pantry, on the other side of Meadfoot Beach, buying food for a dinner party that we were holding for some of Stanley's golfing friends, including our MP, Martin Breville. It was when I spoke to the girl serving me, that Mavis' predictable indiscretion became clear. Emily, the shop owner's daughter, innocently mentioned it to me as she packed away my groceries.

"Last weekend must have been awful for you," she said.

"What are you talking about?" I said, pretending I did not know.

"The stiff," she replied. "Still, it's not the first time it's happened. The Northumberland Hotel had one last year. It was awkward trying to get the body out. They had to stand it upright in the lift, so I heard."

"Oh, that," I said. "He was old, but life goes on. You have to deal with things."

"Well," she said. "The things you hoteliers have to put up with. I'll tell you something—you wouldn't catch me going near a dead body."

"So, I take it this is common knowledge around Torquay, then?" I said haughtily.

"Oh yes, you can't do anything in this town without

everybody knowing. That's two pounds, forty-four, and a half, please."

"Goodness, things are getting pricey," I said, rummaging through my purse for some pound notes. "I've only bought a bottle of wine and a roasting joint."

"Thank you, Marje, that's fifty-five and a half-pence change."

"Good old Mavis," I muttered to myself, loading the shopping bags into the estate. "'I'm the soul of bleeding discretion, I am,' my bloody backside she is. I'll kill her one of these days."

This was the first time that we had entertained friends this year, so I wanted everything to be perfect. I laid the table with our best Wedgwood dinner service and crystal. Christopher brought up my hostess trolley from the basement. Later, he managed the hotel, so that we could enjoy an uninterrupted dinner. The guests arrived at about seven o'clock. It was a small gathering that included Martin Breville and his wife Tannis, Robert and Virginia Grainger—the owners of Corbyn View holiday apartments—and Dicky Harris, our lawyer, and his wife Evelyn.

The evening was a triumph. We had pâté and Melba toast to start, and I cooked a wonderfully tender rib of beef with winter vegetables for mains. We washed the food down with a lovely bottle of Beaujolais. For dessert, I defrosted a Bejam lemon meringue, followed by after-eights. When we had finished dinner, in true Victorian style, the girls and I sat in the drawing room, whilst the men talked about politics over cigars and brandies. They left about midnight, and we cleared up.

"He's not looking well," said Stanley.

"Who isn't?" I said.

"Martin. I think he's finding the pressures of being an MP quite hard. He says he's got a dodgy heart."

"What did you talk about?"

"This Thatcher woman defeating Heath in the leadership election, mainly. Martin thinks she has less chance of becoming the prime minister than John Inman playing as a prop forward in the five nations. He doesn't think Britain is ready for a woman prime minister."

"Well, I liked her when we met her. She's got common sense. She'll kick that bunch of public schoolboy toffs into touch."

"And how was the mini WI convention in the drawing room?"

"It was very relaxing. We promised ourselves we'd do lunch in town next week."

"Good. Keep close to Martin's wife. They've got connections."

"I'd like to think I'd stay close to her because I like her."

"And do you?"

"Yes."

"That's even better. I'll make you proud of me one day, Marjorie Wilson."

"I already am, dear."

Chapter 21

August 2006: Jez Matthews
One morning in August, I received a telephone call. It was a researcher, calling on behalf of Diamond Aspect Productions, who filmed Channel 4's *Hotel Red Alert* program.

Graham and I were huge fans of this show, in which Carol Thompson, a renowned innkeeper, visits some of the worst hotels in Britain. She would act as a consultant who attempted to transform the fortunes of the struggling proprietors. She would revive their flagging businesses by issuing recommendations and advice that she often delivered using colorful language. These suggestions usually came in the form of sarcasm. Sometimes Channel 4 would pay for a makeover of the hotel. It was a familiar but nonetheless entertaining format, although the show was more about good television than genuinely helping the hapless owners.

The researcher explained that they were filming an episode of *Hotel Red Alert* in Torquay. The featured accommodation was to be a small guesthouse, called Green Palms, situated in the main tourist area, owned by a couple, Wayne and Tracey. They had taken it to the brink of bankruptcy, due to a combination of operational incompetence, profligate spending on refurbishment, and abysmal taste in furnishings. The production company was scouting the area for successful hotels to inspire them.

I enthusiastically accepted the invitation to appear. I was a fan of the delightfully wicked presenter, and I relished the opportunity to appear on national television, along with the positive publicity it would bring to our establishment.

A location scout arrived later in the afternoon and after a brief tour, announced that The Pembroke Hotel matched their requirements. I telephoned Graham to tell him, and he said that he would clear his diary in order to be present for the filming. I had little more than a week to diet, as I knew that television could add ten pounds in weight. I also told Jason, who agreed to accompany me on a shopping trip to help me choose an appropriate outfit.

The following day, Jason and I drove to Exeter, where the shopping experience was vastly more stimulating than Torquay. It was always fun hanging around with him. As usual, he camped it up and flirted outrageously with the shop assistants. It was difficult to keep up with his narcissistic, ever-changing fashions. He had dumped the spiritual look and replaced it with a punk style. He had shaved the sides and back of his head but grown his fringe long, which was gelled into a peak. He wore a winged shirt, a denim jacket, and jeans.

We wandered around the designer clothes shops, and eventually I picked a flannel sports jacket with a blue oxford-style shirt, and some chinos to go with it. It was a little conservative, but Jason thought it gave me a smart casual look, with a touch of class. We enjoyed an al-fresco lunch at a cafe situated in the cathedral square. As usual, I picked up the tab.

The excitement of the imminent filming and the retail therapy had relieved some of my emotional turmoil, and I felt carefree for the first time in a while. When we drove back home, Jason and I chatted in the car listening to pop music and bitching about everyone we did not like in Torquay. You have to believe me that there were many. Then Jason inadvertently brought me down from my pink cloud and back to reality.

"So, what's the situation with Lukas now Kristyna's back?"

"There is no situation, it's over. Everything is back to normal, as it should be. It was a moment of madness, one that I will always regret, but I've drawn a line under it now."

"How did he take it?"

"Well, I haven't told him—yet."

"You haven't told him yet. Oh, Jez, pur-lease!"

"I haven't had the opportunity to! Kristyna's watching him like a hawk. I'm sure she suspects something."

"Ah, the dutiful wife to be, poor cow. Does she know what she's getting herself into?"

"I decided it was none of my business. I think he's got it out of his system. They were making love last night like a couple of rabbits."

"Vile!"

"She seemed to be enjoying herself by the noises she was making. He must be doing something right, bless his heart."

"Well, just as I thought your life was becoming a bit more interesting, doll... Now it's back to garden centers and scatter cushions."

"I prefer my life uncomplicated. It's taken something like this to make me realize how much I love Graham."

"Whatever you say, Dollface, but I've got my doubts that this is the last of it."

"Why do you say that?"

"*Hello?* I've seen the way he looks at you. I notice these things. He's not going away, and I know you don't really want him to."

"You're wrong," I lied.

The camera crew arrived on Thursday. They were a scruffy bunch in worn jeans and T-shirts. The men were unshaven and well built. They set up their equipment whilst guests were eating breakfast. Within an hour, there were powerful lights, burly camera operators, people with large furry microphones on poles, and a couple of runners busying themselves around the hotel. Graham returned from London, having set off from Paddington first thing this morning. We were all set for our television moment.

The producer arrived after the equipment had been unpacked. He was an untidily dressed man in jeans and a tea-stained white polo shirt with the Diamond Aspect Production logo sewn onto the top left-hand side. His name was Bill Stanton-Jones. He was in his forties, lanky, and had a pointed face, long nose, and thinning brown hair tied into a ponytail, which gave him a weasel-like appearance. He spoke with a public schoolboy drawl. Despite his less than appealing appearance, he had a warm, enthusiastic disposition. He gave me a firm handshake, and I felt instantly at ease with him. He referred to Carol Thompson as 'CT' and warned me that her caustic television persona was not really a persona; it was genuinely what she was like.

"She can be very abrasive and doesn't suffer fools gladly," he said. "Oh, and don't mention anything about her affair with that member of the royal family or she'll slap you."

The doorbell rang, and I could barely contain my excitement. It was the national treasure, gay icon, and larger than life character, Carol Thompson. I opened the door, trembling in anticipation. She regally extended her bony hand and introduced herself. I stood there with my mouth open, gaping at one of my television heroes.

"Carol Thompson. Erm, welcome to The Pembroke Hotel. I'm a massive fan!"

She did not reply, but her facial expression spoke a thousand words. It was as though I had farted in front of the queen. She frowned in disapproval, and she looked queasy as though she might vomit on me at any moment.

Carol looked exactly as she did on television, although she was not as tall as I had imagined. She had the same severe shoulder-length straight hair, with grayish roots showing below dyed blond strands. She wore a violet jacket over a black blouse, which covered a generous waistline. Her makeup was very Zsa Zsa Gabor goes to Superdrug, bright pink lipstick on overly botoxed lips and several layers of foundation. However, this was all part of her fabulousness. On her left lapel, she wore a stunning brooch, and I had no doubt the sapphires and diamonds were real. I was in awe that this celebrity and national treasure was in our home. Lukas and Kristyna had wanted to be involved with the program, too, but I had deliberately given them duties that would take up their entire day.

Wayne and Tracey, the owners of Green Palms Lodge, arrived at the same time as Carol but had waited outside to have a cigarette. Classy. I was not impressed when they tossed their butts into the flowerpot by the front door.

On first impression, Wayne and Tracey seemed to be unsuited for the hospitality industry. Wayne looked as though he only washed on special occasions, with a craggy beetroot face, an unkempt mop of graying hair, and an enormous girth. He was scruffy, wearing an ill-fitting gray suit, which I doubt contained any natural materials. His appearance reminded me of the politician Boris Johnson, but he lacked any of the charm, intelligence, or personality. He had worked as a plumber until his fifties then had accepted early retirement on health grounds. He had received a lump sum by his employer, which he invested in the guesthouse. He stank of stale tobacco partially masked with the strong scent of Kouros aftershave. I shuddered at the thought of turning up for a holiday to be greeted by him at the door. I shook his hand, and he smiled, revealing a crooked set of yellow teeth.

At least Tracey was clean, and she was definitely more intelligent. She had squeezed her big-boned frame into a nautical style outfit with a navy blazer. She was a few years younger than Wayne, with red hair that she had tied back tightly into a bun. The couple had relocated from Birmingham and spoke with thick regional accents. Their dream was to run a small guesthouse by the seaside. This was something that they had in common with Graham and I. However, unlike them, we had a sense of style and a modicum of business acumen.

Filming was an interesting experience. There were many takes, especially as Bill was a perfectionist. A few minutes of on-screen footage would sometimes take an hour to get right. The process was exacerbated, because curious guests found it necessary to walk into the rooms in which we were filming. Sadly, Graham proved useless in front of the camera. He stumbled over his words and looked decidedly nervous.

The production team treated Carol like a Hollywood star. She had an army of helpers that would fetch her tea, or light her cigarettes, which she smoked out of a holder. They seemed to obey her every whim. She had an appalling habit of snapping her fingers to attract the attention of the film crew, and her attitude ranged from brusque to downright rude. However, as soon as the cameras were rolling, she abruptly changed, oozing charm and personality. It was extraordinary to watch.

The cameras filmed me conducting Wayne and Tracey on a tour of the hotel. I told them about the refurbishment work that we had undertaken. Carol asked Wayne and Tracey to give their opinion on The Pembroke Hotel compared to Green Palms, and they expressed their admiration, before Tracey broke down into tears, saying that she did not think that they could ever achieve this standard. During her outburst, the cameras were still filming, and I could sense the delight of the production crew, knowing that they had captured a golden television moment.

"Keep filming," mouthed Bill at the camera operators, turning his hand in a circular motion. He picked up a cue card with 'ENGAGE SYMPATHY MODE' written on it.

Like a puppet on strings, Carol put a soothing arm around Tracey. "Darling, this is why I'm here. This is the turning point for Green Palms. Will you allow my team to bring this kind of look to your hotel?"

"Yes," sobbed Tracey.

"The Hotel Red Alert team is going to turn this around for you. It's time for a real-life miracle."

"Cut!" shouted Bill

At this point, Carol withdrew her arm with the speed of a coiled python and reverted to her normal disagreeable personality.

"Tea and biscuits," she barked at one of the makeup girls. "And no custard creams, I hate custard creams. Something chocolaty."

In the afternoon, Graham and I sat with Tracey, Wayne, and Carol in our drawing room, being interviewed about what made us one of the best hotels in Torquay. As soon as the cameras rolled, I simply relaxed and spoke as if I had done it all my life. Graham was awkward and stuttered, whereas I chatted as if I were on the phone to a good friend. At one point, Carol's more cantankerous side emerged, and she started waving her arms and swearing at Wayne for being such a "fucking waste of space," which would ultimately be bleeped out, but we all knew it would make great entertainment.

The filming finished around five in the afternoon. A chauffeur-driven black Mercedes collected Carol. She rushed off without a good-bye or a thank you. We shook hands with Wayne and Tracey and wished them luck. They were going to need it. Whilst the film crew was packing up the equipment, Bill came over to chat to us.

"Jez, Graham, can I just say a big thank you on behalf of Diamond Aspect for being so hospitable? And what a lovely hotel you have here."

"Thank you," said Graham.

"And Jez," he said turning toward me. "You were brilliant on camera. Have you done this kind of work before?"

"No," I answered.

"It's just that you came across so natural, confident, and articulate. Your personality really blossomed on camera. You know, not everyone can do it. Most people freeze the moment that they see that red light in front of them."

I blushed a little. "Thanks, Bill."

"No, it's me that should be thanking you. I may have something of interest to you."

"Go on."

"Well, Carol Thompson is moving onto bigger things. She's got a live chat show starting on BBC1 next year. God help them. I'll get to the point. We're looking for a replacement. You've got the pedigree, the looks, and a great on-screen presence. Would you be interested in auditioning?"

"Would I be interested? You bet I am!"

"Right, I'll be in touch," he said, handing me a business card before he left.

I looked at Graham enthusiastically. "Graham, my God, can you believe it?"

"Don't get too excited," said Graham, bringing me down to earth. "It's an audition, not a job offer."

"Yes," I said. "But I just have this feeling about it. Mavis and Elizabeth do too."

"Who are Mavis and Elizabeth?" asked Graham.

"Sorry, my mind's wandering again."

One of the runners asked us both to sign a legal dispensation form, along with some other paperwork, which meant they could use all the footage that they had shot here and edit it in any way they liked, and then they left. Later in the evening, Jason called to find out how it had all gone, and I could not resist telling him about my conversation with Bill about my forthcoming audition.

"Fucking hell," he said. "You have a blessed life. You lucky sod. By the way, don't forget your friends on the way up."

"Ha ha," I replied. "I won't. They should air the show sometime in November, will let you know the dates, party around here! Bye!"

I locked up at midnight, and Graham and I snuggled up. I lay awake fantasizing about my new television career and all the trappings it would bring, before I fell into a contented sleep.

Chapter 22

March 1975: Marjorie Wilson

There was less than two weeks to go until Easter, when I received a telephone call from a tearful Tannis Breville.

"It's Martin," she sobbed.

"What's happened?" I asked.

"He's had a heart attack. I called an ambulance, but he was pronounced dead on arrival at the hospital."

"Oh my God. I'll be right there." I hung up the phone.

"Is everything all right?" asked Stanley.

"Not really," I said. "Martin has had a heart attack."

"Oh no, I thought he's been looking ill lately. How is he?"

"He's dead."

Stanley went white. "You're kidding."

"No, I'm not. Do you have the car keys? I'm going over now."

"They're hanging up in the usual place. Listen love, take as long as you need. Christopher and I will manage. Tannis needs her friends right now."

I drove to the Breville household in the Warberries neighborhood, a beautiful leafy area situated on one of

Torquay's many hills, where there were several imposing Victorian mansions overlooking the harbor. Tannis' daughter Charlotte answered the door, her eyes bloodshot from crying. Instinctively, I put my arm around her, and she broke down into tears.

"Let it out," I said softly.

"Why did it have to be my daddy?" she sobbed.

We went into the drawing room, where Tannis was sitting in a winged armchair in front of a dying fire. She was leafing through an old family photo album. She showed her typical English resolve and dignity, but her make-up was smudged and she was clearly in shock.

"Let me make you both a cup of tea," I said. "Have you eaten anything yet?"

"I'm not hungry," said Tannis. "But thank you."

"Well, you must eat something. I'll make you both a sandwich. Listen, you don't have to talk about this if you don't want to, but can you tell me what happened?"

"No, it's fine, Marjorie. It helps to talk about it. Martin and I were out walking the dog on Ilsham Common when he said he had chest pains. He said that he thought it might be serious, and then he collapsed. He just... crumpled and fell down."

"You poor thing."

"I ran to the nearest phone box and dialed 999. Thank goodness the one by the common wasn't vandalized, as most of them are. I went back to him and another dog walker tried to give him the kiss of life, but it was no good. By the time the ambulance arrived, he was gone."

She paused and buried her head into her hands. "It was horrible, Marjorie, it really was. He was just lying there on the damp grass in his Barbour jacket and Wellington boots, passing away in front of my eyes. Sophie, our Labrador, was licking his hand and whining. God, I can't even think about it."

"It's all right, Tannis," I said soothingly.

"I mean, he had a bloody heart condition. I told him to cut down on the brandy and cigars. He shouldn't have been working so hard either. Weekdays up in the Commons, surgeries here at weekends, a pile of letters from constituents to deal with daily. I should have seen it coming."

I spent the rest of the day with Tannis and Charlotte, fielding telephone calls, answering the door, and playing counselor. It was a horrible day that I would not forget. One of the callers was the former Prime Minister Ted Heath, offering his condolences to the family. Several journalists had gathered at the bottom of the driveway, including a political correspondent from the BBC. It was a cold day, so I brought them out mugs of tea and a packet of garibaldi biscuits that I had found at the back of a kitchen cupboard. I helped Tannis write a brief statement, which I took with me and read to the reporters.

"If I could have your attention, gentlemen," I said. "Tannis and Charlotte Breville have asked me to read a few words to you."

I cleared my throat. "Martin was a much-loved husband and father, who was tragically taken from us this morning. His devotion to his family was matched by his tireless representation of the interests of Torquay and its constituents. We would like to ask the press to respect our privacy at this time, whilst we come to terms with this terrible loss."

The various columnists scribbled furiously in shorthand as I spoke. I started to walk back to the house, when a ghastly pig-faced reporter wearing a cheap brown suit and a kipper tie shouted at me in a cockney accent.

"How is Mrs. Breville holding up?"

I bit my tongue and turned around to face the crowd of reporters. I felt the press was starting to intrude on my friend's grief. However, I was also aware that there was a camera running, so in spite of my disdain, I retained a polite manner.

"Mrs. Breville is obviously coming to terms with the death of her husband, but she is coping as well as to be expected," I said curtly.

The same journalist shouted again, "You're a close family friend. Who do you think is going to stand for the late right honorable gentleman's seat?"

"I don't think these sorts of questions are appropriate at this time, Mr...?"

"Archer, Terry Archer. Political correspondent for *The Sun* newspaper. Your husband is a rising star in the Tory party. Do you think he might be interested in running?"

"If you would all excuse me. I have nothing further to say on this matter. I would like to return to the house to support my grieving friend."

I walked back toward the house. The audacity of the columnist from *The Sun* had irked me somewhat, as I felt that he had been disrespectful. That was my first experience at dealing with the press, and I understood why they had acquired the name 'news hounds.' Despite their brashness, I had found it exhilarating. I contemplated whether this was a taste of things to come.

My announcement made the nine o'clock news, according to Stanley, but even though Martin had not even been buried, the political chatter had gone into overdrive. The talk was about a by-election in a marginal Tory seat. The commentators were speculating on likely candidates and scrutinizing opinion polls. By-elections did not typically receive this level of press interest. However, this would be the first official measure of public opinion since Mrs. Thatcher became the leader of the opposition. The press saw it as a litmus test of her authority and popularity. Would the public endorse or reject her?

I stayed at the Breville's house until late in the evening. As I was emotionally exhausted, I went straight to bed as soon as I got home. However, I suffered a broken night's rest. Stanley told me that I was talking in my sleep. Apparently, I kept saying "Yes, I understand. I know what must be done," repeatedly. This continued until he became so frustrated at being kept awake that he gave me a hard nudge. After that, I lay fully conscious, my mind racing throughout most of the night.

The Times published a short obituary:

Martin Breville, 57, represented the humanitarian face of the Conservative Party. He represented the constituency of Torquay, where the average income is low and employment is seasonal. He passionately defended the interests of his poorer constituents, whilst recognizing the importance of tourism to the area. His promotion of tourism was at odds with successive governments, whom he believed failed to recognize its national importance as a vital source of overseas income.

His character was a mixture of charm and shrewdness. He was a man with whom you could enjoy a pint at the local pub but would need to remain astute to comprehend the issues that would be fiercely debated. Outside of politics, he was a devoted family man who was passionate about his food and his dog, Sophie. He was an enthusiastic wine connoisseur and kept an enviable collection of vintages stored in his cellar. He did much to promote the embryonic Devon wine industry. He gained the respect of politicians from both sides of the house, and his light-

Ian James Krender

hearted humor will be missed in the bars of the House of Commons. He is survived by his wife of thirty-two years, Tannis, and their only daughter, Charlotte.

Chapter 23

September 2006: Jez Matthews

A secretary from Diamond Aspect Productions telephoned me a few weeks after they had filmed at The Pembroke Hotel. The purpose of the call was to extend an invitation to attend an audition at their studios in North London. I made the necessary travel arrangements. I was able to make use of the Anderson Levy apartment, and I traded places with Graham, who managed the hotel in my absence.

It was now autumn. The trees were shedding their leaves, and the petunias and other garden flowers were gradually dying. Zachary, the gardener, had replaced the summer hanging baskets with winter ones. Thankfully, the hotel was quieter. I could sense that Lukas and Kristyna were starting to struggle with the long hours, made worse because Morbid Maureen had resigned to attend an alcoholic rehabilitation retreat in Spain.

Less staff meant that there was more work spread between us. The nights were drawing in quickly, too, and the dark mornings added to our fatigue. We closed the pool, and the central heating was required in the evenings, to take the edge off the chilly nights. What motivated us to carry on was the knowledge that we would soon be able to close and enjoy a long winter break.

The production studios were in an insalubrious suburb of London, tucked away in a nondescript side street close to Bounds Green tube station. When I entered the reception area and completed a registration form, I felt a little disenchanted, as there were at least twenty people taking part in the screen tests. Perhaps it was naivety, but I was not expecting so much competition. I recognized some of the faces, including Geoffrey Miller from the 1980s children's program *Play House*. Apparently, he was hoping to make a television comeback. The years had not been kind to him. His wrinkled skin still had the orange glow to it that I remembered as an infant. He had paid the price for his obsession with sun beds. Determination and focus soon replaced my disillusionment. This was an opportunity of a lifetime, and I would seize it with both hands.

Eventually, my turn came. Bill sat on a canvas director's chair, flanked on either side by two severe looking women with clipboards. There was a camera operator, whom I remembered was part of the film crew on *Hotel Red Alert*. He gave me a thumbs up and a wink, which I appreciated. The audition commenced. I had to read from an autocue as if I was live on television. Afterward, they wanted me to ad-lib a role-play situation with one of the clipboard women, whose name I learned was Julia. She played the role of an incompetent but defensive hotelier. It was unnerving and new territory for me, but I gave it my best shot. The whole process only lasted fifteen minutes, and despite being out of my comfort zone, I enjoyed every second.

"Okay, that's enough I think," said Bill. "We'll call it a wrap."

I could not resist asking, "How was I?"

"We'll be in touch to let you know," said Bill.

"Thank you for the opportunity," I said, turning away.

I bit my tongue, as soon as I uttered those words. This was not an *X Factor* audition, and Bill was not Simon Cowell. Still, at least I had shown some humility.

I caught an underground train on the Piccadilly line to Kings Cross, changing onto the Circle line to The Barbican. I was a little crestfallen. Bill had sounded very non-committal at best, and my dream of fame seemed to be disintegrating. It had also struck me coming back to London that I missed the place more than I had anticipated. Torquay was a world away from the bustling crowds. I relished the sooty air and that omnipresent smell of burnt rubber and ozone on the underground, but I knew it was no longer my life.

When I disembarked the escalator and exited the tube station, the Barbican tower blocks dominated the skyline ahead like giant tombstones. Their brutalist concrete structures cast long shadows over the lawns in front. Back in the apartment, Graham called me on my mobile phone.

"How did it go, love?"

"I gave it my best shot," I said. "There was a lot of competition and people with experience, so hey ho, we'll wait and see."

"Whatever happens, I'm proud of you. I'm sure you were amazing. They would be fools not to pick you."

"You always manage to say the right thing, Graham. I love you."

"Just get back here safely tomorrow."

A short while after hanging up, I received a text. "Love you, see you tomorrow XX"

It was from Lukas. I felt as if a treasured moment that

should have been mine to share exclusively with Graham had been sullied, and my heart sank.

I arrived back the following evening. The train was delayed at Exeter for almost an hour, due to signaling problems, so it was dark when the train finally pulled into Torquay. I was tired and a little grumpy but looking forward to seeing Graham. However, it was Lukas in the car waiting for me.

"Lukas, hi. I was expecting Graham."

"Mr. Jez, Graham busy in hotel. He asks me to make collect you."

"Thanks," I said quickly, fastening my seatbelt.

"How did it go to, Mr. Jez?"

"So-so. I think I blew it, to be honest, but it was a great experience."

"I wish I could blow you."

"Lukas," I said lowering my voice, even though nobody else was within earshot. "This has to stop."

"But I want you, Mr. Jez," he said, gazing at me with his come-to-bed eyes.

"Watch out!" I shouted, as we nearly collided with another car traveling in the opposite direction. The driver sounded his horn angrily. "Just concentrate on the road, or you'll kill us both. We drive on the left-hand side in this country. I knew Graham shouldn't have insured you on this car!"

Lukas drove silently. When we approached the hotel, instead of slowing down he carried on driving, toward the beach.

"Lukas, no more games, please."

"All I ask is we talk. I drive to beach. It's nice evening. We walk and talk."

"All right," I sighed. "I owe you that."

We parked and got out of the car. Lukas was right. It was a lovely September evening, much warmer than of late, with a humid wind blowing off the English Channel. We walked along the beach, with the sound of waves gently lapping against the shore. There was a full moon, which cast a reflection on the calm sea.

"Mr. Jez, I be honest with you. I can no stop thinking about us."

"Lukas, there is no *us*."

"Please doesn't say that, Mr. Jez. I need you, and must you also want me."

I studied him. He looked so handsome in the moonlight, with his cropped hair and youthful square-jawed face. Whilst I was physically attracted to Lukas, I knew that I was not in love with him and never would be. This was lust, pure and simple. Belatedly, I tried to do the right thing.

"I have been foolish to let things get as far as they did. I have no desire to hurt you or Kristyna, please understand that."

"Enough," he said. "I do this for you."

He pushed me against the stone sea wall with his powerful arm.

"What are you doing?" I asked.

"There is no person around. I blow you. You like."

He knelt on the sand and undid my belt. He unzipped my fly and tugged at my trousers and underpants, pulling them down to my ankles. I could not prevent myself from becoming aroused, and neither did I want to. As I moaned with pleasure, he looked up at me as if he wanted my approval.

"God, that's good, Lukas," I groaned.

He grunted in response. A few minutes later, he stood up and gave me a long deep kiss.

"You like, didn't you?"

"Yes, Lukas, I liked very much. I don't know what I'm going to do about you."

"We go back to hotel now, Mr. Jez, Kristyna and Graham waiting for us."

"One thing," I said. "How are we going to explain all the sand on our feet, let alone your knees?"

We burst into laughter and gave each other a hug, before brushing the sand off us. We drove back to the hotel. I knew this was wrong, but already I was planning in my mind when our next secret encounter would be.

When we returned to the hotel, Graham had cooked us all a lovely Italian supper. He had made my favorite risotto from the *Jamie Oliver Does Italy* cookbook, and I told everybody about my audition. The guilt that I felt regarding my earlier sexual indiscretion rapidly dissolved into a large glass of Chardonnay. Later, in the bar, I found another audience that was excited to be staying with a star of the future, or at least that is what I chose to believe.

Chapter 24

March 1975: Marjorie Wilson

The funeral service took place at our local church, St. Matthias in Wellswood. The elite of Torquay society attended, along with some prominent political figures. This included a former Home Secretary, who served under Heath. It was a somber but dignified occasion. The hymns included one of my favorites, "Abide with Me". Martin's brother read a touching and occasionally humorous eulogy, and Stanley felt honored to read a New Testament verse from the gospel of St John.

The coffin was carried to Torquay crematorium in a hearse, with the wake back at the Breville's residence in the Warberries. Tannis was supported by her close friends and family. Whilst her grief was evident, she was a strong woman. Charlotte was younger and more emotional. She retained her composure during the remembrance service, but at the crematorium, she burst into tears as the coffin disappeared behind the curtains. She stayed for as long as was socially acceptable at the gathering back at the house. The strain on her was evident, when she fled upstairs to the seclusion of her bedroom.

Stanley was networking among our acquaintances from the political set. We had rapidly integrated ourselves into the community since moving to Torquay, and the local party perceived Stanley as a high achiever. Willie

Whitelaw was a senior conservative and an advisor to Mrs. Thatcher. He was a charming man with a wicked sense of humor. He was conferring in a conspiratorial manner with Stanley and Richard Grainger. Overwhelmed by my curiosity, I discreetly moved closer to overhear their conversation.

"Stanley, have you considered putting your name forward to the selection committee?"

"Not really, Willie. It is my long-term ambition to become a Member of Parliament, but I don't have a tremendous amount of experience yet. Besides, I don't have the Eton schooling and Oxbridge education."

"That's the whole point," said Willie. "You have hit on the exact reason why you should put your name forward. There are enough toffs like me in the party. We're after fresh blood, new ideas. We want to appeal to the hardworking types, the aspirational people that want to better themselves, entrepreneurs—the backbone of this country."

"You mean people like me?"

"Like you," he said. "Didn't your family own a newsagent's shop in North London?"

"Yes, my father owned it and passed it down to me."

"That's something that you have in common with our esteemed leader, Mrs. Thatcher. Her father was a grocer," said Robert. "They had a shop in Grantham."

"I know," said Stanley, "I read the newspapers."

"So we have a potential candidate who is a small but successful businessman with conviction," Willie continued. "A God-fearing man, who is a pillar of society. A working class man who has succeeded in life through hard work and determination. I think that's an appealing quality for potential voters."

"What are you saying?"

"Well, it's obvious. You are our man. Will you put

some thought into this?"

"Of course I will. It is a great honor to be asked, but I have to consider carefully whether I'm ready to take this step."

"Well don't take too long, old boy. Things are moving quickly. The election date is going to be announced soon, probably in a couple of months. You've got the support of central office, I will see to that. You have the respect in the local party, trust me. I know these things."

"I take that on board, and I will talk with my wife. There are decisions that will have implications to my family and business that she will need to be involved in. I'll let you know one way or the other."

"Best wrap this conversation up, Marjorie's on her way over," said Robert.

Willie looked at me intensely and spoke quietly and quickly. "You would make a formidable Member of Parliament, and you have a damned fine wife to back you up, talking of whom!"

I walked over and interrupted them.

"Maybe Martin's funeral isn't the time to be talking about politics," I said.

"Marjorie, you are absolutely right," said Stanley. "Willie, I'll call you tomorrow."

"I look forward to your decision."

Chapter 25

September 2006: Jez Matthews
Two weeks had passed, and I had all but written off the audition, so I was pleasantly surprised when Bill phoned on Tuesday morning, after breakfast.

"Jez?"

"Yes?"

"Bill, Diamond Aspect."

"How are you, Bill?"

"Very well, thank you. I'm sure that you would like to know the outcome of the auditions last week. I apologize for the delay in calling. It has been a difficult decision to make."

"Did you give it to Geoffrey off *Playhouse?*"

"That old has-been? No. Bless his heart, he's a nice chap. We felt sorry for him really. That's why we let his agent talk us into giving him a go."

"Isn't that a little cruel, giving him false hope?"

"This is showbiz. Anyway, I didn't call you to talk about him. I'll get straight to the point. We all thought you were the best person at the audition. Whilst you are the wild card, in that you don't have any presenting experience, you've got the looks, the charisma, and you're in the hotel industry. You were professional and came across brilliantly—"

"But you've found someone else?" I interrupted.

"If you'd let me finish. I was about to tell you that the job is yours. We want you, Jez."

"Say again?" I said in disbelief.

"We want you for the job. That's if you want it, of course."

"Bill, can you give me a second?" I asked. I covered the phone's mouthpiece then jumped up in the air in excitement and shouted, "Yes!"

"Are you still there?" said Bill.

"Yes, and yes, I would love the job. When do I start?"

"Well, here are some brief details. Because you are an unknown, we are going to do the new series slightly differently in that you will start by staying undercover when you visit the hotels, pretending to be a guest. Then you will announce yourself in the morning. There are a few other format tweaks, too, to keep it all fresh. We'll tell you more about that when you come and meet us next month. Filming for the show starts this side of Christmas, for airing in the spring. The first establishment we are filming is Number 19. It's a boutique hotel in Stratford-upon-Avon. We'll give you dates and details later. You'll need to do some promotional work, too, interviews, chat shows, and so on. After the filming of course, so we don't blow your cover. Please don't panic about it—we'll give you all the coaching and help that you need."

"Brilliant, just tell me where and when, and I'll be there."

"Which reminds me, the *Hotel Red Alert* episode set in Torquay is due to be aired on Tuesday, the 7th of November. I think you'll enjoy your spot."

"Great, I shall look forward to it."

"I must mention one last thing. CT isn't euphoric about you taking over to put it mildly. She thinks the show was hers and that it should have been shelved, when she left. I'll warn you to expect some bitchy comments in the press. She has a foul tongue when she's riled, and she's got her new column in the *Daily Mail*. She uses it as her mouthpiece to the world, to slag off anybody she doesn't like."

"She'll get over it, I'm sure."

"Our legal department will send you over all the paperwork, which you'll need to sign and return, then we'll discuss your first assignment. Do you have an agent?"

"No."

"You might want to consider getting one sooner rather than later. They'll be able to advise you and deal with all the nasty business of money. I'll email you some names. We'll speak soon."

As soon as I finished the call, I telephoned Graham, who was working in London as usual. Unfortunately, he could not be disturbed as he was in an important meeting. This was frustrating, as I was desperate to tell him. In fact, I wanted to tell everyone, but I wanted Graham to be the first to know, which meant I was like a pressure cooker waiting to explode. I emailed and text messaged him to call me urgently, in addition to the message that I left with his colleague. I had to wait a painfully long two hours before he came back to me.

When we spoke, he was delighted. He also had some good news of his own. Anderson Levy had given him a definite finishing date. This meant that we would share management of the hotel and that particular chapter of our lives would finally be over. The next person that I told was Jason, who insisted that we celebrate at The Horn of Plenty that night. The benefit of telling *him* was that the news would be spread far and wide within minutes of putting the phone down. I called my mother, who had never heard of *Hotel Red Alert*, Carol Thompson, or even Channel 4, but she was pleased nonetheless. She said that she hoped that I would have my hair cut. Lukas and Kristyna were excited, too. This was a dream coming true for me. The house also seemed to signal its approval by fizzing the kitchen lights on and off and smashing a dreadful Lilliput lane collectible cottage that Graham's parents had bought us for Christmas. The ghosts knew that I hated it. I found it on the lounge floor in pieces, with no plausible explanation as to why. I knew Graham would blame me, though.

Chapter 26

March 1975: Marjorie Wilson

The morning after the funeral, Christopher and I cooked and served breakfast for the guests, whilst Stanley went for a walk to clear his head. When Stanley returned, we retreated to the privacy of the study and closed the door. Stanley telephoned Willie Whitelaw at the Conservative Central Office in Westminster to give him his answer. We had discussed it extensively, until the early hours of the morning. It was potentially a life-changing decision that could have significant implications for our family life and the management of the hotel.

Stanley was modest and lacked a certain amount of confidence. I had faith in him, and I knew that he would grow into the role. He had cut his teeth on the campaigning with Martin during two general elections and had amassed considerable experience in local government, both in Torquay and London. Whilst Stanley remained skeptical and would never have believed me, I knew that he had the approval of the house spirits. Assuming that he won the selection and the subsequent by-election, it would be a truly remarkable achievement. It would secure a small place for us in history. I thought of the pride that Stanley's father would have felt had he been alive.

It was no easy task to circumnavigate the overzealous receptionist operating the switchboard. Willie's second line of defense was an uncooperative secretary, but eventually Stanley managed to get the call transferred to his office.

"Willie, Stanley Wilson."

"Dear boy, how marvelous to hear your voice. How are you?"

"I'm a little jaded from a lack of sleep but otherwise fine. Look, Willie, I know you're busy, so I'll get straight to the point. Marjorie and I have talked about this all night. The answer is yes. I would like to put my name in the hat."

"Delighted, dear boy, delighted. I'll speak to my people. We'll be in touch."

Stanley placed the handset back on the cradle. "Well, that's it. The ball is now rolling."

"I'm so proud of you."

"Well, I haven't got the job yet."

"You will," I said, my mind wandering. "Lady Elizabeth promised me."

"Who?"

"Oh, sorry," I said, coming back to reality. "I'm going to drive over to see Tannis. I think she deserves to know about your decision to stand. It would be a real coup to get her blessing."

"Isn't it a little soon?"

"Yes, but I'd rather she heard it from me than read it in the papers."

"Good point."

Tannis needed handling delicately, but I managed to get her on our side. By virtue of her late husband's position, she carried influence in the local party, and her endorsement of Stanley would help his chances of selection. We had a base of district support, plus central office backing, so I felt Stanley's odds of winning were strong. However, there was no room for complacency. Initially, there were four candidates, but one dropped out due to personal reasons, so it was a three-way fight. Our friends, the Grainger's, wielded power in the provincial hierarchy and were endorsing Stanley's candidature proactively. In the end, Stanley won comfortably, with the unanimous backing of the selection panel.

It was an understatement to say that our lives changed following Stanley's selection. Immediately after the results were announced, Stanley had an interview with the *Torquay Herald* and with the Radio 4 local news production, *Morning South West* on longwave. Stanley was a little green on these first interviews; thus, Central Office had arranged some coaching in preparation for the higher-profile media work that would ensue during the election campaign. The by-election date was set for Thursday, the 7th of May. Brian Redhead from Radio 4's Today program had requested an interview with each candidate from the major parties, in the days preceding the election. Stanley was also interviewed by Angela Rippon, on the nine o'clock news. The reality of the high profile nature of being a Member of Parliament was rapidly sinking in.

Voting history had shown that the Labour Party was a minority force in Torquay, and with an unpopular socialist government, they were unlikely to gain much ground. Unfortunately, opinion polls showed that the Liberals were narrowing the gap with the Conservatives, and it was going to be a close result. Stanley coined the phrase 'Every vote counts.' He campaigned vigorously, with my support and a great team behind him. He canvassed door to door, with reactions that varied from streams of expletives followed by a door in the face, to vigorous debates of policy issues and the occasional resounding endorsement. There was certainly never a dull moment. He enjoyed the heated discussions and listening to people's concerns, as he felt these were the wavering voters whom he could win over.

The national press was showing great interest in the by-election. To minimize the impact of Stanley's campaigning on the hotel business, I arranged for the GPO to install a second telephone line. A highly efficient volunteer from the Conservative Club started at nine o'clock each morning. She staffed the telephone, managed Stanley's appointments, and dealt with correspondence. Whilst she was unpaid, Christopher and I ensured that she ate with us, and she always had a glass of wine in her hand after six.

Election Day was only a week away. The atmosphere behind the scenes at The Marstan Hotel was tense. Christopher had taken on most of the front of house duties. During the campaign, we had recruited two extra temporary members of staff. The opinion polls were nail-bitingly close. Stanley was polling thirty-nine percent, but Rupert Taylor from the Liberals was only a percentage point behind at thirty-eight, so it was too close to call. Labour trailed on fourteen percent. The National Front and National Teenage Party were expected to lose their deposits. I had to keep myself in check of course and not tempt fate, but it was very exciting to think of Stanley sitting in the House of Commons. Lady Elizabeth had promised me in a dream that he would be successful, but I would not truly believe it until it happened.

The weeks of campaigning had flown by, and there were now only two days to go before the by-election. To prevent the hotel from becoming too busy, we deliberately kept the 'no-vacancy' sign displayed at the entrance. Breakfast was underway, except that Christopher had not appeared. I felt cross, as I suspected that he had stayed out late with his friends. When he eventually walked into the kitchen, he looked like he had been crying.

"Mum, Dad, I need a word," he said, sobbing.

The staff looked at him inquisitively, curious to know what was going on.

"In private," he added.

"Whatever is the matter?" I asked.

"I think you'd better come with me," said Christopher. "I'm sorry, Mum. I'm so ashamed of myself."

Christopher led us into his bedsit, situated in the extension, and opened the door.

"What in God's name!" said Stanley.

A scrawny, malnourished young man with shaven brown hair, in his late teens, was lying naked and lifeless in Christopher's bed, tangled up in the duvet. His eyes were open and his face contorted in terror, as if he had woken up from a terrible nightmare. Except that he had not woken up. He had a skull and crossbones tattooed onto his neck. The ashtray was full of roll-up cigarette butts, and a sickly sweet smell lingered in the air, like joss sticks.

"Christopher, my darling son. What is this?"

"Mum and Dad, I really am so sorry. You've no idea how much I wish I didn't have to show this to you."

"Stop saying sorry. Just tell me what has happened here," said Stanley.

"Please don't lose your temper, Dad. I was on one of my midnight walks around Daddyhole Plain, you know, to help my asthma. Well, I got chatting to Marcus here."

"That's his name, is it?" said Stanley, raising his voice. "Well, I'm glad you know."

"I was enjoying his company, so we came back here. It was late, so I invited him to stay," said Christopher tearfully. "When I woke up this morning, he was like this."

"You invited him to stay, did you? You invite a stranger into our home, and you bloody well ask him to stay over? I mean look at him. Have you checked that you've still got your wallet?"

"Stanley, please!" I said.

"What do you bloody well expect me to say? Should I get out the bunting and crack open a bottle of champagne? Hurray! There's another dead body in the hotel, the second this year. Only it's not a guest this time, though. Oh no, this is just some random man my son met whilst on a late-night walk in an area renowned for being a haunt for sexual deviants."

"Christopher is not a d—" I coughed. "He's not one of those. He's just cursed with a sensitive nature."

"Do you think I was born yesterday, Christopher? I know exactly what went on here, and it makes me sick to the stomach. If you're going to lie about it, at least have the decency to throw away the empty Durex packets."

"Dad, I didn't mean for any of this to happen. I'm so sorry."

"You're sorry! It's too bloody late for sorry. I'm so ashamed of you. I mean, I knew you weren't into sport. I knew you enjoyed musicals and the theatre, but your mother and I have always let you do as you pleased. I should have beaten it out of you when you were young."

"Stanley, please, this isn't helping."

"And it's not tobacco in those rollups either, Marje, that's cannabis! I know the smell. That's going to go down well when the police arrive. Oh, and I trust he's over twenty-one, Christopher, because he doesn't bloody look it. You know what that means, don't you? It means you've had sex with a minor. That means a prison sentence for you, boy."

"Calm down," I said.

"Look at him, Christopher. He weighs about nine stone. He's got needle punctures up his arms and tattoos all over his body. He looks like he's lived on the streets for years. Was he really worth it?"

"It was dark when I met him. I didn't notice."

"I just cannot believe what I'm hearing. Have you no self-respect?" said Stanley angrily.

I shuddered. I had visions of the pig-faced reporter from *The Sun*, writing a front-page exclusive, "Prospective Tory MP's son in underage gay sex and drug scandal." This would ruin us. Stanley's political career would be over before it had even started. That was not the worst of it either. Our hotel would be swept up in the bad publicity. The bookings would dry up. Who would want to stay at a hotel that had a homosexual living in it? A man who had sordid, drug-fuelled encounters with underage strangers in parks? Our reputations that we had fought so hard to nurture would be ruined. We would lose everything that we had worked so hard to build up. Christopher had a lot to answer for, and I shared Stanley's anger.

"Oh, did I mention there's a by-election in less than a week, or that I have radio and television interviews to do? Did you notice that there are journalists coming around every day? The bloody spotlight is on this house and our family!"

"Dad, I'm sorry," sobbed Christopher.

"Stop saying sorry. You repulsive creature! How many British soldiers died in the war, just so your sort can go around doing what you like? Get out of my sight."

"Dad—"

"I'm going to call the police. Then I'm going to call Willie at Central Office to tender my bloody resignation. My reputation might be ruined, but I'll be damned if I'll drag the party down with me. Let's hope they can salvage something out of this mess."

Stanley stormed off to the study, slamming doors behind him.

My mind went into overdrive. I was full of confused and conflicting thoughts. I could hear the different voices of the house whispering at me, all at the same time. I had not heard them in this section of the house before, but their presence was strong. In fact, it was deafening. I put my hands to my ears to shut them out, but it was to no avail. The chattering died down, and Lady Elizabeth's cut-glass voice spoke, giving me clear instructions on how to proceed. I regained my composure. My mind was clear and logical; it was now obvious how to retrieve the situation with minimal collateral damage.

"Christopher, leave your father to me. Pull yourself together, go and serve breakfast. Mention nothing to the staff. Oh, lock your bedroom door—I don't want anyone to go in there. Your father and I will sort this."

I hurriedly followed Stanley into the study. He had picked up the telephone and had started to dial the police. I took the receiver from him and put down the phone, ending the connection.

"Stanley, think about what you're about to do. Think very carefully."

"What do you mean? We *have* to call the police. There'll be an investigation. We'll pay for a lawyer for Christopher. God only knows. I still love the boy."

"If you make that call, there's no going back."

"What do you mean no going back? We *have* to call them."

"The police will come. They will close down the hotel.

The press will be all over us. Your career will be over, and all our friends will desert us. The business will be ruined—everything that you and I have worked for, will be destroyed."

"We have no choice."

"Oh, but we do, we do."

Chapter 27

October 2006: Jez Matthews

After a long busy season, the hotel was starting to quiet down. We only had three couples due in for breakfast, which would be easy to manage. The weather had turned autumnal, with a noticeable morning chill in the air. The leaves on the trees had turned golden brown and were starting to fall. The swimming pool had its winter cover on, and we had packed the sunbeds away in the summerhouse. Most of the hoteliers in Torquay would trade until the half-term week at the end of October, and then enjoy a well-earned rest until Christmas. In two weeks, Graham was due to complete his contract at Anderson Levy, so finally, he would move permanently to Torquay.

I unlocked the kitchen and lifted the dome on the Aga burner. Lukas was late for work, so I started to cook the sausages. I had heard raised voices coming from his bedroom, so I suspected that he was having an argument with Kristyna. Usually, it was just her time of the month, so I was sure that it would all be fine.

Kristyna stormed angrily into the kitchen, her eyes bloodshot from crying and looking uncharacteristically disheveled. Her hair was a tangled mess, instead of tied into its usual neat bun. I could discern from her body language that a confrontation was imminent. She marched over to me, and without warning, she raised her hand and slapped me across the face. The force behind the smack took me by surprise. I nearly lost my balance, and my cheek stung like it had been scalded with boiling water. She raised her hand again, but I gripped her wrists, holding her arms in place. She struggled violently.

"Let go of me!" she said, whilst kicking at me.

"What the fuck are you doing?"

"You bastard! You fucking bastard!"

It dawned on me that there could only be one explanation for her behavior. Somehow, she had found out about Lukas and me.

"For God's sake, Kristyna. Please calm down and tell me what's wrong."

She broke free from my constraint. She picked up the saucepan of sausages from the Aga and threw it at me. I ducked, and it hit the filter coffee machine, shattering the glass jug, then impacting against the wall behind, creating a large dent in the plaster.

"You *fucking* bastard!" she shouted. "My sister died. I was grieving, heartbroken. You were kind and understanding. All the time, I say to my mother, you are best boss in the world. I say I love my Englishman boss, he so kind."

She burst into tears. "And all the time you were sleeping with Lukas," she sobbed. "How could you be so cruel? You make me sick."

My stomach filled with butterflies, and I felt queasy. *How had she found out?* Lukas entered the kitchen, looking sheepish. Judging by the swelling around his left eye, he had also had a taste of Kristyna's wrath.

"I'm sorry, Kristyna," I said. "I really am. I'm deeply ashamed of myself."

She lunged toward me, her eyes filled with hatred, but Lukas restrained her from behind, pinning her arms against her back, as she struggled to break free.

"I'll fucking kill you!" she shouted. Her words were full of venom, her face loathing and twisted.

"Calm down," said Lukas. "Please listen at me, Kristyna, this no helping. You have to accept, me and Mr. Jez, we love each other."

She bared her teeth like an angry lion struggling in Lukas' grip. I was shaking. I had never seen anybody so full of malice.

"Kristyna," I cried, "I promise you I did not mean for any of this to happen. It wasn't planned. I never meant to hurt you."

"Never meant to fucking hurt me?" she said. "Did you think I wouldn't mind? That I'd say no problem, you go on sleeping with my Lukas. I'll carry on cleaning up after all your guests, iron all your shirts, and be your slave."

"It wasn't like that," I said.

She broke free from Lukas' arms, and, acting as though she were possessed, she grabbed a kitchen knife from the wooden block and swiped it menacingly before lunging at me. I quickly stepped out of the way, and she slipped on a greasy, partially cooked sausage on the floor. She fell forward, and her head made contact with the red hot metal plate on the Aga. I heard an awful hissing noise as her face singed. She screamed in agony and pulled herself away, leaving a layer of her skin stuck to the Aga, which smoldered. Her left cheek was charred black with red, raw skin underneath. The kitchen filled with the smell of burning flesh.

She fell back like a puppet with the strings cut. She hit a shelf full of glasses and plates, which collapsed, showering her with broken glass and crockery. She looked dazed, and then she tumbled forward, impaling herself on the knife clasped in her hand, and slowly slid down onto her knees. Looking disorientated, she stared at me with blank eyes. Her ruined face was hideously burnt all down the left-hand side, with her eyeball exposed ghoulishly through the charred socket. She looked down at her stomach in disbelief and tried to pull out the knife. It had penetrated deeply into her abdomen, and a pool of blood was collecting on the kitchen floor. Weakly, she coughed up more blood. Her hand, lacerated and bloodied from the broken glass, flopped limply over the knife, unable to muster the strength to extract it. She toppled over onto her side, and her eyes glazed over. I could see the life slipping gradually from her, and I acted instinctively.

"Lukas, help me," I said. "We need to keep the oxygen going to her brain."

Using what I could remember of my first aid training, I turned her onto her back and checked for a pulse. There was none. I removed the knife and tossed it away. I exhaled a deep breath into her lungs before I started to compress her chest. Lukas knelt beside me, weeping. I was covered in blood, but I did not care; all I wanted to do was save her.

"You need to dial 999 now! We're losing her."

"Mr. Jez, I no want to."

"For fuck's sake, your fiancé is going to die if we don't get help. Do you understand?"

I continued for what seemed like ten minutes, desperately trying to revive her limp body. All the while, I was praying for her to recover, though I knew that it was hopeless. Kristyna was dead. I stood up. The broken glass crunched under my feet. I picked up the phone and started to dial for an ambulance. Lukas took the handset from me before I could finish dialing and threw it on the floor. The plastic housing broke, causing the batteries to fall out.

"We must not be call ambulance, Mr. Jez."

"Lukas?"

"No!"

"What on earth?"

Lukas wiped away his tears. "She gone from us, Mr. Jez. She gone."

"Well, she might have survived if you'd called an ambulance straight away."

"Maybe, maybe not, but look around you, Mr. Jez."

I surveyed the smashed crockery, the broken coffee machine, the frying pan that had dented the wall, and the shattered glass. I looked at Kristyna's body, lifeless on the kitchen floor in a pool of blood, next to the knife that had killed her, covered in my fingerprints.

Lukas suddenly became very cool, bordering on callous. "You want ambulance men to see this?"

"It doesn't look good, does it?"

"You be arrested. I be arrested. You no longer have your TV show, hotel close. It's no good, Mr. Jez."

"But it's an accident, a terrible accident."

"Is that how police see it? Me no thinks, Mr. Jez. Me think they say you murder her in big fight."

I felt physically sick, like a huge burden had suddenly descended upon me, gnawing away at my very soul. "My God, what are we going to do?"

"We serve breakfast like normal. I hide body and clear mess, then I do you new basement floor. I bury her body under floor. We have concrete we bought do sinking patio. I do this for you, Mr. Jez, for us."

"This is like something from a horror film. I don't know if I can go through with it."

"I no want go prison. You know I right. You be strong for us. You get cleaned up. I clean up blood and mess before guests want breakfast."

I could not quite believe the word that came out of my mouth. "Okay."

Ian James Krender

I hurriedly showered, watching Kristyna's blood run down my arms and legs, diluted by the water. It accumulated in the shower tray, like puddles of cranberry juice, before fading in color and washing down the plughole. Unfortunately, the water did not rinse away the nauseous feeling in my stomach. I could feel my heart racing, and I felt faint. I put my bloodstained clothes into a plastic bag, took them downstairs, and placed them in the washing machine. When I returned into the kitchen, Lukas had managed to squeeze poor Kristyna's body into a couple of bin liners, overlapping back to back. He had fixed them together with gaffer tape that he had wound tightly around her, which meant that you could make out the shape of her body through the thin plastic. He had dragged the body into the pantry, where it would not obstruct us whilst we served breakfast. He had mopped up the blood and swept away the broken glass.

"It's good enough for breakfast service," he said. "I do it properly later."

I waited tables, trying to hide my nervousness. Although agitated, somehow I managed to function in a reasonably normal manner. I smiled and made small talk with the guests, but I desperately wanted to breakfast to end.

When I served the woman staying in the bedroom above the kitchen, my pulse started to race even more.

"What was all the commotion this morning?" she asked.

"A shelf collapsed," I said, thinking quickly. "I'm sorry if it disturbed you."

"I thought there had been an earthquake," she said.

"Nothing like that," I laughed nervously.

"And what about all that shouting?"

I felt weak. "Oh, just some staffing problems. You know these Eastern European types, very emotional."

"They are terribly, aren't they?" she agreed.

"What would you like for breakfast?" I stuttered.

My hand shook as I wrote down her order. I think that she suspected there was more to my tale than I was letting on, but she would have no reason to suppose that somebody had died in an argument. That did not stop me from nearly suffering a heart attack. I decided to shut the hotel for the rest of the week and canceled any preexisting bookings, on the pretext of being ill. I wanted to wake up in Graham's arms, having suffered from a terrible nightmare, feeling the relief of knowing that none of this was real. Unfortunately, it was not a nightmare. This was reality and there was no turning back the clock.

The guests departed, and the hotel was empty, apart from Lukas, Kristyna, and me. Lukas took control of the situation with soulless efficiency. We carried the poor girl's body down into the basement. I hired a small pneumatic drill, and I arranged a skip to be delivered at short notice. Lukas started digging up the basement floor, whilst I shoveled concrete and soil into a wheelbarrow. I took it up the basement stairs, using a long plank of wood as a runner. It would take all day to do the excavation work, and by the afternoon, the skip was full of rubble. We threw Kristyna's corpse into the hole, along with her mobile phone and other means of identification, such as credit cards and her driver's license. It was dark outside when we finally filled the hole with the ready-mixed concrete that I had bought weeks ago, to shore up the garden patio.

In the evening, I scrubbed down every surface in the kitchen with disinfectant, mopped the floor with bleach, and cleared away the remaining mess. If the public health department had inspected us afterward, we would have scored full marks. Cleaning was almost therapeutic, as though I was erasing the memory of the crime with each stroke of my cloth. However, I knew in my heart that this would haunt me for the rest of my life.

I was so engrossed in the grisly work that I missed Graham's telephone calls. I wondered how I would explain Kristyna's absence to him. Finally, at around midnight, I had a bath and went to bed. Lukas came upstairs, and I burst into tears. "What have we done?"

"What we had to," he said, as he climbed into bed, putting his arms around me. "Nobody understand but you and me. They were no there."

"I wish I had never listened to you. Why did I ever employ you, let alone be stupid enough to sleep with you? Then none of this would have happened, and Kristyna would still be alive."

"I love you. I see no harm come to us."

Lukas held my head gently with his palm and started to kiss me, putting his tongue into my mouth, but I backed away. This time I was not merely pretending that I did not want him before reluctantly giving in to my true feelings. Now I really meant it. I looked him up and down. I realized that I no longer found him attractive. I thought about the cold-hearted way that he had let Kristyna slip away without lifting a finger to help. I reflected on his callous indifference to her dead body that he seemed to view as an inconvenience, a cadaver to be disposed of, rather than the woman to whom he was engaged. He was an unfeeling monster, and it repulsed me to think that we had a sexual relationship. The thought of him touching me filled me with revulsion.

I spoke my thoughts aloud. "You really don't seem to care what happened today. You seem indifferent. Do you know something? I don't know what I ever saw in you."

"No say that, Mr. Jez. We meant for each other."

"I need a drink."

I got out of bed and went downstairs to the bar,

followed by Lukas. I poured half a bottle of brandy into a pint glass and downed it in one long gulp, retching on its foul taste. Lukas looked at me disapprovingly. I realized that I was frightened to be in the hotel with him on my own. If he turned violent, I would not stand a chance against him.

"That no help you," said Lukas.

"I don't fucking care," I said, pouring myself another one.

"You no mean what you say that you no like me anymore."

"Oh, fuck off and die, and leave me the fuck alone."

Lukas walked off with his head down. The alcoholic hit from the brandy came a few minutes later. Euphoria was followed shortly by the calming anesthetic effect as it wrapped me gently in cotton wool. That elusive feeling deepened, dissolving my worries and self-loathing. My vision began to blur, and I was vaguely aware of Lukas carrying me upstairs to bed before I drifted into unconsciousness.

I woke up the following morning having experienced disturbing nightmares all night. I was suffering from a severe hangover, which heightened my anxiety. I could feel my heart beating abnormally quickly. My hands were trembling like an old man's, and my joints ached. Lukas had slept with me, against my wishes, and he was snoring gently at my side. I went downstairs in my dressing gown and headed straight to the bar. I poured myself a small brandy to calm my jitters. The first drink led to another, and by midmorning, I was sloshed and almost incoherent. I rang Graham, attempting to disguise my pitiful state but fortunately, he was unavailable. The voices of the house were chattering loudly inside my head. I thought I heard Kristyna say "hell awaits you," but the predominant voice was an upper-class lady who was soothing and told me not to worry. She told me that she would take care of things and that I was fulfilling my destiny. I had no idea what she was talking about. Another voice interrupted her. It was an upper-class older gentleman who warned me not to trust her. I heard a meowing noise following by an angry hiss and the smell of cat pee. I went into the owner's lounge and switched on the television. I turned the volume to the maximum and collapsed onto the sofa, clutching my head, trying to drown out the cacophony of conversations and arguments in my mind.

Chapter 28

May 1975: Marjorie Wilson

Stanley stood by the phone with his shoulders hunched, looking at me with defeated eyes. The strain of the morning, combined with weeks of early starts and late nights during the election campaign, had taken their toll. He looked exhausted and ready to accept failure, but I knew what to do. As his wife, I would not let unfortunate circumstances obstruct his ascension into high office.

"You know how I've always fancied a terrace outside the guest lounge?" I said.

"I recall you mentioning it."

"It's time we built it."

"What?"

"You and Christopher will dig a hole big enough to bury the corpse. We'll bring it out at night when everyone is in bed. There's nobody staying in the rooms overlooking the garden at the moment. Then we'll concrete over it and put some nice crazy paving down. Nobody ever needs to know about what's happened here today."

"Marje, get a grip. We'll never get away with it. The boy will be reported missing, then we would be implicated in his death. I know the timing isn't great, but it's not as though Christopher has murdered him."

"You said yourself—he looks like he lives on the

streets. Who exactly will miss him?"

"How can you be so unfeeling? He may be a street urchin, but he's still someone's son."

"Then ask yourself this: Are you prepared to give all this up? Will you sacrifice our magnificent home and business, the opportunity of a career in government, your golf club membership? Make that call, and it's all gone. Christopher will be branded a pedophile and thrown in prison. The consequences for us as a family don't bear thinking about."

Stanley looked thoughtful. "There is truth in what you say."

"You know I'm right."

Understandably, Christopher had found it difficult to serve breakfast, and the staff had noticed that he was not behaving normally. After we had cleared the dishes, with the staff out of earshot, we told Christopher what we planned to do. He listened in horror and flatly refused to have anything to do with it, until I put the fear of God into him.

"Our lives will be ruined. You could go to prison, and everybody there would know why. He is underage, Christopher. I doubt he's even twenty years old. Jail would be a living hell for you. Is that what you want, to be the bitch of the east wing? Don't even answer that. Besides, your father and I have discussed it, and it's the only way."

Reluctantly, Christopher agreed, and in the afternoon, he started to dig out the foundations for the garden patio. Stanley helped him as much as possible, given his heart condition. Stanley phoned the local builder's yard to get some aggregate, ready-mixed concrete, and paving slabs delivered.

"They can do early next week," said Stanley.

"Well, that's no bloody good," I said. "He'll be smelling by then."

I rang them back and offered them an extra twenty pounds in cash for delivery today, and it was sorted.

Christopher worked until the sun went down, having moved a ton of soil. It was going to be the most over-engineered patio in history. We planned to smuggle the body out in the early hours of the morning, then cover it with the aggregate so it would not be visible. Christopher had arranged for the gardener to come over and lay the slabs down the following day.

We waited until one o'clock in the morning. The atmosphere was tense, to say the least. Christopher was especially nervous and had broken out in a cold sweat. The stress had also affected his asthma, and his breathing was wheezy. Stanley and Christopher wrapped the body in sheets and took it into the garden. Stanley had remarked that it hardly weighed a thing. The pit was about six feet by twelve feet, and waist deep. I provided illumination from a small flashlight. We whispered quietly as we worked, through fear of waking up a guest or alerting a passer-by. Once the body was in the pit, Christopher and Stanley started to shovel the gravel over it. Although they tried to be quiet, there was inevitably some noise.

I stood there impassively, listening to the chattering of the souls that occupied the house. Their presence was not as strong outside, but I knew that they would see us through this. Everything seemed to be going according to plan, until the garden gate swung open. It was Mavis, wearing her dressing gown, curlers and slippers, drenched in cheap perfume.

"Darlings, I saw you from my bedroom window. I thought, what are you all doing out here at this time of the night. There must be something wrong, I thought. Are you all okay, not burying any bodies?" she said, unaware of the irony of her remark.

Stanley spoke first. "Hello, Mavis. No, we were, erm, badger watching."

Mavis shone her flashlight at the pit. The hand of the corpse was poking out from the gravel in a motionless wave. She looked at me with wide petrified eyes.

"Oh my God, what is going on here?" she said, slowly walking backward.

"It's not what you think," said Christopher.

"Not what I think?" she said. "That's a dead body in there. For pity's sake, what have you done? What is this?"

"Shush," said Stanley. "You'll wake the guests."

I grabbed Christopher's shovel. I mustered all my strength, swinging it around, and whacked her on the head. She looked confused for a second. Her eyes rolled upward, and she fell face-down onto the ground. She was still alive, although barely. She was unconscious, her breathing sounded strained, whilst blood poured out of her head and soaked into the grass. I hit her again, as hard as I could, and I heard her skull crack. Finally, she was dead.

"Marje, what have you done?" said Stanley, shocked.

"What I had to do," I said.

"You've killed her," whispered Christopher.

"I had no choice," I said, dispassionately. "If I hadn't, the whole of Devon would have known about this by morning."

"Oh joy," said Stanley. "Special offer at The Marstan Hotel. Two corpses for the price of one."

"Well, try to look on the positive side," I said. "It could have been worse. At least the hole's big enough to take her as well."

"This is madness," said Christopher. "We'll never get away with this. Someone will report her missing, and the police will come looking."

"Be quiet, Christopher," I said. "All this is down to you anyway. Help your father get her body into the hole. Oh, and by the way, I've chipped a nail—I only had them done on Tuesday."

Stanley and Christopher picked up her body from either end and threw it into the pit. Stanley jumped down and tried stamping on her, to push her further into the ground, grimacing as her bones cracked under his weight. They worked for several hours, filling the hole with gravel. The sun was rising. I hosed down the bloody trail from Mavis' body. Our macabre task was completed. It was a night that none of us would forget as long as we lived, but the important goal of retaining our family's honor and reputation had been achieved.

Jack the gardener, oblivious to what lay buried underneath, finished laying the patio with Christopher over the next couple of days. The unseen benefit to this horrible affair was that we ended up with some lovely paving outside the guest lounge, and I bought a beautiful set of table and chairs with a parasol from the local ironmongers.

Chapter 29

October 2006: Jez Matthews

I woke up on the sofa with a sore head, still feeling drunk. It was late afternoon, and Lukas brought me a strong coffee.

"You must stop this much too drinking," he said. "It's no healthy."

I gratefully accepted the coffee. "I don't know any other way to clear my head of these thoughts."

"We had do what we did. You know that. It was accident."

"You should have called an ambulance," I said. "It was madness not to. What about Kristyna's mother and her family? They're going to be asking after her. How are you going to explain that?"

"I think of something."

"Well, you'd better think fast. I also have another thought for you to digest. What am I going to tell Graham when I speak to him?"

"You tell him she left and move away from Torquay. You say she finished with me. You say I heartbroken."

"You have this all worked out, don't you...? How did she find out about us? We were discreet!"

"I tell her."

"For God's sake, Lukas! What on earth possessed you?"

"She find text on phone I sent. So I just told truth."

"That was really careless."

"Maybe I want her to find it deep down. You no understand, I could no go on living lie like this. Nearly every night she want me. She paw at me in bed. I pretend I have headache. I no want her. I want you."

"And what do you think is going to happen when Graham moves back permanently from London next week?"

"We can put him down gently."

"I don't want to put him down gently. I don't want to put him down at all. I love him."

"No, Mr. Jez, you love me. You confused."

Lukas started to nuzzle my neck and ran his hand along my thigh.

"Stop it!" I demanded.

"I know you want me. It will all to be okay."

He pushed me back into the sofa and cupped my face in his hands, pressing his lips against mine.

"I said no!"

He carried on, ignoring my protests. I slapped him across the face, and he immediately backed away.

"Why you do this?"

"Because I'm not a sex toy for you to abuse whenever you're feeling a bit randy. I told you no. I'm tired, and I feel about as sexy as Sadaam Hussein at a nudist retreat. I don't love you. In fact, I don't think I even fancy you anymore."

"Don't say that."

"Lukas," I said sympathetically. "You are very young. When you get older, you will learn to understand the difference between love and lust. I'm the first man you have slept with. You think you love me, but there are millions of single, attractive gay men who would fall for your Eastern European looks and charm. Men your own age, for a start."

"I no want anyone else. I only want you."

"But I'm not single. I'm spoken for. Look, I know I'm partly to blame for this. I was drunk, I should have said no, but you must understand this can't work. As a result of all this sordidness, someone is dead."

"If we be together, then it worth it."

"Look, please try to understand. I don't think realistically that you can stay living here. It might be best if you get another job and a new place to live. I'll give you two weeks' paid notice and references."

He looked at me with those huge brown eyes, the pain in them was clearly evident. Then he stood up silently and walked out of the lounge.

The telephone rang, and it was Graham.

"Graham, thank goodness. It's so good to hear your voice."

"Steady on, soldier," he said. "Where were you yesterday? I rang and tried to Skype you. You didn't respond to any of my texts either. I was worried sick!"

"I'm sorry," I said. "It was a stressful day."

"I'm just tying up loose ends here. I've packed most of my stuff in the flat. It's only a couple of weeks now."

"I can't wait, really I can't."

"So what's up there then? Why are you so needy today?"

I braced myself for the lie. "Kristyna, she's finished with Lukas. She's packed her bags and moved out."

"Oh, that is a real shame," he said. "They were a lovely couple, but you know, they were both very young. How is Lukas?"

"He's bearing up," I said.

"Is the hotel busy? Why don't you and Jason take him out for a drink?"

"I'm not sure what he'd make of The Horn of Plenty."

Graham laughed. "It might be good to broaden his

experience. Then again, perhaps not. He'd probably get gangbanged in there with his good looks."

"I've also given Lukas his notice."

"Bloody hell, Jez. Why did you do that? We'll have no staff!"

"His work has been below standard for quite a while now," I lied. "I thought with Kristyna gone, we could have a clean sweep."

"Whatever you say. You'll be off filming soon, so I'll take over the management side for a while."

We chatted for about a quarter of an hour before Graham had to go into a meeting. I found Lukas skulking in the kitchen. He looked angry, and I prepared myself for yet another argument with this petulant young man.

"You used me, Mr. Jez. You used me for sex."

"Lukas, we used each other. You were the one that made advances on me. Every time we had sex, you were the one that instigated it. You have always known that I'm with Graham. I never said I was going to leave him."

"I no leave house. I no resign. When Graham comes back from London, I tell him everything. I fuck your life up like you fuck mine up."

"Look, just think about this for a moment," I said, panicking. "If not for me, then for Graham. What has he ever done to you? I might deserve this, but he doesn't."

"Then be with me. Even if we do behind back of Graham."

"No," I said firmly. "I should never have let this situation get so out of hand. I should have known better, but I'm sorry. This ends right here and now. Whatever I may have felt for you just isn't there anymore."

"So you did have feelings?"

"Well, yes," I said exasperatedly. "I did, but not the same as I feel for Graham. This is why I feel it's best all round that you move out as soon as possible. If you like,

I can give you some money to put a deposit on a flat."

"I no wants your money!" he shouted. He stormed off, slamming the kitchen door.

It was a feeble excuse to hide behind Graham's feelings, and I did not expect it to work. I hoped that throwing some money at the problem might be a solution. If I gave him a deposit to put down on a flat and a few thousand pounds in cash, he might just leave me alone. However, I knew that it was a risky strategy. Lukas was no fool, and he was fully aware that I would very soon be in the public eye, when *Hotel Red Alert* screened next year. I wondered what the *News of the World* would pay for kiss-and-tell stories. My career would be finished before it even began.

I had a microwave meal and an early night with a bottle of vodka taken from the bar. I lay in bed trying to block out the voices and dissolve the stress into my glass of neat spirit.

As I began to slip into an alcoholic coma, four smudged black-and-white figures slowly appeared in front of me like upright shadows. One was a woman in a flowing, floral seventies dress. Another was a scrawny street kid with a tattoo that I could just make out on his neck. There was a woman in a dressing gown and slippers, with her hair in curlers, and, lastly, a Victorian lady in a black dress with a pretty but severe face. They stood there, watching over me. I tried to shout, but I was immobile and my voice silent. I shut my eyes, and I heard them say in a chorus of whispering voices in my head. "Do not fret. The house will take care of you. We will take care of you."

Chapter 30

May 1975: Marjorie Wilson
After a long campaign, the polls opened on the 7th of May. The by-election had created a lot of interest, and the turnout was above expectations. It had been a long drawn-out night, but the votes were finally counted and the results would soon be announced, ending weeks of fevered speculation.

Stanley was wearing a smart black suit, with a blue rosette representing the Conservative Party pinned on his left lapel. He looked apprehensive, and he was glancing nervously at his watch. He was standing on a podium, flanked by his chief rivals, Rupert Taylor from the Liberals and John Connaught, the Labour candidate. Screaming Lord Sutch from the National Teenage Party was seeking attention as usual. He was grinning inanely, and he looked ridiculous, wearing a large multicolored hat. He smelt like a brewery, and whilst it could be argued that he was politically ignorant, Stanley thought he added a welcome dash of fun to an otherwise staid event. I was pleased that the National Front candidate did not show.

Both BBC and ITV had a camera crew and their respective political correspondents in attendance. All the major national newspapers sent reporters. The journalists covering the event included the odious Terry Archer, from *The Sun*. This newspaper was supposed to be on our side, but Stanley and I regarded them as unsavory allies at best. The wait was finally over when Christian Mackay, the returning officer, walked onto the podium to announce the results of the vote count. He moved toward the microphone, deluged with camera flashes, as photographers began taking pictures.

"Ladies and gentleman. It's been a long night," he said, pausing for effect. "But the counting has now finished, and I can announce the results of the Torquay by-election on Thursday, the 7th of May, 1975."

The crowd clapped.

"Screaming Lord Sutch, National Teenage Party, 203 votes. Rupert Taylor, The Liberal Party, 21,468 votes."

I heard Lawrence Chadderton, the BBC commentator, say, "That's a strong showing from the Liberals. This is going to be a closely fought contest."

"The National Front, 587 votes."

"No surprises there," said Chadderton, talking into his microphone on behalf of Radio 4. "The Teenage Party lost its deposit, though the National Front clung onto theirs by the skin of their teeth."

"John Connaught, Labour 12,716 votes."

"As expected, Labour fared poorly in this seat," said Lawrence. "But behind the headline figure, their vote has fallen substantially. This will be bad news for the Prime Minister."

I held my breath and crossed my fingers behind my back. "Come on, Stanley," I said under my breath. "This is it."

"And finally, Stanley Wilson, Conservative Party..."

Christian adjusted his glasses and squinted at the paper. "21,732 votes."

Most of the people present in the room erupted into a round of applause, which drowned out a minority of boos. There were several camera flashes, as the press jostled for position to get a shot of Stanley.

Raising his voice above the hubbub of the excited crowd Christian said, "I declare Stanley Wilson as the elected representative of the constituency of Torquay."

I was unable to approach Stanley to share his elation, due to the well-wishers and journalists who surrounded him.

Lawrence Chadderton thrust a microphone in front of Stanley's face. "Mr. Wilson, do you have anything to say?"

Stanley looked uncomfortably at the microphone and froze on the spot.

"Come on," I said under my breath, mentally urging him to say something inspirational.

After a short pause, he spoke slowly and deliberately.

"It is an honor to be chosen to serve the people of Torquay. I thank all those who have voted for me. I will endeavor to do my best to represent the interests of my constituents across all parties at local and national level."

I took a deep breath. Stanley had taken a conciliatory tone rather than a triumphal approach, trying to reach out to all voters across the political spectrum. This was entirely appropriate, given his slim majority.

He continued in his bipartisan tone.

"Torquay has many problems associated with coastal towns. I pledge to work with the opposition parties and the government to promote tourism in the area. I will be taking a proactive approach to removing the homeless from the streets and reduce poverty and its associated impact on crime. Where there are opportunities, I will work with our partners in the private sector to promote inward investment and prosperity."

After the press had taken their photographs and conducted their interviews, I waded through the crowd toward my husband. Instinctively, I put my arm around him and kissed his cheek.

"I'm so proud of you, Stanley," I said. "You even sounded like a politician! This is just the beginning. We all have big plans for you."

"I love you, Marjorie Wilson."

A local party activist handed us a flute of champagne each. We turned to the cameras with our glasses raised, and that photograph was the one that appeared in the newspapers covering the story.

Chapter 31

October 2006: Jez Matthews
I woke up with another hangover. They seemed to be becoming a daily occurrence. The hotel was to reopen today, and we had guests arriving this afternoon. Despite our best efforts, the excavation work in the basement had spread dust throughout the hotel, so it needed a deep clean. To add to the workload, it had been a windy night and the swimming pool looked unsightly, being full of leaves. Thus, I asked Lukas, who was sulking, to clean it, whilst I concentrated on the inside. It was good to get away from him, as I was in no mood for his company. Zachary, the gardener, was coming in later to mow the lawns and do some general weeding.

I still could not quite absorb the horrendous chain of circumstances that had unfolded that hateful morning. When I woke up that day, I did not expect it to begin with a member of staff bleeding to death from stab wounds on my kitchen floor after attacking me. Even though Lukas had made a pertinent observation in pointing out how suspicious the scene looked after the fight, I still regretted not calling the police. The consequences of that fateful decision to acquiesce to Lukas' wishes would no doubt haunt me until the day I died.

I felt that I no longer knew Lukas. In fact, I wondered

if I ever had known him. I had suspected he was manipulative for a while, but he also had an even darker side, which I was only just beginning to uncover. My only real bargaining card was that we shared culpability. The inescapable impasse was that our shared knowledge of this dark secret bound us together. To contribute to my precarious situation, I had the threat of Lukas telling Graham about our affair. It was a tangled web. I tried to put it out of my mind whilst I set about my dusting and vacuuming. I played some upbeat music in an attempt to distract me and lift my spirits.

The doorbell rang at midday, and it was Zachary. He looked shocked, his face was drained of color, and he was soaking wet.

"Jez, you need to come into the garden," he said. "It's Lukas."

"What's wrong with him?"

"Just come!" said Zachary. "Please."

I followed him into the guest garden, and before I even walked through the gate, a sense of inevitability fell over me. Nonetheless, I was still shocked by the scene awaiting me. Lukas was floating face down in the pool, his head partially submerged. His T-shirt wallowed around him in the water. The vacuum hose trailed over the decking, and the pole had sunk to the bottom of the pool.

"Oh my God!" I gasped.

"He was dead when I arrived," said Zachary. "He's been gone a while. I jumped in and tried to give him the kiss of life, but there's nothing I could do. I'm so sorry, Jez."

I leaned over the edge of the pool and grabbed Lukas' saturated T-shirt and pulled his limp body toward me. I turned him so he faced upward. His mouth was wide open, but his eyes were shut. He looked as if he was asleep, but he was as cold as stone. His handsome face had a blue tinge to it. I tried to pull him out of the water, but he was too heavy.

"Help me, Zach!"

Together we hauled him out of the pool and laid his soaking wet body down on the decking. My tears were genuine as I absorbed the sight of this beautiful, handsome young man, snuffed out of existence. The extent of my anguish confused me. Perhaps I felt something for him after all, yet moments earlier I had felt nothing but loathing.

"Can you call the emergency services?" I said.

"Yes, of course I will."

He went back into the hotel to use the phone. I found myself instinctively give Lukas a kiss on the forehead.

"Rest in peace," I said, quietly stroking his head.

The ambulance arrived, and the paramedics pronounced Lukas dead at the scene. They said that he had probably been in the water for a couple of hours before Zachary had found him. The police arrived shortly afterward. Scenes of crime officers took statements from Zachary and myself and took numerous pictures of the swimming pool. Lastly, Torquay Health and Safety Executive made a report to ascertain whether we had been following the recommendations in the pool risk assessment and if we had not, were there were grounds for prosecution. Another worry on top of everything else.

I called Graham in tears, who immediately left work and headed down to Torquay. Zachary was a star. We postponed our reopening once more, and he kindly telephoned the arriving guests, telling them a white lie that we had a flood and that regrettably we had to cancel their bookings.

Graham arrived late in the afternoon and hugged me as soon as he walked in through the door. I was a mess. I decided that I would see the doctor on Monday and ask him to prescribe something to help me sleep. Graham undertook the unenviable task of informing Lukas' parents, and telephoned them in the Czech Republic that night. It was a horrible call to have to make, made more difficult because they spoke virtually no English. Eventually, one of their neighbors called us back, who had a rudimentary grasp of the English language. He translated what Graham was saying. Then the unbridled grief and floods of tears followed, the emotions pouring out of the telephone into our lounge on loudspeaker. Graham promised Lukas' family that he would arrange to have the body transported back to Pribyslav, once the police had finished with their inquiry.

The police coroners provided an educated speculation to the cause of death from the bruising on Lukas' head. They believed that he had tripped over the vacuum hose on the wet decking and had fallen into the pool. Whilst this in itself would not have been fatal, he had suffered the misfortune of hitting his head on the edge of the pool. This had rendered him unconscious, and he had subsequently drowned.

The coroner recorded a verdict of accidental death. The Health and Safety department was satisfied with this explanation and decided that there were no grounds for prosecution.

The next day, Graham had to travel back to London to tie up some loose ends at Anderson Levy. It would be another week until he moved into the hotel permanently. It was the end of an era for him. The tiresome weekly commutes to London would finish, but also there would be no financial security from his well-paid job in commodities. We were now almost entirely dependent on the hotel for our income. The only other source was from my forthcoming television work. I was turning away valuable bookings whilst we remained closed, but the unfortunate reality was that I could not face the public in my current mental state.

Lukas' death had taken away the only other person with knowledge of Kristyna's body, but also the only witness to the events surrounding her accidental stabbing. His passing had meant that, assuming Jason kept his mouth shut, our affair would now never be discovered. This should have provided some mental relief for me, but it did not. The affair paled into insignificance in the light of Kristyna.

When I visited the doctor, he was shocked at my blood pressure reading and advised me to relax, eat well, and exercise. Unfortunately, I ignored his recommendations. He prescribed me some Temazepam. I took double the prescribed dose, often with a shot of alcohol. This seemed to take a pleasing edge off reality, and it would keep me functioning for the time being.

Chapter 32

May 1975: Marjorie Wilson

The elation of Stanley's success in the election was tinged by the dark secret of the two bodies buried under the patio. The three of us had to bear this guilt between us, which was not easy, as none of us were cold-blooded murderers. We presumed that the young man, Marcus, had died of natural causes, although according to Christopher, he was a drug addict, so his death may have been connected to his habit. We could not be sure. Mavis left me with no choice. Her constant snooping had caused her downfall. Had we let her go, she would not only have called the police but given interviews to the press and spread gossip far and wide for decades. She was collateral damage. She had to die, and it was as simple as that. Whilst I did not wish it to happen, I would not hesitate to do the same again, if the circumstances justified it.

I heard Sir Wilfred and Lady Elizabeth constantly quarreling in my head, the voices discordant, inhuman, and contradictory. The spirits had become more daring and less elusive. Christopher and I now saw them regularly. They floated around at night in the corridors, disappearing behind closed bedroom doors. Albert Henderson's soul had joined the existing spirits. He appeared as a younger version of the man whom I had met when he was alive. He wore an impeccably pressed butler's uniform. He would usually materialize after midnight, when the guests slept, holding a tray of drinks where the lounge fireplace used to be. He had an ethereal glow about him, and his presence emanated an aura of calm. He was not a prankster, like some of the other souls, but I still blamed him for smashing my prized Toby jug. I tried speaking to him, but all the spirits were silent whenever I saw them. I only heard their voices without a visual presence. I do not confess to understand much about the afterlife, but my library book speculated that it might involve too great an effort on their behalf to do both, or maybe I had to build on my relationship with them further. The emboldened spirits were bridging the gap between the living and the dead. I felt their presence growing stronger daily, and I became aware of greater numbers of them. We had a handsome Mediterranean-looking man, who occasionally popped by in one of the bedrooms in the East Wing. I took an educated guess that his name was James. His image seemed to match the voice in my head. It was of a confident aristocratic male in his twenties. He was a teaser, and I often heard Lady Elizabeth chide him affectionately. He often spoke to me in my dreams and reassured me that Lady Elizabeth had my best interests at heart.

I was unsure as to what would become of Mavis and the young man Marcus. Would they stay at the house in which they died, or would they move on? They had little connection with the place. Mavis would certainly not be best pleased with me. However, I could imagine that she would be enjoying herself in the next life, spying one everyone. If she did settle here, I expected a few more broken ornaments.

The spirits were wise enough to ensure that none of the guests ever saw them directly, though we often had reports of strange happenings, mainly odd noises. Occasionally, the afterlife residents would take exception to a guest, who would usually check out after the first night. Stanley remained completely hostile toward the idea and refused to speak about it. Christopher and I would share our experiences, but we did not tell anybody else, save we be committed into a mental institution. The ghosts had become used to us and we to them. They trusted us, and they even helped and guided us.

The recent deaths had negatively impacted Stanley's emotional well-being. He was not sleeping well, and he was suffering from high blood pressure. Fortunately, his new role was keeping him busy, and he was due to travel up to London later today to sit in the Commons during a debate about trade union relations. It would do him good to get away from the hotel. He had taken over Martin Breville's office in the Commons, including a small team of highly efficient staff to help him with his parliamentary duties. Tannis was kind enough to offer Stanley the use of her London residence, near to the Embankment underground station, convenient for Westminster. Tannis was very supportive of Stanley and myself. I had always tried to be sensitive, as whilst it was an exciting time for Stanley and I, this opportunity would never have arisen if not for her husband's premature death. She told me that Martin had respected and admired Stanley and would have approved of his selection.

Stanley reciprocated her kindness by fulfilling her desire to maintain an insider's link to Parliament. She enjoyed hearing about the Machiavellian political maneuvering that was part of behind-the-scenes life in the Commons. Although Stanley would not disclose information in the way that a husband and wife would share pillow talk, he had promised to keep her informed on the issues close to Martin's heart.

Stanley packed the Volvo with his luggage and clean shirts for the working week ahead. He was about to enjoy a cup of tea with me before leaving when the doorbell rang. Stanley followed me out of the kitchen into the hallway, and I opened the front door to find that it was a uniformed police officer. Stanley's face drained of all color, and my heart pounded.

"Yes, constable. How can I help?"

"Good afternoon, Mrs. Wilson," said the officer. "I'm sorry to bother you, but we've had a report of a missing person."

"Oh, really?" I said, feigning surprise. I was anxious to find out if they knew anything.

"Yes," said the officer. "It's your neighbor, Mavis Patterson. She hasn't been seen for over a week now."

"Oh dear, she's an acquaintance of mine. I wondered why I hadn't heard from her recently."

I noticed Stanley was frozen on the spot, looking terrified, as though he were about to break down and confess. I had to get rid of him.

"Stanley, why don't you finish making that pot of tea? Can I offer you a cup, Officer?"

"That would be nice," said the police officer.

"Come into the garden," I said. "It's a lovely day. We'll take tea on the new patio."

We sat down at a table, and he placed his helmet underneath his chair. He retrieved his pocket notebook. Stanley brought out a tray of tea and a plate of custard creams.

"Stanley, why don't you head off to London, darling? You've a busy day ahead of you. I'm quite capable of dealing with this."

"Yes, love," he said.

I gave him a peck on the cheek and whispered. "Don't worry."

"My husband is a Member of Parliament," I said, out loud.

"Yes, Mrs. Wilson, I know. I voted for him. I love the crazy paving, is it new?"

"Yes, we only had it laid last week."

"It looks lovely, very fashionable. My wife and I are thinking of having it in our semi."

"So, how can I help you?"

"Mavis was due at a bridge evening on Saturday. She didn't turn up. Neither was she at church on Sunday, where she is a regular member of the congregation. She has not been answering her phone either. One of the other neighbors had a spare key, and she wasn't anywhere in the building, including the holiday apartments."

"Oh dear," I said.

"The thing is, you see, her bed had been slept in and was unmade. There was a full mug of hot chocolate in the kitchen, and her cats were starving. It's all very strange."

"She certainly never said anything to me about going on holiday, Officer."

"Did you know her well?"

"No, not especially. My husband and I rented one of her apartments whilst we had this place refurbished. We knew her to speak to. Occasionally, she'd pop over for a cup of tea."

"Did she have any problems, anything that might make her want to get away without telling anybody?"

"Not that I'm aware of, Officer."

"We have to check these things. It's more than likely she'll turn up sometime. They usually do."

"I'm sure she will be fine."

"The answer's probably right under our feet," he said.

"If you hear from her or anything that might lead us to find her, can you give me a call at the station?"

"I will do, Officer."

He gave me a business card with his name and the police station's telephone number printed on it, and then dunked a custard cream into his tepid cup of tea.

"On another note, Mrs. Wilson, I don't want to alarm you with this, but please make sure you lock your windows and doors at night."

"Why is that?" I said.

He reached into his tunic pocket and took out a crumpled black-and-white photograph. "This man has jumped bail from Manchester, and we believe he is hiding in this area." He showed me the photo. "Ugly little blighter, isn't he? His name's Marcus Cox. He's nineteen years old with a criminal record as long as your arm. He's got a drug problem, injects heroin. He's wanted for supplying firearms up there. He's quite a dangerous man and must not be approached. He has a tattoo of a skull and crossbones on his neck. If you see him, call 999. The *Torquay Herald* is publishing a warning tomorrow. We're asking hoteliers to be especially vigilant."

"Goodness me. He looks so young," I said. "Do you think you'll catch him?"

"Don't know, ma'am. These people have a knack of going underground, but we're doing everything we can." He stood up. "Thanks for the tea, Mrs. Wilson. You will excuse me, duty calls."

He walked out of the garden gate and headed off to speak to the other neighbors. I breathed a sigh of relief and cursed Mavis. If she had kept her bloody nose out of things that did not concern her, we would never have had that copper coming around. She caused trouble, even when she was dead. At least, I now knew why Marcus had died. The house was protecting Christopher. Goodness knows what could or would have happened to him with that thug in his bedroom.

Chapter 33

November 2006: Jez Matthews

Graham answered the telephone, which rang while we were in the middle of serving breakfast.

"Jez, I know we're busy, but you might want to take this call. It's your producer, Bill."

He handed me the telephone handset and gave me a wink.

"Bill. Hello, good to hear from you," I said.

"It's good to speak to you, too. We need you to start filming next week."

"Did you say next week?"

"Is that a problem?"

"No, I've been waiting for your call, I've kept my diary clear!"

"Good. I'll email you all the details. Oh, don't miss the show tonight. It's Wayne and Tracey from Green Palms."

"Brilliant! I shall look forward to it."

I put the phone back on its charger, and, after many weeks of feeling depressed, it was as though I had been given a shot in the arm. I felt alive again, as if I had been given a new purpose.

"I start filming next week!" I said excitedly.

"Fantastic. I'm so proud of you. It'll be the distraction you need after the horrendous few weeks we've had here."

"And Bill said it's the Green Palms show tonight, too."

"Should we have some friends around for a few drinks and make a night of it?"

"No. I just want us to be on our own."

"Go on, I'll get some nibbles in and some champagne. We'll invite Jason over and some of your mates from the pub. It'll do you good, after all this stress."

"No," I said firmly. "I just want you to myself tonight."

After *Coronation Street* had finished, we switched over to Channel 4 and waited in anticipation. The adverts seemed to last an eternity, but eventually, after the sponsor's message, the familiar *Hotel Red Alert* theme tune started. We sat with our eyes transfixed to the screen. The calm voice of the narrator began, with differing shots of Carol Thompson uncovering various horrors from previous hotel visits, such as pubic hairs in shower trays.

"Carol Thompson, renowned hotelier and restaurateur of twenty years, is on a personal crusade to improve standards in the British hospitality industry. From avocado bathrooms, unconventional owners and no-frills sausages, nothing escapes her beady eyes."

The scene switched to some footage of Wayne and Tracey. The camera panned around them from a low angle as they stood outside their hotel with their arms folded, looking fed up.

"Tonight we visit Wayne and Tracey, the owners of Green Palms in Torquay. A hotel where time seems to have stood still since the 1980s. The desperate owners risk losing everything, unless things change very soon."

Once the titles and theme music finished, the cameras showed Carol Thompson walking up an untidy driveway, with weed-filled plant pots. She turned to the camera and spoke, with her swear words bleeped out.

"I mean for f**** sake. They knew I was coming, yet they can't do a bit of bloody weeding." She went to the front door and rang the doorbell, and Tracey answered, wearing a purple shell-suit. "Good afternoon."

"Good afternoon. Carol Thompson from Channel 4," said Carol.

"Would you like to come in and have a look around, my love?"

"That would be a good starting point."

The next scenes showed Carol being taken on a tour of their run-down hotel, screwing up her face at the décor, and telling the owners how awful it all was. She played up to the camera in the typically prickly style that her viewers adored. She was the villain whom we loved to hate.

"Darling," she said. "The only people likely to stay here are those that have had a frontal lobotomy."

The show followed its usual format. Carol was confrontational, dishing out bile to the distraught owners. When her sarcasm had finally reduced them to tears, she switched tactics and became the caring but stern matriarchal figure. She presented them with a tailor-made recovery plan that she pretended she had written herself and a free makeover for one of their bedrooms. The redecoration would provide a template for the owners to follow, when they had the funds. After a commercial break, Carol said. "Now I want to take you to a nearby hotel that is trading very successfully, to show you how it should be done!"

The camera cut to an exterior shot of The Pembroke Hotel. The sign was in focus, but I noticed that they had blurred our telephone number and email address. I was watching the program with a critical eye and saw that our hedges were untidy. Graham and I appeared on the screen, showing the mesmerized Wayne and Tracey around our beautiful hotel and boasting to them about how all our guests loved it. I felt very self-conscious, watching myself on television. Graham thought he looked fat and sounded weird, and I wished I had picked a different colored jacket, as the one I wore clashed with the scatter cushions in the lounge. The entire day's filming at the hotel produced about five minutes worth of video footage. It was a great episode though, and a good advert for Torquay.

Wayne and Tracey were very entertaining to watch, owing to their eccentricity. They had a wonderful dynamic to their marriage that the production team's ingenious editing enhanced. Wayne was the henpecked husband who was more interested in betting on horses and going to the pub. Tracey was the long-suffering but nagging wife.

In the final part, Carol hired a refuse skip for them and insisted that they declutter the hotel and give it a deep clean whilst the makeover took place. They filmed Carol leading Wayne and Tracey into the newly decorated bedroom for the first time, with their eyes closed. The room had been reinvented for the twenty-first century, with a lovely new bathroom. However, if you looked too closely, the finish was mediocre. The poor couple cried with happiness when they opened their eyes. Carol smiled warmly and told them to decorate all the bedrooms in that style and maintain the new levels of cleanliness, and they would have a thriving business. Channel 4 failed to publicize that two months after filming finished, Wayne and Tracey went bankrupt.

When the credits rolled, we received numerous congratulatory texts and e-mails from our friends and family. Watching the show had given me fresh impetus, and I was looking forward to taking the reins from Carol the following week.

Chapter 34

May 1975: Marjorie Wilson
Stanley telephoned me as soon as he arrived in London. The line was poor, but I could still detect his nervousness. His voice quivered, and he stumbled over his words.

"I've been worried sick the whole drive up," he said. "I nearly stopped off at a telephone box on the A30 to call you."

"It's all going to be fine," I said soothingly. "It was just a routine visit. Mavis has been reported missing. They're only doing house to house inquiries."

"You've no idea what this is doing to me. I don't think I can keep this up."

"We're in too deep now. If you crack—you, me, and Christopher, we all go down. I'm guilty of murder, and you are both accessories. Is that what you want for us, for your son?"

"Of course I don't."

"Well pull yourself together then. We'll get through this as a family. We've survived much worse than this in the past."

"Much worse? Like the dry rot we found in the roof? Or when your Victoria sponge didn't win first place at the Barnet young wives bake off? This is hardly the same thing."

"The judge at the bake off was biased. She had it in for me, ever since Christopher beat her son to play Joseph at the parish nativity play."

"Marjorie..."

I changed the subject.

"Have you parked the car somewhere safe?"

"Yes, it's in an NCP car park, two streets away. The thieving bastards want three quid a day for it."

"Never mind, you'll be able to claim it all on expenses. Now, what's it like up there?"

I managed to distract Stanley, which seemed to calm him down to an extent. He started to tell me about London. The Breville's apartment was compact and spartan in one of the old mansion houses along the River Thames, but it was comfortable enough for his purposes. It had the advantage of being situated within walking distance of parliament. The cleaner had kindly left a pint of fresh milk in the refrigerator and some staples, such as bread and eggs. Stanley would be attending a large number of meetings tomorrow, and the Conservative head office had assigned him a mentor to guide him through the workings of parliament. This was an acquaintance of ours, Geoffrey Bathurst, the MP of the neighboring constituency of Newton Abbott. Stanley's first sitting in the house was to be a debate over a minor piece of legislation, so it was a gentle introduction to parliamentary processes.

In the morning, he rang me from his office in the Palace of Westminster. His team was close-knit and loyal to Martin Breville, so Stanley felt that he had to win their respect. They were crammed into a tiny office at the end of a long corridor, with barely enough space to swing a cat. However, they were moving to the newly refurbished Norman Shaw building next month. This would offer more space and better facilities and had the convenience of being a few hundred yards from parliament. His private secretary was called Rebecca Waters. I met her briefly at Martin's birthday at the Conservative Club in Torquay and later, at his funeral. She was pretty, blond, and coolly efficient. She was not particularly likeable, but she was a safe pair of hands and I was sure that she would work well with Stanley.

He telephoned me again in the evening. He told me that sitting in the chamber of the Commons was an extraordinary experience, despite the debate being prolonged and rather dull. He ate a light lunch in one of the canteens and enjoyed dinner in one of the bars. Apparently, it was very segregated along both partisan lines and in terms of political seniority. Ministers and shadow ministers had their respective bars and restaurants, opulently decorated and overlooking the River Thames, whereas the backbenchers were kept to the more ordinary areas. Geoffrey apparently described it as Claridges for them, the Wimpy for us. Stanley said that the political discussions in the bars were vigorous and often belligerent, being fueled by alcohol. That was just within the party itself, so he understood why the opposition politicians chose to separate themselves from the government backbenchers. As he was a newcomer to the house and did not arrive in the post general-election intake, he found his first day a slightly lonely experience. He compared it to being like a child joining a new school, halfway through the term, when everybody had already made friends. I reassured him that this would soon change.

I rapidly became used to life as an MP's wife. He commuted to London on Sundays and returned to Torquay every Friday. He held weekly surgeries on

Saturdays, at various Church Halls and venues around Torquay. He had taken on board what Martin Breville had told him—never forget your roots and who put you into power.

Life in the hotel continued as normal. We deliberately traded with fewer rooms, as we were one man down, although extra staff helped alleviate the increased workload for us. Stanley's salary and expense account more than covered the reduction in profit.

The *Torquay Herald* had launched a campaign to help find our neighbor Mavis, which the national newspapers subsequently picked up on.

Unbeknown to us, she had massive debts and was in mortgage arrears. What started as a missing person search turned into more of a manhunt. There were unverified reports of her in Spain and Cyprus. Whilst we all knew the truth, this alleviated some of the pressure on us. Christopher seemed to cope reasonably well, but it was Stanley who I could tell was at breaking point. In his capacity as a neighbor, friend, and Member of Parliament, he was asked to issue a statement on behalf of the appeal. It seemed that every time we began to move on with our lives, the past would rear up its ugly head to haunt us. Nonetheless, I instinctively knew that the house would protect us all.

Chapter 35

November 2006: Graham Austen

I had the customary exit interview with Theresa at Anderson Levy and handed back my security pass, the keys to the flat at the Barbican, and the company laptop. She thanked me for my dedication and commitment and gave me an uncharacteristic peck on the cheek. I noticed her eyes were a little watery. We had worked with each other for over ten years, and this little chink in her corporate armor made me realize that she was not as hardnosed as I thought.

When I entered the elevator at our offices on Bishopsgate Avenue, I knew that it would be for the last time. I felt a mixture of excitement, relief, and fear, as I descended from the twelfth floor.

A great weight had been lifted from my shoulders, in terms of the physical and mental demands of working in the city, in the uncompromising business environment that I had been a part of for so long. I would no longer have the burdensome commute every Monday morning. Gone would be the shallow materialism and office politics that came as part of the compulsory package of working in the City of London. I was looking forward to living with Jez again, on a full-time basis. I knew that we had been drifting apart recently, and rebuilding our relationship was my number-one priority. The stress of Lukas' death on Jez was clearly evident. He seemed to have aged ten years in the last few months. I was pleased that I would now be there to support him. On the debit side of the equation, I had left an extremely well-paid job and all the security that it provided. Jez and I would have to accept a substantive fall in our living standards. That meant reining in frivolous spending on clothes, restaurants, and furniture. More frugal lifestyle choices were required, and whilst I was relaxed about that, I knew Jez had become accustomed to the finer things in life.

As I sat on the train, watching the view of the dirty gray London estates replaced by green fields, I felt a sense of excitement. I had finally escaped the London rat race for good. Jez had done a competent job of managing the hotel, although our experience with Kristyna and Lukas had taught us some valuable lessons. We would not employ couples, especially youngsters, and we would not offer accommodation as part of the package. We had not heard anything from Kristyna. I had thought that we would receive a reference request at some point. Her work had been exemplary, and she knew that we were pleased with her. I wondered where she was now. Perhaps she had gone back to live in her little village in the Czech Republic, to be with her mother. She must surely know about Lukas dying. Even though their split was acrimonious, I could not imagine that it would be easy to know somebody that you had loved and slept with for the last two years was dead. I felt sure that we would hear from her at some point.

Jez's upcoming television career provided a source of great delight for both of us. Although I was surprised how poorly remunerated presenting work was, it would hopefully open other avenues such as press columns and interviews. He was looking forward to filming in a few weeks' time. We knew that life would never quite be the

233

same, given the popularity of the program. He would soon be a household name. I was pleased for him, as he had always been in my shadow from a career perspective and this would put us on an equal footing.

We planned to reopen the hotel for Christmas week, and then spend January somewhere warm. This would be our last indulgence using my final salary check. It would be fun planning the break, and we could manage the business remotely via email and telephone.

I arrived in Torquay with two heavy suitcases full of belongings that I had managed to accumulate up in London. It had finally sunk in that I had left that life behind for good. Jez cooked my favorite meal, rib-eye steak and chips. We sat in the kitchen and enjoyed dinner and a bottle of wine together. Later, we made love, and for the first time since we had owned the hotel, I honestly felt like it was home.

Chapter 36

November 2006: Jez Matthews
I drove to Stratford-Upon-Avon, the medieval town famous for being the birthplace of Shakespeare. I battled some horrendous traffic on the M5, arriving at midday. I met Bill and the television crew at the Premier Inn, close to Number 19, the hotel featuring in the program. I spent the afternoon receiving briefings and rehearsing. They taught me how to operate the hidden camera concealed in a specially adapted rucksack. I would have a second camera concealed on my jacket lapel, but this would only have a short battery life and produce grainy, poor-quality video. I would stay at Number 19 the following afternoon.

My clandestine visit to this hotel would include an inspection of the bedroom, covering key points such as cleanliness. Whilst I was still incognito, Bill had asked me to be irascible, in an attempt to antagonize the owner. It was cruel, but it would make good entertainment if it provoked a bad reaction caught on camera. I would only reveal my true identity to the unsuspecting hotelier the following day, after breakfast.

The film crew would arrive shortly afterward and shoot the primary footage. I would discuss with the hotel proprietor the critical areas that were causing the business to fail. Then I would act as a consultant to initiate a mutually agreed recovery plan. My brief was to do this in a way that would be entertaining, so the producer advocated that I made use of my acerbic wit.

Number 19 struggled with pitiful occupancy rates and was in financial difficulty, despite being in a thriving tourist town. The reviews that the hotel had received on various websites carried a common theme. It was clean, but the single male owner was peculiar and the Shakespearean themed rooms were over the top.

I had reserved the Macbeth suite, which turned out to be aptly named. My spy-cam was running as I parked on the road in front of the hotel. It was on a residential street of imposing three-story Edwardian terraced houses, near the town center. I rang the doorbell and waited.

The owner opened the door and said, "All of God's greetings upon thee."

"Hello, I'm Jez Matthews," I said. "I have a room booked for tonight."

"Come-hither, young lad. Entereth into my humble abode."

The owner was called Mark Davies. He was a retired thespian, a bachelor, and a Shakespeare fanatic who insisted on talking in a strange pseudo-Elizabethan dialect. I thought he was a complete fruitcake, but it was immediately evident that he would make brilliant television. He was a gangly looking man, towering in height at about six foot eight. He had long untidy white hair, a huge nose that would benefit from the use of a nasal hair trimmer, half-moon glasses, and crooked teeth. He wore dark-green corduroys and a brown checked shirt. When he moved closer to me, I detected that he suffered from halitosis.

A fair description would be to compare him to an eccentric geography teacher, who did not get out much. I tried to ignore the two cameras running, so that I would come across naturally.

"Dost thou thirst for refreshment?" he said.

"Well, I wouldn't mind a cup of tea if you don't mind," I said, twisting my shoulder at an uncomfortable angle to get a shot of Mark with the lapel camera.

"Tush, sire. Tis the time of day for beverages more medicinal in nature, yet thee hath a tea requested so a tea shalt it be."

"Is there any chance you could speak English? I might have a small chance of understanding you," I said, playing to the hidden camera.

"But thou art in the house of Number 19."

He walked off to make the tea, and I looked directly into the camera in my lapel.

"He's a nutter," I said softly. "I mean no bloody wonder he gets bad reviews, and why does he keep saying Tush?"

I discreetly panned the luggage camera around the room. It was like sitting in a library. There were shelves packed with leather-bound books, and the room was full of lovely antiques. There was a large wooden globe of the Earth next to the green chesterfield sofa that I sat on. Closer examination revealed it to be a cocktail cabinet. The rugs were well worn but quality Axminster's sitting on exposed polished oak floorboards. A grandfather clock ticked away sedately in one corner, and the room smelt pleasantly of beeswax tinged with wood smoke from the cold embers in the fireplace.

"So far so good in terms of the decor," I said. "It's a shame the ambiance is spoiled by the weirdo in cords."

Mark returned to the lounge carrying a silver tray of tea and homemade shortbread, served in a floral Royal Albert teapot with a matching cup and saucer.

"Delicious," I said with my mouth full. "So how long have you owned this place?"

"My family inhabiteth this house for three and two score years. I have owned it for the last two."

"And what made you decide to start taking in house guests?" I asked.

"A magnificent residence such as this requires numerous persons to enjoy its many charms," he said dramatically.

After finishing my tea, Mark showed me upstairs to my room, and I immediately unpacked the camera. I set it up on the tripod and played amateur cameraman/ television presenter.

"This is the Macbeth suite," I said quietly. "And as you can see, it has a theme based upon the play."

I zoomed in on a large plastic cauldron in the middle of the room.

"I mean, okay, I get it, the cauldron that the three witches used, but what is it doing in the middle of a bedroom?"

I took a quick shot of the bathroom, which had a bright pink suite with beige tiles and brown towels.

"Well, they say Macbeth is a tragedy, and looking at that bathroom I would agree. I've not seen diarrhea-colored towels before."

The metaphors and catty put-downs flowed out of my mouth naturally, as though I was reading from a script, except it was all genuinely adlibbed. I recorded an hour of pithy comments and the odd innuendo, hoping they would come across as witty rather than just plain nasty like Carol Thompson's. I knew that only a few minutes of the footage would be used, but this did not dampen my enthusiasm.

The bedroom was generally acceptable, with just a few minor housekeeping issues. The brown towels would have to go. I lifted up the bed and ran my fingers along the skirting, which revealed a minimal amount of dust.

When I tested the bed, I noticed that there were murals of Macbeth characters painted amateurishly on the ceiling.

"Try sleeping with that peering at you," I said, focusing the camera on the ghost of Banquo staring down from the ceiling.

"I think that's supposed to be Banquo's ghost, one of the characters in the play that was murdered," I said for the benefit of viewers that may not be familiar with the story of Macbeth.

The tacky ornaments and dubious artwork aside, there were some clever little touches to the room, such as the leather-bound book of *The Scottish Play* on the bedside table. I liked the crystal decanter of sherry with a stylized picture of Shakespeare's face frosted into the glass. The Shakespeare theme for a hotel in the town that traded so much on his name made commercial sense. It just needed executing with a little more subtlety.

I finished off by saying. "Well, it's goodnight from me until tomorrow morning when I will be sampling breakfast. Will Mark wow me with his Cumberland ring, or will his tempestuous temperament bring double double toil and trouble to the dining room experience? Goodnight until tomorrow."

In the morning, I switched the camera on once again and reported that the bed was comfortable and that I had slept well. I was the only resident, so I dined alone at breakfast. Mark served it in his lovely old kitchen at the rear of the house. Mark continued to speak in his strange Elizabethan dialect.

"I trust thou hast a pleasant night of slumber?"

"I slept well, if that's what you mean," I replied sarcastically.

"Helpeth thyself to the selection of sundry items therewith," he said. "Whilst I prepareth for thee thine choice of cooked items."

I looked at the menu, and ordered some poached eggs. It was difficult to talk to the camera in Mark's presence, so I just put my thumbs up within view of the rucksack camcorder to indicate breakfast was good.

I handed Mark the keys and checked out. Mark presented me with the check.

"Do you accept florins?" I asked.

"Of great wit you possess, Master Matthews," he said. "MasterCard, Visa, or American Express."

"May I give you this business card?"

I handed him my 'Hotel Red Alert - Undercover Detective' card.

"Oh my God," he said talking in normal English. "Well, I never. How did I do? They told me there would be someone undercover coming to stay, but I would never have guessed."

We shook hands.

"It's very good to meet you properly," I said warmly. "Sorry for all the subterfuge!"

"No problem, I hope you're nicer than Carol Thompson. What's she doing now?"

"She's defected to the BBC. She's got some sort of magazine chat show," I said. "I'm the new boy, and you are my first project!"

"I prostrate myself at thy feet."

"Listen, Mark, any chance we can dispense with the bizarre language. I'm not a tourist, and frankly it's just plain weird."

"Erm, yes, okay."

"The camera crew are on their way, so why don't we have a cup of tea and get to know each other a bit before they start filming?"

"Sure," he said.

Chapter 37

May 1975: Stanley Wilson

My London existence provided me with a glimpse of the bachelor lifestyle. This was something of which I had no experience. Before I married Marje, I lived with my parents. After the wedding, we moved into the spare bedroom at her parent's house, before eventually buying our own home.

Whilst I would take my laundry home at weekends, during the week I had to fend for myself. The canteens at Westminster Palace were useful, but I was acutely aware that my suits were becoming uncomfortably tight. I started to cook for myself in order to avoid buying an entirely new set of clothes. At first, I lived off Marks and Spencer ready meals that I just had to put in the oven for thirty minutes. However, over time, I became more adventurous. I soon learned that I could create a decent bolognese or even a curry, and I found it an excellent way to unwind after the rigors of the day.

Tannis and I entered into a formal agreement over the apartment. I rented it from her, and the taxpayer picked up the tab. It was a convenient arrangement, and she would still be able to use it on the odd occasions that she would be visiting London.

I was glad to be away from Torquay. The occurrences of the last few months regularly played on my mind and

I never felt at peace. Nightmares perpetually disrupted my sleep. Marjorie seemed to have accepted the situation and moved on, but I would never forget the sight of Mavis' face. The sound of her skull cracking haunted my thoughts. When I closed my eyes, I relived the picture of the bodies covered in gravel. The scene replayed through my mind repeatedly in slow motion. I had paid a heavy price to gain success at the election. During the working week, I had enough distractions to keep my mind off the morbid recollections of that night, and sometimes I even managed to enjoy my life here in the city.

There was no doubt that London was an adventure for me. Living in the center of the capital was a completely different experience to our drab life in the leafy suburb of Barnet, which had more of a small-town atmosphere. The apartment fronted the main road on the embankment of the Thames, and the traffic flowed twenty-four hours a day. You would often hear police sirens in the middle of the night. At first, this contributed to my already poor sleep, but I soon became used to it and also the gentle clatter of trains crossing the bridge into Waterloo station. When the wind was in the right direction, I could hear Big Ben chiming. It was also in total contrast to Torquay, where it was the sound of seagulls and surf that woke me in the morning. I had the privilege of living close enough to the Palace of Westminster to be able to walk into work. It was a daily battle with the crowds of pedestrians, but I preferred it to the claustrophobic London Underground.

Sitting in the Common's chamber was a surreal experience. I had seen photographs and I had listened to the debates on the wireless, so physically being there sat on the green leather benches was as disconcerting as it was exciting. It felt like being on a film set. The boisterous backbenchers from all parties shouted and jeered at each other, and it was not dissimilar to being at a football match. The omnipresent speaker would occasionally rein in the unruliness, with his shouts of "Order!" but the rambunctious lawmakers would soon rise back to a crescendo of finger wagging and insulting gestures or raucous chants of "Here, here!" I was grateful that there were no television cameras in the chamber, given the behavior of some of the politicians. Whilst I had never seen any physical altercations, they were not unheard of in the bars.

I spent my first few weeks finding my feet, building alliances and trying not to make enemies. Parliament was like a nest of scorpions. You could trust nobody. Everything was very cloak and dagger; there were backroom deals and compromises. The twice-weekly Prime Minister's question time saw the chamber at its most vocal. I always attended this debate and admired Mrs. Thatcher, who performed her role as the leader of the opposition with panache. I swiftly concluded that I was wrong in my original assessment of her. She was determined, shrewd, highly intelligent, and she had conviction. I was sure that she would lead us to victory at the next general election. I rarely had any interaction with her in my role as a backbencher, but I was determined to get myself noticed.

Willie Whitelaw had encouraged me to stand as an MP, citing that the party needed more grounded people who lived in the real world. He felt the party needed to be more inclusive, and that meant attracting people who had worked their way up the system, instead of the mollycoddled public schoolboys who dominated our side of the house. Nevertheless, I still felt an outsider. Sitting on the benches were lawyers, millionaire businessmen, and scholars. It was essentially the cream of society. Most of them were Oxbridge educated, so as the son of a newsagent with little formal schooling, I will freely admit that I had a minor inferiority complex.

It was the Tuesday sitting of Prime Minister Questions that I finally got the opportunity to speak in the house. I had come into politics with a desire to fight the corner for the people of my adopted town of Torquay, a town that I now called home and cherished greatly.

To an outsider, Prime Minister Questions might seem to be one of the great pillars of our democratic process. What one realized when participating, was that it was a very stage-managed event. The Prime Minister would have a copy all of the questions in advance in order to prepare his answers. This tradition was on the pretense that answers that are more constructive could be provided if there were time to undertake adequate research. There was some merit in that argument, admittedly.

Question time started in its usual vociferous manner, with the Prime Minister hauled over the coals and interrogated about a number of current issues. Eventually, the speaker called out my name.

"I call upon The Right Honorable Stanley Wilson, Member of Parliament for Torquay."

I nervously turned toward the nearest microphone suspended from the ceiling.

"Could the Prime Minister explain to the house, why in the face of tremendous competition from Europe, and rising unemployment in the West Country, he has cut funding to the tourist board by twenty percent in the last year, with further undisclosed cuts to follow?"

It was terrifying, but I had done it. Harold Wilson gave a scripted response that as usual did not answer the question at all. He dodged around the issue by talking about regional enterprise zones. He read a list of statistics that successfully changed the answer into an advert for government achievements in bringing down crime rates in the region. That, I had learned was British democracy. Marjorie called the office in the afternoon to say that she had heard me speak on Radio 4 after *The Archers* and was very proud.

My team at our tiny shoebox office in Westminster was finally bonding with me. Rebecca Waters, my secretary, was an absolute diamond and a damned attractive woman, too. It was surprising that she was a spinster given that she was in her early thirties and stunning. Her long slim legs, large breasts, petite body, and short blond hair did not go unnoticed by myself or other male members of the house. She always wore expensive makeup and crisp designer suits. She used her beauty shamelessly to her advantage in the male-dominated environment of politics. The other two members of my team were an intern called Piers Burgess, and a general clerk called Mike Welsch. Piers was a typical floppy-haired ex-public schoolboy. Harrow educated, he had graduated the previous year with a first-class business degree from the London School of Economics. He spoke eloquently, dressed in pinstripe suits and double-cuffed shirts, and was highly intelligent. He was an asset whom I have no doubt would at some point embark upon a very successful business or political career of his own. However, he was also a liability from the perspective that he was tactless. He was keen to learn, and I wondered with my lack of experience in politics whether I could teach him anything at all. Despite this, he proved to be a loyal and willing helper with contacts in high places that may prove useful.

The workload I had as a member of the House was immense. This meant that we all worked long hours. In particular, Miss Waters and I would work late into the night. We would often grab a light dinner or a sandwich in one of the canteens, despite my newfound ability to cook. Rebecca was a private person, who was very guarded about her home life and her background, and it was difficult to build a rapport with her initially. Despite this, over the months, a level of trust and understanding developed between us. I realized that she was far more than a proficient typist. She had become indispensable. If I was to be honest, I had developed an attraction to her. Being married myself and being in a workplace environment, I kept our relationship on a professional footing. I was also acutely aware that there was a considerable age difference. What would a slim, attractive young professional woman see in an aging, portly, and balding man like me? I endeavored to keep an emotional detachment, but I knew in my own mind that I was fighting a lost cause.

Chapter 38

November 2006: Jez Matthews

Bill and the production crew arrived in a large Transit van. Within minutes of unloading the film equipment, they were crawling all over Number 19 like ants. They were doing much of the preliminary filming work, such as checking light levels with portable meters and capturing still shots. Bill was in the van selecting clips of my undercover footage to show Mark. The van was like something from James Bond. Apart from the mini radar dish on the roof, it looked like an ordinary Ford Transit. However, inside it was packed with state-of-the-art broadcast and editing equipment.

Mark and I spoke, off camera, in some detail about the hotel and its problems. In my opinion, he was a hair's breadth from having a successful operation; he just needed a dose of sanity. We sat in the hotel lounge, and the cameras started rolling.

"So, Mark, why did you contact the *Hotel Red Alert* team?" I asked.

"Because my business is failing. I can't pay the bills."

"How much are you losing?"

"I would say about a thousand pounds a month, give or take."

"And how long can you sustain that?"

"Six months at best. The bank wants to see things turn

around, or else they will take possession of the property."

"And this has been your family home for how long?"

"I've lived here since I was a boy. I inherited the house from my parents."

"So this is more than just a building to you? There are a lot of memories tied up in these walls?"

"Yes, my whole life has been spent here."

"How do you think you would feel if you had to hand the keys to the bank and lose everything?"

"I would be devastated."

"What do you think you are doing wrong?"

"I'm not sure, I mean I think it's a characterful place in an internationally respected town, and I enjoy doing it."

"Okay," I said. "Now, let's have a look at some video clips on my laptop. These were filmed using a hidden camera."

I turned the laptop toward him, and the second camera zoomed in on his face. "The first clip I want to show you is how you greeted me when I arrived."

I began playing back the first recording.

"All of God's greetings upon thee."

"Hello, I'm Jez Matthews. I have a room booked for tonight."

"Come-hither, young lad. Entereth into my humble abode."

I clicked on the pause icon.

"Now, how do you think that went?"

"Perhaps I need to tone down the Shakespearean dialect."

"Mark, that is the bloody understatement of the century. I mean, it's totally weird. If I'd turned up on spec and been greeted like that, I would have walked straight to the next hotel. You sounded like a complete prat."

We went through a couple more clips. They were embarrassing to watch, and I could see Mark's discomfort clearly visible on his face. At the end of each section of footage, I would humiliate him further, with scornful comments.

Afterward, he took me on a tour of the hotel. There were four more rooms in addition to mine, which were all named after Shakespearean plays. They were called Hamlet, King Lear, and Othello. The fourth room contained a four-poster bed and was called the Romeo and Juliet Suite, being aimed at those looking for a romantic break. It was not really a suite, though; it was just a room that was marginally larger than the others, which he had managed to squeeze in a tatty second-hand sofa. As we walked around, I became increasingly pithy.

"Mark, where the bloody hell did you get that sofa from? It looks like it has mange," I said, playing to the camera. "And what the fuck was going through your head when you put those frumpy lace fairies on top of the toilet rolls? It's like going back to the seventies. Aside from being shit, they're the worst dust collectors."

All the rooms paid homage to the genius of Shakespeare, and they had provided a literal canvas for Mark to indulge his other passion—painting. Each bedroom had murals of the various play's characters painted on the ceiling. This could have been a good idea if Mark was a talented artist, but they just looked gaudy and in some cases a bit scary, like Mark.

"And this is the Hamlet room," said Mark opening the door. "And may I introduce you to Yorick. Alas, poor Yorick. I knew him well."

Mark burst into laughter, pleased with his puerile attempt to tell a joke. I use the word joke in its loosest possible meaning. He then pointed to a plastic skull on top of a half-sized coffin and an imitation gravestone.

"Tasteful," I said rolling my eyes in a camp manner. "Why in God's name do you think having a coffin in a hotel bedroom enhances the ambiance? Is it in case your older guests don't make it through the night?"

As we walked around, it was the same story in each bedroom, from plastic cauldrons to thrones made from chairs fit for the skip, and painted gold with some costume jewelry stuck on them.

"Mark," I said. "The word boutique hotel is a much-overused term, and quirkiness can be good in small hotels. But there is a thin line between eccentric individuality and tackiness. Number 19 is like Disney does Shakespeare on a fifty pence budget."

"I don't think that's very fair," he said defensively.

"The bedrooms demean the inherent character of this lovely Edwardian building. I mean, the color themes you've chosen are garish. The furnishings are chintzy. It's a design disaster darling. To be frank, Mark, it's pants."

"Well, I don't agree," he said visibly riled.

"Well, let's have a read of your online reviews," I said. "'Number 19, I couldn't wait to leave.' Hardly a satisfied customer. Here's another one, 'Avoid the Hamlet Suite—the coffin put me off.' And another: 'Creepy Owner.' Kind of says it all, really."

We spent the rest of the day filming. Mark was stubborn and it was going to be a fight to get him to change his ways, but I knew that Number 19 had the potential to do well. I presented him with an action plan, which included toning down the Shakespearean theme, and speaking modern-day English. We also had a team of decorators, who were going to refurbish the Hamlet Suite to my design. This would be contemporary, without taking away the Edwardian character and still paying homage to Shakespeare. I would return in two months to check on his progress.

I spent my third night in Stratford-Upon-Avon, staying at the Premier Inn with the production crew, an extrovert and fun bunch of people. In the evening, we went for a curry in the town and bonded over drinks. We agreed that Mark was weird but in a wonderfully outlandish way. Bill said he was delighted with the first day's filming and that he thought I was an asset to the show. The camera operators and the runners were also supportive. They said it was nice to have someone down to earth to work with, instead of the tyrant queen. Although I did not see it, apparently Carol Thomson had made some malicious remarks about the show in the *Daily Mail*. She said that she felt it had run its course, and that was why she left. If anything, it gave me more determination to help reinvent the show and make it better than before.

I drove back to Torquay the following morning, looking forward to telling Graham all about it. Even the heavy traffic and overcast skies could not dampen the euphoria that I felt.

Chapter 39

September 1975: Stanley Wilson
Parliament returned from recess in early September, whilst Britain was enjoying an Indian summer. Thankfully, we had moved from our cramped and stuffy office in Westminster Palace to the refurbished Norman Shaw Building, which was a few minutes' walk away. This was a beautiful old Portland stone building formerly occupied by Scotland Yard. The government had restored it back to its former glory, with extensive repairs to the facade and a comprehensive internal modernization. Unfortunately, the work was not quite finished, so we had to endure contractors hammering and drilling throughout most of the day. Despite this, the offices were an enormous improvement. Unlike our broom cupboard in parliament, they were fit for purpose. We each had our own desks instead of having to share. There was adequate filing space, natural light, and we had modern conveniences such as a telex, push-button telephones, and electric typewriters. There was access to a photocopier on the first floor, which was a very useful contraption. We had some American students from Harvard on a work/study placement in the building, who insisted on calling it a 'Xerox' machine.

Rebecca was sorting through the numerous cardboard packing boxes full of documents, which a removal company had transported across from Westminster Palace. Piers and Mike were sifting through my correspondence, and I noticed that my in-tray was overflowing with letters and memorandums.

In Torquay, the holiday season had been frenetic, and whilst Marjorie and Christopher managed the hotel with a contingent of staff, I had inevitably been drawn into helping out. I juggled this with my constituency surgeries and other duties as an MP. People are misguided when they imagine us spending eight weeks of the summer on a beach.

My biggest challenge as the elected representative for Torquay was to try to secure funding from central government for the Kingkerswell bypass. This we hoped would relieve some of the traffic congestion coming into Torquay, which was one of the largest urban conurbations not served by a dual carriageway. It was an uphill struggle, and I had not enjoyed much success. This was despite all the evidence that it would spur significant growth for the region by boosting tourist numbers.

The Commons provided me with constant challenges. However, rationality and good humor accounted for much, and I had a strong team working for me.

One of the big dividing issues within the party was Europe. However, Mrs. Thatcher was proving to be a formidable leader of the opposition, and thus, backbench discipline was strong. We saw her as our key to gain power at the next election and would back her without too much arm-twisting for now.

In the evenings, I regularly worked late with Rebecca. Our conversations were initially work-orientated. I found her guarded about her personal life, but as the weeks went on, she opened up somewhat. Duties had dictated that we still had contact throughout the recess, and although she would unfailingly address me as Mr. Wilson publicly, in private it was invariably Stan. She had stayed with us at The Marstan Hotel for a three-day stopover, and Marjorie had taken an intense dislike to her. I think that she sensed my attraction, despite my denial. I assured Marjorie that even if there were a scintilla of truth in her accusation, it would never be reciprocated. I was after all a balding, middle-aged man with a potbelly. She was a beautiful young woman more than ten years my junior. If there were any feelings on her side, it would be that I was like a favorite uncle to her.

Rebecca led the life of a spinster who was married only to her job. She was ambitious with aspirations to run as a Member of Parliament when the time was right. She owned a small basement flat near Hammersmith tube station that she shared with a tabby cat called Truffles. She was Jewish by birth but considered herself an atheist, which was very modern, I thought. She enjoyed the theatre, and I promised her that I would take her to see a show.

I bought a copy of *Time Out* magazine, and we discovered on a cigarette break that we both enjoyed Andrew Lloyd Webber. I had his greatest hits' collection on my eight-track in the car, and we both fancied seeing *Jesus Christ Superstar* at the Palace Theatre. I booked two tickets using my Access card and made a dinner reservation at L'Escargot on Charing Cross Road for after the show. I hoped that Marjorie would not scrutinize my credit card statement too carefully, although I was sure that I could explain it as staff entertainment.

We went on Tuesday night. The show was good, and I was familiar with most of the music. Nevertheless, it brought another dimension to it to see it on stage with live singing. Dinner afterward was also very enjoyable. It was agreeable to be out of the office in more relaxed surroundings, and Rebecca had exchanged a business suit for a black low-cut evening dress that bordered on being provocative. She was a picture of elegance. She sipped her wine in a cultivated manner, making effortless conversation as she gracefully nibbled at her starter. We spoke about the musical, about my family, and about Torquay. My life down there seemed a world away. I was glad to escape from the house that hid the dark secret underneath the patio, and I enjoyed being apart from Marjorie and her controlling nature.

As the waiter opened our second bottle of wine, I could not help but think that Rebecca was probably the most beautiful woman I had ever met. It was unfair of me to make comparisons to Marje, but it was becoming apparent to me that my feelings toward my wife had changed.

The woman I had once loved so dearly had murdered our neighbor in cold blood. I would never forget the way in which she lunged at Mavis and the methodical and calculating manner in which she organized the disposal of both bodies. When we had met, she was young, slim, and a little shy but great fun with a naughty streak. Now she was plump, wrinkled, and ambitious to the point where there no longer seemed to be boundaries. At some point, I had become a mere tool to further these aspirations. I wanted to confess to Rebecca, but despite the quantity of wine I had consumed, I still had a grasp on reality. Even if she did not go to the police, it would not be fair to burden her with the knowledge of what I was involved in. I did talk to her about Christopher, though. I had kept my feelings on him bottled up for some time.

"I feel I no longer know my son," I said, trying a sip of Riesling.

"Is the wine to your liking?" said the waiter.

"It's exquisite," I said. The waiter poured us a large measure.

"What makes you say that?" said Rebecca.

"Well, he's a pansy, isn't he?"

"You've never mentioned it before."

"Well, it's not something you broadcast, is it?"

"I suppose not, but it's not illegal anymore is it?"

"Not illegal but, well, it's disgusting the thought of it. I mean, we knew he wasn't going to make captain of the rugby team, or even badminton for that matter. We knew he was more interested in the theatre and music, but I never thought he was..."

"Gay?"

"I can't bring myself to say it."

"Do you still love him?" said Rebecca.

"Of course I do," I said. "He's my son. It's unconditional. More than anything, I worry about him. It's no life for him, no children, and no marriage. Every time he goes out, I worry about him being beaten up. Then there are my beliefs as a Christian."

"Have you spoken to him about it?"

"I just can't, Rebecca. I want to understand. I want to accept it, but I just can't."

She offered her hand across the table and I clasped it firmly.

"Silly me," I said. "I don't know where all that came from. Let's talk about something different, like are you dating anyone at the moment?"

"No," she said. "But I have met somebody I really like."

"Oh," I said. "Do I know him?"

"That would be telling," she said, her eyes lingering on mine.

I quickly changed the subject to work related matters. Eventually, we finished our main course

"I think it would be rude not to have a pudding. Waiter, can we have the dessert menu, please?"

Rebecca smiled at me as we both ordered.

I wolfed down my profiteroles whilst Rebecca gracefully ate her crème brûlée. When we came out of the restaurant, it was pouring with rain. I put Rebecca in a black cab and gave the driver a wad of pound notes, which would cover the cost of the journey. She gave me a lingering kiss on the cheek before I made a dash for the Underground.

I found women almost impossible to read. They were such complicated creatures. I thought I had sensed body language suggesting that she might be interested in having some kind of relationship with me. That surely could not be right. She could have anyone she wanted. What could I offer her? Besides, I was married.

As the Northern Line tube train pulled out of Charing Cross station, I started to play with my wedding ring. I had a sudden desire to take it off. I twisted and pulled at it, but it was stuck fast behind the knuckle of a finger that was much fatter than when I had married all those years ago. My thoughts were interrupted when a passenger asked me for a light. I obliged, and then I picked up a copy of the *Evening Standard*, left on the seat opposite me. The pages were full of depressing articles about strikes, inflation, and unemployment. I disembarked at Embankment station, wondering why I had not invested in an umbrella and walked home, rather than bother to travel one stop and suffer the inconvenience of traversing all the escalators.

Chapter 40

November 2006: Jez Matthews
I arrived home just after lunchtime in a state of excitement. I was looking forward to telling Graham all about my adventure. I found him sitting in the kitchen, his face a picture of worry.

"What's wrong?" I asked.

"Kristyna has gone missing. Her mother was here earlier today, distraught. I've never seen anybody as distressed as that. She was beside herself with worry."

"Her mother was here?"

"Yes. Lukas told her before he died that she'd left Torquay, but he didn't know where she'd gone. He said that he had tried calling her on her mobile phone, but it was dead. Apparently, he thought she changed her number so he couldn't pester her."

A wave of panic swept over me. In the last few weeks, I had managed to bury my emotions about Kristyna, but now they came flooding back, stronger than ever.

"What does she know? I mean, have they called the police? How long is it since anybody's heard from her?"

"They've had no contact with her since October, when they split up. That's over a month ago. The police are treating it as suspicious."

"There must be a simple explanation. Maybe she's gone abroad," I said.

"Apparently they can tell if she's left the country, because the border control agencies can check passport records. And there's no evidence of her bank account being used."

"Oh no, this is awful. First her sister dies, and now she vanishes. Her poor mother."

"Her poor mother indeed. She was in a wretched state. Her English was very basic, but she was with a friend who was translating. Even so, you didn't need an interpreter to see the agony in her eyes. The police are coming around later to take statements from both of us."

"The police are coming here? Why would they want to do that? I mean, we don't know where she is. I mean, I don't think we can help?" I said, waffling.

"It's routine. We were her employer, and this was where she used to live. You were one of the last people to have seen her."

"Yes, I suppose that makes sense."

"Are you okay, darling? You look as if you've seen a ghost."

"Yes, of course I am, just a bit shocked about Kristyna."

"So how was the filming, then?"

"It was brilliant. I mean, totally amazing," I said distractedly. "Listen, can I tell you about it later? I'm feeling a bit tired after the drive. I'm going to have a lie down."

"No problem, love. I'll bring you a cup of tea shortly."

Two plain-clothed detectives visited the hotel later in the afternoon, just as it was getting dark. Graham talked to them for about half-an-hour in our private lounge, telling them what he knew about Kristyna. I was sweating profusely. My mind was a jumble of confusion and emotions. The excitement from yesterday's filming seemed a lifetime ago; now I felt nauseous with fear.

My turn for questioning soon came. I went into our lounge and sat on the wingback chair opposite the officers. They sat on the sofa with various forms spread over our coffee table. A cut-glass voice inside my head that I knew to be Lady Elizabeth told me to "remain composed, and everything will be fine." The two detective constables introduced themselves as DC Ward and DC Hemming from Devon and Cornwall Missing Persons Department. Both were balding and middle-aged men with large beer bellies and wore polyester suits. DC Hemming had a bushy moustache and round glasses.

I answered their questions as best I could, but I was fidgety and I felt sure that they suspected something. DC Ward had an unnerving habit of eyeing you up and down, as if looking for clues in your body language. I gave my answers succinctly, being honest where I could. To start with, they were mainly simple queries like how long did she work here or did she have any friends in other cities. They asked me if I had any idea of her whereabouts, to which I lied through my teeth. Although they may have been innocent questions, it still felt like an interrogation. Then they threw in some unexpected details.

"Did you know that Mr. Lukas Kopecky was having an affair?" asked DC Hemming.

I hesitated. To my surprise, Lady Elizabeth had materialized beside me. She stood next to my chair, wearing a smart black Victorian dress. She was monochrome and semitransparent. I looked up at her severe features.

"Is something wrong?" asked DC Hemming.

"No, why?"

"You appear to be staring to your left?"

Why could nobody else see her other than me? Lady Elizabeth raised her finger and put it to her mouth and shook her head, then disappeared.

"We were talking about Mr. Kopecky having an affair?"

"Erm, I didn't know he was. Lukas, an affair? Really?"

"Yes," said DC Hemming observing my face. "She called a friend of hers in the Czech Republic in tears saying she'd found text messages on Lukas' phone. He had deleted the contact so she did not know who they were sent to, but they were enough to guess he was seeing somebody else. She was going to confront him apparently."

"Oh my God, that would explain why she left so quickly. I mean, I knew they split up, but I didn't realize that was the reason."

"So Mr. Kopecky didn't confide in you?"

"No, he was staff. He lived here, but he spent his evenings in his bedroom. He certainly didn't speak to me about things like that. It was none of my business what he did in his personal life."

"Is there something the matter, sir, you look distracted?"

"No, I'm fine. Just tired, I've had a long day."

"Do you mind if we have a look around?"

Lady Elizabeth's voice entered my mind. "Let them," she said. "Offer them a cup of tea."

"Yes, Elizabeth."

"I beg your pardon?" said DC Hemming.

"Sorry, Detective, no problem," I said hurriedly. "Would you like a cup of tea?"

"No, thank you, sir. We'll have a quick look around, then we'll be off."

I showed them Kristyna and Lukas' old bedroom and gave them a brief tour of the hotel.

"Can we see the basement?"

My face turned white. "Yes, of course. I don't think

she's down there, though," I said, laughing nervously. "Let me just get the key."

I was in the verge of mental collapse. Lady Elizabeth reappeared and glided behind me into the study where I picked up the key.

Her presence was becoming corporeal, her shape more solid, I could make out more features in her face, and for the first time I heard her speak at the same time as seeing her. It was if she was feeding on my emotions. "You are doing well," she said, in a detached, inhuman voice. "Trust me, they are both stupid. They suspect nothing."

"Thank you," I said to the blurry apparition beside me. I noticed she wore a beautiful diamond necklace.

I walked back to the officers, opened the basement, and led them downstairs.

"New floor," remarked DC Hemming.

My heart stopped. "Yes," I said. "We had a damp problem. It's all been tanked, and new concrete laid down."

"Good job by the looks of it."

"And Mr. Kopecky, Kristyna Chladek's ex-partner, he died suddenly, didn't he?"

I sighed. "I've been through all this with your colleagues weeks ago. The postmortem confirmed he drowned as a result of being knocked out by a fall. It was a freak accident, quite horrible."

"We've seen everything we need to see for now," said DC Ward. "Should you hear from Kristyna or think of any other useful information, please call me on the number on this card."

"Sure," I said. "If you hear anything, we'd really like to know. We thought the world of her."

"There is going to be a television appeal tomorrow, so we hope that will bear some fruit. Good-bye, sir, and thank you for your time."

I shut the door behind them and breathed a sigh of relief. Lady Elizabeth promptly vanished into a wall. Graham came out of the kitchen into the hallway.

"You look awful, what's the matter?"

"I just don't like the police."

"Since when?"

"Since they come crawling around our home asking questions, like I'm some kind of criminal."

"Oh, for God's sake, it's not as if we've got anything to hide."

"I know that. I just didn't like the way they looked at me, as if I'm involved somehow."

"Now you're being paranoid. She's probably working on some farm in the country where there's no phone signal. It'll all be fine. It's not as if we've killed her and buried her in the basement."

I suddenly felt sick to the bottom of my stomach.

Graham went to bed early. I told him about the filming, but the police visit dampened my enthusiasm and it had given me a headache. I felt worried and anxious. I could not sleep, so I went into the study with a triple brandy and opened the desk drawer to retrieve my tranquilizers. I swallowed double the prescribed dose with a large swig of brandy and waited impatiently for the combined effects of the alcohol and drugs to kick in. I opened up the drawer again to put the bottle back and stupidly pulled it out too far. It came off the runner and fell onto the floor, tipping the contents across the rug. Cursing my clumsiness, I began to pick up the various items, realizing where all the paper clips and sticky notes that I could never find had disappeared.

Nestled among the office paraphernalia, I spotted a

crumpled envelope with "A message for the future owners" scribbled on the front in blue fountain pen. It had slipped my memory that during the refurbishment last winter, the builders found a letter under the floorboards in the old master bedroom. I had put it away for safekeeping and forgotten about it.

I opened up the creased envelope and switched on the desk lamp, which bathed the writing paper in a green glow. The writer had scrawled notes in fountain pen onto headed Marstan Hotel notepaper from the 1970s. The writing was spidery and barely legible, as though the person that had scribbled it was drunk or had a shaking hand. There were splatters of blue ink where the author had pressed the nib too hard against the paper.

Some words of truth—

My time is short, so I will be brief. I need to tell the truth before I die. I was nineteen when I started to work for the Kingsley family as a footman. I became deputy butler five years later, and when the head butler died in 1918, I was promoted to that role.

Sir Wilfred and Lady Elizabeth's marriage was a sham. The marriage gave her a title, great wealth, and a lifestyle that she would not otherwise have enjoyed. Hers was a marriage of convenience and nothing more. She never loved him. I have no idea why Sir Wilfred tolerated her infidelity, but he turned a blind eye.

Things took a turn for the worse when she started dating James Partridge. Their affair progressed beyond Elizabeth's usual short-lived flings.

A year later Wilfred became seriously ill, and despite my prayers he never recovered. Elizabeth banned me from being alone with him, in the latter stages of his illness. He died during the winter of 1919 in the room in which I am now staying.

When Wilfred died, James and Elizabeth were killed

in a fire caused by an ember spitting out from the hearth, which set alight their clothes. It was a one in a million accident, and I now know it was not just a coincidence.

Weeks later, I cleared the room and packed Wilfred's belongings. I kept his watch, bequeathed to me, which I still wear today in his memory. He was my employer, but I was his confidant and dare I say it, we were close friends—or as close as etiquette in those days would allow. When I sorted through the dressing table drawers, I found an almost empty bottle of arsenic. Whilst I lay no claim on being the most intelligent man in the world, it was clear that Elizabeth had poisoned Wilfred over a period of months. She would have inherited a considerable fortune and been free to remarry.

I should have told the police, but something stopped me. Maybe it was because I did not want the Kingsley name blighted by scandal. Perhaps I was worried in case I may be implicated in some way. Whatever the reason, I did not and I regret it deeply. I tipped the remaining arsenic down the sink and later went to Meadfoot Beach and threw the empty bottle into the sea.

I intend to hide this letter, and I hope that one day it will be discovered. My last words are probably the most important. I want to give the reader a warning:

If you are living in this house, I urge you to heed these words. In the weeks after the fire, I saw and heard things that I cannot explain. There is an evil presence in this house. Fifty-six years later, I can still feel it. I feel the malevolent spirit of Lady Elizabeth Kingsley, marauding around this room, bitter and resentful for being taken before her time. There are other souls, too, trapped within these walls.

This must all seem unbelievable to anybody reading this, but I swear to almighty God: This place is cursed.

Albert Henderson, 2nd February 1975

I finished reading the letter in amazement. If I had read it a year ago, I would have thought it the ramblings of a lunatic. I clasped my hands together, then had a thought. I turned on the computer, which beeped and whirred as it booted up. I clicked on Google and typed "Pembroke House Torquay" in the search box.

The first few pages were articles about our hotel and links to our website. Our web designer was doing his job well. I scrolled down; finally, when I got to the seventh page, I saw a link to an old article from the Torquay Museum archives.

"LADY ELIZABETH KINGSLEY KILLED IN MYSTERIOUS CIRCUMSTANCES: Calamitous fire at Pembroke House in Torquay takes the life of Lady Elizabeth Kingsley and Mr. James Partridge minutes after Sir Wilfred Kingsley lost his battle against an unknown illness. Inquiry confirms it was a tragic accident."

I entered another phrase into the search box, using the words "Albert Henderson Marstan Hotel." This time on page two, there was a short archived article in the *Torquay Herald* about his death in February 1975.

"Oh my God!" I said. "What have we got ourselves into?"

The room became icy, and Lady Elizabeth appeared in front of me, stroking a headless white cat. A handsome but badly scarred man, whom I instinctively knew was James Partridge, accompanied her.

"You are ours now, Jez Matthews," she said. Her voice sounded hollow, as though she were speaking into a long cardboard tube. "You belong to us."

She laughed as her beautiful face transformed into a hideously burnt ghoulish monster, and then they both metamorphosed into a wisp of smoke. The gray vapor twisted and descended rapidly like a whirlpool into a point in the floor, as if a powerful extractor fan was sucking it out. An old man appeared in their place wearing a butler's uniform and carrying a bottle of wine on a tray. He was smiling kindly and was joined almost immediately by a distinguished old man in gentleman's clothing. Unlike Lady Kingsley's spectra, they emanated an air of benevolence.

"We all have a choice in life, and we are judged by those decisions," said the butler.

"I guess you must be Henderson."

"You are correct. I am Henderson, and this is my master, Sir Wilfred Kingsley. He still expects me to wait on him hand and foot, by the way. At least my arthritis has gone."

Sir Wilfred spoke up. "Remember, Jez Matthews, you have a choice. You can do the right thing." His deep voice seemed to reverberate around the study. "Your soul can still be saved."

They both dissolved into the night. The air went cold again, and a middle-aged translucent woman in a floral dressing gown, curlers, and slippers appeared accompanied by a whiff of cheap perfume.

"I would never have told," she said earnestly. "I promised I wouldn't."

Her head split open and brains started pouring out, and she made a gruesome gurgling noise before vanishing into the wall. A painfully thin, tattoo-covered young man replaced her. He scowled at me angrily before disappearing.

I drifted into a semiconscious state and found myself standing in the master bedroom. My presence was seemingly invisible to the occupants. The curtains were different, thick red velvet drapes in place of our cream swags and tails, and there was a fire raging in the hearth. The door to the en suite was not there, and the decor was unrecognizable, old fashioned with oppressive colors.

I saw Sir Wilfred Kingsley laying on his bed, clinging tenuously onto life. His breathing was labored and his face deathly.

People looking concerned, surrounded his four-poster bed. A young lady in a nurse' uniform patted his sweaty forehead with a flannel. I noticed a copy of *The Times* on a table, dated the 23rd of February, 1919.

Lady Elizabeth was dressed in a black skirt and blouse, with a pearl necklace and matching earrings. Her face was pretty but severe. She pulled the cord that operated the bell in the servant's quarters, summoning the maid. A young girl answered, whom Elizabeth beckoned to draw the curtains to keep out the draft. As the maid pulled the drapes across, I looked out of the window, but all I could see was an impenetrable gray fog.

"Fetch Sir Wilfred's supper," she instructed.

"Yes, m'lady," the maid replied. "Mrs. Jones said that she has made up the green room for Mr. Partridge, who has telephoned to say he will be on the twelve thirty train from London."

"Thank you, O'Connor."

The maid bowed her head and went downstairs to the kitchen. She returned a few minutes later with a tray bearing some buttered bread and a bowl of soup and handed it to Lady Elizabeth before discreetly leaving the room.

Lady Elizabeth turned to the nurse and a tall man in a three-piece suit, identifiable as a doctor due to the stethoscope around his neck and the medical bag he carried.

"Please," she said. "I would like to be alone with my husband."

With due respect, they left and Lady Elizabeth placed the tray on the walnut dressing table. Shielding her actions from Sir Wilfred with her body, she removed a small brown bottle from the back of the drawer where it had been hidden. The bottle was labeled "Arsenic" and bore the skull and crossbones symbol with the word "POISON" underneath. She shook out a tablet into her hand and crushed the pill into the soup, stirring it until all signs of this addition had disappeared. She put some extra pillows behind Sir Wilfred's back to enable him to sit upright in order to feed him the soup. Cautiously, she began spooning the toxin-laden broth into his mouth.

Desperate to warn Sir Wilfred, I shouted at the top of my voice, but my cries were silent as if I were trapped in a glass bubble.

"Elizabeth," he croaked weakly. "My love, come closer."

"Eat your dinner," she said, her lips displaying a thin wicked smile. "You need your strength."

"I need to tell you something," he said rasping. "I know... I know about... James and you, I know."

"Goodness," said Elizabeth whilst wiping soup from Sir Wilfred's chin. "All this chatter. You're dribbling everywhere. Hardly appropriate behavior for a knight of the realm."

Sir Wilfred, his face pallid and his eyes sunken into their sockets, looked defeated.

Lady Elizabeth whispered soothingly into his ear. "Not much longer to wait now, my sweet."

Lady Elizabeth seemed to become aware of my presence and looked at me with her steely eyes. She smiled and burst into inhuman laughter, which echoed around the room. It became distorted and distant as though being played backwards on a record player at the end of a tunnel.

The room swirled into a kaleidoscope of color around me, and I felt like I was falling from a great height. I felt dizzy as the room spun, as though I was on a merry-go-round, and then I was back in the study in my own time.

"What do you all want with me?" I pleaded, before collapsing unconscious onto the floor.

Chapter 41

pril 2007: Jez Matthews
I finished filming *Hotel Red Alert* in February.
It was now April and the first episode would air at
the beginning of this month. It was an absolute ball being
a television presenter. I still could not believe my luck that
I was being paid to dish out well-timed innuendoes and
bitchy comments, since this all came perfectly naturally
to me. I was appearing on the Kenneth Adams show on
Radio 2 on Monday afternoon to promote the new series,
the day before its inaugural broadcast. The following
week, preceding the second episode, Jim Lockton was
interviewing me. I was excited about meeting both
celebrities. Kenneth Adams was a colossus of the radio
world, and Jim Lockton was hugely popular in the UK.
The publicity should help reignite interest in *Hotel Red
Alert*, which had been waning in popularity for the last
few years.

Jason and the crowd from The Horn of Plenty were
following my career with interest and a touch of envy.
They arranged to show the first episode on one of the
big plasma televisions in the pub, with a complimentary
buffet. I was asked to provide some commentary during
advert breaks. They also requested that I host bingo
afterward. I agreed to the commentary but not the bingo.
I had to draw the line somewhere. There were only so

many times that you could regurgitate the same-old line 'eighty-eight, *two* fat lesbians.' It had not raised a laugh in the five years since they opened the pub, so I doubted I would have any success.

The police had called the hotel to tell me that Kristyna had not 'resurfaced.' It was an unfortunate choice of words, and if it were not for the fear that the call invoked, I could have almost laughed at the irony. Graham had a very unpleasant call from her mother, who was shouting down the phone in broken English.

"You know something, you no tell, you know something."

There was a thing called a mother's intuition, and although Graham was totally innocent, I could tell that Kristyna's mother knew something did not add up. Unsurprisingly, the television appeal was not successful.

Aside from that, our life was relatively uncomplicated. In January, we enjoyed three weeks traveling around Florida. We would have stayed longer, but I had to fit the holiday around my filming schedule. Graham had taken charge at the hotel, and things were running efficiently.

Morbid Maureen had returned from her retreat in Spain, and we employed her on a permanent basis. Although she drove us mad and walked around in a dark cloud of despondency, she was great conversational fodder and proved reliable.

Graham was hyperactive, and he chose to be hands-on with the work, even though much of it was menial. I had not had any strange visions or supernatural encounters since before Christmas, apart from a second Lilliput Lane collectable miniature cottage, which I found shattered in pieces on the lounge floor one morning. I put it down to an act of kindness from the spirits, but Graham's mother would be devastated.

I went to London the day before the radio show. I stayed in a shabby hotel, close to Oxford Circus tube station. In the morning, I walked to Western House near Marble Arch to meet Kenneth Adams. The interview was going to be live, and it terrified me. There was little comparison to a prerecorded television episode with a few camera operators present, who could second take if you fluffed your lines. I told myself that I could only do my best. Kenneth and his motley crew, as he referred to them, were great fun. There was an electric atmosphere in the studio that came across on air. I met them a couple of hours before the show started, and we had gone over the questions that Kenneth was going to ask me. He was very reassuring and told me not to worry. If I froze, they would work around me. The preparation was a big help. However, as the time approached for my spot, my nerves were taking over. My agitation made me feel queasy, and whilst I craved a tranquilizer, I knew that I could not risk taking one. I needed to be energetic and vivacious, not sleepy and relaxed. I went to the toilet, shaking. This was when I met Brett, who was about to change my life forever.

I stood bent down over the sink, splashing my face with cold water. I glanced in the mirror and noticed how tired I looked. I had dark bags under my eyes. I was glad that it was radio and not television. I became aware of someone standing close behind me. He was tall with a wiry frame and multiple piercings in his ears. He wore a grubby blue polo shirt showing his tattooed forearms. He had cropped black hair, framing a thin, pointed face and steely gray eyes.

"All right, mate," he said in a thick east-end accent. "'Ows it going?"

"I'm a little nervous," I confessed. "I'm promoting the first episode of *Hotel Red Alert*. It's on tomorrow."

"Ah," he nodded understandingly.

"What do you do here, then?" I asked.

"Me? I'm only the cleaner," he said pointing to a mop and bucket in the corner and a yellow 'Caution Wet Floor' sign. "That's me official job. I'm also the morale officer."

"Morale officer?" I queried.

"I 'elp keep up the morale of the joint," he said. "That's me unofficial role."

"And how do you do that?" I asked.

I wondered what he was about to do when he put his hand in his pocket. He passed me a small plastic wrap of white powder.

"Little somefing for ya," he said. "On the 'ouse."

"Oh no," I said. "I don't really think..."

"Listen mate, if you don't want it, chuck it down the toilet—but you're on air in twenty minutes, trust me. This'll 'elp."

"What is it?" I said examining the packet.

"Blimey, you are new to all this, int yah?" he said. "Only a bit of charlie, mate. It's showbiz. Everyone does it, just go into a cubicle, roll up a note, snort it up your nose, and enjoy."

"Right, I get it."

"First one's free—want any more, here's me number. I supply the best names in showbiz." He handed me a cheap business card. "All good stuff. Pure, not cut with flour and shite."

"Okay, thank you, erm, Brett," I said reading the card.

After he had left, I pondered on the conversation, rolling the small wrap of cocaine in my hand nervously. Then I went into a toilet cubicle. I wanted to flush it down the pan, but an invisible hand stopped me. I had never been into the drug scene, but I had seen it on television enough times, so I gently tipped out the packet contents onto the top of the cistern. I took a ten-pound note from my wallet and rolled it up, and then I took a good long snort.

I was unsure of what to expect, but my nostril felt unpleasant, as though it was burning. Following the burning sensation, it itched like mad for about a minute, and then it felt numb. Aside from that, I did not feel any different. I went back up to the studio, a little let down. I wondered if it was all some kind of joke, and I had just unwittingly sniffed baking soda. Then about ten minutes later, it hit me. All my angst vanished. More than that, though, I felt it replaced by a sense of euphoria and confidence. I felt exultant and invincible. The fear of doing a live interview disappeared, replaced by excitement, a desire to tell the world about the story of my brilliant television show. I could not wait to get on air and speak to the nation.

Kenneth played the Gorillaz song "Dare", and after two minutes of banter with his cohosts, he introduced me.

"And we have sat in our studio on my right, the new Hotel Detective, from Channel 4's *Hotel Red Alert*. A big welcome to Jez Matthews."

I sat in front of a large oval microphone on a stand on the desk, and a red light came on indicating that I was now live on the air.

"It's good to be here, Kenneth."

"So *Hotel Red Alert*, great show, used to be hosted by the rather abrasive Carol Thompson. Where are you going to take us with it?"

"Well, Kenneth, I've been a fan of the show myself, and I have my own hotel."

"Let me just tell the viewers," he interrupted. "Jez owns an award-winning hotel in Torquay with his partner.

It's not Fawlty Towers, is it?"

"Ha ha, no, not at all. Well, sometimes behind the scenes it can be, we had a rat in the kitchen once. Whoops, did I just say that on national radio?" I laughed. "Please, can you edit that out? Oh, we're live, aren't we? Anyway, to answer to your question about the new show: The format is tried and tested, so it's evolution, not revolution."

"I like that—evolution, not revolution, must remember that one!"

"Ha ha," I laughed nervously. "The main difference in the first series is—"

"So you've been asked back for a second?"

"Yes, I signed a contract almost immediately after filming the first series."

"So they're confident of it being a success."

"Well, I hope so, I'm pleased with it. As I was saying, the main difference is that as I am an unknown, I go undercover. I try to catch them out a little."

"Brilliant."

"And catch them out I do. You would be amazed by the way that some people behave, when they don't realize a camera is filming them."

"Don't you feel a bit sneaky?"

"I certainly do, but I love every second of it."

"And what's the worst thing you've come across in this series?"

"The worst one was this lady who owns a guesthouse in Somerset."

"What did she do?"

"Well, it was a bit like staying at boot camp. When she checked me in, she gave me a book of rules a centimeter thick."

"You're kidding me!"

"No, I'm not, I swear. Then she told me about the

red and yellow card offences. Not taking your shoes off indoors was a yellow card offence, being more than five minutes late for breakfast, yellow card. Get two yellow cards and you would qualify for a red card which meant you'd be asked to leave with no refund."

"Seriously?"

"Seriously!"

"What did you have to do to get a red card?"

"The list included bringing back prostitutes, wetting the bed, and being drunk."

"So did you get a red card?"

"You'll have to tune in and see," I said.

"So what do you hate most about British hotels?"

"Many things... bad service, poor hygiene, deluded proprietors, but also when they waste their time doing stupid things like make elephants out of towels. I mean, get the bloody basics right first."

I could very easily have jabbered on for hours on my chemical-induced high, but Kenneth was experienced at managing his guests and reining in their egos.

"When does the show start?"

"The first episode will be aired tomorrow at nine o'clock, then every week until midsummer. Please watch it, everyone, it's great, and I've a huge mortgage to pay."

"Okay, everyone, big thank you to Jez Matthews, the new presenter of *Hotel Red Alert*, which will start tomorrow night at nine on Channel 4. Now for a bit of an oldie."

He faded in "Come on Eileen" by Dexy's Midnight Runners, and with the microphone switched off, turned toward me, smiling, and shook my hand.

"You were great, Jez, pleasure to have you in the studio."

"Thanks, Kenneth, it was an honor. Really, it was."

I left the studio buzzing, partly from the adrenaline rush but also from the cocaine. I felt invincible and carefree. I had another night in London before getting the early morning train back to Torquay, so I thought I would journey across town to the gay village in Soho and visit a few of my old haunts on Compton Street. As I walked along Oxford Street, I dug out Brett's card from my trouser pocket and called him.

He answered, "Who's this?"

"It's Jez Matthews. We met earlier today at the radio station."

"All right, mate, what can I do for yah?"

"That stuff you gave me today, got any more?"

"Plenty where that came from."

"I'm back up next week to do an interview for Jim Lockton, could do with some more."

"No problem, mate, suppose I'd better talk about prices."

"I don't care about that," I said. "Whatever it costs, it costs."

"Good lad," he said. "Call me when you're up in London, and we'll meet."

I reached Compton Street in London's gay village, probably the most diverse stretch of tarmac in the world, and picked my favorite bar, The Admiral Duncan. I thought to myself that this was possibly one of the last times I would be able to drink anonymously without anybody pointing at me or asking for an autograph. I found a quiet corner in the pub and enjoyed my night of freedom.

Chapter 42

September 1975: Stanley Wilson

When I walked into the office on Wednesday morning, Piers, Mike, and Rebecca were already there, working industriously. I had a minor headache from the quantity of wine that I consumed the previous night. I was also in a state of mild confusion. Did I imagine the conversation at dinner last night with Rebecca? Was my judgment clouded by alcohol and wishful thinking, thus leading me to misread the signals? It was infuriating to realize that I would have to be patient and wait until the end of the day to speak to Rebecca, when there would be nobody else around to overhear.

I felt slightly awkward in the office but managed to hide it from the staff. Rebecca was coolly efficient, as always. Fortunately, the Commons were sitting today, and I was due in the chamber in about an hour. The legislation being scrutinized was the sex discrimination act, effectively a debate on equal pay for women. There were a few dinosaurs in my own party that still thought that the old days were best. These types felt we would be better off going back to living in Victorian England, where the working class knew their place and rickets was just a fact of life. However, the bill had cross-party support, and it was a case of rubber-stamping the legislation. Then it would be a tedious afternoon of self-congratulation on how progressive we all were, putting the welfare of the public before the selfish interests of large corporations.

Rebecca gave me a cardboard wallet full of briefing papers, handed over with a charming smile and a discreet wink. She mouthed 'speak later' to me. I felt a butterfly in my stomach upon realizing that last night was not just my mind playing tricks. I realized that she was interested in something more than a professional relationship. A sense of excitement came over me, instantaneously replaced by a wave of guilt, when I thought of Marjorie back in Torquay. Nevertheless, the situation now had a certain inevitability to it, and my mind began working overdrive to make plans.

As it transpired, the debate in the chamber proved to be more protracted than expected. Some of the older members of the house seemed to hold the attitude that men were the breadwinners and the stronger of the sexes. Therefore, it was only right that they received higher salaries. This was a spurious argument, in my opinion. However, there was a genuine concern over the additional burden on industry and its possible effects on employment. In the end, the bill passed comfortably, with only nineteen MP's voting against and three abstentions. The women's suffrage movement would have been delighted.

I returned to the office at six o'clock, and Rebecca was typing up some letters for me. The rest of the team had already left.

"So does this mean I get a pay rise?" she said, laughing. "I listened to the news on the office wireless."

"Strangely enough, I think it does," I said. "Either that or the other two get a cut."

"This is the last letter I have to do tonight," she said. "Unless there is anything else you would like me to do for you?"

"There is one thing," I said.

"What's that?"

"Join me for dinner? Please?"

"Two nights in a row? This is becoming a habit."

"Sorry, Rebecca, you probably have plans. It was only an idea."

"No, I didn't mean it like that. I would be delighted to," she said. "I haven't brought a change of clothes or anything, though."

"You look perfect the way you are," I said.

"Flatterer. Just give me five minutes. I'll nip to the ladies' to freshen up."

I lit up a cigarette and waited for her to return, lost in thought.

She came back, having put on some fresh makeup and tidied her hair.

"Where are you taking me?" she asked.

"How about the Park Lane Hilton? It's such a lovely evening. I thought we could have a walk around Hyde Park afterward."

"That sounds lovely."

We caught a black cab, in hindsight a poor decision given the London rush-hour traffic. On arriving at the Hilton, we took the elevator to the restaurant on the top floor. I had the waiter put us at a table tucked into a cubicle hidden away from curious eyes. There were stunning views of Hyde Park and across London. We enjoyed a lavish dinner of foie gras, lobster, and chocolate-dipped strawberries to finish. Over the course of the evening, we drank an entire bottle of Moet and a half-bottle of Beaujolais. However, the most enjoyable thing about the meal was the company. We had set ourselves a new rule that we would not allow ourselves to talk shop. As well as getting to know each other and finding that we had many common interests, we also discovered that we shared a sense of humor.

After dinner, we enjoyed the remainder of the autumn evening burning off the calories by walking around Hyde Park. As we strolled, I timidly held out my hand, which she clasped. The sun had set, and whilst not completely dark, the moon was in the sky. A warm gentle breeze carried the muted hum of traffic from the Kensington Road. The smell of flowers and freshly cut grass masked the air pollution. We stopped walking and sat on a bench overlooking the Serpentine Lake. The park was quiet. There were a few families dotted about, a group of lads kicking a football, some amorous couples, and the odd vagrant. I decided that I had to grab the moment; it was now or never. I leaned over and kissed Rebecca, half expecting her to push me away, but she reciprocated. As our lips met, she put her arms around my back, pulling me in closer. It was a moment I did not want to forget. It felt like my pent-up desires were being released like floodwater out of a dam. After a few minutes, we stopped and I held her head against my neck, feeling her soft blond hair that smelt of roses.

"I'm old enough to be your father," I said.

"I don't care," she replied.

We kissed again for a few more minutes.

"You could have anyone you want," I said.

"I only want you."

"Come on," I said. "We need to get back home. I need to phone Marje. She'll be calling the flat wondering where I am."

"Do you have to mention her? It kind of spoils the moment."

"I'm sorry. I don't know what to say. You know my circumstances."

"You could do better than her," she said.

"She's why I'm where I am today," I said. "It's her that has pushed and supported me."

"Do you love her?"

"What sort of question is that?" I protested.

"It's one I want you to answer honestly. Do you love her?"

"Truthfully, I don't know. I know that I did once. I loved her with all my heart, but times have changed. Things have happened, horrible things." I managed to stop myself from confessing, even though I wanted to.

"What do you mean horrible things?"

"Oh, nothing you need to worry about," I said. "All I know is that when I am with you, I don't care about them anymore. Coming to London, well, it's been amazing. Torquay is a different life."

"It's a life that you return to every weekend."

"Yes, that is true, at the moment."

"So where do I stand?"

"I don't know what you want me to say. I've known you for four months. I find you extremely attractive. I enjoy your company, and I have to confess that my feelings for you have been growing. If you're asking me to tell you where this is going, I can't give you that answer. I won't blame you at all if you want to call this off before it has even really started."

"I don't want to do that."

"I was praying you would say that," I said. "I want to be honest with you. I desperately want to carry on seeing you outside work, but we have to be discreet. Marjorie cannot know. I will tell her at some stage, but it has to be on my terms."

"I see. I'm to be a bit on the side, am I?"

"It's not like that, Rebecca."

"It sounds like it to me. Listen, the last thing I want to

be is a home wrecker, so I'll follow your rules for now."

"It's a lot to ask, and I know I am being selfish... But can you do that for me, for us?"

"Yes. I don't like it, but I will do it for you."

"Come on, it's dark and it's starting to get cold," I said, taking off my jacket and putting it around her shoulders. "I'll put you in a taxi."

Chapter 43

April 2007: Jez Matthews

The Horn of Plenty was buzzing as usual. It was smoky and difficult to reach the bar through the crowd. Both Graham and Jason were present to give me moral support. I was unsure as to what was more nerve racking, watching myself broadcast to millions of viewers on national television, or watching it in the presence of a hundred bitchy queens.

Jason had dyed his hair black and was now a goth, with dark lipstick, pasty white foundation, and heavy eye shadow. I did not think it suited him, but I was wise enough to keep my mouth shut. Dave, the barman, was pulling pints and dishing out venomous insults like a puff adder, under the watchful eye of Michelle. Steph was gliding around in a black ball gown and wig, sipping Babycham. The buffet was up to the usual low standards that I had come to expect from The Horn of Plenty. It consisted of sausage rolls, vol-au-vents, and mini scotch eggs from the Iceland value range. A lot of it had freezer burn, so I suspected that it was leftovers from last Christmas. I had thought the cheese and pineapple hedgehog was for kitsch effect, so I managed to upset Michelle. He had put a lot of effort into making it, and my scathing comments about his proud creation had not been well received. It was amazing what you could do with a can of Del Monte pineapple chunks and some no-frill's cheddar.

The television was on, and they had piped the sound through an amplifier to lend a theatrical atmosphere to the occasion. It was the first time I had seen the show in its entirety myself. I had seen clips and pre-edited scenes without narration or incidental music, so although I had an idea of what to expect, it was going to be new to me, too. They had filmed the series out of sequence, so I knew my debut episode was going to be a hotel near Cardiff.

Steph had asked me to sit on a high stool next to the television and had provided me with a microphone to voice some additional commentary during the commercial breaks. He had also instructed Dave to provide Graham and I with as many drinks as we wanted, and we were both taking full advantage. It was the first—and I would imagine the last—time that tight cow would put his hand in his pocket. The chairs and tables were arranged cinema style, in a semicircle around me. There was not enough seating for everyone, and some people stood at the back.

The familiar theme music of *Hotel Red Alert* began, played by a string quartet, met with a round of applause from the entire audience. The introduction started.

"Jez Matthews is an award-winning hotelier from Torquay, who single-handedly turned a decrepit Victorian villa which was overdue for demolition into an award-winning, five-star boutique hotel."

It was inevitable that there would be a few spiteful comments from the pub audience, and they did not disappoint.

"Single-handed with the help of a rich boyfriend," said Millicent. Millicent, or Miles as he was actually called, was a bitter queen who had somehow washed up in Torquay in his youth and had never escaped. Now he was old and wrinkled and spent most nights propping up the bar drinking Stella, wondering what had happened to his life.

"Don't worry about that vile queen," said Jason. "Last thing I heard, she'd gotten drug-resistant syphilis from some bear she picked up in a lay-by."

The narrator continued, "From tempestuous thespians, plastic coffins, and all manners of holiday horrors, Jez Matthews brings his expertise to struggling hoteliers and is on a mission to improve standards of hospitality."

The program showed a clip of me lifting up a duvet and sheets to reveal a filthy stained mattress while shaking my head disapprovingly to a round of applause and laughter in the pub. I looked over at Graham, who winked at me encouragingly.

The narrator continued. "Tonight we visit The Gallifreyan Citadel, a three-bedroom bed-and-breakfast just outside Cardiff—a hotel that is literally out of this world."

The music faded into the 'Waaa Waaaaaah' *Doctor Who* theme, and the picture switched to me driving along in a little open-topped sports car that Channel 4 had leased for me. I drove up the hotel's shingled driveway. The flowerbeds were overgrown and full of stinging nettles. The dashboard-mounted car camera showed my surprised face, as I noticed about ten half-size plywood Daleks with lopsided heads and broken suckers on sentry duty on either side of the drive.

Again, there was a roar of laughter from the pub and a shout of, "No way!"

I got out of the car, wearing a designer jacket and jeans. I had picked a different outfit for each episode.

"Well, that's an entrance I won't forget," I said on the show, sarcastically. "I mean, they used to film *Doctor Who* in old quarries, and this certainly looks like a wilderness. Is it deliberate? Perhaps it's laziness that they can't be bothered to mow the lawns and do a bit of weeding."

Next, I was shown walking up to the old stone

farmhouse, which, although neglected, was full of character, made from dark Welsh limestone with a moss-covered slate roof and tiny leaded-light windows. I walked up to the front door. It was painted blue with a homemade sign reading, 'Police Pubic Call Box,' stenciled above. I rang the bell and rolled my eyes as the *Doctor Who* theme tune chimed electronically out of a cheap speaker inside.

"I think they meant public, not pubic," I said sarcastically, pointing at the misspelt sign.

Someone shouted, "Thought this was s'posed to be undercover, where are the camera crew hiding?"

"Yeah!" shouted somebody else.

I spoke into the microphone, and my voice reverberated around the pub. "They filmed these bits afterward, Kyle. It's called editing."

"Shame they couldn't edit out your face," he said evilly.

I ignored it, but Steph gave him a look, which could strike fear in hearts of much braver men than Kyle. He would suffer for that comment later.

The hotel owners, Mike and Shelia, answered the door, and I could sense the reaction from the pub audience, who stared at the screen in open-jawed disbelief. Mike was wearing a long multicolored scarf and hat, inspired by Tom Baker's Doctor. Shelia, his overweight wife, had squeezed herself into a scaly green homemade Ice Warrior suit with red tinted sunglasses. Apparently, Ice Warriors were a race of reptilian soldiers from Mars, bent on galactic conquest. If a spaceship full of what was standing in the doorway arrived on Earth, we would not have much to worry about.

"Good afternoon and welcome to Gallifreyan Citadel in the constellation of Kasterborous, also conveniently situated twenty minutes from the M4," he said. "Don't worry about her, she's harmless."

The papier-mâché Ice Warrior hissed, "Mars shall conquer."

They gave me a cup of 'Usurian' tea with 'Zygon' milk, as they described it.

"Very much like PG Tips," I said onscreen, noting the chipped mug with the *Doctor Who* logo on it.

The secret cameras recorded the check-in, then once alone in my 'Mondas' themed bedroom complete with bits of tin foil stuck randomly on the wall and a pair of what I could only describe as Cyberman fetish outfits in the wardrobe, I set up the HD camera on its tripod and let rip.

"I mean, WHAT THE BLOODY HELL IS GOING ON HERE? This place is a lunatic asylum."

Then the commercial break started, and I received another round of applause. Jason came over with a glass of wine for me and gave me a hug.

"Dollface, you were brilliant," he said. "Remember me on the way up. I always remember those that have been up me."

I was suddenly surrounded by twenty or more queens clamoring for my attention. All of them were gushing with praise.

The broadcast continued. There were claps, whoops, 'oh my God's, and raucous laughter. I knew that it had been well received, and I knew that I had made my stamp on the program. I also knew that life would never be the same again.

The hotel newspapers were delivered the following morning. I had ordered extra copies of *The Guardian*, *The Mail*, and *The Times*, as Bill had told me that there would be reviews by television critics. I also bought *The Sun* and *The Daily Mirror*. My experience of unpleasant online reviews about our hotel had mentally prepared me for what I knew would inevitably come, so I braced myself as I sat down with Graham at the kitchen table after serving breakfast.

Sreeta Malik from *The Guardian* gave me five stars in her 'Last Night's TV' column. In a short article, she wrote:

Jez Matthews, the undercover hotel detective, has taken the program in a radical direction, breathing new life into a tired format. With his pithy put-downs sometimes bordering on camp, he is often outrageous but invariably funny. Not standing for any nonsense, he soon exterminated the apathy from Shelia and Mike, who were using up their savings to subsidize their failing business. Their Doctor Who-themed hotel was an interesting if not eccentric idea but poorly executed. A lack of attention to detail combined with poor marketing was quickly diagnosed with his astringent put downs, tempered by gentle encouragement. Putting aside the often-scathing humor, Mr. Matthews' passion for the industry shines through. Whilst I enjoyed his disparagement of the strange couple running this odd business near Cardiff, he was never cruel and displayed a genuine desire to help. A reassuring written message at the end of the broadcast stated The Gallifreyan Citadel had been receiving favorable comments on review websites, and bookings were fifty percent up since the show had been recorded.

I smiled and handed the paper to Graham, who read it approvingly. *The Times*, *The Sun*, and *The Mirror* also contained complimentary articles. It was only the *Daily Mail* that stuck in the knife, courtesy of Carol Thompson.

Her article was entitled: "Does Britain really need another camp TV presenter?"

I would not have minded so much, if I *were* camp. She then went on and used her column to write an acrimonious passage spewing vitriol all over the page:

When I filmed my third and final series of Hotel Red Alert, *I gritted my teeth until the end. A program that started as innovative and groundbreaking descended into farce, despite my best efforts. The last series slipped into a lethargic, repetitive routine regurgitating the same laborious weekly format. I was often ashamed to have my name associated with it. This dinosaur should have been made extinct when I quit, but Channel 4, ever hungry for a cheap buck, commissioned a new series. Now it is hosted by the ridiculously camp and rather silly Jez Matthews, 38. His cheap, arrogant shots at the owners of the failing Gallifreyan Citadel Hotel were both tiresome and cruel. He shows little comprehension of the basics of hoteling, and his barbarous and constant derision of the near-destitute owners made for uncomfortable watching. I hope for the sake of the viewing public that Jez Matthews' television career is a short one.*

My blood boiled as I read it, but Graham reassured me. "She's riled, because you're two hundred times better than her."

"I've never seen so much venom printed on a page."

"It's the *Daily Mail*, what do you expect?"

"Yes, but Graham, it's not about you. Imagine how you'd feel if you were me?"

"Just rise above it."

"How can they be allowed to print such rubbish? It's just vindictive. And she deliberately got my age wrong, by five years, the silly tart. She knows full well I'm not thirty-eight. I barely look thirty. I don't spend thousands every year on moisturizing products to hear things like that!"

"You're in the public eye now. This won't be the first time you get something horrid written about you. Besides,

Carol Thompson has done herself more harm by writing that. She just comes across as bitter."

I knew that Graham was right, of course, but I was enraged by Carol Thompson's rant. It rattled me and knocked my confidence. However, later in the week, the viewing figures were released. Carol Thompson had been averaging about 1.5 million viewers; on my debut show, I achieved an audience of 2.8 million. This was nearly double. The first episode received an unprecedented eighty-two percent approval rating on TVyousay.com. It seemed that Graham and the critics were right, and Carol Thompson was wrong. I was talented, and I had a great future in television.

My life had indeed changed beyond recognition. Torquay was a small town, and I was their homegrown star. Everybody it seemed now recognized me as I walked down the street. In particular, I was popular with old ladies who always stopped me, wanting to chat. The mayor of Torquay called to wish me well. The flip side of it all was it became impossible to go out for a quiet drink in the town without people wanting photographs on their mobile phones. I had to watch my behavior in public, which meant drinking responsibly and not letting the occasional heckler wind me up too much.

The Horn of Plenty offered a safe haven, though; Michelle and Steph protected me as best they could, and I could enjoy a drink or two without being too bothered by unwanted attention.

I started getting fan mail. Some of it was via Channel 4, though often it was sent directly to the hotel. Whilst it was concerning that so many people knew where I lived, I understood that it was an inescapable consequence of having the hotel plugged on the program credits. It was easy for people to obtain the hotel email address, so I had the mammoth task of sorting through the emails. Most of the messages I received were complimentary, though it rapidly became tedious to sift through them all. Inevitably, some of it was nasty, including a loathsome note from a *Doctor Who* fan who claimed I had been disrespectful about Jon Pertwee's hairstyle and thus deserved to die.

I also acquired a stalker. He was a lonely gay man who sent me pictures of his genitalia with a page full of pornographic sentences about his fantasies. He clearly got some kind of a kick out of it. I just threw them away. Even more worrying was that I received letters from female fans that sent photos of their vaginas. It felt a bit like being flashed by a stranger in the park. I received a pair of knickers and a proposal of marriage. I acquired the granny brigade admirers. I received numerous knitted items from this section of the audience, including a jumper with a picture of a fried egg and a sausage embroidered on it. At least, that is what I thought it was.

Despite the minor drawback of receiving dubious knitwear, I would not have traded my new life for anything.

Chapter 44

September 1975: Marjorie Wilson

The weekend arrived and I was looking forward to seeing Stanley, who had been away in London all week. During the summer parliamentary recess, our family life had regained a sense of normality. Since parliament had recalled, I found it difficult waving him off every Sunday as he commuted to London. It was only five days, but prior to Stanley becoming an MP, we had not spent more than a day apart since our wedding.

I heard him pull up the driveway at a quarter to ten, having suffered extensive delays due to the road resurfacing work on the A380. He looked exhausted and disheveled. Torquay was still attracting large numbers of holidaymakers wanting to escape from the oppressive heat in the cities. Whilst that was good for business, it meant that the roads struggled to cope with the high volume of cars. The situation was worsened, due to the fact that every utility company seemed to want to dig up the streets.

"Go and get out of your work clothes and take a shower," I said. "There'll be a gin and tonic waiting for you in the bar. I want to hear all about your week."

"Yes, mein Fraulein," he said, doing as he was told.

Ten minutes later, he came downstairs wearing beige corduroys and a casual short-sleeved shirt.

"Your dinner's a little dry," I said. "I was expecting you back at nine, so it's been in the oven for an hour."

"No problem," he said. "What is it?"

"Pork chops and mash."

"You do spoil me. That's my favorite."

He finished his gin quickly, and we went into the kitchen together.

"Where's Christopher?" he asked.

"Amateur Dramatics. They're rehearsing *The Pirates of Penzance*. He's playing the pirate queen."

"Don't you mean king?"

"I wish I did. They've adapted it somewhat."

Stanley rolled his eyes at me. "Well, at least he's not down at that God-awful pub."

"So tell me about life in London," I said. "I tried calling you on Thursday, but there was no reply."

"Sorry, love, I worked late. I meant to call you, but, well, you know how it is."

"My husband, the Member of Parliament for Torquay," I said proudly.

We sat and chatted. He seemed a bit detached, but I put it down to a hard week, followed by a long commute home. I had to leave Stanley, as I had some guests waiting at the bar who wanted a nightcap. When I finally locked up, Stanley had gone to bed and was snoring loudly. I changed into my nightdress and snuggled up to him, but he pushed me away.

The following morning, we served breakfast to the guests as normal. Afterward, we sat down at the kitchen table to enjoy some scrambled eggs on toast. Stanley still seemed to be a little cool toward me. An outsider would not have noticed as he remained courteous, but I had been married to Stanley for over twenty-five years. His body language was standoffish, and he did not make conversation in his customary way. My questions received monosyllabic answers, and I instinctively knew when something was not right.

"Have I done anything wrong, dear?" I asked.

"Hmph," he replied.

"Come on, dear. I've been married to you for too long not to know when something isn't right. Please tell me what's wrong? Have I done something to upset you?"

"Oh, nothing much, love, only murdering our next-door neighbor and burying the body in our garden along with some poor waif whom our homosexual son Christopher picked up in the middle of the night on Daddyhole Plain."

"Don't be beastly, dear."

"Beastly? I find you incredible. You have murdered a poor woman in cold blood, yet you carry on with your embroidering and cake baking as though nothing has happened. Two people are dead—does that mean nothing to you?"

"The first one was the house. It was looking after Christopher. Lady Elizabeth thinks the world of him."

"The house? What are you talking about, woman? Will you please stop this nonsense!?"

"It's not nonsense. He was a criminal. The spirits were looking after your flesh and blood. You should be a little bit more grateful. They don't ask for much."

"Now listen here, the only spirits in this house are in bottles behind the bar."

"Christopher has seen them, and so have I. They talk to us."

"Please, Marje—I can't go on like this. You need help. I'll call Doctor Woodfield tomorrow. I'm sure he can prescribe something to—"

"It's true! They show themselves from time to time. You don't know how much we both owe them. Your political career for starters."

"What are you saying, they won me the election?"

"Well, no, but Martin's death was a little unexpected, don't you think?"

"Please don't tell me you had something to do with that."

"No, of course I didn't, not directly, at least."

"Well, that's something."

"But I think Lady Elizabeth did. I don't know for sure, though. Her influence is mainly confined to the house, but I know she used to walk on Ilsham Green. She keeps her cards close to her chest."

"This is like living in a lunatic asylum. Who have I been married to all these years? What is going on here?"

"We are fulfilling our destiny," I said. "From the moment we viewed this house, I knew we were meant for great things. The house protects us. It nurtures us. It has been here for over one hundred years. We are becoming part of its history. Don't you understand?"

"I can't listen to this rubbish anymore. I've had enough," said Stanley. "I'm going for a very long walk."

Stanley put on a jacket and stormed out of the hotel, slamming the front door behind him. Elsie came into the kitchen.

"Is everything all right, Mrs. Wilson?"

"Not really, Elsie, but I'm sure it will be."

"Let me make you a nice pot of fresh tea."

"You are kind, but I've a mountain of paperwork and Stanley's washing and ironing to do. If you could start the rooms, I'll come up shortly to supervise."

I brought down the laundry basket from our bedroom and started loading Stanley's whites into the twin tub. Then I came across a shirt, which had what looked like a bloodstain on the collar. I assumed that Stanley had cut himself whilst shaving. I put it in the sink to rub it with some laundry soap and give it a presoak. It was then that I realized it was not blood. It was lipstick, and the shirt also reeked of perfume. I recognized the scent immediately. It was the fragrance that Rebecca Waters wore. I scrunched up the shirt angrily in my hands and threw it to the ground. Everything suddenly started to make sense. Stanley's mood swings, his changed attitude toward me, and my midweek phone calls being ignored. I felt anguish, followed by disbelief at his betrayal. How could he do this to us, to me, after all that we had been through together? Then I felt a fury beyond anything I had ever felt in my life. I let out an angry scream and collapsed to my knees, sobbing into my hands.

Chapter 45

April 2007: Jez Matthews

I was due in London to meet Jim Lockton for my publicity interview. This was hugely exciting for me, as I was a tremendous fan of his television chat show. *Attitude* magazine had also been in contact via my agent. They wanted to do a topless photo shoot of me with an accompanying article about the show. It was going to be whimsically titled "Between the sheets with Jez Matthews!" I was supposed to have photos taken in a five-star hotel holding a pillow over my privates, among other things. They said that I would "put the pecs into peak time television." I was also doing something similar with *Heat* magazine to appeal to bored housewives and the like.

I was concerned as to whether this kind of publicity would demean the series, but Bill had said to go for it. Apparently, I had the looks and the body, so I might as well flaunt it, and they had been doing it on Emmerdale for years. Diamond Aspect took the view that it would widen the gay fan base of the show. It felt a little like prostituting myself, and I was self-conscious over having my semi-naked torso on the front of a popular magazine. However, my agent had negotiated me a fee of £15,000 for a day's work, so I could hardly say no. I had spent many hours in the gym to prepare for it.

I caught the fast train up to London on Tuesday. I spent the morning in Harvey Nichols choosing an outfit for the show. In the evening, I arranged to meet Brett, my dealer. He waited for me in a tatty backstreet pub, near to Covent Garden. We sorted the money out over a pint, and we exchanged the goods in the gent's toilets. Apparently, the pub landlord was tolerant of this behavior. He sold me enough coke to see me through the TV show and the photo shoot, plus a bit extra to take home. Additionally, he gave me some cannabis that he suggested would help to alleviate the comedowns from the cocaine. It did not even cross my mind what would happen if I were discovered with it all. I had never dabbled with narcotics before; this was a learning experience for me. I had always been judgmental of people who used drugs and even a little afraid. However, I now understood why they were so popular.

Filming was on Wednesday for airing the following evening on BBC2. The photo shoot with *Attitude* was on Friday. I stayed at the Travelodge near to Oxford Circus. Sadly, showbiz was not all glamour and meals at The Ivy. Channel 4 were as tight as a badger's butt, and it was all about money onscreen. The lucrative employment was from the spin-off assignments and hopefully the endorsements that my agent was currently negotiating. I was hoping to be the new face for Shake 'n Vac carpet freshener.

I caught a Bakerloo line tube train to Waterloo, where they recorded the Alan Lockton show at London Studios. In the capital, people were much less bothered about seeing a television presenter. I received a few curious glances as I went about my business, but nobody maintained eye contact for more than a few seconds. I guessed I was small fry compared to some of the A-list celebrities who lived here.

Once I had negotiated the tight security at the studios, a stocky man led me to my dressing room. This sounded sophisticated, but it was an unheated box room, with a Formica dressing table, a coat rail, and a shabby chair with foam spewing out of the ripped cushion. The floor was worn linoleum, and there was a strong stench of stale cigarette smoke partially masked by a synthetic pine scent from a plug-in air freshener. I wondered if Jim Lockton's A-list guests had to endure these conditions. I doubted it.

A friendly girl knocked on the door and came into my room, asking me if I wanted anything. I requested a cafe latte. A few minutes later, she came back with a plastic cup of foul vending machine coffee. She told me that she would take me to make-up in an hour.

After ten minutes, there was another knock on the door. A different girl came in and introduced herself as Sharon before handing me a short note.

"It's from Sir Jim," she said. "I'll wait outside and take you to see him when you're ready."

"I didn't realize he had been given a knighthood."

"He hasn't," she said. "But he says that he should have, and it's probably only a matter of time, so that's how he likes to be addressed."

I managed to decipher the untidy handwriting that was almost illegible. The note was written in a rather imperious tone and read, "You are summoned to my dressing room in fifteen minutes. Do not be late!"

Sharon led me to Jim Lockton's dressing room. She instructed me not to say anything at all until Sir Jim spoke to me. She knocked on his door, and a surprisingly deep voice answered, which did not sound anything like the camp Irish comic that I felt I knew and loved.

"Come in!"

I walked into a room of almost palatial proportions. I felt like Alice in Wonderland. There were curtains of fairy lights hanging from the ceiling, faux leopard-skin rugs on the floor, and two luxurious sofas arranged around a frosted glass coffee table. The walls were adorned with dozens of signed and framed pictures of the guests Jim had interviewed over the years. The large window at the far end of the room afforded magnificent views of London. Jim was sitting with his back to me on what I can only describe as a throne. It was ornate and gold in color with rich red fabric. I saw a small disembodied hand extend from in front of the high back and point silently toward the sofa. I sat down as gestured. The hand retracted and picked up a bone china cup and saucer from the dressing table. He took a sip, then put it back. The throne turned around slowly, with a quiet whir from the electric motors. It resembled a scene from James Bond. Jim Lockton sat in his huge ornate electronic chair, like Blofeld but without the cat, the threatening demeanor, piranhas, bald head, or the scar. He was smaller in person than I had imagined him to be and wore one of his trademark flamboyant suits.

"Jez Matthews," he said in his soft Irish tone. "Can I tempt you to a matchmaker?"

He pressed a button on one of the arms of his throne, and a box of chocolate mint matchmakers in a polished silver box rose out from the coffee table.

"Thank you," I said, and bit into a chocolate twig.

"So, you're the new kid on the block, the rising star of Channel 4," he said. "I saw your show last week. Would you like to know what I thought?"

"Yes, I would love to," I said, nervously.

He placed a matchmaker delicately into his mouth and bit off the end. He crunched on it slowly before gradually feeding the rest in. "I think you are an extraordinarily talented young man who will go very far," he said deliberately.

"You've no idea what that means to me, Jim—erm, Sir Jim Lockton."

"You suit that program format perfectly," he said.

"Thank you."

"I don't think that chat shows would be your bag, though—that's presenting them, not appearing in them."

"Well, I mean, I've no plans. I've never thought about it."

"Good," said Jim, his voice softening. "Then I'm sure we will get on famously."

"I hope so. I mean, I'm a huge fan."

"I need to ask you a question. What are your thoughts of the other one?"

"What do you mean by the other one?"

"My nemesis," he said in a menacing voice. "He calls himself Alan Carr."

"Well, I mean, he's quite good, too, but not in your league."

Jim smiled. "Oh, you and I are going to have fun tonight."

He clicked his finger, and the runner entered the dressing room nervously.

"Take him to make-up," he ordered.

She curtseyed and led me out.

I sat in a chair similar to the ones that they have in barber shops, as the chatty make-up girl brushed foundation over my face, talking about some of the famous people that she had met.

"And Brad was marvelous," she said. "He was a

gentleman. Keanu, on the other hand, terrible flirt and kept belching."

I switched my mind off and listened to her vacillate, wondering when the optimal time would be to take a couple of lines. In the end, I managed to get a toilet break ten minutes before I was called to the sofa.

I panicked at first as I thought I had left my stash in my other jacket but was relieved to find that I had stored it in my inside pocket. I snorted a couple of lines, ignoring the tingling sensation that I knew would soon fade to be replaced by a wonderful head rush.

I shared the sofa with a presenter of a popular motoring show, plugging his new series, and a retired actress from *Coronation Street* promoting her spill-all autobiography.

Filming the show was possibly the most euphoric couple of hours of my life. As the effects of the cocaine kicked in, I exuded confidence and charm. The guests I sat next to were far more famous than I, but I viewed them as equals. The audience loved me. Jim was fantastic at weeding out little anecdotes and stories in his wickedly camp manner. He was particularly good at extracting the more racy tales, or perhaps sleazy might be a better adjective. I did a great sales job on *Hotel Red Alert*, essentially by just telling the truth about the mad hotel proprietors I had met and about life in my own hotel. I even received grudging respect from the car program presenter, who had a reputation for being difficult.

Afterward, Sir Jim invited me out to the Shadow Lounge in Soho, where Graham and I had met all those years ago. Apart from a total refit, new bar staff, and a different cocktail list, it had barely changed. We drank champagne until the early hours, interspersed with me sniffing up lines of charlie in the toilets every now and then. It was a great evening full of laughter, and I hoped he would stay in touch. At three in the morning, we caught separate taxis, and I headed back to the Travelodge, wide-awake. I thought about having another line when I got into my room, but when I checked my pockets, I realized that I had snorted the whole lot. That was £100 gone in one night. I messaged Brett and asked him to meet me in the morning to replenish my supply, before the photo shoot. I went into the bathroom to brush my teeth and looked at my bloodshot eyes.

"Let's hope they can Photoshop that out," I said to myself.

I found some tranquilizers in my wash bag and swallowed triple the prescribed dose. Finally, around four in the morning, I fell into a drunken, drug-induced sleep.

Chapter 46

September 1975: Marjorie Wilson

Stanley was gone almost all day. He returned at half-past eight, stinking of beer and cigarettes. He entered the kitchen to find me cooking evening meals for the guests.

"You've been to the pub then?" I said. "You've come back for your dinner, I suppose?"

"I've been driven to drink," he said. "Pushed into it by a mad woman who is living in my house. Forced to do it to block out the voices in my head and the pictures in my mind of Mavis lying on the ground in a pool of blood. To forget the sight of her brains spilling out of her skull."

"You say you no longer know me. Well, you're not the Stanley I married either."

"Now what are you talking about?"

"Was she worth it?"

I looked at Stanley and felt only hatred. I lost self-control and slapped him across the face.

"You *filthy rascal*!" I shouted. "Did you think I wouldn't recognize her perfume or notice the lipstick?"

"Marje, please, this is not getting us anywhere."

"I've been through your wallet and found the receipts for two tickets to the theatre and dinners for two. Who did you go with? That Rebecca woman, wasn't it?"

"Do you really need to ask me that?"

"Now you listen here, Stanley Lawrence Wilson. On Monday, you will sack Rebecca Waters first thing. You will have no further contact with her from then on. Do I make myself clear?"

"Perfectly, and I'm not going to do it, or anything else you ask from this day forward."

"You will do as you are told!"

"Now it's your turn to listen to me. I can't live like this anymore. Rebecca has been like a rock to me these last few months. Despite what you think, we have not slept with each other. We are colleagues. We work closely together, and over the months our friendship has strengthened. Yes, if I'm honest, I hope we become lovers at some point, but whatever happens between Rebecca and I is none of your damn business."

"But I am your wife!" I said angrily.

"In name only," he said. "I know this is hard, and it's hurtful for me to say it—but the truth is, I no longer have feelings for you, Marjorie. You destroyed this marriage during that horrid night in May. You have to understand. We cannot go on like this."

"And what do you think the police would say if I were to tell them about the bodies under the patio?"

"Now you're being stupid. I know you too well. You do that, and it's over for all of us. Besides, it was you that killed Mavis, not Christopher or I. Christopher will vouch for that if it comes to it."

"Try me."

"I want a divorce. You can have the hotel, our savings, the lot. I'll start afresh in London."

"And what will all our friends say about this? What will the newspapers make of it, our friends at the conservative club?"

"Marje, it's the 1970s, not the 1900s. People get divorced. If you want to make it acrimonious, that's up to you—or we can do it in as a dignified way as possible."

"And you think this creature that's nearly twenty years your junior will stay with you, iron your shirts, put up with your bad hygiene, your drinking and smoking."

"This is not about her. It's about you and me. It's over. I wish I'd had the courage to do this months ago."

I picked up a glass tumbler and threw it at Stanley, who ducked, and it smashed into pieces against the kitchen wall.

"You are feeble, Stanley, a weak, foolish man. Do you think this house will let you go so easily after all it has done for you?"

"I'm going to stay in room three tonight. We'll talk again in the morning before I head back to London. Now for pity's sake, calm down and get these meals served."

Stanley walked out of the kitchen, and I burst into tears as the reality of the situation sunk in. The fluorescent lights flickered off, and the room became cold. A shadowy figure slowly faded into view beside me radiating a luminous glow that cast eerie shadows across the walls.

"Lady Elizabeth," I said monotonously.

"You poor dear," she said comfortingly. "Please don't be too upset, we have a plan."

"You can speak to me whilst showing yourself now," I said.

"It takes time to build trust," she said. "And I trust you, Marjorie. You have proven yourself to me, to us. Absolutely."

I nodded slowly. "I love him, Elizabeth."

"I know you do," she said

"He can't leave me, not for her, please, not for her."

"Have faith," she whispered, before dissolving into the shadows.

The lights came back on. Christopher walked into the kitchen.

"Is everything all right, Mum?" he asked. "I heard shouting."

"Yes, everything is fine, Christopher. It's just your dad being silly. You know he can explode sometimes for no reason."

"So long as you're okay..."

"I'll be fine, love. You go back to your bedsit. I can manage tonight."

I took a deep breath and plated up the shepherd's pie and vegetables. I served the guests in the dining room, my inner turmoil disguised behind a warm smile.

Chapter 47

October 2007: Jez Matthews
The morning sun shining through the cracks in the curtains woke me.

"Happy birthday, sexy," said Graham, leaning over me in bed pinning my arms back against the pillow. He planted a big kiss on my forehead.

"Thirty-four," I said. "I feel bloody ancient."

"Wait until you hit forty. It's all downhill from there, darling."

"It's been a long time since we had a party," I said. "I'm looking forward to it."

When we moved to Torquay, many of our London friends had abandoned us. However, since my appearance on national television and on magazine covers, they seemed to have miraculously remembered how to use the telephone.

I had joined a new and rapidly growing website called Facebook and had somehow accumulated four thousand friends in a month. I had no idea who most of them were. A man called Greg Clarke sent me a friend request, then followed it up with an email about how he had never forgotten our time together. I studied his photo and I racked my brains, as I had no recollection of who he was. Then I realized that I met him in a seedy nightclub in Hammersmith, fifteen years ago. We had spoken for about an hour and had a quick fumble on the night bus home. Weird, but it meant a lot to him that I had accepted his request.

As well as *Hotel Red Alert*, which had achieved incredible viewing figures and rated as one of Channel 4's top programs, I did a lot of promotional work for the show on radio and television. It was all great fun. I was also the new face of Shake and Vac carpet freshener, following my agent's successful negotiation. I starred in a series of adverts, sprinkling it over big rugs in stately homes, vacuuming it up, then stating in a camp voice, "That's put the freshness back, darling." Apparently, the brand managers said that sales had soared. Dale Winton was livid, as he was their second choice.

It was all a bit silly, really, except the money was no laughing matter. Rita, my agent, was negotiating ridiculous fees for my doing very little work, and my bank balance was swelling. The promotion and spin-off work paid many times more than Channel 4. Graham was the sensible one of course and had insisted that we pay off the capital on the mortgage and invest in ISAs because we did not know how long it would all last. I let him take care of that side; after all, he was the financial man. I enjoyed fame; I discovered that it opened doors, quite literally. I enjoyed royal treatment in restaurants and could get into The Ivy at short notice when I was in London, but the disadvantage was that I had very little privacy. Nearly everybody these days seemed to have cameras on their mobile phones, and I would be minding my own business browsing through magazines in WHSmiths, and there would be somebody taking a photograph. My high profile necessitated that I was discreet in my dealings with Brett. It seemed that I needed a regular supply of coke to see me through filming. I did not have a habit, as I knew that I could stop any time I wanted, but I did not see the point.

The celebrity lifestyle and cocaine went hand in hand, and everybody did it. My on-screen performances were enhanced by the confidence it gave me. If it started to become an addiction, I would cut down.

During a week with no commitments, a few lines a day would be enough. When filming or holding a party like today, I would want considerably more to keep me on top form. When I was not traveling to London for a while, Brett would journey to Torquay to keep me supplied. I would usually meet him somewhere discreet like the toilets on Meadfoot beach. My doctor was also good. He realized that my sleep suffered from my workload and kept writing me repeat prescriptions for my sleeping pills and tranquilizers.

Graham had planned a big party for me. We had shut the hotel over the weekend, and we had invited about seventy people. We had the usual contingent from the pub, including Jason, a few of our London friends, and the odd celebrity. We had employed caterers, who had prepared a hog roast among other things, and Graham had arranged for the waiting staff to be dressed in fabulous Louis XV footman outfits, complete with high boots and white wigs. A staging company had dressed the hotel in voile drapes and fairy lights in a winter wonderland theme, and the local florist had created some amazing horticultural and balloon displays. A checkered dance floor had been laid in the drawing room and we had a disco later, hosted by Steph, the pub landlord. He had brought up his karaoke equipment. So long as we could keep him reasonably sober, we would be okay. However, it was a vain wish, as he was knocking back the champagne like lemonade. He was attempting to practice his signature tune, Neil Diamond's "Love on the Rocks". He was wearing an outrageous frilly red and white dress, or "strawberries and cream," as he described it. We all knew that the more he drank, the bitchier he would become, and he would try to steal the show if I let him. His partner, Michelle, was looking after the pub, but would come to the party later. The rest of the guests started arriving at about seven. Jason was first, in case the free bar ran dry. For some reason, he thought it was fancy dress and had come as Michael Jackson. I think that was Graham's idea of a joke. Always on the prowl for sex, he had homed in on one of the poor waiters. Thomas was a young, pimply lad in his late teens on a gap year before starting at Bristol University. Graham felt a paternal need to rescue the poor sod and guided him gently away from Jason's clutches.

I was thoroughly enjoying all the attention and flitted from one group of friends to another. As the champagne dissolved barriers, people were beginning to drift out of their cliques. There was an eclectic mix of friends whom I did not think would mix particularly well, but everybody seemed to get on famously.

There were some old friends whom I had not seen for years that I knew from my art course at Leeds Metropolitan University. They were looking older and far more respectable than when I used to know them. They were all smartly dressed and had normal hairstyles, in contrast to the dyed and weirdly sculpted cuts that we all used to sport in the name of art. There were only a few hints of their previous rebellious student lives in the shape of semi-healed ear and nose piercings. Most of them had wives, husbands, or partners, and a few of them had produced offspring.

We all had a good catch up, reminiscing over old times. Some of them were aware of the new Facebook website, so we all promised that we would 'friend request' each other. We also reaffirmed our commitment to the well-intentioned, but so far unrealized plan of having an annual reunion.

Our London friends included some ex-colleagues of Graham's. Unfortunately, he had invited his ex-boss, Robo-bitch Theresa. She stood alone, sipping cordial and bewildered by the fact that people were enjoying themselves without discussing business deals or office politics. Most people seemed to be scared of her. A few of our old drinking buddies from our nights out in Soho were also there. Our friends were standing around, admiring the hotel and slightly bemused by Steph's drunken efforts at being a DJ and lounge singer. Naturally, they all hated Torquay, which they thought was far too parochial and the shopping dreadful. It did not occur to them to go for a walk around the coastal paths or appreciate the natural beauty of the place. Many had booked into Green Palms Guesthouse for the sole reason that they had seen it on television when Carol Thompson was presenting *Hotel Red Alert*, and it was every bit as awful as they had had imagined, despite having new owners. However, I think the irony was that it was so bad it was good.

Every hour or so, I would slip away to take some coke that I had stashed in the medicine cabinet, which would fuel my confidence and conversational abilities. All my party guests wanted to know about *Hotel Red Alert*, and I embellished the filming stories to make out my life to be far more glamorous than it was in reality.

As people became progressively inebriated, they started to dance and try karaoke. I debuted with a reasonable attempt at The Proclaimers' song "I Would Walk 500 Miles", complete with air guitar gestures, and I managed to get the audience involved.

"You were good," said Theresa. "It's agreeable to see you. Happy Birthday."

"Why don't you have a go?" I asked. "You might enjoy it."

"No, thank you," she said icily. "I like to watch."

"Observe, you mean," I said, walking away.

Jason, who had always adamantly refused to have anything to do with karaoke since our duet of "Hopelessly Devoted to You" had consumed so much champagne that he decided to try again. I hope that it was the last time that he ever would sing in public. He destroyed Michael Jackson's "Bad", both musically and visually, with his failed attempt at moonwalking.

Graham came over to chat to me.

"What an awesome party!" he said, shouting over Alison Moyet's "All Cried Out".

"It's brilliant," I said, planting a kiss on his cheek. "Thank you so much for doing a great job of organizing it."

A waiter topped up our glasses.

"I don't know where you get your energy from," said Graham.

"What do you mean?"

"It's like you're on speed or something, just chatting away from person to person. It's great to see you having so much fun."

"Ha ha, as if I'd ever take drugs. It's just great to see our friends, old and new, you did so well to arrange it all."

"Well, it was easy, really, round robin email, sorted in a day. Everyone wants to meet the TV star. Anyway, come with me!"

Graham took my hand, led me towards the raised stage, and took the microphone from Steph, who faded out the music.

"I know you weren't expecting this, Jez, and I apologize in advance, but I'm going to embarrass you," he said, his voice reverberating around the room.

The party guests gathered around us, looking on curiously.

"Oh, God," I said nervously.

"Ladies and gentleman—and Steph—if I could please have your attention. I hope you are all enjoying the party. As you all know, Jez and I have been an item for twelve years now, and I think this is very overdue."

Graham bent down on one knee and took a small box out of his trouser pocket.

I gasped. "Oh, Graham..."

He opened it. Inside, there was a platinum band with six square diamonds set into the metal. It was a bit showy but still masculine enough for me to wear.

"Jez Matthews, would you do me the honor of becoming my civil partner?"

"Yes, of course I would," I said tearfully. "I love you so much."

Graham slid the ring onto my fourth finger then stood up and held me tightly.

"Thank God it fits," he whispered in my ear. "I had to take a guess on the size!"

"It must have cost you a fortune. It's lovely!"

"Thank Anderson Levy."

Steph took the microphone from him. "And who said romance was dead?" he slurred. "Let's have a round of applause for the happy couple."

Everybody present clapped and cheered. Steph put on "Tale as old as Time", from the Disney musical *Beauty and the Beast*, and almost managed to sing in tune. It sounded vaguely like Angela Lansbury, after she had smoked twenty cigarettes. Graham and I slow danced along with the other couples. I felt a happiness and contentment that I had never felt before in my life. As the song reached the final verse, Steph stopped singing and announced.

"Ooh, I wasn't expecting this. Look over there everyone, we've got strippers!"

Two drop-dead gorgeous men in high-visibility police jackets walked onto the dance floor and approached Steph. "Ooh, Officer," he said. "Show me your truncheon!"

"Bloody hell, Graham, I can't wait to see those two with their kit off!" shouted Jason.

"I don't understand," said Graham, looking confused.

"You've arranged two strippers," I said, drunkenly. "They're quite fit, too. Little bit tacky, but I don't mind!"

"I haven't arranged anything. I bet you it's that cow next door that's complained about the noise, the interfering old bat."

Steph gave one of the police officers the microphone, and at his behest turned off the music. The room fell into an uncomfortable silence as the party guests waited to see whether an act was about to start or hear what the police officer was going to say.

"Ladies and gentleman, I'm sorry to say that the party is over. If you could leave by the front door in an orderly fashion, and give your names to the WPC there."

Two police officers walked over to me. One was in uniform and the other was a plain-clothes officer, wearing a gray polyester suit. The suited officer waved his warrant card in front of me.

"Detective Inspector Willets, CID," he said.

I was conscious that everybody in the room was looking at me. I recognized DC Ward among the police officers from the house visit a few months ago.

He continued. "You are Mr. Jeremy Thomas Matthews?"

"Yes," I said, trembling.

"I'm arresting you on suspicion of the murders of Kristyna Chladek and Lukas Kopecky."

There was a collective gasp as I looked around furtively.

He continued, "You do not have to say anything, but it may harm your defense if you do not mention when questioned something that you later rely on in court. Anything you do say may be used in evidence against you."

Events seemed to be unfolding in slow motion, like a nightmare that I wanted to wake up from.

Graham looked at me in disbelief and turned to the officers. "This is some kind of joke, right?"

"I wish it were, sir."

"Graham, do something!" I pleaded.

The uniformed officer pushed my face against the wall and cuffed me.

"Is that necessary?" said Graham. "I mean, he's hardly going to run off."

"Standard procedure, sir," he said gruffly. "We don't make exceptions for C-list celebrities."

"How dare you!" I said indignantly. "I'm on prime-time television."

Steph got back on stage and took the microphone from the officer.

"Well, what a fantastic finale," he announced, pointing at one of the officers. "Aren't you a honey? Any chance I could have your number, constable?"

The police officer did not look remotely amused and pointed to his wedding ring.

Steph started playing and singing the Roy Orbison song, "It's Over", before a policeman pulled the plug.

"Inappropriate, Steph, enough is enough," said Graham. "Please, can everyone just leave?"

"Are you okay?" said Jason, whilst texting furiously. "I mean, what's going on? Murder? I don't get it—"

"Jason, do me a favor and fuck off," said Graham.

The police started to lead me away. "Do you know who I am?" I said angrily. "I am Channel 4's greatest new talent. You have no right to treat me this way!"

"This way, Mr. Matthews. Let's not make a fuss now," said the uniformed officer.

"Graham, stop them. They can't do this."

Graham just looked at me in disbelief, and I realized that even he could not get me out of this one.

"Is there anything I can do, Graham?" asked Theresa.

"Didn't anybody hear me?" shouted Graham, ignoring her. "Please everybody leave, *now*!"

People started milling out of the hotel, chatting earnestly. A plain-clothes officer came over to speak to Graham.

"You are Graham Austen? Mr. Matthew's partner, I believe? You are not formally under arrest at this stage," he said. "However, you will be required to help us in our inquiries. You will need to come down to the station with us so we can take a statement."

"This is all some terrible mistake," said Graham, sobbing now. "Jez wouldn't hurt a soul."

The scene outside the hotel was like that of a movie set. In addition to a police Transit van, there were two liveried cars with their blue lights strobing in the darkness against the painted walls of the building. Four forensic officers in white medical gowns were standing next to an unmarked BMW estate, unloading their scientific equipment. Lastly, the press was there. Presumably, somebody in the police had given them a tip off. There were numerous camera flashes and shouts from the news reporters covering the story.

I was bundled into the back of a police van in handcuffs. Inside, they locked me into a tiny cage that smelt of sick with barely enough room to sit. My cocaine-warped mind was working overtime. What did they know? Did they have any evidence? Could I talk my way out of this, or should I tell the truth? After all, it was a terrible accident, and Lukas had talked me into hiding the body... Would they believe me?

Chapter 48

September 1975: Stanley Wilson
I drove back to London on Sunday. Leaving Marjorie behind in her emotional state was not easy, as I am not devoid of compassion. However, I felt as if a heavy burden had been lifted from my shoulders. It was the right thing to do, no matter how difficult a decision it had been. I had concerns over Christopher as I did not have a chance to speak to him. It would not be easy to break the news to him, as he was a sensitive young man. I am sure that Marjorie would stick the knife in. At least he was no longer a child, and he could form his own opinions as to why our marriage had failed.

I arrived at the flat late in the afternoon after another horrendous journey. The traffic was terrible, particularly around Stonehenge, and the car was baking hot. I took a shower as soon as I walked through the front door and changed into some summer clothes. I sat down at the writing bureau and telephoned Rebecca.

"Rebecca, it's Stanley."

"Hello."

"I have some important news. I've ended my marriage with Marjorie. I'm filing for a divorce."

"This all seems a bit sudden. Is this because of me?"

"Partly, yes, but it was over anyway. I couldn't live the lie anymore, telling myself this was the way all marriages were. It had become a loveless business partnership, and we were barely tolerating one another."

"Have you thought this through properly?"

"I haven't done anything but think it through for the last five months! It isn't a decision I've taken lightly."

"Maybe I'm not the most impartial person to be giving you marital advice, but is there anything I can do to help?"

"Rebecca, I really like you, and I've no idea what you see in me... I'm hoping I'm not being too presumptuous, and honestly, there's no pressure, but I've booked a table for dinner at the Hilton tomorrow night and a suite with views over Hyde Park. I would be delighted if you joined me."

"Of course I will."

"I just didn't want you to think it was... well, you know, all a bit sleazy."

"It's okay. I feel... I don't know. I suppose I feel ready. I never wanted to be your bit on the side, but now that I know you're serious about ending things with Marjorie it's... well, different."

"You are a truly amazing woman."

"I do feel sorry for Marjorie, though. How did she take it?"

"Not great, though I didn't expect anything different. She found lipstick on my collar. She knew straight away that it was you. I couldn't be bothered to deny it. I just told her the truth."

"I feel like a home wrecker."

"You mustn't feel like that. There are things that you don't know, that I can't tell you about my marriage... dark secrets."

"Every marriage has those."

"No, this is different," I insisted. "Marjorie has a side to her that I never knew. She has a vindictive, frightening aspect to her character. I feel I don't know her anymore.

That young, innocent woman I fell in love with has, well she just isn't the same. When I think about it, things haven't been right for a long time."

"Sure..."

"I just know that I don't want her. I want you. I've told her she can have everything. I just want to be free, even if I'm penniless. My MP's salary isn't a fortune, but it's enough to keep me in this flat and run a small house back in my constituency."

"You might want to think things through before you make any big decisions."

"I just want a clean break."

"Stan, I've got to go. Someone is at the front door. I'll see you at work tomorrow. I'll bring an overnight bag— don't worry, I'll put it somewhere out of sight. Adios."

"Adios." I put the phone down. I poured myself a large scotch and sat on the sofa in a reflective mood. I lit a cigarette and took a long drag. This was the beginning of a new life for me.

Chapter 49

October 2007: Jez Matthews

I was transported to Torquay police station on South Street and booked into custody. Whilst the custody sergeant typed in my details on the computer, he mentioned he enjoyed my show. I had offered to give him my autograph, but he was not impressed. I realized too late that his supposedly kind comments were actually sarcasm. The arresting officer removed the handcuffs. They were the rigid type, allowing virtually no flexibility of movement, which meant that they had rubbed my skin raw on the bumpy ride to the station.

"You are entitled to one phone call, free legal advice, and medical help if you feel you need it. Do you have a lawyer?" asked the sergeant.

"No, I've never needed one before."

"We can appoint one on your behalf if you wish. Do you have any medical problems we should know about?"

"Not that I'm aware of, but I am gluten intolerant."

The sergeant shook his head and gave me a withering look. "Would you like us to tell anybody where you are?"

"No need. Graham knows, and I'm sure this is all a misunderstanding. I'll be out soon."

He handed a key to a jailer, who led me to an empty prison cell. The cell was a tiny, brightly lit cold concrete box that smelled of disinfectant. It was painted mint green with a blue rubber mattress and a toilet in the corner. The door was made of thick, riveted steel, with a small shuttered window at face height. The other cells seem to be full of angry drunks banging on the doors and shouting obscenities. One of the jailers kindly brought me a polystyrene beaker of lukewarm tea and passed it through the shutter.

"White, no sugar," she said.

"Any idea how long I'm going to be here?"

She shrugged. "They don't tell me anything, but if I were you, I'd think about getting my head down. I think it will be morning at the earliest."

"Thank you," I said.

I managed to get a few hours of broken sleep on the thin, hard mattress. The shouts of the other prisoners continued throughout the night. When the morning light came streaming through the glass block window and my head was clear of the drugs, the reality of the situation hit me.

A different jailer brought me breakfast. It was a microwave meal of sausage, scrambled egg, and beans presented on a cardboard tray with plastic cutlery. Shortly after breakfast, my appointed lawyer, Henry Jacobs from Lawson, Dell, and Company arrived, and we spoke in a small briefing room, with an officer waiting outside. He opened his briefcase, removed various papers, and put on a pair of half-moon spectacles.

"Mr. Jeremy Matthews," he said with his ballpoint pen poised over a sheet of A4.

"Jez, please," I said. "Only my mother calls me Jeremy."

"Whatever," he said dismissively. "Do you understand why you have been arrested?"

"Yes, but it's rubbish."

He leaned forward over the desk and spoke slowly.

"Mr. Matthews, these are extremely serious allegations. You have been arrested for the murders of Kristyna Chladek and Lukas Kopecky. I believe they were live-in employees of yours. Under disclosure rules, the police have given me details of the evidence they have been building against you."

"Right."

"Things are not looking good for you. The police have been preparing their case for over a year, covertly gathering evidence against you, ever since they received an anonymous letter."

"What letter? What are you talking about?"

"It was written in poor English," said Henry sifting through his papers. "They've given me a photocopy. They received it a week after Mrs. Chladek reported her daughter missing. I suggest you read it. Although it's hearsay and not enough evidence to arrest you on its own, it was the trigger for their lengthy investigation."

He handed it to me, and I read in disbelief:

I need tell police important things you need know. Kristyna no missing, she dead. Killer is Jeremy Matthews. He bury body in basement at Pembroke Hotel, he bad man. He dangerous. I think he plan kill me too.

"What an utter bastard." *A queen is never scorned*, I thought bitterly.

"Can you shed any light on this?" asked Henry.

"Yes, I can. I know exactly who sent this."

"Who?"

"Lukas. The late Kristyna's late ex-partner. I'm not proud of myself, but I was having an affair with him and Kristyna found out. There was a fight—she died because she fell on a knife. Nobody killed her. He's a lying bastard. If he thought I was going to kill him, why didn't he just move out? He was twice my size. Surely they're not taking that seriously."

"Why would he claim that you killed his fiancée?"

"Because I ended our affair, sacked him, and gave him notice to move out. He was mad, deluded. I was just having a casual fling with him, but he thought I loved him and that I would leave Graham. This is his revenge."

"And he's now dead, correct?"

"Yes, he drowned in the swimming pool. I wish he were alive to answer for this. It was he that told me not to call an ambulance. He was covering his back by writing that letter, putting the blame on me if there was any comeback on Kristyna. He was obsessed with me. The bloody two-faced bastard!"

I could not believe Lukas' betrayal and what a poor judge of character I was. What a fool I had been, and what poor decisions I had made over the last year. If I could only turn back the clock.

"Your house has been searched from top to bottom. In addition to finding considerable quantities of class-A drugs, the police have excavated the newly laid floor in the basement. They found the body of a young female. Although a positive identification is yet to be made, the body matches the description of Kristyna Chladek, and her bank cards and driver's license were found buried with her."

"It is Kristyna. God, this is intense. I *am* guilty of going along with Lukas' wishes. He insisted that we buried her, but I swear I didn't kill her, or Lukas, for that matter."

"The police also interviewed the guests staying at the hotel on the day that Kristyna's mobile telephone stopped being detected by the network. One lady claimed that she heard a heated argument in the kitchen. She said in her statement that you behaved erratically at breakfast. Then you asked all the guests to check out early because you were unwell. The other guests confirmed that you served breakfast that morning instead of Kristyna the previous morning."

"I could not face the public, knowing what had happened, so I closed the hotel."

"I am your lawyer, not a police officer, which means I'm on your side. Would you like to tell me what you know and what happened?"

I burst into tears and slumped face down on the desk in front of me.

"Mr. Matthews, please pull yourself together. You are in very serious trouble. You need to be straight with me. To help you, I need to know the truth."

"Yes, of course," I sobbed. "I'll tell you everything."

I started from the beginning and relayed the incredible but true story that I knew my lawyer would not believe. It was strange, confessing my darkest secret to another human being. I talked for an hour, speaking without restraint or censure about the history of events that had led to me being locked in a police cell. Telling someone else was oddly therapeutic. Afterward, it felt as if a giant weight had been lifted from me, as if I had been to church and sat talking to a priest in a confessional.

Henry had sat in the chair and listened to me patiently as I spoke. I concluded my story by telling him about the ghosts in the house and how I had stupidly allowed myself to be influenced by them. I was sure that they were responsible for leading me down this terrible path.

Henry shook his head in disbelief. "In all my years as a defense lawyer, I've never heard anything like that before."

"I swear, it's the truth."

"Are you asking me to offer a defense of diminished responsibility?"

"I know how crazy it all sounds and I know how it makes me look, but I didn't kill Kristyna or Lukas. I give you my word."

"I'll check our legal library to see if there are any test

cases on using paranormal activity as a defense, but I think we're skating on thin ice here, Mr. Matthews."

"But it's the truth!"

"Tell it to the interviewing officers if you must, but God help you."

"Has this made the newspapers?"

"Naturally. It has made the front page on the tabloids," said Henry. "Most of the broadsheets have given it a mention, too. Your television career may have been brief, but you have certainly made an impact."

"Oh my God," I said. "What will my mum and dad be thinking?"

"That's the least of your worries, I'm afraid."

I was put back in my cell for another hour before DI Willets and his colleague DC McGill took me to an interview room with my lawyer. The officers sat opposite me, behind a desk. They had a thick wad of statements and notes. DC McGill put two cassettes into the tape machine and pressed record.

"The time is 11:56 a.m. on Sunday, the 7th of October, and we are in interview room three at Torquay Police Station. I am Detective Constable McGill. Also present are..."

"Detective Inspector Willets."

"Henry Jacobs, lawyer."

"Can the interviewee please confirm his full name and date of birth?"

"I am Jeremy Thomas Matthews, born on the 6th of October, 1973."

"Jeremy Thomas Matthews, you are being interviewed in relation to the murder of Kristyna Chladek and Lukas Kopecky. You do not have to say anything. However, it may harm your defense if you do not mention when questioned something that you later rely on in court. Anything you do say may be used in evidence against you. Do you understand the caution?"

"Yes."

"In the early hours of this morning, our scenes of crime officers found the body of a young female buried under your basement floor. Her dental records have now confirmed the body to be Kristyna Chladek. The body shows signs of severe burning to the face, bruising, and a fatal stab wound. Would you like to explain what you know and what happened?"

I broke down and told the officers everything. I gave them details of my affair with Lukas, Kristyna finding out and going mad, her falling onto the Aga then impaling herself onto the knife. I explained our fear of calling the police when we realized how it looked. I told them about Lukas persuading me to bury the body in the basement against my wishes.

"And of course, Lukas is now dead, too. The only witness to all this," said DI Willets. "Very convenient, wouldn't you agree?"

"Lukas' death was also a tragic accident. There was an investigation, which found no evidence of foul play," I insisted.

"Tragic accident? I can tell you now, that this case has been reopened considering the circumstances," said DC McGill. "Your lawyer has been told about the anonymous letter that we received. We found fingerprints on it. They will be checked."

"Let me put this to you," said DI Willets. "I believe that you think we are stupid. I am not convinced that the unfortunate Miss Chladek's death was an accident. I think you tortured the poor girl before stabbing her, and then buried her to cover your crimes."

"No, it wasn't like that, honestly!"

"What did she do to you, Mr. Matthews? Did she threaten to expose your relationship with her fiancé? Did you fear that she would ruin your television career before it even started? Or was it envy? Lukas came to his senses and finished the affair, and in a fit of jealousy, you killed her."

"No, no, no! She was my friend. It was all an accident, I tried to save her!"

"Do you sleep with all your friend's partners?" said DC McGill. "Do you get a kick out of torturing innocent girls? How did you feel when you burnt her face? Did it turn you on?"

"I think you panicked," said DI Willets. "Fame and wealth were in your grasp, and she could take it all away from you. So you killed her in a fit of rage."

"No, that didn't happen, I swear. I sincerely regret sleeping with Lukas. If I could change things, I would. I told you how Kristyna burnt herself."

"You tortured her, killed her in cold blood, and then attempted to cover your crimes."

"Officer, you are asking my client leading questions," warned Henry Jacobs.

"It's okay, Henry," I said. "I want them to know the truth. Inspector, it was Lukas who wanted to bury her. I wanted to call an ambulance... I tried to resuscitate her whilst Lukas looked on."

"But you didn't manage to revive her or call an ambulance."

"No, because Lukas said you wouldn't believe it was an accident, and that's exactly what you're saying now. He wanted me, but I didn't love him! This is his revenge for my rejection. I'd asked him to move out. He was obsessed with me."

"Let's move on. This wasn't an accident in my

opinion, or an argument that got out of hand. This was a premeditated murder," said DI Willets lifting up a bag of receipts. "You meticulously planned Miss Chladek's demise and the disposal of her body. For the benefit of the tape, I am showing the accused exhibit A. Your credit card receipts show that ten bags of ready mixed concrete were bought two months before the murder—why would that be?"

"It was for a project. The patio in the guest garden was sinking. Lukas was going to put in new foundations."

"But the concrete was used to bury Miss Chladek's body in the basement. The patio was never fixed, but the basement floor is new?"

"Yes, we ended up using it for that, but that's not why I originally bought it."

"Let's go back to Mr. Lukas Kopeky again. He was a good-looking man, but very young, wasn't he? I put it to you that after you had tired of his affections, he was the only person alive that knew of your secret in the basement, so you arranged a convenient accident?"

"Mr. Matthews, I suggest that you reply no comment to that," said Henry.

"No comment," I said

"A convenient accident that meant no witnesses to Miss Chladek's murder were left alive. We received an anonymous letter. Let me show you exhibit B. In this letter it claims that you murdered Miss Chladek. It claims that you are a dangerous man. Do you know who wrote this? Is this a man or woman in fear of his or her own life?"

"I don't know for sure, but it's all lies. I think the writing is Lukas'. He was up to his ears in it. Like I said, it was all his idea to bury her body. He was covering his tracks. Blaming me was his way of punishing me and making him look less guilty."

"Miss Chladek's mother came to see you last year, I believe," said DI Willets.

"Yes, she reported Kristyna missing. Lukas had told her she'd left Torquay."

"And did you feel any guilt when you lied to her about her daughter's whereabouts?"

"I didn't speak to her directly, Graham did. But yes, I did feel awful when he told me. I'm not a monster."

"But you didn't feel awful enough to tell the truth and let her bury her daughter properly and grieve for her."

"I couldn't."

"And what did you tell Graham when Kristyna mysteriously vanished?"

"Now, you leave Graham out of this. He never knew anything that happened, anything! I swear on my life. He was up in London. I told him that Kristyna and Lukas had split up, and she'd moved out."

"What can you tell me about the two bodies under the patio, who are they?"

"I don't know what you're talking about," I said, shocked.

"A man and a woman, quite decomposed, but we'll identify them in due course."

"I give you my word. I really don't know anything about that. I'm as shocked as you are. Maybe that's why the patio was sinking."

"The Pembroke Hotel is turning out to be a proper little house of horrors, isn't it? Any other bodies hidden away that you might like to tell us about?"

"If there are, I know nothing about them."

DC McGill took out a clear plastic evidence bag with a bloodied knife contained within it.

"For the benefit of the tape, exhibit C. Do you recognize this Mr. Matthews?"

"Yes, it's the kitchen knife that Kristyna stabbed

herself with. I thought Lukas had thrown it away."

"It was found in a plastic carrier bag buried in the garden. It has Kristyna's blood on it and your fingerprints. Kristyna's injuries are consistent with the shape and size of the blade. Why would it have your fingerprints on it?"

"Because I removed it before I tried to resuscitate her."

"But why bury it in the garden?"

"I didn't. It must have been Lukas. Don't you see? This proves my innocence! Why was it put in a plastic bag? If I had wanted to cover my crimes, I would have thrown it away."

"And risk your bins being searched, or a member of public finding a knife under a bush," interjected DI Willets. "It was deliberately concealed. You were hiding the murder weapon, in the garden, just in case the house was searched. There were no other prints on it, only yours."

"I tell you I didn't hide it. This is Lukas, putting the blame on me. I was showering when he was clearing up the mess, so we could serve breakfast to the guests. I'm being framed here!"

"Clearing up the mess? Serving breakfast to the guests?" said DI Willets. "You torture and stab a young woman to death, and get her fiancé to cover up your crime, whilst you carry on your business as normal."

"You're twisting my words," I protested. "You must understand me. I thought Lukas was an innocent country boy. Don't you see? He was an evil, calculating man! He planned to seduce me before he even started work at The Pembroke Hotel. Kristyna's death gave him power over me. He used me as a scapegoat in case his plans went wrong. He wrote that letter. He buried the knife and made sure he didn't get his fingerprints on it. My God, I have been so stupid. I trusted him..."

"A fit young man in the prime of his life with a beautiful

young girlfriend. You say he was more interested in you, a camp gay man, ten years his senior with a bottled tan?"

"I tell you, he wanted me! He was obsessed. And I'm *not* camp."

DI Willets showed me a small bag full of white powder.

"I am now showing the accused exhibit D," he said. "This is talcum powder is it?"

"No, look, I've got a mild cocaine habit. It's for personal use. Everyone in television does it. Are you going to arrest the entire BBC?"

"Is that so, Mr. Matthews? You are aware that this is a class-A drug that can bring on episodes of paranoid schizophrenia?"

"I only use it recreationally, before filming."

"I see. And what about all the prescription drugs you're taking? We found significant quantities of antidepressants and sleeping tablets. Having trouble sleeping are we? Difficult to live with yourself, isn't it, when you've murdered someone in cold blood."

"I did not kill Kristyna or anybody else."

"DC McGill, have you any further questions for Mr. Matthews?"

"No."

"The time is now twelve fifty-five p.m. I am concluding this interview."

He pressed the stop button on the cassette recorder, removed the tapes, and signed the label.

"Is that it?" I said naively.

"For now," said DC Willets. "We will be seeking an extension of your custody, whilst we continue with our investigation."

I was taken back to my cell, where I collapsed on the hard bed in floods of tears.

The investigation went on for over two weeks, during which time I had to endure fingerprinting and having my blood drawn for DNA tests. There were constant interviews conducted around the clock. I was severely fatigued due to sleep deprivation. The police holding cell was only designed for short stays. It was a hellish environment, but the worst times were at weekends, when the cells were full of boisterous drunks.

The custody staff were kind, though, and brought me some magazines and books to read, in order to help pass the time. They fed me three microwave meals a day. They were bland and tasteless, and I longed for a decent home-cooked meal. If there were a nice jailer on duty, I would get regular cups of tea and a biscuit. I showered in the morning, but I wore the same boiler suit each day, so I never felt clean.

Occasionally, I would get to stretch my legs in a small enclosed yard for ten minutes whilst an officer had a cigarette break. I would gulp the fresh air down as if I was drinking wine, savoring the smell of the nearby sea. I even welcomed the greasy odor from the extractor fan in the police canteen, since it helped to alleviate my sensory deprivation.

One day, it was an inspector's birthday, and he brought a slice of cake to the cell. I have never enjoyed a Victoria sponge so much. The boredom was so extreme that I had taken to doing press-ups and crunches in my cell at various points throughout the day. I spent the rest of my spare time lying on my hard bed, daydreaming.

The Czech authorities exhumed Lukas' body, which was buried in a Catholic cemetery in Pribyslav. The Czech police surgeon discovered that there was evidence of penetrative sex with traces of my DNA present, which confirmed my story that we were having an affair. The police tried to twist the truth. They suggested that I was sexually abusing an innocent young employee before killing him to avoid the truth coming out. His fingerprints were identified on the anonymous letter. In this note, he had expressed concern for his own life, so I was subjected to a second murder investigation. The police tried to claim that I had bludgeoned Lukas, who had subsequently fallen into the swimming pool and drowned. My lawyer pretended to believe my story—after all, he was being paid to defend me—but I knew from his eyes that he thought I was a liar.

I had little idea of what was going on in the outside world. I had requested to speak to Graham, but the police refused me any contact with him until the investigation was complete. Henry Jacobs mentioned that the press was having a field day. Maybe it was fortunate that the police forbade access to a television or newspapers.

On Thursday, the 19th of October, I was brought before the custody sergeant, and DI Willets read out the charge sheet in the presence of my lawyer. As I listened, it felt as though my life was in slow motion. The words sounded as though they were being played on a record player at the wrong speed.

"Mr. Jeremy Thomas Matthews, birthdate 6th of October, 1973, who resides at The Pembroke Hotel, Meadfoot Sea Road, Torquay: You are hereby charged with the murder of Kristyna Chladek and the subsequent concealment of her body. You will therefore be remanded in custody at Her Majesty's pleasure to await trial. You do not have to say anything, but it may harm your defense if you do not mention now something which you later rely on in court. Anything you do say may be given in evidence."

"I didn't kill her! I give you my word," I said weakly. "This is all a terrible mistake."

Two burly prison officers were waiting by the exit door

to transport me to Channings Wood Prison in Newton Abbott. They led me to a windowless, navy blue van and locked me inside.

The crown prosecution service decided that there was not enough evidence to charge me with Lukas' death. Although it was not an acquittal per se, at least some justice was done. Concerning my cocaine stash, the police decided that given the gravity of the murder charge it would not be in the public interest to pursue this. The bodies discovered under the patio had been identified. The first was Mavis Patterson, a middle-aged woman who had gone missing in the early seventies. It was believed at the time she fled the country to evade her debtors, so the police investigation into her disappearance was archived. In fact, she had been killed by two blows to the head and subsequently buried in the grounds of our house. The other body had turned out to be a young criminal called Marcus Cox, who had absconded from police bail. He had been wanted for various offences in Manchester, and had never been found until now. Since I was an infant at the point in time that these alleged murders had taken place, it was accepted that I could have no knowledge of them. The police reopened the investigation into the death of these unfortunate characters. At least their discovery had provided an explanation for the sinking patio.

I learned that the police were pursuing Christopher Wilson, the son of the couple who bought the hotel in the 1970s. Apparently, he had emigrated to Brazil a few years before the death of his mother.

By all accounts, the police picked apart the old building, piece by piece. The swimming pool had been drained and dug up and a headless cat had been found, but, fortunately, no more human remains. I shuddered to think of my beautiful home being butchered after all the renovation work that we had done.

I prayed to Lady Elizabeth for help, but she never made contact with me. I often thought about the house ghosts. They were truly treacherous in nature, and I had been a fool to trust them. I had no doubt that they were responsible for this whole mess.

After learning about the two bodies under the patio, I deduced who two more of the specters were. The woman wearing a dressing gown and Carmen rollers, with her brains spilling out—this had to be Mavis Patterson. The scrawny tattooed street kid was Marcus Cox. None of it all mattered now, of course. I was determined to clear my name and get my life back to normal. Then I would pay for a priest to exorcise the house to rid it once and for all of these malevolent forces.

My agent had already passed on a message via my lawyer that she was negotiating deals on a biography and a film about the whole experience, for when my I proved my innocence. I still hoped that my life would return to normal, once this ghastly affair was all over. If they did televise my story, I wondered who they would choose to play me and what royalties I would receive.

Chapter 50

September 1975: Marjorie Wilson

Stanley's revelation had taken me completely by surprise. Everything I had done was for him and Christopher. Hiding the boy's body and killing Mavis was my selfless gift, so that my husband could embark upon his dream career. I felt betrayed, and the initial hurt turned quickly to anger, which festered and grew inside me. I felt an all-consuming rage that I had ever experienced before in my life. Hatred dominated my every waking thought, and I was preoccupied with revenge. I loathed the woman who had stolen my husband, and I detested Stanley for throwing our marriage away for some young tart.

I told Christopher, who was naturally upset and blamed himself. There was some truth in this. If he had he not brought back the waif whom he had met that night on Daddyhole Plain, then the subsequent chain of events would not have unraveled. I still could not blame him, though. He was my only son. I loved him and would do anything for him. I would even kill again, if necessary.

Stanley had packed most of his clothes and cleared out his study, so I assumed that he would probably not be back at the weekend. That was most likely for the best. I needed time to adjust to the new circumstances. For the time being, we agreed to keep it quiet and try to work things out as amicably as was possible for the sake of appearances, but I knew that it was not going to be easy.

It was Monday afternoon and a lovely autumn day. I was in the kitchen making a coffee and walnut cake, listening to the afternoon play on Radio 4. As I folded the eggs into the mixture, the radio went silent for a few seconds, and then the somber voice of Brian Perkins spoke.

"We interrupt this broadcast to bring you an urgent news report. At four fifteen p.m. today, a bomb exploded in the lobby of the Park Lane Hilton in London. The IRA has claimed responsibility. Early reports have suggested that two people have been killed and dozens more injured, some seriously. The police have stated that whilst the IRA issued a coded warning, they did not give sufficient time for the building to be evacuated. At this point, the police are not releasing the identity of the deceased until their families have been informed. There will be further details in the five o'clock news bulletin."

The doorbell rang. I opened the front door to reveal two uniformed officers holding their helmets in their hands, looking solemn.

"Erm, Mrs. Wilson I presume?" said one of them awkwardly.

I knew exactly what they were going to say before they spoke.

"Yes?"

"I'm afraid I have bad news regarding your husband."

Chapter 51

December 2007: Jez Matthews
If you could use one word to describe prison, I would say terrifying. There was an ever-present threat of violence and an undercurrent of tension. This was true even at night with the cell door locked. The prison welfare officer categorized me as having a high risk of self-harming, so he put me on twenty-four-hour suicide watch for the first few days. I certainly wished that there were an easy way out.

Everybody in prison seemed to know who I was and had followed my case in the news. My celebrity status meant that there was no hiding. Much of the attention I received was unwanted, but there were some positive aspects, too. Some prisoners, aware of my wealth, attempted to curry favor. They apparently possessed an ulterior motive. Others saw me as good sport to vent their anger upon, and I was a regular target for verbal assaults, mainly revolving around my sexuality. As for the soap-dropping shower scenarios that you hear about, sadly—or thankfully, depending on your point of view—this is a myth. As much as I would have liked to discover that prison was full of sexually frustrated rugby-player types in the prime of their lives, the reality was that we were all under constant surveillance. Additionally, there were few attractive people inside. Some relationships did happen among the prisoners, but they were generally furtive or frighteningly dysfunctional. I tried to keep my head down and avoid trouble.

To complement the official prison rules, there were the prisoners' own laws. A hierarchy existed among the old timers. There really was a 'Daddy' on each wing, and they were usually the toughest, most ruthless lags of all. The wardens tolerated it because it helped to maintain discipline. Prison was about making allies and joining the right gang. My priority was not to upset or annoy anyone.

I perceived my incarceration as a temporary state, since I knew I would soon be acquitted. There were plenty of drugs available in jail if you wanted and even alcohol, though the latter was scarce. However, to obtain them, you would be interacting with unsavory characters to whom it was unwise to be indebted. For the first time in a long while, my head was free of street and prescription drugs. As the fog in my mind cleared, I found myself having to deal with reality, and it was not pleasant.

Whilst on remand, I was permitted to use the Internet under supervision, in the prison library for an hour a day. I finally saw the news stories written about my arrest.

The Daily Mirror had published a front-page article, "HOTEL OF HORRORS," with the strap line "Three bodies found so far!" There were photographs of police and forensic officers scouring my hotel for evidence. The garden resembled a muddy field with a large pit where the swimming pool used to be. They had erected a small marquee covering the patio. A center spread went on to give the background to my two alleged victims. There were interviews with the grieving families in the Czech Republic. The descriptions of their lost ones portrayed them as saints. *The Sun* went for a slightly more imaginative front-page headline, "Shake and Crack," mocking my promotional work for the carpet cleaning company along with my drug habit. They described me as an evil, calculating psychopath.

Carol Thompson wrote a typically gloating and opinionated article in the *Daily Mail*. In summary, it said: *I told you so, I never trusted him. His eyes were too close together, and I warned the producers his shortcut to fame could only have dire consequences for everyone around him. And you, the taxpayer, are footing his legal bills.* When Carol Thompson could claim the moral high ground, you knew that something had gone awry in your life. Like all her articles, it was scathing, self-serving garbage, but it felt as though she had won—and in truth, I knew that she had.

The broadsheets were less sensational, with headlines like, "Talented TV presenter charged with murder" from *The Guardian*. I liked that fact they had written "talented."

My court case was set for February 2008. In the months running up to the trial, tabloid interest remained muted. There were plenty of other things happening in the world, but I knew that would change in February. I had written to Graham many times but had not received a reply, and his telephone was disconnected. Finally, a month into serving my remand, he came to visit me. We sat at tables in a room with a dozen other prisoners and visitors, watched by several guards. Graham looked haggard and disheveled from the stress that this situation had placed on him. It broke my heart to see him in that state. I looked into his tired eyes and realized why I loved him so much.

"It's good to see you," I said.

"I wish I could say the same," he replied. "I don't even know who you are any more."

"I guess you mean the beard," I said, referring to the

bushy growth on my chin.

"I'm not talking about your appearance. Who have I been living with all these years?"

"Surely you don't believe that I could kill anyone? What I told the police happens to be the truth. Kristyna had an accident. Lukas forced me into burying her. I didn't want to. Lukas, well, they know that was an accident, too. He was the only witness to Kristyna's death and the only person that could have exonerated me... I'm so sorry, Graham."

"I don't know what to believe. How could you live with that secret for so long? I mean, why didn't you tell me? You've lied to me for months."

"It wasn't easy, but I had to protect you, to protect us."

"Protect me?"

"If *you* had known anything, you would be guilty of aiding and abetting."

"I feel sick. When I think of you sleeping with Lukas, whilst I was up in London and while poor Kristyna was grieving for her dead sister. I could have been out cruising the bars in Soho every night picking up men, but I loved you. I stayed faithful."

"I said no, so many times! But he kept on pushing me, and in the end, I just... Well, I gave in. It was all him leading it. He was so manipulative. I'm sure he'd planned to get me into bed from the moment he started working for us. You have to believe me."

"What kind of monster are you? Has your mind become so warped that you actually believe what you're saying? You are truly evil."

"Don't say that, please!"

"The tabloids were in bidding war for my story, you know. *The Sun* offered me sixty grand to do an exclusive. They wanted me to spill all the dirt on you. I refused, even though I'm broke and homeless."

"Thank you."

"Don't thank me—I did it to retain the last bit of dignity I have. The hotel is fucked, by the way. The police have ripped it apart. All the floorboards have been taken up. The garden is a bombsite. Not that anybody in their right mind would ever stay there now, given the events of the last few weeks and the morbid history that's been laid bare."

"Graham, the hotel is haunted. You have to understand. You must read the letter from Albert Henderson. He left a warning. The spirits are malevolent. They caused all this!"

"Stop it and face up to the truth. Do you know what I dream about every night in my little rented flat above Oxfam? I see you and Lukas carrying that poor girl's body down the stairs to the basement. I picture you digging out a hole and covering her body with cement, thinking how smart you both are, getting her out of the way. Was I to be next?"

"It was awful, I hated every second. If I could change things... And no, of course you weren't going to be next. I finished it with Lukas. All I have ever wanted is you."

"Yet you slept with Lukas, despite everything we'd been through."

"It was a mistake. I love you. I need you!"

"Well, you can't have me. I came today out of courtesy and respect for what we once had, but I'm telling you straight—it's over, finished, no discussion, the end."

"Graham, please?" My eyes welled up. "You can't leave me. I love you. I can't get through this without you."

"I loved you once, but it seems what we had was an illusion. I never want you to make any contact with me again. No letters, no emails, no calls, nothing. Do you understand?"

"Graham, please!" I sobbed.

"I mean it. You've made your own bed, now sleep in it, and take some responsibility for your actions for once in your life. Good-bye."

Graham stood up and walked out, leaving me in floods of tears. I had expected the meeting to be awkward, but perhaps it was naive of me to think that Graham would stand by me. Hearing him say those words to me was like being stabbed in the chest. I felt grief that held my soul in an iron grip. I could not escape from it, and it was all consuming. That was the last time I ever saw him.

Chapter 52

September 1975: Marjorie Wilson

Stanley's funeral was at our lovely old local church, St Matthias in Wellswood. Christopher was deeply upset over the loss of his father. My emotions were in turmoil. Part of me still hated him for his betrayal. When I heard about his death, I also had to deal with the fact that he was with Rebecca Waters at the time, and that they had booked a suite at the Hilton. This conflicted with the grief I felt for the loss of the man with whom I had spent the last quarter of a century of my life. Despite his infidelity, he was the person that I loved with all my heart, and now he was dead. At least the bomb got her too.

Lady Elizabeth had told me not to worry, she said that the house would sort things for me. I assumed that would mean something would happen to Miss Waters, and that Stanley and I would reconcile. I did not realize that Stanley would be taken from me. I felt a sense of betrayal. The spirits had tricked me. I was trapped in the house, unable to leave with the secrets buried in the garden. It became apparent to me that I had unwittingly done a deal with the devil, and the price was my obedience and my soul. I had succumbed to temptation and allowed my ambitions to corrupt my very being. I now belatedly realized the folly of my ways and the inescapable trap into which I had been ensnared.

Fortunately, the staff at the Hilton were discreet and leaked nothing to the press. An MP killed along with his mistress would likely make the front page of the newspapers. It was the kind of seedy story that their editors loved. The Hilton issued a statement that they were booked in for a business dinner and made no mention of the suite that they had reserved. At least our family had been able to maintain our dignity. Tannis Breville proved to be a rock. She had lost her husband, albeit in different circumstances, but also there were many similarities. Both our husbands were taken from us prematurely, and Martin before Stanley was the MP for Torquay. The funeral service was in the same church, and they would be buried yards from each other. Connie Francis from *The Times* wrote a short obituary about Stanley. The Prime Minster had said some compassionate words, and Margaret Thatcher had written me a kind letter expressing her condolences. She stated that it had hardened her resolve to defeat the terrorists responsible for this and other atrocities. There was a minute's silence in the Common's chamber on Tuesday. Stanley was relatively new to parliament, but he had made some good friends.

The service was touching. I managed to keep a stiff upper lip as best I could. The pallbearers took Stanley's coffin out to the cemetery and lowered it into the ground. It was a blustery day with a damp cold wind. The vicar held the common-prayer book in his left hand whilst making the sign of the cross upon his chest.

"Ashes to ashes, dust to dust," he read. "I heard a voice from heaven saying unto me. Write, from henceforth blessed are the dead which die in the Lord, even so, saith the Spirit, for they rest from their labors."

Led by myself, we threw clumps of dirt onto the coffin. It was at this point, I lost my composure. Tannis held me as I looked at Stanley's coffin in disbelief. I think at that moment I realized that he was not coming back. It felt like I had been struck be a train.

Chapter 53

February 2008: Jez Matthews

The media mostly forgot about me, whilst on remand. The networks took *Hotel Red Alert* off the air. Future production of the program itself was also canned, since Channel 4 felt that the brand was irrevocably tainted. I felt like I had let down the production team.

Although I had no direct contact with Graham, lawyers were untangling our joint financial affairs, so I had to sign various documents. The bank had taken possession of the hotel as Graham had been unable to keep up the mortgage payments, but in any case, it was an unsaleable white elephant of no value. The bank had boarded it up. There was talk of it razing it, to prevent it from becoming a macabre tourist attraction, but that was of little interest to me now.

The court case revived the tabloid frenzy. I chose to cover my head and face with a coat as I was led daily into Exeter crown court, pursued by photographers and journalists. The bitter irony was that in court, I told the truth. I was guilty of concealing a dead body but nothing else. It was clear after a few days that the case was not going my way, but I still clung to the hope that the jury would see sense and believe me.

Whilst I was in the dock, I had hoped that Graham would sit in the public gallery to support me but he did not, and surprisingly neither the defense nor prosecution summoned him as a witness. The prosecution witnesses were mainly the CID and the forensic officers who uncovered Kristyna's body. Apparently, the two plain-clothes officers DC Ward and DC Hemming that had visited back in November 2006 had mentioned the newly concreted basement floor in their statements. This seemed to affirm the accusations in the anonymous letter. The officers also suggested that they felt I had been shifty and evasive. This had been noted when the unsolved missing person's case was reviewed months later by a zealous superintendent. They had spent the last few months surreptitiously monitoring me, which ultimately led to the arrest and premises' search on my birthday. Unbeknown to me, my telephone had been tapped. I discovered that undercover officers had posed as guests. Medical experts gave specialist opinions about the causes of Kristyna's death and argued that they believed her burnt face was the result of a prolonged and cruel torture. One doctor stated to the jury, "The best thing that happened to the poor girl that day was when she drew her last breath."

The defense had no witnesses or anybody that could back my story. All that my lawyer could do was attack the integrity of some of the officers, who had disciplinary black marks on their service records. This compared to my lack of criminal record and previous good character. Thus, they argued, the jury should believe my version of events over theirs. It was a weak argument at best, and I sensed that the jurors were not convinced.

The judge was a wizened old man with a large belly and a complexion that betrayed a love of fine wines and good food. He wore his wig of office and court clothes, a black cloak with a lace cravat. He dominated the courtroom with proprietorial arrogance. He would occasionally look at me disdainfully, peering over his half-moon glasses, and I had the distinct feeling that he did not like me.

Kristyna and Lukas' family were in the public gallery, glaring at me with pure hatred in their eyes. My mother had come to offer support, but my father was too ill and ashamed. Jason was there, his hair shorter than normal, and he was immaculately dressed in a pinstripe suit and double cuffs with a large pink rosette on his left lapel that said 'FREE JEZ.' Bless him. Steph had also turned up in a black lace ball gown, caked in vampish makeup. He looked like something off the Rocky Horror show. I noted that he was also wearing a pink rosette. It was surprising that the judge had not declared him in contempt of court. I found it heartening, though, that a small number of people still had faith in me.

The trial lasted for eight days. The defense and prosecution made their closing statements, and the jury retired to reach a verdict that the judge instructed should be unanimous. In the event, the jury took fifteen minutes to decide.

The jury reentered the courtroom, filing through the small doorway at the back of the chamber. I sat nervously in the dock, the loneliest place in the world. The judge ordered me to stand up. There was no cocaine or a stiff brandy to get through this horrendous moment. Once again, time seemed to have slowed down. Then the judge finally spoke.

"Would the foreman of the jury, please rise," he ordered.

A tall suited man in his sixties stood up.

"Have you reached a verdict?"

"We have, my lord," he replied.

"And are you unanimous in your decision?"

"We are, my lord."

"Please, can you tell the court your verdict?"

"My fellow jurors have instructed me to confirm the verdict of..."

I stood sweating with my heart pounding, and both my fingers crossed behind my back. The juror seemed to be speaking in slow motion. His words were lumbering and slurred. I could barely focus on him.

"Guilty."

I gasped and shouted, "No!"

Kristyna's mother stood up and shouted in broken English. "I knew this! I knew you did it. Rot in hell, you bastard!" She burst into tears and collapsed back into her seat, comforted by a friend. Steph also started crying, causing his eyeliner to start running. He blew his nose loudly, and I saw him take a discreet swig from a hip flask that he had concealed in his handbag. Jason looked shocked, then fainted. He would never miss the opportunity to steal my moment.

"Silence in court," ordered the judge, slamming down his gavel. "I thank the jury for their decision. Mr. Jeremy Matthews, I order that you return to this court one week from today, for sentencing. I have no need to tell you that you should expect a lengthy custodial sentence for your appalling crime."

He glared, continuing, "You had many opportunities to tell the truth and help the Chladek family piece together the facts surrounding their child's death. Instead, you chose to continue to weave a web of deceit, even bizarrely claiming at stages during the investigation that the tragic events were the result of paranormal activity. I shall be recommending the full force of the law be applied in your case. Take him down."

I was taken to a holding cell and then back to Channing Wood. A week later, the judge issued my sentence. I received a life tariff with no possibility of parole for twenty-five years. This meant that I would be in my sixties before being released from prison. When he issued his verdict, I collapsed to my knees, holding my hands over my face, before the prison officers standing either side of me dragged me away. The paparazzi were waiting outside the courtroom snapping away. When I arrived back at Channing Wood, I realized that this would now be my home for virtually the rest of my life.

Chapter 54

June 1979: Marjorie Wilson

They say time is a great healer. I would say that the pain never completely goes away, but it has become manageable. There is not a day that goes past that I do not think about Stan. Over the years, I have forgiven him his affair. It was not easy at first. The spirits in the house have not shown themselves to me since Stanley's funeral. I am unsure as to why, but I am glad. Occasionally, at night, I feel an atmosphere of malice in the lounge area, and the stain in the old master bedroom reappears from time to time, accompanied by a smell of charred flesh, but things seem a lot quieter.

Stanley had good life insurance cover in place. That combined with our savings and a widow's pension meant that Christopher and I have been financially secure since his death.

We operate the hotel at a reduced capacity and take longer holidays, but I know I will have to live here until the day I die in case the two bodies under the patio are ever discovered.

I was careful to visit the Breville's London residence after Stanley's death to collect his belongings. Thank goodness I found his diary. The safest thing would be to burn it, or remove the implicating pages, but I do not have the heart. It provides me with comfort, as it is a window into his memories. It is locked securely in my safe, away from prying eyes.

Margaret Thatcher won the election earlier this year and embarked on a radical reform agenda. There were many champagne corks popping in the Conservative Club that night. For me, it was a bittersweet moment. I wish Stanley had been around to see it and that we could have shared that particular journey together. After Stanley's death, they held another by-election, which Jonathan Townsend won. He was our man. I did not know him well, but I approved. He recaptured the seat again at the general election.

Christopher finally seems to have grown up. A couple of years ago, he met a young Brazilian man at The Horn of Plenty public house, who works as a doctor at Torquay General Hospital. Whilst having a relationship with another man would not be my first choice for him, they are both discreet. I also have to say that I like Felipe. He is handsome, educated, and very courteous. Such a waste, really, but I know they are both happy and in the end that is all a mother could wish for. I accepted that I would not be having grandchildren some time ago.

Felipe rents a small terraced house in Babbacombe, and the two split their time between there and Christopher's little bedsit here. It is good to see Christopher smile again. He was devastated by his father's death. Their relationship was strained during the last six months of Stanley's life. Stanley did not approve of Christopher's leanings. They never had a chance to resolve their differences. Following his sudden death, it remains unfinished business for Christopher. At some point, Felipe's visa will run out. I am not sure what will happen at that point in their relationship, but Christopher seems relaxed about it.

I have three arrivals in the hotel today, including a young family. It will be nice to have some children around the place. I feel it brings back the life into the old building. That will mean cooking supper for eight people tonight. As the expression states: 'Life goes on.'

Chapter 55

October 2007: Christopher Wilson
To whom it may concern,
My apologies to the staff of the Hotel Marina Palace in Rio de Janeiro. If things go according to plan, they will find my body tomorrow morning. I leave a substantial tip that I hope will cover any inconvenience to you, and I was diligent in settling my account in full when I arrived.

To my darling Felipe, I love you more than anything in the whole world, and I am so sorry to be leaving you in this way. I am sure you will understand the circumstances as to why I had no other choice. I cannot subject you or myself to the events that will be unfolding over the coming weeks. Believe me, this is a better option for all of us.

I have been following the news in England on both the Internet and the BBC world channel that we receive via our satellite dish. The news about my old home, The Marstan Hotel—or as it is now called, The Pembroke Hotel—has not escaped me. It would only be a matter of time before the police came knocking on my door, and I cannot face the questions and accusations that will follow.

I hope that the families of Marcus Cox and Mavis Patterson will find some closure. I can only give you my word that this is the truth; after all, I have nothing to lose.

I met Marcus Cox whilst cruising for sex on Daddyhole Plain, just around the corner from my home. It sounds seedy I know, but it was how gay men met in those days. Whilst consensual homosexual sex was legal behind closed doors, attitudes toward us were not tolerant. I had not met him before, and I knew little about him except that he was broke and homeless. I brought him back to my flat at The Marstan Hotel where he showered, and I fed him. We had sex and smoked weed. I think it is inappropriate to go into any further detail. I am unsure how he died, but when I woke up in the morning, he had passed away.

My father was running as the Conservative candidate for Torquay at a by-election at that time. This would have been a nationwide scandal, especially in those days and circumstances. My father and I both wanted to call for an ambulance and do things correctly. My mother, God rest her soul, had other ideas. She suggested that we bury the body under a newly built patio, so my Father could go on to pursue his career in the House of Commons.

Mavis Patterson was our gossipy next-door neighbor at Delamare Court. Unfortunately, she was in the wrong place at the wrong time. She saw flashlights in the garden and came to investigate. We could not disguise what we were doing, so mother killed her with a shovel. It was a horrendous moment that I have had to live with for over thirty years. My mother lived in the house until she died. I moved to Brazil with Felipe in the early 1980s. I became estranged to my mother then, and I have not spoken to her since.

In retrospect, I wish I had possessed the courage to stand up to my mother and do the right thing. However, she was a domineering and controlling woman, who persuaded me to act against my wishes. This I regret with all my heart, and I apologize unreservedly for my role in this affair. I also want to clear my father's name that will no doubt be slandered over the coming weeks. He was an unwilling participant at best, led astray by an ambitious, unfeeling woman.

I have consumed a large quantity of sleeping pills and alcohol that are beginning to take effect. The quantity of the dose will be sufficient to induce organ failure. My partner is a doctor, and I have forged his signature to obtain the drugs without his knowledge. I know this is an easy way out and that there is nothing courageous or admirable about suicide, so I will finish this note off by saying: God forgive me.

—Christopher Wilson

Chapter 56

April 2034: Jez Matthews
As I sit and write the last few pages of this book, the evening sunlight is fading through the sash windows. There are still bars in front of them, but the open prison in West Sussex is a world away from the austere life at Channing Wood. My room has a decent bed with cotton sheets and a duvet. There are curtains hanging on the window. I would almost go as far to say that it has a homely feel.

I placed Marjorie's memoirs and Stanley's diary back into a cardboard box full of my few possessions. Christopher's partner Felipe posted them to me about five years ago, a few days before he died of cancer. I was surprised that the guards had not confiscated the package, since the contents were both controversial and evidential. However, a cursory glance at the diaries would reveal a great deal of day-to-day humdrum spanning over a decade, and nothing of great interest. One of Stanley's early entries stated, "Marje burnt the shepherd's pie tonight, I must remember to water the hanging baskets tomorrow." This was hardly worthy of censorship. Many people would not have read past the first few pages. Felipe had also enclosed Christopher's suicide note and a short letter stating: *Christopher left specific instructions to send you these journals, which he found in his mother's safe. Marjorie's notes are more of a memoir, written retrospectively in her years as a recluse. I am sorry I have left it so long. You may find some answers among the gibberish, but in any case, I hope this helps you make sense of all this, because I never could.*

I have daily visits from people in the probation service, helping to rehabilitate me back into regular life. For nearly thirty years, I have never had to think about putting a meal on the table, what to wear, or how I would travel to work. The open prison is my first step toward returning to freedom in a few weeks. People are critical of the prison system, but it has done an enormous amount for me. Although I still maintain my innocence, during my incarceration, I accepted that I had a drug and alcohol problem. I have received help for this, and I have been clean and sober for over twenty-five years. I have exchanged it for a smoking habit, though, but whilst this might eventually kill me, it is preferable to using mind-altering drugs, and it is legal. I blame it on boredom, but no matter how hard I try, I seem to be unable to stop for more than a few days.

I often reflect on my poor judge of character, and the bad decisions that I made all those years ago. I am still serving a life sentence for a crime that I did not commit. I have learned to accept this, save bitterness infect every part of my being.

The uniformed guards are still present here, but there is a more relaxed atmosphere. They even address you by your first name. I am permitted to leave the prison for a few hours a day. At Channing Wood, our access to the outside world was mainly via television; even so, much has changed that I had never noticed. The money is still pounds and pence, but it all looks different with the elderly King Charles III now pictured on the coins and notes. Until last week, I had never seen a ten-pound coin. The cars look and sound different, powered electrically, since petrol is now the preserve of the super-rich. Hairstyles and fashion have changed, but the countryside remains as beautiful and timeless as I remember. Nobody recognizes me now. I am just a footnote in history. So far, there have been no press murmurings about my release. I am a forgotten, lonely frail old man for whom people open shop doors. When I shave, I look into the mirror, and I still see the handsome blond-haired young man from yesteryear. The true reflection is a wrinkled, white-haired stranger with sunken-yellowed eyes that look back at me with immense sadness, betraying a promising life wasted.

The probation service has found me a small, furnished flat in a modern block in Brighton, all courtesy of the taxpayer. It will be a new town for me, a new beginning away from Torquay, though I know I will go back one day. There is unfinished business that I need to deal with.

Jason sold his story to *The Sun* newspaper a few days after my trial concluded. It was disappointing but unsurprising. The headline was typically childish: "The Hotel of Death: My dalliances with the devil." All those confidential conversations regarding my affair with Lukas were laid bare. The rest was the work of pure fiction, with manufactured stories and invented scenarios that never happened. He had even claimed that I tried to seduce him. I never heard from him again, though I learned that he had died in Torquay hospital of hepatitis-related complications in his early thirties; his hedonistic lifestyle finally caught up with him. Steph and Michelle retired to Gran Canaria. Steph lived into his seventies before succumbing to lung cancer. Michelle survived him for a couple more years. They wrote to me every Christmas. I would look forward to their letters; though infrequent, they provided me with a window on the outside world and helped to alleviate the boredom. All my other friends and family deserted me. At my parents' request, I did not attend either of their funerals. That was hard to come to terms with.

As a lifer in prison, I have managed to make a few acquaintances, though I know that once on the outside, I will lose contact. Maybe that is for the best.

I thought about Graham every day whilst serving my sentence, even though I had completely lost contact at his behest. Many years later, I discovered that he had settled down with someone else a couple of years after we had split up. They emigrated to Brisbane, Australia where Graham had reinvented himself as a math teacher. He always had a flair for numbers. He passed away peacefully in his sleep last year, aged only seventy-two. Though it was distressing, I could not resist trying to gather information about his new partner, and his life in the Southern Hemisphere. I was not able to glean much. Through a bit of research, I found out his name was Andrew. He was fifteen years Graham's junior. He liked them younger, so nothing had changed. Graham's death affected me in ways I did not expect, given the passage of time. He had been my one and only true love, and I grieved for him within the confines of my prison cell. This meant hiding my tears and crying silently at night. It did not matter to me that he had moved on and grown old with another man. In my mind, he would forever be the well-kept thirty-something that I had met in the Shadow Lounge in Soho, all those years ago. It pained me to think that I would still be with him, had we not both fallen in love with that damned hotel in Torquay.

Chapter 57

May 2034: Jez Matthews

I was finally released on the 9th of May, 2034. There was no fanfare, crowds of protesters, or indeed supporters. I walked out of the main gate, alone, wearing secondhand clothes donated to the prison by charities. I caught a bus to Brighton, following the directions that the probation service had provided me.

My flat is basic but modern, quite close to the town, with glimpses of the sea from the kitchen window. The social security system gives me enough money to feed and clothe myself and afford the occasional treat, though I intend to get a part-time job to supplement this money. I am so institutionalized that it is difficult to function in the way that I used to, but I have rediscovered my love of cooking.

On the outside, I attend Narcotics Anonymous meetings in Brighton, of which there are many. In these places, I can be honest about my past and not face judgment. I have started to make friends—sober friends—and I am gradually rebuilding my life. It is infinitely less exciting than before but better for it.

There is one thing that I know I have to do, and it is not going to be easy. I have to go back to Torquay and deal with my demons.

I ascertained that The Pembroke Hotel had lay

boarded up and derelict since 2007. The bank sold it to the local authority at a knockdown price. I assumed it would have been demolished and the site developed, but during the year after my conviction, there was a global recession and property prices slumped. The council had allowed it to fall into disrepair. The Hotel of Horrors, as it became known, was a liability that nobody knew what to do with.

By contrast, 2034 was enjoying a runaway property boom, and it had returned to the open market. Though I knew I could never afford to buy it now, I arranged a viewing with the estate agent under the pretense of me being a wealthy pensioner. Fortunately, he had no idea who I really was.

It took nearly four hours and three changes to get across the south coast from Brighton to Torquay by rail. The trains were as overcrowded and unreliable as I remembered them. At some point whilst I was being held at Her Majesty's pleasure, the train company had sensibly extended the line into the heart of Torquay town center. I decided to walk from the station to Meadfoot Sea Road. The shops had changed in the town. The only one I remembered was Starbucks, but the facades were still recognizable; most of the old Victorian buildings remained. I walked along Meadfoot Lane. The Horn of Plenty was still there. The current owners had painted it yellow, and the rainbow flag swung proudly from a pole over the front door. No doubt, the latest generation of gays would be partying every evening. I peered inside the window. There were only a handful of people inside. Memories of Dave pulling pints behind the bar and Steph singing on the karaoke machine flooded back.

I continued up the hill until I reached my old home. Kelvin Saxon, the estate agent, was waiting for me with his flashy Tesla sports car parked in the drive, holding an iPad and a flashlight. He warned me to be careful and watch my step as much of the woodwork in the building was rotten. This was compounded by that fact that it was dark inside due to a combination of no electricity and the windows being boarded up. I followed him in and felt goose bumps prickle up all over my body.

"I'm afraid that the house has a pretty grisly history," said the agent. "They found dead bodies here, about thirty years ago. It spooks many people—I guess that's why it's not sold, even though it's so cheap. That being said, we do have a young couple interested. They want to buy it and turn it into a murder-mystery hotel... Quite fitting, really."

The police had ripped apart the building all those years ago during their forensic search of the premises. The beautiful Axminster carpets were rolled up and had disintegrated in the damp. The sofas were rotten and covered in mildew. My sense of smell was very poor, but you could feel the mustiness in the air.

"Despite its condition, it is in a prime location and is overdue refurbishment. It just needs somebody to love it again."

"History repeats itself," I muttered under my breath.

He led me into the old private lounge. The plaster was hanging off the ceiling. It was a picture of decay and neglect, and it certainly was not habitable.

"Strange, there's a slight whiff of gas in here," he said. "I'm sure it's nothing to worry about. All the services have been shut off."

"Could you leave us alone, please?" I asked.

"Us?"

"Sorry, me." I snapped. "Can I just have a moment to look around on my own?"

"No problem, Mr. Matthews. Just remember what I said, though, be careful, and please don't go upstairs, it's not safe. Here, take my flashlight."

I walked into the guest lounge. There were cracks of sunlight bleeding through the edges of the windows where the plywood did not quite fit. All our furniture was there in situ, as if we had just gone out for a walk. The beautiful walnut grand piano that I had bought at an auction in Exeter, stood there frozen in time, covered in thick dust and cobwebs. I went over and pressed a key. It was hopelessly out of tune. There was a framed picture of Graham and me on the top. I blew off some of the dust and looked at it. We looked so young and happy, full of energy, life's dreams and hopes. A tear came into my eye, and I touched Graham's face. He beamed at me through the thin glass. His eyes had that look of the boyish mischievousness that I loved so much. The picture was taken when we were on holiday in Province Town, Cape Cod. We were holding flutes of champagne, celebrating three years of being together. The lovely clapboard guesthouse that we had stayed in was behind us. They were happy days. I wiped off some more dust with my thumb and felt a sharp pain. I had cut it on a crack that ran vertically up the glass, which spliced Graham and I into two separate parts. It left a bloody stain on the glass, covering my face. I sucked my thumb dry and wrapped it in my handkerchief. I removed the back of the picture frame and took out the photo. It had been fairly well protected from the damp, and, though faded, it was in generally good condition. I folded it in half and put it in my wallet. This was one record of those happy memories that I wanted to keep forever.

The set of Russian dolls that Lukas had proudly presented to me all those years ago were still on the mantle. Even though they were tacky, Graham had refused to let me throw them away because of the sentiment behind them. I remembered Lukas giving them to me when he had returned alone from Pribyslav. That was in the days when I thought he was an innocent, handsome country boy. I preferred to remember him that way. I shone the flashlight on them. Their gaudy painted faces leered back at me, devoid of expression.

I went into the orangery. This had not been boarded up, so it was light. A decomposed seagull lay on the floor. It had met with a premature death, presumably by flying into a glass pane that was smashed. This had allowed water to flood in whenever it rained. The whole structure was so rotten that you could push your finger through the wooden frame like papier-mâché. The terracotta tiles on the floor were powdery and cracked by the frost. The tables were all laid as if breakfast was about to be served.

The white tablecloths were riddled with mildew, and the crockery covered in dust. I closed my eyes and imagined how it used to look when it was all newly painted and full of guests making conversation whilst tucking into their breakfast.

I went into the kitchen and shone the flashlight around. The Aga stood in the chimney breast, unlit and cold. I shuddered when I thought of poor Kristyna burning herself on the ring. I heard muffled chattering emanating from the walls.

"Who's there?" I shouted. "It's okay. It's Jez. I'm back... back where I belong."

The whispering reached a crescendo, then was replaced by a cat hissing angrily, followed abruptly by silence.

"You don't have to be afraid to show yourselves," I said. "The agent is outside, it's only me."

A shadow briefly darted across the beam from my flashlight, and I heard a fluttering noise, like a startled pigeon. I walked out of the kitchen, through the door leading into the bar. Like the rest of the house, it was covered in decades of accumulated dust and cobwebs. The bottles of spirits were still in place, and the inoperative glass fronted refrigerators were fully stocked with beers and wine that would be long past its sell-by date. I last consumed an alcoholic drink twenty-five years ago, in prison. It was homemade hooch, and it nearly blinded me. I looked longingly at the grimy bottle of Remy Martin Brandy sitting on the bar. The golden-brown liquid tempted me. It called out to me, enticing me to pour myself a glass.

"My old friend," I said. "I've missed you so much."

I placed the flashlight face up on the bar counter so the light beam shone against the ceiling. The diodes were fading as though the battery was about to fail. I took a crystal tumbler from the shelf, wiped off the dust with my shirtsleeve, and poured myself a large measure of brandy. I noticed a smudge of blood from my thumb on the side of the glass. I took a swig. That elusive and immediate sense of well-being that alcohol gave me was back within seconds.

In the corner of my eye, I saw a shadow and looked up. I could see Kristyna, disfigured, with burnt skin hanging off her face. She was almost solid. She stood next to Lukas, who looked as stunning as I remembered him, with his cropped hair, square jaw, and perfect teeth. He was wearing soaking wet clothes, and his face was covered in beads of water. They appeared as two monochrome silhouettes standing in the corner of the bar. Unlike me, neither of them had aged a day since they died.

"Cheers," I said raising my glass. "Is anyone else going to join us today? It's a shame you can't drink this stuff. It's rather good. I'd offer you a glass."

They stood there impassively, silently observing me. I poured myself another large measure of brandy, and I sat down in a damp armchair, in front of the cold fireplace.

"Aren't you going to say anything, then?" I said.

I retrieved a packet of Golden Virginia tobacco from my trouser pocket and started rolling myself a cigarette. I took another swig of brandy. I surveyed the decaying scene around me, remembering the happy drunken nights Graham and I had enjoyed with the guests. I could almost hear the sound of Vivaldi played through the HiFi, mixed with the sound of laughter, convivial conversation, and clinking glasses. A tear came to my eye. I remembered the time when Graham and I had locked up the bar and had made love on the rug. I relived the mornings when Kristyna and Lukas would be busying themselves polishing the glasses behind the counter.

The darkness in the bar seemed to dissipate, and the room filled with light. The mildew on the chairs vanished, and the room became pristine and freshly painted, as it had been when we had refurbished it. A vase of fresh flowers appeared on the coffee table, and the fire was lit. The logs crackled, giving off an inviting orange glow. The room felt warm, and the smell of mold was replaced by the scent of lilies intermingled with wood smoke. I could hear chattering and classical music, but the music was distorted, as though the speaker was underwater and the voices were disturbingly inhuman.

"You know, Kristyna. I never meant any of this to happen. I always thought you were a sweet girl. I'm really sorry that I slept with your fiancé."

Kristyna stood motionless and silent, smiling malevolently.

"As for you, Lukas, you brought this all on yourself. You wouldn't take no for an answer. You were nothing compared to my Graham. You weren't even that good in bed. I wanted you to know that because after today, you will never see me again."

Lady Elizabeth came into view, giving off a sinister aura and stroking the body of a headless cat that I could hear purring unnaturally. She stood there impassively. Marjorie appeared beside her. She was plump and wore a light blouse and a dark skirt. She smiled evilly. An icy chill fell over the room. The fire extinguished itself, replaced by cold ashes, and the flowers withered and died in seconds. The light vanished, and the room returned to being dank and musty. Mavis Patterson materialized, wearing her dressing gown and Carmen rollers. More ghosts came into sight. Marcus Cox stood there, scowling aggressively. A young Albert Henderson in his butler's uniform, James Partridge looking charming in an oily way, and Sir Wilfred Kingsley. Albert, Wilfred, and Mavis stood back looking concerned; they were trying to tell me something, but I could not hear their voices. Their mouths moved silently, and they pointed toward the door. The others stood motionless in a semicircle around me, staring menacingly. Their eyes were jet black. Led by Lady Elizabeth, they joined their hands and closed their eyes.

"I'm not afraid of you. I hope you know that," I said calmly. "Your influence is limited beyond the boundaries of this property. So long as I don't die in this place, you can never hurt me. I may be stupid, but at least I managed to work that out."

I struck a match.

CPSIA information can be obtained at www.ICGtesting.com
Printed in the USA
LVOW06s1508040915

452608LV00016B/116/P